Colusa County Free Library

P9-AFO-648

Colusa County Free Library
738 Market Street
Colusa, CA 95932
Phone: 458-7671

CUB

TICKET HOME

ALSO BY JAMES MICHAEL PRATT

The Lighthouse Keeper
The Last Valentine

TICKET
HOME

JAMES
MICHAEL
PRATT

Bookspan Large Print Edition

ST. MARTIN'S PRESS
NEW YORK

COLUSA COUNTY FREE LIBRARY

This Large Print Edition, prepared especially for Bookspan, contains the complete unabridged text of the original Publisher's Edition.

TICKET HOME. Copyright © 2001 by James Michael Pratt. All rights reserved. Printed in the United States of America. No part of this book may be used or reproduced in any manner whatsoever without written permission except in the case of brief quotations embodied in critical articles or reviews. For information, address St. Martin's Press, 175 Fifth Avenue, New York, N.Y. 10010.

ISBN 0-7394-1521-2

**This Large Print Book carries the
Seal of Approval of N.A.V.H.**

In memory of my uncles,

NORMAN AND LUCIAN PRATT

*who personified love, kindness, and the gentle
nature of true manhood. They have long been
deceased but they left a legacy of love and
service to God, family, and country.
The world is a better place for
these two men having
walked among us.*

ACKNOWLEDGMENTS

I express my gratitude to my family, friends, and reading fans who continue to urge me on in my pursuit of inspirational love stories and moral fiction. I receive so many kind letters and e-mails. Thank you! Please keep them coming. I promise to write back.

I also owe a continued debt of gratitude to Kenneth Atchity and Chi-li Wong and their team of *AEI/All Media* of Beverly Hills, California, and New York, who have enthusiastically endorsed my work all along.

To Mr. Joel McKuin, entertainment attorney, a special thank you for being there from the start and for all the work performed so professionally for me on this and other books.

The world has never been more cynical about basic goodness in the human character, the enduring nature of love, and "old-fashioned" values. I express my sincere appreciation to Jennifer Enderlin, senior editor with St. Martin's Press, who is a true believer. She has shown the courage to take her beliefs in my storytelling of love, faith, and hope to print.

It is Jennifer and others at St. Martin's Press, including publisher Sally Richardson, who understand that stories filled with the basics of human nature, life, and honest love are perennial winners.

To my radio syndicator, colleague, and friend, Mitchell Santell of PCBroadcast.com, who also shares his vision in my nationally syndicated weekly radio show *The Bestsellers*, a special thank you for personifying excellence in attitude, honesty, and performance.

My new friend and public relations confidante for *The Bestsellers Show* is the marvelous Donna Gould of Phoenix Media. Donna, the personification of kindness, is at the top of the game in media and publishing, and I feel fortunate and blessed to have her friendship and wisdom in my professional life.

Leo Weidner, personal success coach and friend—and Mark Kastleman, fellow writer, speaker, and longtime friend and confidant— are enthusiastic cheerleaders for my writing, my health, and my personal growth. These are great men of the success culture who live what they teach and devote their lives to inspiring others. I love you guys!

A special thanks to John Rimmasch of Heber Valley Railroad in Heber, Utah, who provided valuable insights into steam locomotives, their operations, and the romance of the great train era. From engineer to fireman I was taught the secrets of the "short-line railroad" through his generous sharing of time and resources. Also of Heber Valley, Mr. James Ritchie, an early supporter of my creative efforts, deserves my thanks and appreciation for his long-standing belief in me. Thank you, John and Jim!

A special acknowledgment is owed to Dr. Neil Whitaker, for whom the character "Neil" of *The Last Valentine* was named. He was there in the critical times with my health challenges of the past. He interceded to help save my life not once but twice! I wouldn't be here today penning these novels without his observant wisdom. I cherish our lifelong friendship.

Love wakes men, once a lifetime each.

—COVENTRY PATMORE, *THE REVELATION*

PROLOGUE

"Once upon a time," Lucian Parker read from the fairy tale at the prompting of his preschool-aged granddaughter as she climbed up on his lap.

The padded rocker was positioned in front of the voluminous picture window to take in the Oklahoma ranch he loved so well. *Whoever coined the phrase "there's no place like home" was truly the first wise man*, he mused.

Now his mind suffered the inquietude of a condemned man. Time, precious as it was, was short. Life, as good as it was, was draining from him daily. He felt it. Now for the first time in his mortal existence he couldn't control events around him.

And eating at him always was the one thing still left undone in his life, a secret he had so successfully buried that he had reasoned no one need ever know. Not that he hadn't lived an honorable life, it was just that a secret lay buried in the Philippines, left behind by war, and that secret was something even he had believed, until now. Now there was one more item of honor he must fix, God willing, and then he could rest in peace.

"Grandpa!" the tiny blonde with ponytails and a lively bounce announced, alerting him that his precious little girl was still in need of storytelling.

"Oh yes." He smiled, returning to the present. *"Once upon a time . . ."*

His voice trailed off after a few sentences and he fell silent. His focus was far away from this, the sweetest place on earth. He couldn't seem to help it. He wondered about time, where it had gone, why it had suddenly passed like an unsuspecting breeze does— so silently, quickly, wafting across the brow, at once hot, sometimes cold.

His health had been good for so long, he wondered and felt puzzled by the news the doctor had given him days before. "I'm sorry to tell you this, Lucian . . ." he had said.

"Lucian, it's time to slow down," Mary Jane had said as they left the doctor's office in Oklahoma City, a three-hour drive from Warm Springs. "You've lived your life like you're trying to make up for something," she added as he opened the car door for her. He couldn't let her know the bad news.

"I am," the seventy-nine-year-old responded in a deep, reflective tone of voice. He gazed into the azure eyes of the silver-haired, slender, and stately seventy-seven-year-old love of his life and stared as if he were looking through her and into the past— far beyond where he now stood.

"I am," he whispered as he closed the door for her.

That was two days before. A routine physical last month revealed why he was suffering so much fatigue and loss of weight. He had promised a concerned Mary Jane that it was the malaria that visited him every now and then. The test results were not characteristic of his normal vigor, however, and malaria it wasn't. The tests showed startling revelations of a virulent disease that had silently, and without noticeable pain, crept into his life, sentencing him to a fate no one returns from.

Now days later he still hadn't told her the truth, though he suspected she had checked up on him, had called the doctor's office herself since their visit.

"I want you back in this office the minute you get home from that trip to the Philippines," the doctor ordered. Mary Jane seemed to know about that, reminding him just this morning of the fact. She had remained in the outer waiting room while the doctor gave him the troubling report.

"I don't know any other way of telling you this, Lucian. You are an older man. You have had a longer life than most. Men in this advanced stage simply don't get much more time. I'm sorry," he had said and then gave an indication of what "much more time" meant, what to expect.

What was I supposed to do? he questioned himself, mind wandering. *Walk out of the doctor's office and say to Mary Jane, "I don't have much time left . . ."*

Lucian Parker had been aging, yes, but "older"? No, not an "old" man. Old men retired. Old men sat on their porch rockers and whittled, they didn't work. He still worked every day—running the depot. Taking people from miles around for rides on the steam locomotive down the line to Redemption town.

The water tower was thirty years his senior. The steam engine had two decades on him and it still ran. They held up with regular maintenance. So could he, he concluded. If he died, so be it, but he would die on his schedule, his way, working and living life, not on some doctor's timetable.

But he would see the doctor when he returned, especially if it made Mary Jane feel better. He would rope the moon for that girl. He had always felt that way. Guessed he always would.

Lucian was the switchman on the shortline railroad he had owned for more than fifty years. He could still pull the levers changing the direction of the train to switch from one rail to the other. He had just done so today, although it took considerable effort. Even today the rails in shortline country weren't automated like the mainlines.

Being the small country depot owner, engineer, and mechanic on this railway from the farmland of Warm Springs to the Santa Fe mainline south meant he knew everyone and everything that moved in and out from these parts. *Mostly a switchman though.* He nodded ironically as he contemplated this day.

"Ha!" he laughed out loud as if in dialogue with himself, his granddaughter still on his lap contented in turning pages. "Switchman. Now if that don't beat all! Haaa!" he cackled long and loud for anyone to hear. *I'll be damned and guess I am*, he thought. *Now that takes on a whole new meaning— switchman . . .*

If he had taken a short and direct line to truth fifty-five years ago he wouldn't be so worried about the outcome of his trip to the Philippines. But this day had to come. *Should've come sooner*, he reasoned.

His beloved twin brother was there. Buried. Left behind by war. And he had to make a final visit to find his peace with him, to talk to him, figure out how it all ended like it did, and make amends somehow. Then he'd straighten out this whole fifty-five-year-old secret—his quiet affair—with his precious Mary Jane.

His granddaughter had waited, patiently flipping the pages, talking to herself as children do while his mind had wandered.

"Grandpa?" She nudged him, looking up at him from a wide set of tender and penetrating blue eyes. "Grandpa!" she pleaded, jostling him awake.

"Oh, yes. Yes indeed. Eyes like Grandma's," he said smiling, giving her a tight squeeze and tickle around the middle. *"Once upon a time,"* he again began in a reverent whisper, but trailed off as suddenly as the word "time" issued from his lips.

It was a word playing tricks on him, teasing him, and his secret was like a balloon ready to burst. But then he and Mary Jane were leaving for the airport today. Then on to take care of this nagging matter.

His tiny granddaughter eagerly went ahead of him, turning the frayed pages of the colorful and well-worn fairy-tale picture book he had read to his offspring for five decades.

His mind drifted plaintively back making it hard to focus on the words of the children's story. He knew his inner turmoil, a private hell, would soon end—one way or another.

The child impatiently took over in a sweet high-pitched tone as she made her own story up from its pages, contented and lost in them, as a child does when absorbed in so much fantasy.

His faculties had abandoned the rocking chair this day, and left his granddaughter there to fend for herself. He went back to another time and place during the Great Depression of the 1930s. *Was that when it all began?* he mumbled to himself. *It was then, wasn't it?*

The rocker had slowed to stillness. The family patriarch had been lost in remembrance for minutes, no more, but long enough for his darling granddaughter to fantasize, turn each page, and happily contemplate the ending of the fable.

"*And they lived happily ever after,*" she squeaked in guileless innocence, reaching up to touch her grandfather's whiskered cheek. Seeking his attention, she grabbed onto his right hand and patted the gnarled work-worn hands, playing with the wedding band, causing it to turn around his finger.

"Grandpa?" she called. "Grandpa!" she demanded, waking him from his reverie.

"Yes, sweetheart?" he answered, breaking his solid stare out the living room picture window. For minutes it had painted a panorama of his past life and final deeds with his dying brother at the end of their private war in 1945. He blinked at the moisture unexpectedly welling in the corners of his eyes.

"Grandpa, how come all the stories end the same?"

"How's that darling?" he responded throatily.

"*Happily ever after*," she answered. "Do all stories end 'happily ever after?' " she quizzed innocently, still playing with his thick hand many times the size of hers.

He couldn't quite muster an answer. He watched her playfully manipulate the ring on his finger. It had replaced another one long ago, one inscribed with a deeper meaning than he could ever have imagined, until now.

That ring had been passed down to Parker men for two generations. First to him from his father, then to his brother, and then . . .

He could barely remember now, just that Manuelito, their faithful wartime Filipino ally against the Japanese, had it last on that fateful day in the Philippines. The ring, a symbol of faith, was lost for fifty-five years now.

He was old, more confused than ever about how stories ended, but he didn't lack for a memory. He had a good memory. And that meant he must not lie to her, nor tell her the truth . . . damage innocent hopes and dreams.

"If you do what is right and *keep the faith* then all stories end 'happily ever after'," he finally offered, hiding his true emotions behind a kiss on her soft cheek, a tickle to her tummy. "Run along and play now darling," he encouraged.

"Thank you, Grandpa," she yelled, as the screen door shut behind her petite and bouncy little body.

"You're welcome darling. You're welcome," he spoke softly.

His mind lingered on the happy scene of playfulness then moved on. It was as a convicted man does. Knowing he was about to be set free from a prison sentence he had brought upon himself and returned to his former identity—a man freed from his prison but on probation. Even the probation would end if . . . No, impossible. His brother was dead.

That is how justice works, he mused. It comes no matter if you want it or not. Maybe delayed, but certain to have its day. But he had *kept the faith*, hadn't he?

He had done all he could to make up for the lie he had lived. He was a servant to the townspeople, benefactor to many causes, an elder of his church—the one in the small neighboring town of Redemption just a hike down the road.

But all that didn't matter to him now, not if he couldn't be forgiven. He wondered if he could be absolved—if his one glaring fault of character could be erased.

My twin brother would want that, wouldn't he? And even at this late day in his life, would Mary Jane understand and release him from the weighty burden he had lived under?

He was determined to follow through with his final visit now. Mary Jane had consented to go with him. Outside Manila in the Philippines were the graves of seventeen thousand servicemen who died freeing the island country from the Japanese during World War II.

He had something to say to his twin, something that would set the record straight and resolve the deepest wound of the war. He could close that wound now, and at least offer this token of honor even though it was late, so very late in life.

He gazed intently through the large paned-glass window and thought he saw his brother's face smiling that silly grin from their youth. He smiled back but felt ashamed. He knew in his heart he had let him down, and that it should have been his twin, not he, who was sitting here now hearing a granddaughter sweetly voice the words of childhood innocence, *"Once upon a time . . ."*

CHAPTER 1

Summer 1939, Warm Springs, Oklahoma

"Don't you want to check out the springs? That's what this place is all about," Lucian said grinning, tugging his shirttails from his trousers as they stopped the ten-year-old Dodge stake-bed truck at the end of a dirt road outside of the small town named for the natural hot springs.

"Lucian, we promised Pa we'd check out this land—see if it was the one for grazing livestock. It looks like maybe the only one worth something in these parts. We got to go back to the county clerk and submit the bids while Pa works with the Santa Fe man on those contracts. Come on," Norman urged.

"It won't hurt nothin' to take a peek. We've come halfway across Oklahoma to take this job, and I hear these hot springs make your body sort of tingle when you're done. Besides, them years as boys down in Redemption? Pa always promised to bring us up here. Remember? We moved back in thirty-two and never got to. Now's our chance," he grinned, "to do some skinny dippin'."

"Yeah, I recall all about Pa's promise. But we made one to him too. Lucian, we got a deadline to meet."

"It won't hurt to take a dip. You want to, don't you?"

"Sure, I'd like a dip in the springs, but we can come back tonight," Norman protested.

"All work and no play makes for a dull boy, Norman." Lucian grinned.

"Yeah, well, playing is just fine, but 'there's a time for every purpose under heaven,' the good book says. You aren't the only one that can quote," he replied, surrendering to Lucian's whim by untucking his shirt and stripping it off. "I'll race ya," he laughed.

"Hey, Norman, that's not fair. You're not supposed to be so spontaneous," Lucian laughed, racing to catch up with him.

"Which way did that drug store clerk say to go once the road ended?" Lucian asked, huffing and coming to a stop.

"Straight ahead and then toward a path jogging off to the right by a clump of trees," Norman answered, breathing huskily.

"Clump of trees? There's nothing but trees. Off to the right? Come on." Lucian waved as he took off through the open meadow to his right.

A short distance later a path developed and they found themselves under a thick canopy of green willows making their way to the pool of water for which the small whistle-stop town was named.

"There it is," Norman pointed out.

"Well I'll be," Lucian said. "See that?" he said lowering his voice.

"What?"

"That. There." He smiled as they drew nearer the vapor-producing pond. "In the steam . . . over on the other side. Is that a woman?"

"Sure looks like it," Norman agreed with a sheepish grin.

"Let's hunker down here behind the bush. Come on," Lucian whispered, smirking and motioning with his hand for Norman to join him.

Norman hesitated. It wasn't like him to take advantage of a young lady . . . but in the heated mist coming off the pond she was a vision of a goddess if there ever was one. He stood there transfixed, staring at her slender back. Her tender curves were unlike anything he had ever seen and his heart beat loudly enough for her to hear it, if she listened close.

He could tell she wasn't wearing anything below the water-line either as she stood waist-deep, bending forward to rinse her long autumn-colored hair. At least her hair, as wet as it was, reminded him of autumn with its golden hues.

"Norman, sit down," Lucian commanded. "She is the prettiest thing I've ever laid eyes on," he whispered as he peeked through their bushy hiding place at the teenage girl enjoying her bath in the hot spring. "Norman!" he growled with another movement of his hand. "You're going to give us away."

But he stood there, contemplating more than her beauty. What should he do . . . follow Lucian? Where would that get him? He pondered. How could he meet her?

"No, Lucian. This isn't right," he whispered back. He was excited, a normal testosterone-driven eighteen-year-old as he supposed, but . . .

He watched a moment longer. She was turning to the side. The sight of the pale-skinned and innocent blonde bather dropping down into the water caused him to tremble. He recognized her now! He had seen her in town earlier that day and had sworn he would find a way to meet her. He hadn't shared that with Lucian—yet. Oddly, she sparked something else in him he couldn't quite finger.

No! Courtesy. Privacy . . . it wouldn't do for her to see him gawking like this. He had to give her respect or he'd never get anywhere with her. He'd never heard her voice, knew nothing of her life, but *this must be love*, he mused silently to himself.

"Naw, Lucian. This isn't fair. We can't stay."

"Are you nuts? We're not hurting a thing."

"Yes we are."

"No, we're not. Now stop. You're ruining this."

"It's not right."

"Well wait then. Just wait 'til she gets out of the water!"

"We've come here on business for Pa. The land is priced the lowest ever in decades, people are just givin' up and walkin' away and there is a county bid for it . . . we got to hustle, not let Pa down. Suppose some other bidder gets theirs in and we get back too late?" Norman answered.

"You ain't sane Norman. Now hush!" Lucian urged.

"Who's there?" the girl screamed, startled at the sound of men's voices on the far side of the pond.

"There you go, Norman. Now look what you've done," Lucian spit out, disgust in his voice.

Norman stood frozen, unable to move, apologies written on every crease of his face. Lucian stayed put.

The pretty girl submerged herself up to her neck in protest . . . and Norman could tell, fear. She glared at him. "You boys just get on out of here. Go on! Leave me be! Go on! You know the rules, or don't ya?"

"What rules?" Lucian called back from his hiding place.

"Don't give me that. You know what I'm talking about," she called back angrily.

Norman turned two shades of red and walked toward the truck parked on the dirt road, certain he had never seen anything more lovely in all his days. His heart raced, wondering how to make up for the embarrassment and meet her.

Lucian remained content to have some fun. "You didn't answer my question," he called back from the bushes.

"I'll scream," she said.

"No need, ma'am. But I have just got to say we were innocent of any bad intent. You're just so pretty. Guess we couldn't help ourselves."

"You have a smart mouth. Now go on! Leave me be! The rules are rules and you know darned well everybody gets their privacy."

"Very well, ma'am." Lucian grinned as he stood and bowed. "I humbly apologize."

She couldn't make out the distinct features of the young man but he was almost a double for the other man who walked off. She froze her gaze, momentarily confused.

"Humph," she snorted. "You aren't sorry. And your teasing, walking away, then hiding down like that. You're not bein' a gentleman neither."

"Well then. Let's leave it at that," he laughed as he turned to follow Norman.

Norman sat on a tree stump away from the hot springs pondering that face . . . and more. But it was her face, eyes, something he recalled from his youth—from years before.

They had lived in Redemption as boys. Their father had brought Mother there and they had eyes on making this part of Oklahoma home. Working for the Santa Fe, his father had been the youngest country station manager this side of the Texas border. That was until the 1920s roared into 1930 and then whimpered into the Great Depression of 1931.

Norman had gone to school with the prettiest blond-haired girl he had ever known. When he first laid eyes on her in 1930, his nine-year-old heart had fallen hard for the little girl from Warm Springs. For the entire year they attended school together he sought ways to be near her, fantasizing about carrying her books, holding her hand.

He even wrote love notes, undelivered, and looked for ways to get noticed in the school yard during recess and lunch.

Lucian was less stealthy in his ways. More direct. He had a teasing way. And Norman had noticed how it worked on her. He suspected Lucian had fallen just as hard but was showing it in a different way. They were twins, as close as two brothers could be, but Norman could never bring himself to pull pranks, tease, or be as carefree as Lucian.

He thought his young heart would break when his pa was forced to go into the big city in Oklahoma to look for work on the rails. About the same time he heard the blond-girl, two years his junior, had moved with her family in the great "Okie" migration to the farmlands of central California. Seemed everyone was moving somewhere else which made Warm Springs and Redemption darn near ghost towns for all these years since.

Now he smiled at this turn of fate. His heart picked up the sprinter's pace he had formerly known, as if time had been erased, and it was 1930 again. In his mind he was there, gazing across the country school classroom totally hypnotized by the prettiest seven-year-old girl in Oklahoma.

"Hey Norm!" Lucian called laughingly as he stumbled from the wooded glen out of breath. "Did you get a load of that? Wow! I never seen anything like that before. Whew!" he roared, happy with himself. " 'You boys know the rules or don't ya,' she says." He laughed gleefully. "Well I know one thing. I'm coming back tomorrow and this time with Pa's binoculars!" He snickered.

"You've got no shame, Lucian," Norm scolded. "It isn't right to do that. She's not an object to—"

"Oh, hush, Norm! What's wrong with you? Don't you think she's the prettiest thing you ever laid eyes on? You need your head examined, brother," Lucian added as they both made their way down the path to the parked truck.

"She's pretty, that's for sure. But it isn't fair and I just can't take advantage of a woman like that . . . even if . . . even though I'd kind of like to sneak a peek too."

"Now there you go. You *are* human," Lucian chuckled as they both hopped into the old Dodge pickup and started down the road.

"There's the house," Norman pointed out. "Must be hers."

"Looks abandoned," Lucian observed.

Norman's head turned against the progress of the truck as he drove. He was memorizing this road and how to get back here.

"For gosh sakes, look out, Norman," Lucian demanded and tugged at the steering wheel to get the truck back on the road. "Watch the road," he added.

Norman could tell that Lucian wasn't taking stock in who this girl was. He was too interested in the fun. He hadn't put two and two together. Didn't place her face in the past like he, Norman, had. *Typical for lighthearted Lucian*, he thought to himself. *That's why he can't see who she is. He's always looking at the wrong things*, he mused silently.

"Well this land is for sale by government auction for back taxes and we definitely are going to get that bid in," Lucian offered cheerfully, finally breaking the silence as they entered the small town. "I didn't think I'd like Warm Springs. Missed the city life too much. But I could really get used to this swimming hole." He smiled.

Before Lucian figured out who the blonde was, Norman would have to make his move, or he'd be out in the cold when his brother used his slick ways to dazzle the young lady.

Norman gazed over at his grinning twin whose mind was obviously at work, but differently from how he was thinking. He'd find a way to meet that girl, apologize, and make things right. He'd have to sneak back, break away from Lucian and his pa—who was waiting down at the depot. Before Lucian figured things out he'd find the pretty blonde . . . today.

CHAPTER 2

"The station manager just up and left for California, the Santa Fe man said. Says all we got to do is sign this here contract and we got ourselves a steam engine, two flat cars, one boxcar, and a depot on a ten-year lease, renewable after that. The house is ours at the end of the lease. What do you boys think?"

They looked at each other. Norman could read Lucian's mind. He wasn't ready to become a hick. They all sensed the Depression was turning a corner. City life, college was on Lucian's mind. Not to mention the girls.

Lucian smiled at Norman. He knew his brother was a country yokel at heart. Except for that pretty blonde and the interesting idea of a daily visit to the hot springs, this dusty one-horse town was going to be in his rearview mirror if he could get a ride out of here soon enough.

"Well?" Jason Parker, their father, prompted again.

"Well, Pa, there ain't much in the way of farmin' goin' on. And with no product to ship, how do we pay those Santa Fe folks?" Lucian drawled as he stuffed chewing tobacco in his cheek.

"Norman, what do you think?" Jason turned to his other son.

"Lucian's got a point, Pa. All the folks are leavin'. Why? The land here looks good. There's water down at the springs. It don't look so bad. It isn't any dust bowl like further on north and west in the panhandle. Why they all left for California them eight years back or so I can't figure."

"Big promises, son. The prices don't pay good here. The yields were down. A man can only take so much. A couple bad years in farming and you're all done. The government don't pay ya to grow low yields or high.

Nothin' they can do. This damnable depression doesn't offer men the work it used to. Men are paid less for the same work they used to do. It's not just Oklahoma. California may seem like a dream, but those wages out there are just survival wages, like everywhere else.

"It's land, this train, a business such as this that gives a family roots, stays with ya, becomes part of the heritage and good name. I swear, I do feel sorry for all these folks. It ain't been easy for us, boys, but we've made do. We are luckier than most. Come on over here, Lucian. Got somethin' to show ya."

Norman kicked at the old steamer and held back, leaving the two to do some talking, him to do some thinking.

Iron beast, this locomotive was a good solid workhorse. He'd loved trains as much as his pa, as much as any child ever did. He grinned watching his pa take Lucian on a guided tour of every working part inside the engineer's compartment and outside. Lucian was bored. Not that he wasn't a good trainman, just that his heart wasn't and never had been in it.

His pa was doing a sales job on Lucian.

Trying to convince him what a grand life country train-working could be. Surely trying to sell him on the greatest opportunity to ever come to this family of two children— owning their own steam engine. Running their own train depot! He smiled overhearing his pa's country drawl as enthusiastic as a revival preacher proclaiming salvation in Jesus.

His pa was a work of art. His mama too. He thought of her now. She was down in Albuquerque, New Mexico, at her widowed Spanish-speaking mother's, Grandma Violeta. Grandma "Leta" as everyone called her, was of Mexican-American and Native American stock. And with that mix, as pretty in her old age as many women could ever hope to be in their youth. *A real looker*, his Eastern born-and-bred granddad Lawrence Mead used to say.

His mama, the sparkle of his pa's life, was a princess to him. He treated her royally, yes sir. Pretty pitch-black hair common to mixed blood Mexican-Americans. Green eyes from the Irish blood in her. High cheekbones, characteristic of her Pueblo Indian grandparents on her mother's side. Ivory skin inherited from her father's crimson-haired and fair-skinned Irish mother. A mix that the universe had blessed and his pa had fallen madly in love with when he started working on the rails in 1915.

She was wheelchair bound now. Polio struck her hard just the year before. But she was spunky and loved life . . . she was the kind of woman Norman imagined he'd marry, with one exception. His woman was a blonde. In his mind she'd always been a blond girl. And he found her again today.

Norman couldn't help having his daydream shattered by the loud banter going back and forth between his pa and Lucian now that they had cranked the steam engine up.

"If everyone packs up and goes, who's gonna be supplyin' the goods to make this train-run worth operatin'? If Santa Fe is pullin' out, how are we to make it work out?" Lucian countered.

"I got contacts up north a ways," Jason Parker loudly answered above the noise. "Oklahoma City, Tulsa, even Kansas City," he yelled. "There are still folks who will never give up. We just got to stick it out, stick together, that's all. This depression, this weather—these things change. God won't punish a people forever. He just likes to wake 'em up now and then.

"Besides, we got the land and nobody can take it from us. I'm sorry for them who sold out, but they are gone West and aren't comin' back. Might as well farm and ranch it best we can."

"Norman always wanted to be a cowboy," Lucian grumbled, so low his brother could barely hear it.

"Santa Fe is still movin' out, Pa. Aren't ya a bit concerned we could lose everything here?" Lucian prodded.

Jason studied his boy's responses by gazing at his feet as he walked, as if the wood planks they stood on held the answer. "Santa Fe is just cuttin' their losses. These shortlines don't have the value. Just the mainlines. But they got value to me, to us. Your mother will be proud when she sees what we've done. Those are my thoughts on the subject.

"I'm thinkin' we could offer cheaper shippin' if we line up with a trucking outfit from here to Oklahoma City north and to Fort Worth south. Plus now I got this side deal cookin' over in Albuquerque with old man Monroe. You remember him?"

"The old codger who nearly fired you for the mistake that no-good-for-nothin' warehouse manager made up in Oklahoma City last year?" Lucian spit tobacco juice disdainfully on the ground when he finished.

"The same." Jason nodded. "Wish you wouldn't chew that stuff, son," he added.

Lucian nodded and turned away. "That man isn't honest," Lucian added. "It wasn't fair dockin' your pay neither."

"It wasn't that, son. He's just a hard man—fair but hard. I should've caught on to the warehouse tricks being played. He thought I had run them cars empty to Wichita without checkin' on the bill of lading first. He found out what caused it. He even apologized, sort of. Knows it wasn't my fault. Knows that warehouse manager, Calhoon, was skimmin' off the top—takin' goods each load.

"It don't pay—dishonesty don't. He got his due for that. I hear he's lost his home and packed up headin' out West. Old man Monroe, he's hard but fair. He has a couple runs a month I could make from Albuquerque to El Paso way. He says the Santa Fe won't even charge for them, if we piggyback on some of their runs. He says it's government work, that it'll pay four hundred dollars a run on top of expenses. Too small for the Santa Fe to handle, just right for us.

"With a little bit of work from the small farm here—if we get that land on the bid—we'll make the six month payment and have some cash to spare. You and Norman got that bid in to the county man, didn't ya?"

"Just got back from the office that county fella set up next to the barber shop. Pa . . . not much social life around here," Lucian complained and spit again.

"Not like it was in Kansas or Oklahoma City when you two were just little scrappers. A dream come true for your mother and me."

"I like it fine, Pa," Norman offered. "We'll make a go of it," he announced, rounding the corner.

Jason smiled approving of what lay before him. "Your mother needs this, she deserves this. It'll bring her peace of mind to be out here in clean fresh country air."

"Yes, sir," Lucian answered, resigned to his fate of becoming a country hick in a one-buggy town. "There's always the springs." He brightened and poked Norman with a raised eyebrow.

"Yeah," Norman smiled. He was thinking of the pretty blonde now. *She's mine*, he whispered under his breath. *She's mine.*

CHAPTER 3

Jason Parker was off walking the depot grounds, inspecting the turn-of-the-century loading dock and train station, savoring this once-in-a-lifetime opportunity.

"Great day in the mornin'! We got us a railway station!" he turned with a triumphant grin and thrust his fist in the air.

"We got to do this, Norman," Lucian whispered. "Look how happy he is. With Mama in that wheelchair, polio gotten to her the way it has, it's like he's got hope again." He spit his tobacco chew out, a sore look on his face.

"We'll make this place purr like a kitten,

Lucian. Come on. Let's get on over to the drug store. Get us a cold Coke and check this town out some."

"You go along. I'll stay here with Pa. I'll be by later. I want to figure out what he's thinkin' on this farming stuff—I'm not a farmer. I got plans for college next year. Maybe I can work something out to do both. You go ahead."

Norman jumped off the wooden platform and into the dusty unpaved road that led up to the main street. His mind was heavy with the vision of the girl. He'd never seen anything lovelier.

Main Street was two blocks long and ran east and west and then to a small town square with a general store, one room post office, and a half dozen other shops. The drug store and one-pump gasoline stop was on the east edge of town. All a ten minute walk one end to the other.

"You one of them train boys?" the old man sitting in a rocker called from the porch of a small cottage off the main street. He spit tobacco juice, hitting just next to Norman's feet.

"Yes, sir," he answered politely. "Norman Parker is my name."

"Well, it means a lot for us to see new blood comin' to rescue this old station. Worked it for forty years myself," the aged man said as he rocked and whittled on a stick of spruce, spitting and hitting the same spot with no apparent effort.

"That so? Well, we aim to make a go of it. What did you say your name is?"

"They call me Harry. My great-grandpa was a Cherokee, Grey Wolf was his name. My grandma was one-half Kiowa, married a white man. They used to call me "Chief" but that was long ago," he laughed. "Almost all them folks is now dead and buried. My woman was the prettiest blonde in these parts. Harriett and Harry. We were H and H," he laughed, slapping his knee. "A real team, yes sir. Harrison's the last name. But you can call me Harry."

"Thank you, sir. I'll be sure to. Bye now." He waved. *Nice old man*, he thought to himself. *Good spitter.* He smiled.

He crossed the street to the almost-deserted town square. The sound of commerce had slowed to an occasional door opening or a car passing through town headed somewhere else.

He wandered slowly, thoughtfully, down

the single-lane road noticing faces peering out from behind drawn curtains in a shop, at the general store, a tired and worn looking gasoline station—faces wondering, no doubt, who the stranger was, why he had stopped in Warm Springs.

Suspicious.

Curious.

Faces. Nameless faces so far—except for Harry.

Norman stopped outside the one room post office and decided to check on the number of boxes in town. The number would more than likely indicate the number of homes. *See how many closed out, how many available*, he thought.

He counted thirty-five exactly. A red note, VACANT, was spelled out and taped to one half.

"Excuse me," a young woman happily announced, standing behind him as he peered into one of the boxes, trying to read a name on the mail.

"Yes, ma'am. Sorry," he offered, politely removing his worn brown fedora, more cowboy-style than city.

"You!" she gasped.

Norman smiled, shuffling his feet nervously. "I apologize, miss. I wasn't aware of the rules."

"I ought to smack you across the face for scarin' me today. You left me nothin' private . . . nothin' at all," she fumed. "How am I to be a lady if nothin' private is left? Who are you anyway, and why did ya have to be so mean?"

"Norman, miss. My name is Norman Parker and my pa and my brother have come to buy the old train depot, on a note from the Santa Fe, and that land out by the springs . . . we bid on it—come here to buy it out. Some folks lost it to the banks and we . . ."

"My folks that's who! Just 'bout broke their hearts. They had that land for thirty years! Now you're buyin' it for practically a song?"

"I . . . uh . . . had no idea. We are comin' from Oklahoma City for a new life. No way to know—well you know how it goes. I am sorry. Granddad, he left my mother a small piece of money in his will or we wouldn't be here. A bit of good fortune in bad times, I know. And about the springs—I, my brother, we apologize. Sincerely, we do."

"Humph! Brother. You are foolin' with me. Messin' with my mind. I saw ya there. I saw ya walkin' off and then comin' back to the bushes to play with my mind."

"I have a brother. See, we are twins. I'm Norman. He's Lucian and . . ."

"I think I'll just get my mail and be leavin' if you don't mind," she said, furrowing her brow. Suddenly coming to her was a memory of two boys, schoolboys older than she, when she lived here seven years ago. "What did you say your name was?"

"Norman. And you are Mary Jane. See, I remember you from when we went to the county school down in Redemption but I wasn't sure you'd remember me."

"And you say you got a twin brother?"

"Sure do. Lucian. He was out there today with me. See we were innocent of any spying on you. It was more Lucian and . . ."

"Lucian Parker?" She smiled.

"You remember us?"

"I remember Lucian and you well. But you always were so shy." She smiled, suddenly aware of an old interest stirring in her. "That brother of yours was such a tease." She grinned with a shake of her head.

"Today, well it got out of hand. See he was the one stayin' and I was the one leaving . . . to give you respect, see. I humbly apologize. Lucian is just that way," he added, making his case.

"Well, maybe I'll forgive you. Let me think on it," she replied, trying to act reproving, not showing her approval at meeting the handsome boy like this.

"I would like to offer to make it up to you. May I stop and see you? Make it up some way?" His heart was beating so hard he was sure the blond-haired blue-eyed beauty could tell.

"I'm leavin' soon for California. I haven't seen the folks for some time. Needed to take care of Grandpa out here. But I'm going back now. We up and left about seven years ago."

"I remember. We did too. My pa ran the Redemption depot," Norman offered.

"We ran the farming land out by the springs. It about killed my folks to lose this land here in Warm Springs. Now I'm goin' to join them again in four weeks. I've got work out in California. If you really want to make it up to me, you'll make sure that you show it by helpin' out once I'm gone."

"What can I do?" he stammered.

She walked outside.

He followed.

"See that old house? The one with the worn paint on the siding?"

"That's where the old man Harry lives." Norman smiled.

"Yes. Grandpa. I see you have met."

"He is a very nice gentleman," Norman observed, trying to cover his tracks. He was caught off guard by the rush of emotions capturing his mind and tongue as his eyes froze upon the full pink lips, the fine, almost perfect facial features. Skin so delicate, soft, made of ivory without a blemish, almost too perfect. Eyes set apart like innocence with narrow brows accenting them. Eyes that smiled with the hue of blue like a clear sky— free of trouble.

She looked at him—grin mixed with furrowed brow—a weak attempt to act stern overcome by her interest in the handsome young stranger. "He won't leave. He's stayin' in Warm Springs. He can't keep up the place alone. You promise to check on him and I will think about forgivin' you."

"I think he has a new friend." Norman smiled. "Can I come and visit?"

"I don't see why not. Supper is five o'clock, right after we get back from church tomorrow. You can call then if you like."

Norman smiled. "I look forward to it, Mary Jane. I don't recall your last name," he stated, anticipating her response.

"Harrison," she answered.

"Well, Mary Jane Harrison. Again I apologize for earlier. I promise I will be more honorable. I hope you will forgive me," Norman urged, trademark fedora to his chest.

"I'm considerin' it. Five o'clock. Supper will be ready," she finished and moved to leave.

"Allow me," he offered, opening the door ahead of her.

She brushed lightly against his arm, a bounce in her step as lively as the rush of excitement running through him now.

"Five o'clock," he called to her as she walked off. He placed the worn brown fedora back on his head and turned around struggling to contain his new energy. "Five o'clock!" he whispered triumphantly.

CHAPTER 4

Norman strolled back to the depot on a cushion of air. He glided along taking his hat off to every passerby, smiling, introducing himself, as cheerful to know he'd be part of this Oklahoma town as any time he could recall being happy in his entire life.

Maybe I could convince her to stay, he thought. But she must be just sixteen if he was eighteen now. He couldn't marry her, not yet anyway. *Maybe I could write her and then visit her out in California. Ride the rails on a slow week. Court her long distance and when she turned eighteen . . .* His mind fantasized the possibilities.

Better she leave town before Lucian makes his move, he thought. *Yes sir. Far better for me to make my impression upon her and then keep at it. Better stake out my ground with her and let Lucian know not to cross the line*, he contemplated. Four weeks to do it and keep Lucian away.

He bounced up to the loading dock with one leap and looked for his pa and brother so he could announce his happy intentions of making Warm Springs his home. He couldn't help overhearing the lively debate going on around the corner. He leaned up against the building and listened.

"There are still some farms, some livestock going on. We got us enough money from your Grandpa Mead's inheritance and estate sale last year in New Mexico to make a real go of it! It's just been waitin' for the right opportunity.

"Son, I've been workin' the rails my whole life. Lucian, it's time to settle down. This place is about to turn around—everything does. We just got to have enough patience.

"Old Roosevelt, he's startin' some government work projects. The wages aren't bad. You boys could get yourselves workin' this summer and then . . ." His voice drifted away with his thoughts.

"Pa?" Lucian drawled, spitting some tobacco juice with it. "Pa?"

"Come fall we get those Santa Fe short runs goin', put everything back into this; pay her off—owning the land—maybe pickin' up some more—who knows? By the time you boys are all grown, you won't have to work like I've done. You'll be sittin' real pretty. Your Grandpa Mead was a right smart man to put that money in them bank bonds, scrimping and saving. We owe it to spend this right, not squander it. No sir."

"Pa, I was thinkin'," Lucian finally broke in as they both stood there looking out from the loading dock to the farmland bordered by trees near the hot springs.

"Pa, I had this idea when Norm and I graduated from high school last year in Oklahoma City of maybe goin' out West to work and gettin' into college. I could work the docks on the Santa Fe or Union Pacific at night, and maybe go to college in the day . . . makin' something of myself."

"So you don't think this is something?" Jason Parker waved his arm in a broad survey of all that stood before them.

"With a farm, some of the spring water, good luck, our own line—after I give the Santa Fe man ten thousand dollars we still got five thousand left for that land and a good head start on some cattle, some seed, a year of money.

"We could be landowners and own our own steamer—she's old, some forty years—turn-of-the-century, yes sir—but a real beaut, a classic. They don't make 'em like this Baldwin steam-driven beast no more. Diesels maybe pull more, but nothin' beats a real honest-to-goodness workhorse. A Baldwin Steamer! Nothing beats her, no sir. This is something, boy." Jason Parker turned happily as he ran his hand across the hull of the black engine that stood proudly against the loading dock. "This is really somethin'," he repeated with deep reverence for the forty-year-old locomotive.

Lucian judged the reaction his father had just displayed. "Yes, sir. I do think this is something. But Pa, I had this idea, see I'm real good at math and chemistry," he started.

"They got this engineering course at the University of Southern California and with my grades—I got a notice right here from my school counselor," he said as he reached into his back pocket. "It says that the government helps out some with tuition, and I join ROTC or the National Guard or something to help my payments out and . . ."

"I know, I know." Jason waved him off. "Your mother and me, we've been talkin'. I just think its best you put to workin' for one year son." He turned. "You could help build a real future and there is still time to go off to the city and do that schoolin' and city life you want so bad."

"I know, but . . ."

"Just give it some thought. That's all I ask. I know all of this is new to you, but maybe if you just slow your mind down, give it the summer, then you could have something to compare it to. Country life is a good life, son. It's healthy. I surely have looked forward to building a business with my two boys. If after you work a bit here and know it still ain't right, I'll understand."

"I guess so, Pa. I want your blessin' and I do want to see you and Mama happy." Lucian gazed around, coughed as a truck stirred up dust on the road nearby. "I know how happy you are, Pa. I surely do and I'll give it the summer."

"That's my boy. Why don't you run along, find Norman, and let's go on down the road a piece to Redemption town. Let's get a real good look at our neighbors. What do ya say?"

"Yes, Pa." He turned and jumped off the dock to the dirt road. "Pa?"

"Yes, son," he answered with a smile of contentment.

"Thank you. Thanks for hearin' me out."

Jason Parker winked and flicked his hand as if to let him know all would turn out. He stroked his hand across the black hull of the reliable iron steamer and smiled.

Lucian turned to watch the love affair his father had with the steel beast. "He's worked hard for it," he muttered to himself as he walked away toward town.

"Hey Norm . . . you been here long?" Lucian asked as he turned the corner and bumped into him.

"Heard the whole thing. So what do you say, Lucian?"

"I don't know. We're leaving next Monday for our first train run over to Albuquerque to pick up Mama. Maybe the old man will see how bad I want out."

"Look, brother. I support you. Just pack

your bags. I can handle it. I'll talk to Pa for you."

"You'd do that for me?" Lucian smiled as they jumped off the loading dock and headed down the dirt road leading into the town square.

"You bet. I think you should go to school. Besides, what's to do here? No girls you know," Norman added with a wink, baiting his brother into thinking miles ahead of the hot springs and the pretty blonde he'd set his heart on.

"You know Norm." Lucian grinned as he put his arm around him. "You are a real square sometimes. I swear if we didn't look exactly alike I'd say we had a different mama and papa. Thanks for the vote of support. Let me buy you a beer."

"Lucian, I don't drink. Knock it off. When are you gonna quit and just accept me for being different?" Norman asked heavily.

"See? There you go. You can't ease up, let loose, just be carefree. Always serious Norman. Proper dignified Norman," he laughed, slapping his twin on the back. "Okay, a *root beer!* Geez, you'd think I was temptin' ya to go to some big city bordello house with me." He spit his chewing tobacco out and continued to tease his somber brother.

Mary Jane peered out from the kitchen window facing Main Street. She shuddered at the sight of the two dark-haired handsome boys walking into town. The only way she knew who was who was her certainty that the boy she had just met at the post office didn't chew tobacco, and he wore a hat, turned up cowboy style.

But he was interesting, the tobacco chewing one, she thought to herself. Dangerous, carefree, laughing. She gazed intently at the twins who had caught her undressed at the springs. It was innocent of course, but now she was glad for the excitement. This boring town hadn't offered her so much as a date to the movies down in Redemption.

She wondered if the other brother, Lucian, was a bit more exciting, liked the city life. The two disappeared around the corner but not before Lucian caught a glimpse of her peeking out from behind the lace window curtains.

"Is that the young blond chick we saw earlier at the springs?" Lucian asked, poking his elbow into Norman's rib and pointing to the small white bungalow with worn siding.

"Could be," Norman answered flatly, seeking to distract his brother's attention. He still didn't recognize her for the little school-girl he used to tease years ago.

"Come on, Lucian," he poked back. "I'll race ya for the root beer. I win, you pay. You win, I pay." He took off. Lucian hesitated. He was already going to pay.

Now a love affair just might convince me to stay. He smiled at the thought of the blond-haired beauty in the steaming vapors earlier that day. *Yes sir. Might just convince me.*

CHAPTER 5

Sunday couldn't come too soon. Norman took the well-worn dark brown fedora off his head and straightened his tie. He reached up to the cottage door then pulled his hand back. He felt his heart racing to the beat of the pistons on the old steamer when she was cranked up full speed. He thought he had control . . . until now.

He took a step back to consider his nerves, what he would say, do. This girl scared him as much as anything—she was the prettiest picture of a woman he had ever seen. She messed him all up inside. He stammered to himself just thinking about her. No telling how he'd come off trying to spit two intelligible words out, one following the other, that is.

Dazzling azure eyes and fully flaxen gold streams of fine fiery strands cascading upon her slender shoulders like the perfection granted to mythical female figures from classical stories. He imagined every beautiful woman he could rolled into one with her. His father seemed to feel this way about his mother. He had overheard him admiring her so often. Now he understood love. If this was a fraction of what his own pa felt for his mother, then God in heaven was smiling on him now.

To find the love of a lifetime here in this two-horse town of south central Oklahoma was the least he had expected from this move his family was making. And to *fall in love*, it was something he hadn't given any thought to just days ago. And he had fallen hard—real hard—for this girl.

He was afraid of his feelings. It felt good, but he couldn't help the fear—maybe of rejection, acting foolish. It had him all in knots. Falling in love didn't seem so sane in an uncertain world with the Depression and all, and she was moving out to California. Foolish it was, to fall in love.

He cleared his throat and practiced his line. "Hello, Mary Jane. I brought you these," he would say as he extended the spring bouquet to her. He straightened himself and reached to knock on the considerably paint-worn raised-panel door once more.

Maybe she had come to her senses. He had seen her without a stitch on . . . at least a good part of her.

Maybe she would slam the door in his face. He had embarrassed her so out at the springs.

Maybe she would be so embarrassed after all that she wouldn't be angry, just unable to cope—like someone had taken something precious from her, something very private.

Then if he tried to explain, what would he say? "I thought you were beautiful?"

No, if he said that she might think he was a pervert, a no-good-for-nothin' peeping-Tom. It was Lucian making all the fun, but he couldn't tell her that.

Better to say, "Mary Jane I want to apologize and hope you never think I was acting interested out there at the springs. I'm not that kind of boy."

If he said that she might think that he thought she wasn't attractive, gorgeous, beautiful. Then she would be offended anyway.

He turned his back to the door to try one more line—"*Mary Jane, I . . .*"

"Hello, Norman Parker," Mary Jane called from the door as it opened. "I thought I heard someone out here on the porch. Won't you come in?"

"Sure. I mean, yes," he stammered in return.

"For me?" She smiled, noticing the bouquet.

"Yes. Yes indeed." He smiled, holding them out to her.

She raised the wildflowers to her face and inhaled. "Thank you, Norman," she said, offering a coy glance upward into his frozen admiring gaze.

"I picked them from the garden. My mother is crazy about flowers. She can't walk much—polio, see—but she gets a lot of joy from flowers, so we tend to them with her, and, well she's comin' to her new home next week, so I prettied up the garden a bit."

He stumbled on his words, self-conscious now because of his rambling utterances— his heart was skipping to a dance he didn't know existed—until now. "The flowers at the depot needed tendin' and I want them just right when our mama arrives . . ."

"How sweet," she cut him off, noticing his awkwardness, shyness. "The poor dear must struggle with polio. I surely would like to help her some. At least I'll have one month to know her before leavin' to help my own family in California . . . Grandpa, Mr. Norman Parker is here to have supper," she called into the parlor.

"That train-engine boy?" he called back.

"Uh, yes, sir. Sure am. And a real good engineer to boot," Norman chirped, happy to know the friendly old man would be there to help him feel more at ease.

"You can hang that hat on the coatrack if you like." Mary Jane smiled. "I'll go put these in some fresh water while you and Grandpa get to know each other."

"Yes, ma'am. I mean, Mary Jane." His heart stumbled to a jazz drummer's beat.

She winked.

"Howdy-do boy?" the eighty-year-old called in an unusually loud tone of voice.

"Grandpa doesn't hear too well. You'll have to forgive his loud talk," Mary Jane whispered as she returned with the wildflowers arranged in a vase.

"Oh. Well, I hadn't really noticed. Trains are so loud, you know. Everybody just kind of talks loud at my home," he countered. "I'm good. Real fine, Mr. Harrison," he said directly to the old man busily rocking in his parlor chair.

"Well you are the best specimen of a man this poor country girl has laid eyes on in some time. I told her that her train would come in one of these old days. Hee, hee," he laughed loudly slapping at his knees.

"Grandpa!" Mary Jane scolded with eyes focused tightly on him.

"Well, sir. If a boy were to have an interest I haven't seen a finer flower in this whole state. I guess the right boy might be real lucky," he offered bravely, unusually smooth. *More like something Lucian might say*, he thought to himself. "So how are you feeling today?" Norman asked, hoping to change the direction of the conversation to something more general.

"A bit ornery, I guess. Have a seat. Don't jus' stand there lookin' lost." He motioned with a wave of his hand to the small time-worn cushioned sofa.

Self-conscious, Norman positioned his left arm on the white doily on the armrest and leaned into the afghan draped over the back of the earth-tone love seat.

"Grandpa, I'll be fixin' supper. Please *try* to behave yourself," Mary Jane urged with a pleading voice.

He smiled and looked out the window trimmed with lace curtains. "Been here the better part of fifty years. Before that steam engine of yours arrived. Before most steam engines were ever built. New territory, Oklahoma was then. Yes sirrey."

"That is real interesting, sir." Norman intimated interest with one eye on him and one on the back of Mary Jane just feet away in the cozy country kitchen.

"Yes sirrey," he continued. "Long before you were a sparkle in your pa's eyes I suppose."

"My father wasn't even a sparkle fifty years ago, sir. He's all of forty-six years old. Mother is forty-five. She's gotten polio," he added, trying to make something of this conversation.

"Humph," he snorted. "Can't figure how a

man can come here to take over a town at such a tender age."

"Me, sir?"

"No. Not you, boy. Your pa! He's got to be a hard workin' man, that one," he offered. "Most men work themselves into a grave hopin' to pay off a small piece of land, and he's in his prime buyin' a shortline railroad. Now figure, I says to myself, he must have some powerful good connections."

"He's a real hard worker, sir. Started railroading at age fifteen. Married Mother at eighteen and her father, my granddad, wasn't too keen on him. He was an original Westerner. The original stockholder in a start-up bank in Albuquerque, New Mexico. Owned businesses and such. Wrote her out of his will when she married Pa. Then he up and rewrites her back in a few years ago, without tellin' no one. So she has this piece of money from the bank stock that was good cause Granddad made it through the bad years, made good loans—a shrewd man he was."

"So that's how your pa got this shortline and our old piece of land by the springs?" the aged man asked directly.

"Yes, sir. He is real aware of his good fortune. But now we got to make it pay off. We got to find some side jobs, and such."

"Well a boxcar of good luck and some Sunday prayin' would do ya good. Nothin' good has come out of this town for on to seven years now. Not since the crash of 1929 and then the drought. We're lucky we held on this long. I guess you might as well have the land as the next carpetbagger," he grumbled.

"Grandpa!" Mary Jane scolded. "It doesn't do any good talking like that. It's not Norman Parker's fault, his pa's neither. You know the county took it back for taxes owed. I won't hear another word!"

Norman looked puzzled. He wasn't expecting such complications. He was wishing to add some defense but changed course. "Smells real fine, Mary Jane. What is it you're cooking up?"

"Special chicken recipe with dumplins. My mama made it each Sunday after church. I didn't see you today at service in Redemption."

"No, ma'am, Mary Jane. I was wantin' to go. We almost regularly do. We had to put all our effort into the engine overhaul. Seems we got us our first haulin' job starting tomorrow. We're goin' all the way to Albuquerque and bringing Mother back. She's been there waitin' for near a month now visitin' Grandma and such."

"Poor excuse for breakin' the sabbath," she countered.

"Well yes, maybe so. I mean the *ox was in the mire*, see. And, well, the good Lord understands that. But you can count on seein' me there every week that ox gets unstuck." He smiled.

"Well put, boy." Old man Harrison laughed heartily. "Seems as a lot of that ox miring is due to how high the dung gets at times—don't it, boy?" He smiled.

Norman blushed a deep shade of red.

Mary Jane gave the old farmer a stern look. Her slender facial lines which followed to a delicate pointed chin tightened as she locked her jaw, pursed her lips. "Supper is on. Both of you wash up and sit yourselves over at the table, please."

"Oh that young woman can give the look," the old man chuckled. "Just like her grandma," he said, thoroughly enjoying the moment. "Now that's what I call fixins to satisfy a grown man's appetite," Grandpa called out loudly so Mary Jane could hear in the kitchen as he took his chair. "You do us the honor of sayin' grace?" He nodded to Norman.

"Please . . ." Mary Jane said, coming in from the kitchen shaking her head in displeasure toward her grandfather.

"Yes, sir. I'll be happy to." Norman watched them bow their heads and followed, cupping his hands together on the table:

"Oh God our redeemer; we give thee, the Almighty, honor and thankfulness this day for this food and all we have. God bless the hands that provided and prepared it. May we always remember your grace and goodness to us. In Jesus' name, Amen."

"That was beautiful, Norman." Mary Jane approved with a wink.

"My pleasure." He smiled. *I've won her over*, he mused excitedly.

CHAPTER 6

"Times are harder than many a man can re-member—boy," the old farmer everyone in Warm Springs knew as "Harry" said as he patted his abdomen appreciatively. "Very fine dumplins, granddaughter." He smiled with satisfaction. "Don't know what I'll do without her." He sighed as he moved from the table to a small desk where he retrieved his smoking pipe.

"Grandpa won't go with me and the rest of the family to California," Mary Jane replied simply. "We held out five years longer than anyone else that got up and went. But he's stubborn. Won't budge."

The old man nodded, winked at the young man and sat back down at the dining table. "Cal-ee-forn-aye-ehh," he grumbled accentuating the West Coast state's name, making his displeasure known. "Runnin' off scared. Darn near the whole state of Oklahoma," he groused.

Norman sat silently. Maybe the old man was right. He wished Mary Jane wouldn't go. Wished she were as stubborn as Grandpa Harrison too. He'd like to see Lucian go, but not Mary Jane.

"Yes sirrey, hard times these years have been," the old man added with a sigh.

"Yes sir," Norman finally offered. "Seems Mary Jane is needed here," he added hopefully.

"I've lived in this boring one-horse town most of my life. Now that we have lost everything, there is no reason not to go. California might be hard work—I've been there most of the past two years since the folks up and left—but it isn't this boring. Not even the country towns of Fresno, Bakersfield, and Modesto are this boring. Least ways they got movie theaters and dancing."

"I don't think it's so boring," Norman countered. "What with some land and some travel on the rail line. You could ride with us from time to time," he eagerly offered.

"Wouldn't be right. Mother and Father needin' me to work and all. Besides, California seems so thrillin' now that I can go out on dates. I was too young before. Why don't you come out there?" Mary Jane suggested.

"I can't leave my pa. He's so excited. And with Mama in a wheelchair and all. Guess it wouldn't be right."

"Good for you, boy. Now that is the proper Oklahoman attitude." Grandpa Harrison pointed. "This here is a real man," he added, shaking his finger toward Norman.

Norman sat up with pride, took in a deep chest-filled breath at the old farmer's comments.

Harry suddenly countered with a remark that shook Norman. "Then again, you've never lost land, home, everything you ever worked for, have ya boy?"

"No, sir."

"Well, I have lived long enough to know all things turn around eventually. But I never thought I'd see whole farms, towns, just dry up and move West like they've done. Might as well go off to search for the dream somewhere else. California is far enough away from the pain."

"Mighty hard for folks too, I'm sure," Norman added.

"Humph," the old man groused. "You know why we still got this house and can eat so good even in bad times?"

"No, sir."

Mary Jane now began to clear the table.

"I wouldn't let my children, Missy's parents—that's the name I give this youngin'—convince me to sell this old three-room shack and move out to the farmland. If I'd sold when they wanted me to, we'd have lost everything. At least I still got a roof over my head. Paid for and no taxes owed. More than I can say for most folks."

"A mighty good decision, sir," Norman responded approvingly. "Pa has never owned a home, never purchased anything until this old depot came up with the small cottage attached. Just rented until now. Saved all he could. Promised my mother her own place someday. A place out of the city. We're mighty grateful to God for it."

"Funny how it goes. One man's loss is another's gain. God blessed ya. Humph. Mighty strange how one gets hurt for another to get blessed. But you're a strong boy."

"Grandpa, don't be so sarcastic," Mary Jane interrupted.

"It's true," he countered.

"I didn't literally mean . . ." Norman stammered, seeking a way out.

"No, it isn't true. It's just life. You can't blame God for bad luck. But it's foolish to not give Him glory for good fortune. We all need to be grateful for what we got," Mary Jane expounded.

Norman's head went back and forth during the exchange, wondering what he should say. He had already fallen for the strikingly beautiful girl Grandpa Harry called by the family nickname of "Missy." He fell deeper in love with every word now.

"We are grateful, sir, and mighty sorry for them folks who suffered. All we can do now is better the situation. I hope to help all those I can. By the way, 'Missy' is a real pretty name."

"Well, I prefer Mary Jane but Grandpa is an allowance I make. And you're right, Norman. We all can do what we can and that will have to be enough."

"Well, we got more than most, I suppose,"

Grandpa Harry countered. "But it's because I used this old noggin', the clickity-clank of the wheels turning up here," the old-timer said, tapping at his skull with his index finger. "Come with me, Norman." He gestured, pushing his chair back from the table.

"Pudding is almost done. Don't be too long," Mary Jane said with a disapproving shake of her head toward her grandfather.

"Thank you for the wonderful meal, Mary Jane," Norman answered with a smile as he followed Harry out the back of the Main Street homestead.

"See that shed over yonder?" Harry pointed as he reached into his overalls pocket and pulled out a key.

Norman nodded.

"Follow me."

Norman followed the spry but aged man down some wood stairs to a root cellar under the shed. "Wow, it's got to be ten degrees cooler down here," he said.

"Twenty degrees on good days," the old-timer pronounced proudly. "Lookie here," he said, opening a hatch that led down another flight of stairs to a small chamber lined with boards and mortared bricks against an earthen wall. Both men stooped under the floorboards of the first level that became the underground level's ceiling.

Harry struck a match to a lantern hanging on a hook suspended from one of the overhead beams. "Watch out for black widdas," he warned. "This is enough for one family for an entire year. I never needed money as long as I had a roof over my head and a good supply of foodstuffs," he proudly stated.

"This is incredible. Grain, corn, beans, potatoes, beets . . ."

"This, my boy," he pointed out with a wave of his hand in a circular fashion, "is real wealth. Security, yes sirrey. Peace of mind." He winked. "If you fancy that young lady up there you'll remember what I am tryin' to tell ya." He grabbed a handful of dried corn from one of the barrels then blew out the light. "Now follow me," he said as he turned to go back up the stairs and out into the sunlight.

"Feels good, the cool moist earth on a hot summer day, don't it, young man?"

"Yes, sir. Surely does."

"Well, come on now. We are going to get some free meat for tomorrow's supper."

Norman was beginning to feel kindly toward the old man and grinned at his boyishness. "So where we goin'?"

"You'll see," Harry answered as he swung open a creaky picket fence gate, waist high, and whitewashed recently. They exited out the backyard that opened to a dirt road bordering a field and a grove of trees. "The quail love it out here. Pheasant too," he said in lowered voice.

"You going to throw corn at 'em or such?" Norman laughed.

"Don't be so impertinent, young man. Follow me an' hush."

Norman followed, reminding himself that Mary Jane and dessert yet awaited him.

Harry began by dropping one corn seed after another across a small clearing until he reached an old stovepipe some five feet long. He then threw some corn in the pipe and beckoned to Norman to hide himself in the bush at the front of the pipe and he would put some seed out the back.

"Here is a board to cover the pipe opening. Once that bird is in, you slap it shut. See that square wire cage at the end? I'll be there to shut the door once the greedy bird is happy and feedin' on the corn inside."

"Gottcha," Norman grinned.

"See there?" Harry smiled. "Now hush. Here they come out of the bushes. They can't resist. Even though it's a trap. Dinner for them today is supper for us tomorrow. Shhh," he put his finger to his lips.

Norman smirked at the joy this brought the old man. He enjoyed it too. All the years growing up alongside railroad tracks was in the big cities. This country trickery was fun.

The small flock of quail approached the seed which had been generously spread out before them on the ground. One eagerly fought off the rest and greedily found himself pecking at the seeds inside the rusty stove-pipe tube.

"That's right, come on now my fine feathered friend," Harry coaxed. The quail, followed by two more, scrambled for the seeds and came out the stovepipe into the chicken-wire box Harry had set up. He slammed the metal trap shut, sliding the door down with the pine branch he held in his hand. "Fine lookin' birds, wouldn't ya say, Norman?"

"Mighty fine," Norman laughed. "I can't wait to try this out on a bunch of them quail hanging around the depot. Suppose it works on pheasant too?"

"Why sure does only they seem a bit smarter than quail. Can't make too much noise and only the greediest get trapped. Serves 'em right though."

Norman nodded his head in agreement. He really enjoyed the trick. "I don't suppose these are going to turn into chicken dumplins next Sunday?" He smiled.

Harry grinned and patted him on the back. "Most people don't mind. Chicken. Quail. Dumplins all the same. And that granddaughter of mine sure knows how to fix 'em."

"Don't suppose you'd convince her to stay here in Warm Springs and cook them each Sunday for say, one year, do ya?" Norman quizzed.

"She's a headstrong one. Until you boys showed up there weren't no prospects here in this town," the old man commented as they walked with the cage full of squawking, irritated birds. "Can't really blame her for wantin' something better, seein' California and such."

"No, sir, guess not."

"Unless of course . . . " He sized Norman up and down with his eye. "How old are you, boy?"

"Eighteen," he said, inflating his chest and rounding his shoulders.

"Humm . . . Well she needs a real man or none at all. Come on in and let's show Missy what we got. I'll feed 'em real good this week and then next Sunday you and me can have roast duck." He laughed loudly. "Just a little imagination is all it takes, son . . . Just imagination."

Norman winced. He had imagination all right. Enough to wrap his arms tightly around that pretty blonde, convince her to stay, if he could find the way. He had one month to try.

CHAPTER 7

"What are you seein' that's so all-fired inter-estin', Missy?" the old man questioned, entering the small country kitchen for a slice of homemade bread and jam.

She fluttered the window curtain as if straightening it. "Oh, nothin', Grandpa."

"Them Parker boys ain't exactly nothin'." He grinned, leaving her flushed with embar-rassment.

She couldn't deny her interest and now reached back into the recesses of memory where the heart had locked up a childhood crush she had for one of them. She glanced back out the window as the brothers continued their walk into town.

"Hey, Mary Jane. What did you say to that one Parker boy?" Vera Scott asked as she came stomping back to the small country classroom from recess. "They sure are cute." She giggled.

"Oh, nothin'," she answered.

"You did so. You said somethin'."

"Oh, hush, Vera. I got my peace said is all."

"What peace? Did one of them boys tease you again?"

"That Lucian. Always gettin' in my way. Making some remark. Then he writes a note on my new paper book cover. See?" she showed. "Now I got to do it all over again. Make a new one," she complained.

"I think it's cute!" Vera squealed. "He wrote something in Spanish?" she quizzed.

"Yeah. He says his pa says it to his mother all the time, though he won't tell me what it means."

"So. Maybe it's a love note or somethin'," she whispered from her seat at the same time a small paper airplane hit Mary Jane's desk. "Look!" Vera pointed.

Mary Jane, blushing, opened the small paper airplane to discover a note. "Sorry," it read simply. She turned her head to see Lucian Parker looking around the room, with a silly grin plastered to his dimpled face like he was totally unaware of where the glider came from. Norman shrugged his shoulders toward her with embarrassment. *He was the gentler, kinder of the two,* she thought.

"Mary Jane, we should go ask Annabella Garcia what this means before the teacher gets here. Don't ya think?" Vera asked, smiling and waving to get Lucian's attention. He looked away.

"Don't, Vera. I don't want him to notice me."

"But he is the cutest boy in the class," she protested.

"His brother is just as cute," she replied.

"That's because they're twins, but there is something special about Lucian," Vera assured Mary Jane. "I'm showing Annabella," she said, grabbing at the math book.

"No, don't," the pretty blonde replied.

The two girls with the book held hands over their mouths, struggling to suppress the giggling while pointing to Lucian who now wore a wide smile of victory.

Unashamed of his pranks, this one was his last way of trying to show the blond-haired girl from Warm Springs he cared for her as much as his more polite brother Norman did. They were moving out of town next week and he figured it couldn't hurt.

"Mary Jane," Vera whispered excitedly. "Do you know what this says?" the freckle-faced flaming red-haired girl announced in a quiet breath of glee.

"No, what?"

"It says, *'Yo te amo, yo te adoro. Tu eres la vaca, yo soy el toro!'*" She cackled, becoming hysterical—doubling over in spasms of laughter because of the translation given by Annabella.

The entire room now circled the two girls hoping to be in on what was so funny. *"I love you! I adore you! You are the cow and I am the bull!"*

"Stop that! Vera Scott, you stop that right now!" Mary Jane protested. "All of you leave me be!" she cried, getting up from her seat and heading for the door.

"Lucian loves Mary Jane . . . Lucian loves Mary Jane . . ." the children sang. Another shouted, "Mary Jane the cow!" The room erupted in commotion-filled laughter.

Lucian slid out of the room ahead of the girl while Mary Jane suffered the wisecracks as she headed to the back door.

"I'm sorry, Mary Jane," Lucian announced as she flew down the back steps where he now stood. She charged past, determined never to speak to him again.

That was seven years before, the last time she had seen the daring twin, until this week. His family went to Oklahoma City for work and hers to California grape and citrus fields for labor wages. Norman was the obvious gentleman of the two and equally as handsome, but Lucian had a spark. She wasn't sure what. She would be polite to Norman, maybe even end up liking him, she thought. But Lucian intrigued her in a way she was eager to understand.

CHAPTER 8

Maria Linda Parker was grateful for her husband and two handsome boys. They were her light, her life, and her joy. She had wanted more children but the doctors warned that her fragility wouldn't allow another childbirth.

Now, in midlife, with so much life and happiness ahead of them, the plague that tormented so many families each year had knocked on their door. How she got the virus that caused her legs to stiffen with polio she wasn't sure. Only that the contagion was one of the most feared each winter.

She longed to feel life there again, to hold

her darling Jason in her arms and allow the lovemaking to happen that she was sure would last forever. Through all the years of poverty, the travail of the Depression, they always had love, the thrill of each other's embrace and the intimate moments. Nothing could take that simple pleasure from them, until this.

Now when their trial of shortages and privations was at an end, a new trial had stolen the former simple joys away. So ironic, she thought. But they had their dreams and whatever she could do to make Jason and her sons happy also fulfilled her now.

Jason had always wanted the dream of a country railroad job. But his own depot and locomotive with four rail cars! This was more than he ever could have hoped for. It wasn't every day in the Depression of the 1930s that a boon so grand was realized by a family. Jason had never asked for a handout, had worked for years, six, sometimes seven days a week. There were times that a dollar per day was all he had made, but he never gave up on his dream.

She was so very proud of her father for finally understanding how much she had loved the poor rail-hand from Oklahoma. For having willed her and Jason the money sufficient for this dream. She adored him for that. She figured her banker father had finally seen what a good man he was and was sorry for the alienation he had created. The inheritance was a message of love but she would have preferred the real thing.

"Mamá?" Maria Linda called gently to her mother at work in the kitchen. "Mamá? *Te necesito*. I need help," she announced gently.

Since last year her polio had subjected her to life in a wheelchair, and her arms were just now regaining much of their former strength. But she still couldn't quite budge the chair over the threshold. She wanted some fresh high desert air, the kind that a rainstorm cleanses and causes new life to blossom in the New Mexican high country.

"*Querida*," her aging but sturdy and stately Mexican-American mother answered. "Let me do it," she said, pushing the chair over the hump in the floor to the covered patio that looked upon the mountain range in the distance.

"The lightning is beautiful Mamá." She pointed toward the mountains. "The thunderheads are like giants in the sky. See there's one. Beautiful. No, Mamá?"

"Ahh, truly. But beautiful is a word God created for my baby." She smiled, kissing her child, now a woman in her forties.

"Mamá?"

"Sí hija?" she answered in Spanish, easily mixing the two languages.

"Is it hard? I mean missing Papá and knowing he isn't coming back," Maria Linda asked, knowing the answer but looking beyond it for something else.

"Aye, hijita," she replied with a long release of breath from her lips. "I thought I could maybe love again once. But now? After forty-five years of marriage he was my partner, part of me. When part of you leaves . . . yes *mi hija*, yes my daughter. Yes, it is like losing a limb, like losing eyesight, like losing a friend all in one."

"Oh . . ." Maria Linda sighed looking down at the legs she had lost. "I see." She stared with glazed eyes fixed upon the lightning show in the distance.

"It is almost *La Pascua* . . . Easter, Mamá. My boys are coming this week. All three boys," she said laughing. "Jason teases me so much every year with this stupid Easter egg joke about me being the best hen in the henhouse." She laughed tearily.

"I always scolded him for it—so improper—maybe I'll tell it to you sometime." She laughed. "But now," she shook her head looking down at her rigid, motionless, paralyzed limbs, "I can't offer him love," she cried softly in the comforting arms of her mother.

"*Querida*. Is that all a woman is good for? To give part of her body? No *hija*, but this you have." She pointed to her heart. "And this you have." She pointed to her mind. "And this you have." She pointed to her lips. "And soft hands you have. A lovely figure you still have," she added. "To say love is only given to a man in one way is to miss all of the other ways, *hija*," she admonished. "*Hija mia*, remember *tu padre*? What he would say? He would say that '*any cup with love in it is always full.*' "

"Thank you, Mamá. I had forgotten," she said, wiping at the tears. "Mamá, do you believe we see our loved ones again when they die? You know, do you believe in resurrection, the promise of Easter? Seeing Papá again?"

"*Por supuesto hija!* Of course!" she returned in both languages. "Now you are thinking very deeply. What makes you think this way my always carefree, cheerful Maria Linda?" She knew the answer to the question but allowed her daughter to speak, talk it out.

"Papá, you know, wasn't a very religious man but I love him and want to see him again," she answered. "Then polio. And the thoughts of the holy words *en la Biblia* which say *as in Adam 'all men die, even so in Christ shall all men be made alive.'* If we all be made alive someday then we shall be perfectly reborn, made new and never lose our loved ones. No, Mamá?" Maria Linda asked innocently, childlike.

"*Sí, sí. Querida hija mia,*" she uttered tearily, kneeling next to her deeply reflective daughter. "You are so wise in your age!" she announced, proudly placing her head next to her girl's cheek. "See the rays of sun come from behind the dark rain cloud?" she pointed to the mountain. "So shall our love be again after this life, scattering all these miseries of this time on earth forever away. So shall it always be for those who love truly."

"That's what I think too, Mamá. Yes that is what my heart tells me," she smiled. "You know how Papá always taught us to *keep the faith*? Gave us each a ring with the initials 'KTF' on the cross so we would always remember the family motto? I always knew he taught that it meant we should stick together, do what is right to others, being proud of our family and name. I wonder if he understood the deeper meaning?" she pondered. "He never talked about the symbol on the ring."

Maria Linda's mother shook her head with a smile. "He knew. That man of mine, he just was too *macho* to let anyone know how much he cared."

"Thank you, Mamá." She smiled. "I made Jason a ring, you know, when we got married. Even though Papá disowned us for so long I wanted our boys to understand they must stand together, keep the family name proud. But also look to God."

"It is so good to have you home, *hija*." Her mother smiled contented, and pulled a deck chair next to her daughter. "What will I do when you are gone?" They held hands and together watched the daylight turn amber, a rainbow accenting the horizon.

As the rainbow faded, the deep fiery orange sunset blended to a star-filled night sky reminding them both how small they were, and yet how each soul was watched over. They had lived fully by the simple motto of the ring and now lived in the hope offered by the upcoming *La Pascua—life and love everlasting*.

CHAPTER 9

"One month since we called this Warm Springs place home, *Maria Linda*," Jason softly whispered as he nuzzled her neck. She smiled broadly at his tenderness and at knowing how all this made up somehow for her sickness.

"I'll miss you every hour you're gone," she responded, tugging him closer and bringing her lips to his from her seat in the wheel-chair. "Stop that!" she scolded with pretense of disapproval as his hand slid to a spot re-served for more private places and mo-ments.

"Just checking. Making sure all is in order."

"Everything *was* in order," she replied and wriggled to straighten herself out.

"No place like home." He winked then blew her a kiss. "You sure you'll be okay getting in and out of the house now with that ramp?" he called from the dock where he now stood.

"Do I have to show you for the hundredth time?" Maria Linda asked with exasperation but grateful Jason cared so deeply for her safety. She wheeled herself around from the walkway on the front lawn to the entry door of the cottage standing ten feet from the depot. Easily she maneuvered the chair over the ramp and into the house then back again. "See? Perfect. Now go and don't trouble your mind."

Norman both smiled and winced at the tender scene between his parents. He had grown up secure in their love for each other but also felt the fear his father must have to leave his beloved mother alone. He'd never known a man who showed his love and affection more often than his father had for his mother.

"Pa, maybe I ought to stay," Norman offered in low tones. He knew if he did he would lose the opportunity to be with Mary Jane traveling to Redemption where she was headed on her first leg of the planned trip to California, but his folks came first.

"Son, I think your mama has a point to make with us. I would feel more comforted but she knows we got to work as a team and wants to prove she can handle it alone while we're gone. Besides Claire from Kelly's Drugs has promised to check on her two times, morning and afternoon."

"*Te amo!*" Jason yelled, grinning to his pretty but disabled Maria Linda.

"I love you too, darling." She waved and then wheeled herself to clip and tend to the roses.

Lucian was busily engaged at the water tower filling the tank on the tender car down the tracks. Norman had just about finished loading the coal tender from the shed nearby.

Lucian had noticed how Norman strutted, paced. Norman had been acting nervous all morning as they loaded the steam engine coal box and filled the boiler tank with enough water to make the run down the tracks to Redemption.

They had fired the train up now and moved it up the track to check off final preparations at the depot dock. "That Mary Jane sure is a pretty sight. Too bad she isn't stayin', Norman," Lucian drawled with indifference in his voice as he chewed on tobacco, a habit he was determined to master. "With this right arm I'm gonna be a pitcher when I get accepted to college." He smiled. "A good pitcher has to chew good and spit even better. Watch this." He spit out the engine door and hollered, "Beat that if you can." He laughed, looking toward Norman who brought another wheelbarrow of coal to the loading dock.

The young lady stood there looking at the near miss before her and then at Norman's twin. She shook her head in disgust. "Some things never change," she remarked with a touch of sarcasm.

Lucian removed his work cap and smiled a stained-tooth grin. "Mighty sorry, ma'am. Didn't see a woman. Norman and I were just having a spittin' contest."

She looked over at Norman with a stunned expression. She had already come to know Lucian for the wild side and his mocking her, weeks earlier at the springs where she bathed. She even suspected he had been there spying on her since. She tried to act bothered, ruffled, but silently felt something else.

"No, Miss Harrison. You don't need to pay him any heed. I don't do that. I don't chew," Norman offered in defense.

"That's good. I'm glad one of you has manners," she said as she walked her bag over to the seat where she would wait until the train was ready for the trip.

"Here, let me help you with that," Norman offered eagerly.

"Thank you, Norman," she said politely in deference to Lucian's snickers.

Lucian mocked her actions and voice behind her back from the engineer's seat where he readied the gauges. He was attracted to her, had made sure to keep an eye on her for weeks every chance he could but knew Norman had made his claim fair and square. If he could, he'd do something about that but there was nothing to be done now except admire and feign sarcasm, indifference.

"How long before we begin?" Mary Jane

asked Norman, who brushed at the coal dust on his trousers, hoping to appear magically presentable somehow.

"A few minutes is all. It appears Pa has gone back to tend to some item with Mama. Helping her get situated and all. He sure does love her, yes sir. I guess a man ought to love his woman with all he's got," Norman observed, making sure she noticed his answer. "All three of us are needed this trip, but we'll be back before nightfall, God willin'," Norman added.

"Poor dear. I must go tell her good-bye," she said, dropping her luggage on the ramp while she went to the small house to pay her respects. A few words, a womanly embrace, and some advice was exchanged obviously about Norman, for both women looked in his direction.

"Good," he said triumphantly under his breath. "Real good!"

"I will miss Grandpa," she said, returning to the dock. "I will miss you too, Norman," she added, reaching out to touch his hand while glancing over to Lucian, who was busy in the cab.

"Same here," he said, clearing his throat.

"I'd better finish loading. It takes a good box-ful of this coal to get the fire hot enough."

"Well, I'll just wait and watch."

Lucian was quietly jealous of the scene. He watched Norman strut and strain over the loads as he worked at impressing Mary Jane. It would be nice to find something to redeem himself with, some way of showing he wasn't a total jerk.

"Boys, you all about ready?" Jason called as he came out from the tiny depot holding a sack full of meat sandwiches and baked potatoes for the trip.

"We're just about there, Pa," Norman grunted, shutting the compartment door to the coal box. "Got us a payin' passenger too," he added with a smile.

"How far you say you was goin', Miss Harrison?" Jason asked.

"As far as you are, I guess. At the junction to Redemption I can catch a bus, then on to Amarillo where I'm supposed to catch the Santa Fe line clear on to Los Angeles."

"Well we got just the setup for you in the caboose. Norman, you show her to the car while Lucian and I finish the checklist. We'll be ready to roll in no time," Jason Parker finished.

"Sure thing, Pa. This way, Mary Jane." He smiled.

"Norman sure looks happy. Don't he, Lucian?"

"Sure, Pa."

"Well then. Let's do our checkoff. Tender been coaled and watered?

"Yep."

"Running gear oiled?"

"Yep."

"Checked dynamo?"

"Yeah, Pa. Checked," Lucian said with head craned to the caboose watching Norman give a hand to Mary Jane.

"Hydrostatic lubricator?"

"Yeah it's filled, Pa."

"Sand dome?"

"Filled."

"How's our boiler pressure?"

"Fine. Checks out fine, Pa."

"Pressure   gauge   at   two-hundred pounds?"

"Yep." Lucian was having a hard time keeping his mind on the checkoff. His head was clearly turned by that pretty blonde Norman had taken to. It bothered him to feel this way. But she did something to him hard to describe.

"Son, we are on our way. Let's make sure that fire is ready."

"Yes, sir," he replied, turning his head back to the coal box and shoveling coal into the fire. *Hot. She really is*, he thought as he shoveled.

"Here let me help you with that," Norman said, taking her two suitcases and trunk. "Looks like you mean to be gone for some time with all this luggage," he added.

"I don't intend on ever comin' back I guess. Except for a visit to Grandpa, that is once I get established and can earn my way out here again."

"Well, I hope that isn't too long."

"Me, too," she shyly agreed. "That brother of yours—Lucian. He sure is a sore-head. Most disagreeable. Why's that?"

"He's just embarrassed I guess. Bein' the situation and all at the pond. He really doesn't mean to be so smart and tough. He's just sore about a lot of things, I guess."

"Like what?"

"Like wanting to go to school. Not be a railroader. Wanting to be a college boy. He likes city life, see. Me, I care more for all this. This land. This peace and quiet. I'd like to settle down someday. With the right person, of course."

Mary Jane was now settled in on a cushioned seat with a table in front of her. She patted it nervously with her fingers as Norman finished stowing her baggage away.

"Here's the washroom. It's got all the facilities you may need. I hope you find it agreeable."

She peered over to the small closet door he held open. "I'm sure I will."

"I guess I'll be back here with you, if you don't mind. My job, see, is to look out for trouble, rest, be ready for a shift up front, change tracks, be a switchman while Pa and Lucian load coal and run the engine."

"Oh, I see. Will you be trading off with your pa or Lucian?" she asked.

"Both I guess. The run to Redemption should be all mine back here. Then we have a short run beyond to deliver some goods for the government."

"Oh," she replied simply. "What's big city life like?" she asked with a brightened look. "It seems so thrilling and exciting; all those trains, cable cars, shops, lights. Why don't you care for it?"

"I don't know why exactly. Guess I get

tired of the fast pace. All the runnin'. There doesn't seem to be a place to stretch out and lay back and just find quiet after twelve hours of work. It's got some dangers too. I don't think it's so great for kids. The country is better."

"But it's exciting?"

"Sure, to visit. Anytime you want a little excitement just hop a train and on into town you go. Nothin' to it. Since we own this line, I figure I'll be seeing enough of the city life. My wife and kids too," he added, hopeful she felt the same.

"So you plan on getting married? You have a girl or something back in Oklahoma City? Tulsa maybe?"

"Nope. Just thinkin' ahead is all."

"It's good to think ahead." She sighed, leaning her back into the leather cushions of the seat, closing her eyes, dreaming, no doubt, of some exciting big city far out West. "You're a sweet young man, Norman Parker. You deserve a good girl too. But then I'm sure you and Lucian know a girl in every city, travelin' like you do."

"Well here we go," he mumbled. *Couldn't she see plainly? Couldn't she see he was attracted to her, that she was the "good girl" he had longed to meet?* He doubted it even though he'd tried to make it obvious.

"All clear," he shouted out the window of the caboose to his father who waved a hand. The steam locomotive lurched forward.

Norman gazed at the face of beauty that beamed from the corner of the car. He admired her in a way he'd never admired a woman before. He tried to settle back across the aisle watching her contentment at leaving the whistle-stop town behind.

He noticed his soiled clothing, wishing he could change into something more suave . . . something clean and citylike. He doubted that any girl this attractive could take interest in a simple train man. *But then maybe . . .*

After all, she was a country girl too. He reasoned she liked the fact that he had known so much about the city life.

He gawked unashamedly at the serene repose settling upon the girl from Warm Springs. *Missy*, her grandpa called her. All of the shoulder length, flaxen locks and azure eyes that smiled but changed with the whim of colors she wore was more fair to gaze upon than anything he had seen or imagined.

He was smitten bad, real bad, by this Oklahoma belle. Falling asleep so easily—she must have stayed awake all night excited to leave this place. *Maybe she is just playing with my mind*, he thought. *Knows what she's doin' to me . . .*

Her lips opened slightly, a full pout that stirred him up crazily. He couldn't resist the thought: *What would it feel like to kiss lips like that?*

So content to be leaving. He wished she were contented to be with him now.

CHAPTER 10

Lucian exited the engine compartment and climbed up on the coal stack in the trailer car.

"Lucian? Where you think you're goin'?" his father, at the throttle, yelled above the hiss of steam and the crackle of the furnace. "You aren't going to do that asinine trading-places-with-Norman trick are you?"

He flushed red. *How'd Pa figure me out?* He questioned himself as he looked back at his father at the controls. "Just gonna ask if Norm wanted a break."

"Leave the boy alone. Can't you tell what

this means to Norman? I can read your mind even before it thinks, son."

"Awe, Pa, I'm just needin' to tease him a bit. I'll be right back."

Before his father could answer, he scrambled out into the tender and onto the water tanker walking on top like a man doing the high wire act at Barnum and Bailey's. He'd seen that once when the circus came to town in Oklahoma City.

Scrambling across the top of the rounded tank he felt like a bird in flight. The train motion was at thirty miles per hour now and he was walking the opposite direction. *Dangerous*, he thought. *Fun dangerous.* He grinned to himself.

Norman shouldn't be the one having all this fun. It isn't fair, he thought. Maybe it's justice for having been the one willing to linger in the bushes at the springs that day, willing to risk the embarrassment of the pretty country girl. But he knew she wasn't right for Norman. She was too excited about the city life. *More like me*, he thought as he scrambled across the two boxcars connected finally to the lonely caboose.

He had overheard her talking to the grocer a couple days before. She hadn't no-

ticed him in the next aisle behind the front
counter cash register until she checked out.
He had quickly scrambled to the front door
of the tiny store and held it open for her. She
had become more friendly, smiled, said,
"Thank you, Lucian."

How could a girl do something so inno-
cent and make a man fall so fast? He
couldn't mess with his brother's dream, but
he could flirt with it, he decided.

CHAPTER 11

Fall 1939, Warm Springs

"I guess this is good-bye, Mama," Norman said in reverence, kneeling at the base of the headstone. He gently stroked his hand across the words, then wiped at his eyes.

Maria Linda Parker. Loving wife.
Loving Mother.
September 1, 1895–October 5, 1939
RIP

His father Jason, and his twin Lucian, had each taken their time to be alone with her.

There was no explaining what had happened that day.

Sunshine-filled sky.

Enjoying her flowers.

The trip to Redemption was a one-half day's journey with the small load and deadheading back. Just two were needed for the journey but Norman had chosen to ride along that day. It had been weeks since Mary Jane had left for California and he had a gift ordered at Paul's General Store to pick up for her and send on to some place called Santa Paula, California.

The weather was calm, eerily so, as he now recalled. When they returned home to a stormy afternoon, darkened clouds had filled their horizon as they pushed the steam engine to get back to Warm Springs. A sense of foreboding had swept over all of them. How could they have known?

They found her there, in the rubble of the cottage, dead, next to a crumpled wheelchair. Their small home had been blown to pieces as a house of cards crumbles with so much as a flick of the finger.

The twister gave no warning. None at all. Funny how the water tower got missed. Real strange how the depot stood practically untouched by the deities of thunder and lightning. Why those powers didn't choose to protect the only human at the depot he couldn't understand.

Nature was allowed to take apart their home like it was a rag doll; she shook the stuffing right from it and a precious life was snuffed out as if Mama were an annoyance, in the way.

Skipped right over old man Harrison's, hit a shed, a barn, some out-buildings; on the other side of town, uprooted one-hundred-year-old willows and cottonwoods, and then flattened the dream Jason Parker had for the life he had planned—a dream of lovingly caring for his sweetheart stricken by polio and building a business with his boys.

"Time to go, Mama. I got me and Lucian a job on the Santa Fe. Pa asked old man Harrison—you know Harry, Mama? He's gonna be the lookout in the caboose and Pa says he can hire a boy now and then to shovel—be the fireman up in the cab. Things have slowed down considerable. We'll be out in New Mexico, Lucian and me, for the time bein', anyhow.

"Gonna put up with Uncle Sammy Mead, your brother near the tracks in Albuquerque.

We can stay for free for the time bein' and can work the warehouse for old man Monroe and do double the money earnin' by takin' shifts on the rail lines. Me and cousin Johnny Mead will be joinin' the New Mexico Guard together. Kinda makes me a New Mexican and Oklahoman. I thought you'd like that.

"May even get to go to California for at least once or twice each year. Least Lucian says he's gonna go as soon as he's got some money. They say there is a big harvest out there in citrus and they were lookin' for some boys to go; the Santa Fe warehouse folks and Monroe, that is. Lucian likes the idea—says he can be seein' California, big cities and such all the sooner. But I guess you know all that, bein' you are lookin' down on us and all. Right, Mama?"

Norman knelt down on both knees and bent over the headstone. "Bye, Mama. I love you, Mama," he offered as he gently caressed the stone marker with her name on it. "Mama, I never knew love like you and Pa gave each other. I'm hopin' for your blessin'. I want the girl Mary Jane to be my wife and I'm hoping you'll smile on us, Mama. I won't forget. Not ever. You were a beautiful woman, Mama. Pa, he loves you so. It'll be real hard . . ." He choked on his words and wiped at his eyes with the back of his hands as he made an effort to offer his final thoughts.

"I'm goin' now, Mama," he said, his voice, husky with emotion, struggled. "I love you," he added almost inaudibly. "I'll keep the faith. Don't you worry. I won't let Lucian forget neither. We'll both *keep the faith*."

CHAPTER 12

Jason Parker, red-eyed and slow of pace, walked up and down what was left of the depot boarding and loading dock. Lucian had the steam built up in the reliable, but forty-year-old engine. The twister didn't even touch the tracks it sat upon. *Why take a life and not this worthless hunk of metal,* he struggled to think.

He couldn't seem to comprehend what was happening. How so many years, such a grand dream, well within his reach, could be snuffed out in an instant—as if it didn't matter, as if the dream didn't count for anything.

"Her name was *Maria Linda,*" he voiced

roughly. He blinked at the incessant moisture stinging his eyes. "You know what *linda*
means in Spanish?" he asked Norman who
stood nearby, helpless at the sight of the
broken man he revered. "Of course. I've told
you boys a million times."

"Tell me again, Pa," he answered.

"Well, *linda* means beautiful. If you call a
woman *linda* you are saying she is pretty.
My wife was *Maria Linda* for a reason," he
said. "Pretty Mary. Oh, son, she was so very
beautiful," he whispered.

"We best be goin', Pa," Norman offered
gently as he reached for his father's elbow.
"Mr. Harrison . . . You know, Harry? He's here
now. Guess I'd like to train him as the fireman
helper. He sure is a sturdy old coot." Norman
smiled through oppressive gloominess, trying to lighten the moment the best he could.

"How you boys gonna make out? I mean,
you are gonna be fine and all, aren't ya?"
Jason muttered low as he pensively sought
solace gazing deeply into the boardwalk.

"You know we will, Pa," Norman feigned.
He really wasn't sure.

"I mean the Santa Fe line, they've sure
been good to us. Takin' you boys on, givin'
you and Lucian jobs and such. And you, Nor-

man, stayin' nearby in Albuquerque, means a lot to me. Sure gonna miss that Lucian when he goes on out to California. Wish he'd stay put and work with you," Jason sighed.

"I know it, Pa. I know how ya feel. Lucian has just got to see things—the world—a bit, I guess. He'll be back. He'll settle in. We'll still make this place go. You'll see."

Jason cleared his throat, tongue set in cheek, and paced looking for the right words. "I don't know what to say to you boys. How to tell ya what you mean to me," he answered. "You are the pride and joy of your mother and me," he said wrapping his arms around his son's neck and tearily giving him a moist kiss on the cheek.

"Sorry, son," he said as he reached into his overalls and wiped at his face with a considerably worn handkerchief. "You've made me proud, Norman. I want to thank you for all the extra you are doing, joining the National Guard down in Albuquerque with your cousin, Johnny Mead.

"That extra fifteen dollars a month is gonna just about cover the remainder of the land payment. Just wish Lucian was there to look out for you. Guess he don't care much for horse-riding though, does he?"

Norman grinned through the weightiness of the moment. "He doesn't care much for cow-pokin', Pa. You know me. That Guard unit is one of the best and last cavalry units in the country. The money, a place to stay for free at the armory while working the warehouse on the Santa Fe docks—it's a good deal. I believe in this place, Pa. I believe in you. I'm glad I can put the money back here to help out."

Jason Parker, head hung lower than his round shoulders, surveyed the ground for a response. He finally nodded and again studied his boy. They reached for each other in the same instant and embraced strongly. No words exchanged. None were needed.

"Let's round things up, son," Jason remarked as he pulled himself together to greet the old man stepping up onto the platform.

"Mighty fine sermon and mighty fine service for your missus, Jason. I surely do appreciate your sorrow," Warm Springs' most senior citizen offered genuinely, grasping hands with the depot owner.

"Thank you, Mr. Harrison."

"Please call me Harry." He smiled.

"Harry it is."

"Hello, Harry. Let me help you with that,"

Norman offered, taking his lunch pail and thermos jug. "We'll stow it right up here in the cab. Guess you are ready for fireman training?"

"You bet I am." The eighty year old winked.

Jason turned to his son, his back to the old man. "That old fella will do fine. He'll be good company too, while you boys are gone. And I'll bet he can shovel coal as good as many a man."

Norman knew what his pa was up to, as if in saying so, it would make everything all right. "But you watch out and let me know how it goes to Redemption. Don't want him tryin' to do too much—overdoin' himself. I'll get settled in the caboose, try to get some shut-eye. Send Lucian along to keep me company, will ya?"

"Sure thing, Pa." Norman would live the illusion for a while and then pray to God that his pa could handle the load he and Lucian would be leaving him.

"Always wondered what it would be like to run one of these things." Harry smiled as he took the engineer seat from Norman.

"You look like a real old-fashioned steam-engine man, Harry. It suits you."

The steamy noise from the boilers, the roar of the coal fire burning, and the clack of the rails drowned out most small talk. The old man nodded in agreement to whatever was said and waved out the window to some children who stood by the rails.

Norman smiled. Harry had found a pleasure that little boys feel when they get their first train set under the Christmas tree. It wouldn't be the same for his pa as when he and Lucian were there, but the older man had a quixotic energy and vitality about him. It livened things up to be with him. Even if his pa would have to shovel most of the coal—Harry would be good for him and he would be good for Harry.

"How's Mary Jane?" Norman mouthed loudly.

"Ehh? What's that son?"

"I say, how is Mary Jane?" he called above the roar.

"Oh, Mary Jane. Well then. The letter just came day before yesterday. She arrived to some place called Santa Paula, out in citrus growin' country north of Los Angeles somewheres. She likes it fine. Says to say hello. I think she likes you."

"Really? You think so?" Norman perked

up. "Well I got to write her then. You wouldn't have that address, would ya?"

"Sure. Back at the house. Don't you worry. I'll give it to your pa. She is a feisty lady, that granddaughter of mine, but worth every ounce."

"Yes, sir. She surely is."

Mary Jane was a dream wafting across his mind every hour or so it seemed. He couldn't put her out of his head. He was going to stay out here over fifteen hundred miles away in New Mexico while Lucian worked a month for traveling money and moved on to California.

Well, he wouldn't allow Lucian any slack on this one. He'd keep this information to himself. He should've laid Lucian out for that trick he pulled the day they took Mary Jane to the Redemption train depot. But then came the tornado and all. The weeks had gone by in a blur of emotion trying to figure out what each of the three Parker men would do.

He knew one thing he'd do for sure. He'd take a week off right after National Guard training. He'd ride the rails out to California, see Lucian and find Mary Jane, and ask her to marry him.

CHAPTER 13

Santa Fe Line, San Diego

"Tryin' to get me up to the Santa Fe loadin' docks in Ventura County," Lucian called with a grunt. "Pretty blonde up there I'm fixin' to see. At least I think she's still there. Santa Paula is the town."

The big man grunted and passed the next crate along to Lucian who fit them neatly on pallets in a boxcar. "This military stuff gets old. Might as well join up for all this stuff we've been packin'," the big man answered.

"Yeah. I don't care so much for the way these sailors and marines get all the girls neither. Don't really seem fair that a uniform can do so much to a fella," Lucian drawled with tobacco stuffed in his cheek.

"Guess I should join up," the big man reminded himself aloud. "I mean the pay isn't much less than I'm makin' now and they get free room, free food . . . and girls. Sure is temptin'."

"Yeah, guess so." Lucian stopped and wiped at his brow. "Weather can't be beat here in San Diego. Folks say it's just as nice up the coast too. Like it a whole lot better than Oklahoma in the summertime. Nice cool breezes, salt air, and lots of bathing suits to ponder on down at the beach," he smiled.

"Yeah. Minnesota don't have too many of them," the big man said, pulling an apple out of his lunch pail.

"Want a Coke?" Lucian called above the noise of a passing train, boarding calls, passenger talk. He walked a few paces to the cooler, flipping a nickel into the honor jar. The big man nodded.

"What ya say we catch the late train up to that skinny dippin' cove past La Jolla ways? Pretend we are marines on leave. We got a place back home in Warm Springs where bashful people don't dare show up. The prettiest girl I ever laid eyes on . . . yes sir . . . not a stitch to her name when I first laid eyes on her. They say a dozen or so romp in the surf about midnight. Drunk as skunks on a hot August night . . . so they say. Heard some sailors talkin' about it."

The big man grinned as he bit heavily into the crisp red apple. He slugged the Coke down without a breath and wiped at his mouth. "Be back by mornin' shift?"

"Just hop the Coastal Express there at Del Mar." Lucian smiled. "Always a couple of flat cars to ride on."

"I could sure use a good—" He coughed choking on a piece of apple.

"Swim?"

"Yeah. Swim." The big man laughed.

"How long we worked together?" Lucian asked.

"Three hours," the big man answered. "You're trouble in blue jeans. Know that?"

"The name's Lucian. Oklahoma is home," he said, extending his hand.

"Albert Handy from Minnesota," the big man said. "Didn't know if I was gonna like you at first."

"Me neither," he laughed. "Look. You just get here to San Diego or what?"

"No. I been working out on the line up in Imperial Valley. Talk about Oklahoma heat! Whew! It gets a hundred and twenty degrees in the shade some days. I got me this cushy loading job on account of the new government contracts happening all of a sudden. All this Jap attacking the U.S. bases talk. Just talk. Just rumors. But them boys are really mean son-of-a-guns, killing Chinese like swatting at flies. Know what I mean?"

"Yeah. But they would be stupid—performing a monumental stupidity if you ask me, to think they could attack a U.S. base and win," Lucian returned.

"Yeah. Still the same, this old stuff left over from the last war is going to Philippines and Hawaii like it was going out of style. I was in the Guard back home. Still am, I guess. This stuff ain't worth horse . . ." Al yelled above the noise.

"Say what? What was that?" Lucian yelled as the sound of a passing train drowned them out.

The big man mouthed it back louder. "Said I was in the Guard back home and this stuff ain't worth jack . . ." More noise drowned him out. Al continued, "Fuses don't blow, bullets don't fire, rifles missing springs, rusty bolts . . . you name it. We aren't ready for no war."

"My brother is in the Guard. New Mexico. I almost joined with him," Lucian replied.

"Thought you said you was from Oklahoma."

"I am. But the closest outfit is New Mexico. Besides, he works for the Santa Fe there and we got kin and all who were joining up."

"So why didn't you join?" the big man asked, still yelling above the sounds of passing trains.

"Don't care much for the military life, but just in case something hits the fan I might go back and join him for a while. For now I'm a college boy at night. Going to school at San Diego State nights, up in Los Angeles next fall if things work out. Gonna look that girl up that ways too."

"Just as well. If we got attacked and the Japs or Germans didn't kill ya, this stuff probably would."

Lucian understood. His father had gone to battle in the First World War. The present gear, ammunition, boxes of aged bolt action Springfields, old grenades, weren't comforting—no match for the new German weapons. That concerned him some, but not the Japanese. They were no threat. *They were butchers just killing their own kind*, he thought.

"Well. Guess we best finish this up and get on to acting like marines on leave . . . what ya say, Al?"

The big man threw a crate marked FIELD RATIONS and grinned.

"Some say a man should take it nice and slow. Women like that. So they say."

"Suppose so," Lucian answered not wanting to tip his new friend off. He'd had no experience. Nothing to base how to treat a woman on, except for some outings in groups in high school and watching how his pa treated his mother. Acted like a darned fool around that pretty girl in Warm Springs. At least Norman had been cool—collected, a gentleman.

"They say women like to talk a lot, feel understood," Al muttered.

"Who says that?"

"Some woman writer in *Life* magazine.

Read it just the other day. Says they like to be noticed for looks, but need understanding," the big man added as the train clicked off another mile north along the Pacific Coast. "Sure pleasant out here. A man could live forever in this sunshine." He smiled and lay back, head on the small duffel bag he had brought along.

"Would need someone to share it with. Sure enough could be pleasant," Lucian agreed as he cast his gaze out to the blue waters shimmering with a tint of orange as the sun pulled the shades of evening down with her.

"How far is Encinitas?" Al asked, relaxed now as the flat car clanked along the tracks.

"Oh, I'd say fifteen minutes and we best be ready to roll off into the easiest sand dune we can land on. We are in La Jolla now." Lucian pointed at the sign.

"So these bathing beauties are a sure deal?"

"Every Friday night—so says those sailors I talked to at the station." Lucian smiled.

"Boy . . . I haven't seen anything prettier than these California girls," Al pondered aloud.

"I have," Lucian said under his breath. "I surely have."

CHAPTER 14

"Some cove. Some beach loaded with skinny-dippin' mermaids anxious for a little fun," the big man grumbled.

"I could have sworn them sailors said Encinitas. Come on, let's ask around."

"No way I'm gonna make a fool out of myself. There a good bar around here?"

"Awe, come on, ya sore-head. This ain't no time to get drunk. We gotta find some women, catch a midnight swim. Maybe we just got off the train too soon," Lucian assured, slapping the big man on the back. "Come on," he said motioning with his hand.

The two men ran across the highway to a

small grocery store. The whitewashed door swung open on creaky hinges, the only sound disturbing the faint crashing of waves on the beach across the road.

"Hello!" Lucian called. "Anybody here?"

"Don't get rattled. Hold your darn horse. Might know someone would call the same time Mother Nature did. Now what can I do for you boys?" A slender, bespectacled man in country overalls came from the back of the store to the front counter.

"Kinda lonely out here." Lucian smiled.

"Just this time of night," the store owner replied. "What you boys doing way out here on foot?" he asked, looking out the window, noticing no sign of a car.

"Just hopped a train from San Diego. Lookin' for some sailor buddies. They told us to meet them and some girlfriends here. For a swim." Lucian smiled.

The store owner nodded, appearing not to grin. "The cops run them off two weeks ago. Indecent exposure, they called it. Handcuffed a few sailors then let 'em go. I think that party moved to La Jolla Cove back that-a-way." He pointed south.

"Much obliged. Say you got some cold drinks of some sort?"

"You boys servicemen?" the store keeper asked, heading for a cooler.

"We're military ammo loaders on the Santa Fe. Servicemen? We sure are." Lucian grinned.

Al looked on admiringly at the smooth ways of his new work associate.

"Here you go. On the house. You boys just keep them Japs way out there in the Pacific where they belong and you can have a soda on me any time."

"Sure thing, mister. That's mighty kind. You must be an Oklahoman. Friendly as you are and such."

"Nope. Ohio is home. Seems everybody around here is from somewhere else. But don't suppose that means much to you boys just yet. Settle down some, and you'll find this to be the best mix of people under God's great sun."

"I hope to settle down soon. I sure do like California and all. Well, we best be goin' to find our friends. Say, you sell Lucky Strikes? For my friend here," he said digging in his pocket for a quarter dollar and laying it on the counter.

"Two bits will do it," the proprietor said, handing him the pack with the big bull's-eye.

"Whew. Them just got expensive. Here ya go, big Al." Lucian smiled. The store owner didn't blink.

"Consolation prize," the big man grumbled breaking the pack open and pulling his lighter out of his trouser pocket.

It was sunset and the next train wouldn't be by for another couple of hours.

"Guess we try to hitch a ride," Lucian suggested as they crossed the highway to the beach side of the road.

"Not much traffic." Al nodded at the northbound lanes, blowing smoke in puffs as he contemplated the ruined evening.

"Best be walkin'. Hear any sound of cars, stick that big thumb out of yours. I'll do the same."

A half-hour went by with two cars headed in the opposite direction. The sound of an approaching vehicle prompted the two to turn around and toss their thumbs out begging for a ride to La Jolla. The tan Packard convertible skidded to a halt yards ahead and the two ran to find three females giggling and fighting over how to share the space.

"Howdy," Lucian drawled. "You girls can't be offerin' us fellas a ride now, could ya?"

He grinned. Al threw down his cigarette and crushed it under his foot.

"You boys look like you could use a ride into town. What ya say girls?"

The big man hopped into the backseat with a pretty redhead before Lucian could muster up a word of thanks or ask where they should sit.

The brunette at the wheel with her hair pulled back was laughing as she looked in the rearview mirror to see her friend setting the big man straight about how close he was to get.

Lucian hadn't been able to make out the face of the shy girl, the passenger who began to scoot over in the front, making room for him to take a seat. He threw his small bag in back with Al and looked at her, trying to get her to reveal a turned-away face. "Hi, my name is Lucian," he offered with an outstretched hand as the driver pulled back onto the road.

Stunned, the reluctant blonde with a red scarf covering most of the wavy golden locks turned abruptly to the man seated next to her. She wore sunglasses concealing her eyes. Removing the eyewear she looked intensely into his smiling eyes. "You!"

Lucian's smile widened. "Well, how do you do, Miss Harrison?"

CHAPTER 15

Four Months Later, Santa Paula, California

"Loading oranges on the Santa Fe is fine for some but I'm goin' to school in L.A. next month. Picked me up a job at the downtown warehouses with the company. USC accepted my San Diego State credits. Gonna go to school days and loadin' nights. Yes sir . . . I'm stayin' out here, Norm. And ooh la la, the California girls!" He grinned.

"I got to be back for training in thirty days. The Guard unit is heading down to Fort Bliss for regular training. You ought to join up."

"Norman, you're too serious about workin'

and what is all this playin' army about any-way? There isn't gonna be no war."

"Lucian, there just might not be. So what's with your ROTC classes you just said you enrolled in at USC if you don't think it's pos-sible? Besides twenty-five dollars extra per month is twenty-five dollars extra and it puts me near Pa and home. I can send him the fifteen dollar land payment and go home just about once a month, and I'm fixin' to buy me the abandoned Dearborn spread the other side of the springs. This Depression is tur-nin'. Things will get better, be pickin' up. Gonna find me a good woman and settle down."

"Mary Jane?" he quizzed nervously with a feigned grin, tossing a plump orange to his fellow worker Al, who had followed him from San Diego.

"Nice ripe one," the big man grinned, peel-ing and then biting into it.

"You haven't seen or heard of her yet, have you?" Norman quizzed, tossing a crate of oranges on top of another.

"I hear she has gone to work in Los An-geles. Waitin' tables and goin' to school," Lucian tried to say without interest in his voice.

"Who says?" Norman quizzed.

"Folks here knew her folks. They moved on to Fresno awhile back."

"Well. I think I'll pay a visit on my way back to army boot camp. Won't hurt. Guess old Harry Harrison could tell me where she is if I put in a call to the depot back home," Norman mentioned casually as he tossed another crate onto a pallet headed for the cooler.

"How's Pa, anyway?" Lucian asked changing the subject.

"Guess the whole town turned out to help him put the damaged walls to the depot back up. No house, just a couple rooms for living quarters attached to it. He's a real proud man; but he accepted the help. We should've been there," Norman added, grunting as he laid another crate up in the stack.

"Guess so," Lucian replied.

"Hey, what's the big idea," Al growled, spitting out the pulp and a large portion of a worm with it.

Lucian backed away slowly, laughing. "Now see here, Al. Can't blame me if it's extra juicy," he said laughing, as he took off with a leap from the warehouse loading dock followed by the big man through orange trees nearby. Al in his overalls was no match for Lucian's lightness and speed.

Norman smiled as he finished loading the crates, listening to Lucian's mischievous taunting off in the distance. He had known enough of his brother's playfulness to last a lifetime. It was time to get serious though. Glad his brother was chasing his dream, but he could find no way in his soul that he would let his pa down. He figured Lucian just didn't feel the same, but didn't blame him. He was working for a bigger dream anyway. A house, a woman, and a long future with the business of railroading once this Depression turned around.

And the woman. Mary Jane nagged at his mind constantly. She bent it and twisted it all up. He'd like to forget her but she was there, always there. Smiling with those azure eyes that could turn a man to mush, and dipping her shoulder just so as she relaxed cross-legged, engaged in some interesting conversation about life and such.

She was slender. So slender she would break in a strong wind if he wasn't there to hold onto her. And that was exactly what he planned to do. Embrace her, love her, and lay down everything he was and would be if he had to for that woman.

The army pay would give him a good boost. He could work the Santa Fe docks down in Albuquerque until he had enough money to pay off the Dearborn place in Warm Springs. Be near home too. The Guard would give him a free place to sleep.

It was working out perfect in his mind. His pa had survived the worst of it with the help of Harry, and his and Lucian's extra money was goin' home to pay off the debts to land and depot.

Just one thing left to figure out and do. He was in love or a fool. Either way he needed to see Mary Jane. And seein' her would only make his sickness worse.

He needed her. She might be willing to marry if he laid his plans out right. There was something between them. He could feel it.

Tomorrow he'd hitch a ride on the Southern Pacific line up to L.A. and call his pa, get the address of where she worked from her granddad, Harry.

He looked at the loaded pallet with satisfaction. They had run out of work in Albuquerque. Now they need him back, and of course so did the Guard unit he was training with.

He liked the orange-growing country of rolling Ventura County hills. The cool Pacific breeze was pleasant. But he had to get back, keep working to have the girl of his dreams go with him too. He hoped she hadn't become too attached to all this California pleasantness, the city life she had found in Los Angeles.

Slapping his time card through the clock, he headed for the company phone. Then, after packing, he'd say good-bye to his brother, this stint on the rails in California, and look at the future with Mary Jane's shining eyes and smiling face staring back at him every day of his life.

Love hurt bad. But nothing hurt so good neither. He never knew a pain like this one. They don't make pills or tonics to make it go away, he reasoned. Nothing lasted more than wanting this woman Mary Jane. And nothing felt better than believing he would have her forever. *God made bliss but he surly made a man to hurt too*, he thought to himself.

Not having her was like a sore spot that festered in his heart. All wound up like a spring, his heart felt like breaking at the same time. He wanted his heart back. She could hand it to him. He was glad this misery was about to end.

CHAPTER 16

Lucian didn't know what to do. Al finally quit chasing him, gave up, and he caught his breath. He had faked being fun-loving, raucous, playful, just to get away from his brother and the emotions welling inside of him.

He wouldn't hurt Norman for the world. But he couldn't stop seeing Mary Jane. And he couldn't tell Norman about him and Mary Jane.

That night on the beach, after the three girls had picked him and Al up, was a night for the books. He thought he had felt something for her before, but walking through the surf, hand in hand, talking more seriously about life . . . it was a feeling he hadn't ever tried on before. He was acting more like Norman than himself. He even kept his chew in his pocket so as not to embarrass himself with spitting all over the place.

He pondered what to do as he found the comfort of an oak tree on the lawn where the small red schoolhouse sat. He had Al chase him that far, darn near a mile, and needed at least that much space from his brother, that much time away to sort this thing out.

She had kissed him that night and he never knew it could be so good, so honest. He was sure he was going to have to marry her.

He knew he was betraying Norman while it was happening, but he couldn't stop the feeling, the emotion—and Mary Jane? She melted him. He forgot everything when she was within eyesight of him. He couldn't muster one level-headed thought within touching range. And kissing and hugging . . . *Well I was just plumb lost. A goner*, he silently reasoned.

He was caught up in that night. It was two

months ago now that fate had handed her to him, causing all this mess.

"Lucian," she said turning to him. "I wondered what it would be like. You know, being here in California, the ocean. It's so, so, vast and mighty. It just goes forever," she said, kicking happily at the surf with her bare feet.

"Pretty big. Never imagined anything so big. A lot bigger than that bathing hole back home." He smiled.

She pushed at his arm. "You better not start now."

"I was just thinkin', that's all."

"Keep it there," she reminded him.

"Yes 'em, ma'am." They walked on in silence. The sun, already set, had spent her light upon the water like the last hot glimmers of coal burning . . . embers so hot, yet dim in the steamer that the locomotive engine stayed revved up an extra mile anyway. His engine was churning terribly and he couldn't run. All he could do was just fake control. His heart was ablaze, and nothing was going to put it out.

"Thought the Oklahoma sky went on forever," he finally said, trying to keep up in the conversation, act smart, take his mind off the manliness overcoming him. *Norman was better at trying to sound interesting*, he thought to himself. A momentary twinge of guilt swept through him upon thinking about his brother.

"I was mad at you, you know," she laughed, interrupting his private ponderings.

"You mean about . . . about the first time we met?" He smiled.

"Something like that," she responded playfully. "I wasn't really, really mad exactly, just embarrassed I guess. I thought you and Norman were the same, person, and I tried playing angry 'cause you startled me so."

"I would have done the same, I guess."

"No you wouldn't. You're a man. Men don't care. They'd probably like girls catching a peek." She laughed at her own remark.

"Well, I, uh, I'm not too sure. That all depends."

"Depends on what?"

"Oh, I don't know. You know Norm, he's a shy one; I am too, I suppose."

"You?" she laughed.

"Well, yeah. Maybe less. Well, less formal, less a gentleman sometimes, but I can be shy too," he argued. He knew she had appreciated Norman's quiet dignity.

She stopped him and looked up into his eyes. "You're different. But you look exactly alike. Sad eyebrows that look so thoughtful, dimples that smile before your lips do, strong jaw line." She softened her voice as she went on. "Exactly the same, but you're different," she continued.

"Guess so," he answered nervously, feigning indifference.

"You know how different you are?" She ventured closer.

"Oh, I suppose." He gazed into blue eyes locked into his. He connected to those eyes like a a bad habit he didn't want to break.

She leaned up and reached her slender, tanned arms around his neck. She offered herself softly, gently pressing against him for his arms to reach back around her.

He didn't resist.

She started the kiss. His cheeks first, moving slowly, carefully toward his lips.

They fell to the sand eagerly and hungrily kissed until there wasn't anything left.

He was at a loss. He sat up stunned as she nestled against him. Both of them wanting more. Both constrained by proprieties they had been taught about intimacy. It had to be right. Married right. He knew it, so did she.

He'd never done this and as much as he'd imagined it and wanted to, he couldn't have known. No words were good enough to tell a man how it would be. And if kissing and holding her were this good . . . His mind wandered through the fire.

The other girls, with Al and a sailor friend of the pretty brunette, were making their way back out of the surf from their swim.

They made a fire in the sand. She sat with his arms surrounding her as they sang, laughed, shared the food and drinks. He was forced to retell how Mary Jane and he had first met, to the approving laughs of the nearly-drunk Al and the more sober girls.

Now he sat under the oak tree pondering this peculiar challenge, how to love her and yet warn Norman. Norm was headed up to L.A. to see her. It had his mind all messed up like too many drinks. It was foggy. Not clear what he should do. A fire had built up so hot that night on the beach he didn't think he could live without it. To tell Norman the truth would kill him.

CHAPTER 17

Norman sat on the flat car, listening to the clanks of the wheels on the Union Pacific rails. He was somewhere near Los Angeles now, headed toward some rocky peaks and a long dark tunnel. The sign posted read SANTA SUSANA DEPOT. He liked this place. Not at all like Oklahoma, but so pleasing. Fertile land, mountains that jutted up into the sky like stony sentinels—guardians surrounding the tiny valleys. Now he was just a few miles north of the L.A. county line and then on up to Los Angeles Union Station, where he'd stay the night and look for Mary Jane.

The train entered a tunnel leading to the L.A. county side. It was dark but relaxing after the heat of the sun had baked his face and exposed arms a reddish brown. He closed his eyes and tried to imagine this meeting with Mary Jane. *Would she be surprised?*

His mind wandered over her exquisite lines, curves, the slenderness, the tenderness of an ivory skin that played his mind like the melodies of a soft piano strain. She seemed to have a music to her walk, the way her eyes glanced at him—they smiled and danced at the same time. He knew he was welcome when her eyes smiled like that.

He wondered if Lucian knew what seeing Mary Jane meant to him now. He tried being coy about it, not offering too much information. He loved his brother but didn't exactly trust him. He'd played tricks with a girl he was in love with once before and it had hurt. She fell for him . . . his twin. The girls always fell for him.

Doggone it! Not this time, he assured himself.

The tunnel opened suddenly to noonday brightness that caught him off guard. The tracks descended into the San Fernando Valley heading southwest to Los Angeles.

Another hour will just about do it, he thought.

Los Angeles Union was a new station. He was friends with one of the warehouse managers there. The man had offered to let him stay in one of the sleepers sitting off the tracks; a real luxury car that was being worked on. It had plumbing, a bed, the works. He'd smell good, get a shave, stow his gear, get to a phone, then find the west Los Angeles café where Mary Jane was said to work.

Lucian had seen his brother off without warning him about the relationship he had with Mary Jane. He wondered how to reach her since he didn't have the phone number where she was working. A new place, somewhere on Santa Monica Boulevard.

He wasn't a praying man like Norm. Lucian wished he was now. Not so much for the hurt he might feel, but for Norman's feelings. He wished he knew a prayer. Norman was good. A lot more sensitive in his ways.

He pulled his wallet out of his baggy trousers and took out the photo of him with Mary Jane taken just the week before down at the Santa Monica pier. *"Ah, hell!"* he whispered in frustration. Being a twin stunk sometimes. *It just plain stinks*, he thought, silently kicking at a stone as he walked back to the bunk house at the citrus packing plant in Santa Paula.

Putting the photo away, he thought the best he could do now was hope for the best. He walked the dirt road from the loading dock down to a gray barracks-style bungalow he shared with other men working the rail lines.

He'd better hit the rails on up to L.A. and see if he could salvage this. Tell the truth. Break the news. Help Mary Jane out of this sticky mess and hope that Norman would understand somehow.

Norman pulled the crumpled note with the scribbled address from his shirt pocket. The diner was two blocks from the sound of crashing surf. Red flashing neon lights accented the name on the sign. JERRY'S DINER.

He entered nervously, his heart pounding one hundred beats faster than regular when he thought about her. He sought to hide himself in the crowded doorway while setting one eye to the task of finding her.

Every table was taken. *Maybe this is a mistake*, he thought. *No, I can't back out now. I won't get up the nerve again. I won't have a chance again.*

Debating with himself, the pros and cons of seeing her like this, was a useless pursuit. She appeared suddenly, plates in hand, through the swinging doors that led to the kitchen. There behind the counter she stopped, called back into the kitchen, swung her blond hair back, blew some puffs to remove golden strands from her eyes, and had him mesmerized. He couldn't move now if he tried.

He noticed there were stools vacant over at the counter. Maybe he could get a seat, act casual, like he didn't know she worked here. Explain he was just visiting town, wanted to see the ocean, got hungry. That would work.

"Uh, hum," he cleared his throat. "Miss?" He directed himself to a busy waitress. "The counter over there. Is it okay to take a seat?"

"Go ahead." She nodded.

He walked, head bowed slightly, not wishing to expose his identity or act too interested. He took the last seat at the farthest end from the kitchen doors and quickly occupied himself with a folding menu. His eyes met the top of the page and he gazed over it toward her. She was serving the far end of the counter now and looked his way.

He buried himself in the menu once again and wondered how he was going to respond. He couldn't seem to keep a clear train of thought. His heart managed his mind, and seemed stuck in his throat.

He sipped at the ice water placed there by another waitress, glad that maybe she wouldn't be his. She passed by him, apparently headed for the soda fountain farther down the wall across from the counter.

He found himself absorbed in her graceful movements. *She looks good! So mighty fine!* He gazed at her easy walk, the way she handled pressure, the ease at her handling the tasks. This distracted him, but his heart sent spurts of blood even faster into every artery and then some. Maybe she'd be first to say something.

She turned and stopped. Her mouth unhinged, then smiled. "Hi!" she squealed.

She recognizes me, he thought. "I was just in town and thought . . ."

"Sure!" she teased. "Don't order anything. I'll be off in one minute. We can go down to the pier." She winked, grinned, and acted as if seeing him was as natural and right as serving dinner.

Man this is easy, he smiled, satisfied with

the way things were going. He finished his drink, watched her talk to another waitress and noticed her explain something while nodding her head his way. The waitress smiled and waved. Norman waved in return. Mary Jane gave her a hug and took off her apron, disappearing into the back of the packed restaurant.

He waited.

"Hey you!" She poked at him from behind. "Come on. I have something special for you." She grinned as she placed her arm in his and pulled him through the crowded diner to the street.

"I knew you would be coming, but thought it would be next week."

He didn't ask how she knew, just went along with it.

She stopped, leaned up against the wall in the alley where deliveries were made and teasingly pulled him to her. "Well?" she asked, then went ahead without waiting.

Norman was frozen stiff but willing as lips met. He forgot anything he would say, think, or feel, and hungrily added his passion to hers. She allowed him to find her ears, neck, and shoulder before he pulled back, suddenly, to her voice.

"What?" he asked, stunned. "What did you say?"

"What do you mean? I just said your name. I just said your name, and said you've never kissed me like this before." She studied his shock, then his face carefully, and felt the heat from his embarrassment as he pulled away completely.

"Mary Jane. I thought . . . You think I'm . . . ," he said with a strained voice as his words trailed off. "You thought . . ." He stopped without saying his brother's name then nodded with the sudden realization. "I'd better be going," he added, turning from her.

"Norman? Oh my gosh, Norman! Come here. Please?" she pleaded. "I am so, so sorry. Norman, I didn't know. I was so excited to see you, I mean . . . Didn't Lucian say anything to you? How we met?" She stumbled as her face flushed crimson with discomfort.

He shook his head in silence, examining the sidewalk, looking for a better response. Angers that lay hidden just beneath the surface, the ones going all the way back to childhood that reared up when Lucian interfered, stalked him now.

"Norman, I was so excited to see you . . .

you and Lucian look so handsome, both of you are, exactly alike, and I just wanted to . . . ohhh, this is a mess. I'm so embarrassed. You must believe me, I would never intentionally hurt you."

"It's okay, Mary Jane. I'll just be on my way. I'm embarrassed too. It was good to see you. I best go. Got Guard duty to report to in New Mexico." His face showed the red of anger, the paint of embarrassment, and the hurt of someone who had been treated meanly, unfairly. "I'll be seeing your granddad soon. I'll tell him how mighty fine you looked," he offered in an attempt to mask his emotions, recover ground he had suddenly lost. He turned and began down the sidewalk away from her.

Mary Jane witnessed the pain Norman was suffering and realized that she was helpless, but for words, to fix the damage. "Norman," she pleaded, running to him, tugging at his shirt sleeve. "I love you, Norman." She was as shocked at saying it as he was at hearing it. But it was true.

He had never heard those words spoken to him. His eyes burned and he didn't want her to see his torment, his bruised ego, his pain.

"I love you both. You in a different way from Lucian."

He turned again to face her. His eyes gleamed wet like a hurt child. His countenance was hard, rigid, stern like a man. "I've never said this to another woman and might never say it again, Mary Jane," his eyes glistened. "I love you. I love you like a crazy man without any common sense at all. It was from the first time. I love you like a hot fire burning up all the fuel it can find. I guess I always will. If I didn't say that I think I'd burst. But I can't . . ."

She reached up to him and kissed him gently on the lips, a parting kiss, the way only a woman can. "If I had it to do all over again Norman, I would never have hurt your feelings," she offered softly, tears now coming freely. She reached her soft hand up to his face and stroked it gently. "I'm so, so sorry."

He produced a weak smile, a silent thank you, and began to walk away, then stopping, he turned around to face her. "Did I kiss good?"

Tears welled in her eyes and she nodded, adding with a voice strained to almost inaudible. "Too good."

CHAPTER 18

"You sure got here in a hurry. What's that all about?" Norman sneered from the door of the sleeper car as Lucian approached.

"Oh, knock it off, Norm. It ain't worth it." He climbed up to the car to face him.

"Seems it was worth you catching the next train up here to L.A. to try to stop me from embarrassing myself . . . not to mention . . ." He didn't finish.

"Did your mind ever burn so hot it felt like a fever . . . like it would melt?" Lucian shot back.

No response. He continued packing.

"So hot you couldn't douse the fire? A fire

so big that ten horse-drawn fire engines couldn't put it out?"

He kept his back turned and shoved the last shirt into the duffle bag.

"Good gosh, Norman. Aspirin won't help, getting stone cold drunk won't help. My mind is burning up trying to figure out how to fix this. I didn't mean for none of this to happen. She . . . Mary Jane . . . it wasn't supposed to be . . . I wasn't lookin'. It wasn't as if I came out here to California ahead of you lookin'. I was in San Diego workin'. It was all an accidental meeting. She was with some friends down there for the weekend and . . ."

"Shut up Lucian. Just . . . Shut! Up!" He grabbed his duffel bag and tossed it out of the sleeper. "Stay the night. It's all arranged. I'm headed back to training for the Guard, then home."

His twin didn't try to stop him.

Norman brushed by him, hopping the distance from the car down to the rails, picked up his bag, and started in the direction of the next train headed southeast—Arizona, then El Paso, and finally Fort Bliss, Texas.

"Norman!" Lucian called, beating his fist against the wall of the sleeper car. "Norman!"

Lucian leaped the distance to the ground and ran after him.

"What!" Norman turned on him.

"It ain't worth it, Norm."

"Oh, that's real easy for you to say! You always do this to me, Lucian. You always have a way of getting what you want. Right?" He was angry and letting it show as he stared his brother down, nose to nose.

"I didn't mean to hurt you, to hurt nobody!" he yelled back. "Ah, horse collar, Norm. What we arguing about anyway?" he said, backing away.

"About lying! About telling the truth, Lucian! About other people's feelings!"

"I got feelings! You don't think it hurt thinking about how I was gonna break this to you? You don't think I knew it would hurt you? I'm no good at lying, and, it appears, at telling the truth neither, but you gotta know, I didn't want any of this to happen!" His eyes begged for understanding.

"What's the difference? You didn't want it to happen, it did. I got to go."

"Don't leave mad like this."

"Why? You can't enjoy yourself so much if I do? You can't feel free from guilt when you're *making out* with Mary Jane? I got news for you. I'm not giving up. I won't just roll over for you. If there's a chance . . . well, may the best man win, brother."

"Okay. You want it that way? Okay then. All right. May the best man win!"

"See ya, Lucian." Norman waved, as he turned away from his brother and walked down the tracks.

"I'll be here. Don't you worry about that. I'll be right here!" he yelled back.

CHAPTER 19

"My name is Skully. What's yours, boy?"

"Parker. Norman Parker." He scowled.

"You hurtin' pretty bad, boy," the grimy old-timer stated matter-of-factly from across the boxcar they both bummed a ride on.

Norman whittled on a piece of willow as the tracks turned into miles east of Los Angeles.

"Good thing it's night. This desert gets a hundred and ten in the daytime," the rail bum added.

A grunt, wood shavings flying, implied Norman's response.

"Where ya headed, boy?"

"Nowhere special," he mumbled.

"A man of the rails? Nowhere special? That's my usual destination."

The clack of wheels turning against a tired iron rail line underscored the noise going on in his brain. It was a dialogue with Lucian that wouldn't quit. He argued, Lucian countered. It was driving him crazy.

"Got some food in that bag of yours?" the grizzled veteran of the railroad tracks asked, pointing a gnarled finger to Norman's duffel bag. "Got cut off, trying to hop my first train. Works just fine," he said, bending it. "A little shorter than it was, that's all."

Norman shuffled through his bag and picked out a couple of oranges and tossed them to the old man.

"I just love California oranges. I first went to California to pick 'em. From Oklahoma," he added.

Norman raised an eyebrow and nodded, continuing with his pocket knife against the twig.

"Don't know how a man lives without one of these," the traveler said, pulling his own knife from well-worn trousers and slicing the first orange evenly. "Sweet," he slurped as he sucked the juice out and ate the pulp.

"Yes sir," he continued, noisily sucking at the orange meat.

Norman glanced at the man, seemingly contented to make his presence known with each bite.

"Must be a woman. That or death. Nothin' hurts more than bein' a man in love or losin' someone you can't live without. That's why I travel."

Norman threw the stick off into the passing night. "Shut up, please."

"You must be educated. Shut up, *please*," he mimicked with a laugh.

"Look, next stop, I'll just get off and find my own car. Until then, just shut up! Suck the darned orange and shut up!"

"Well, a man can get lonely sometimes. Hope someone treats you better when you got somethin' to say," the old traveler said diffidently.

He had cut Norman to the bone with the remark. He was angry with his brother and the circumstances and didn't mean to take it out on the man.

"Still, I forgive ya. You're hurtin' and I can see that plain enough. Had plenty hurt in my life. Yes sir."

Silence rode between them like a deaf and mute companion would for the next hour. The veteran rail bum slumbered against his pack and the side of the boxcar he sat up against. Norman was sorry he had bit the old codger's head off. He just didn't want to talk. That was all there was to it.

He looked through his pack and found a can of Spam and a half loaf of bread still good from the day before. Scooting over quietly, he set it next to the man and went back to his place on the car and engaged in gazing out at the crescent moon from the open boxcar door.

"I was about thirty-two at the time," the old man started suddenly, as if nothing had happened between them. "I was fixed pretty well for a young man from the sticks in Oklahoma. Had me a mechanics shop, a small plot of ground too. Wife, three youngins.

"Had been to the big war and all. Did my part, came home, and won the hand of the prettiest girl in Seminole County. I thought if she ever could love me I would be the happiest man on God's green earth," he sighed.

Norman winced, knowing all too well the feeling. The aging rail bum was starting to look human to him as he rambled on, eyes meditatively closed as he related his story.

"It must've been the uniform when I got back from the war. That, and her beau was killed. The war got him, and I was happy. Not that he was dead, but that I had a chance. He was my friend, but that didn't matter. I was glad I was alive, and he had been in my way."

Norman eyed the man in surprise. This tattered old fool was talking love, life, jealousy . . . things bums don't usually spout off about.

"Felt mighty guilty, though. Here's my buddy, all shot up, was dying in my arms. No doubt I loved him too. You get like that in war. Like brothers, see?"

"Yeah. I see."

"Well, he was ramblin' on about his woman, the girl I secretly loved, and how I was to look out for her if he didn't make it back, and well, I sat there with his head in my lap knowing that was exactly what I was gonna do . . . made me feel awful guilty at the time.

"The thing I had for that woman was so pleasin' it hurt. I got so bad over her I thought my mind would burn up if she didn't have me.

"Once she knew I was there to stay I finally got the nerve to ask her out. Kept wearing my uniform, just to impress her, ya know. She went out with me and by and by she kissed me. It was all lost for me then. I was a lost soul without her from then on. Yes sir, a damned fool puppy dog lost soul.

"But—" He coughed. "I had my sights set on winnin' her heart. I knew she married me 'cause I was kind to her and bein' no other offer made in our town, well I knew in my heart that I didn't have her love like she had mine. It kind of hurt. All the time, this pangin' ache that just wouldn't go away. So knows what I do?"

"Nope," Norman obliged, finally acknowledging the old-timer.

"Well, I said to myself, 'Skully you got two hands and one brain. Get to work day and night and build somethin' for this woman that would make her glad she married you. Make her a fool to leave you too.' "

"So what did you do?"

"I fixed everything that people needed to have fixed. Everything in sight. Farmed too. Got me a small spread of land with my war earnings, built a one room house at first. Then two. And so it went. Built a work shed off the barn and turned people's problems back to them fixed. If it were broke I found a way to fix it. I was good with these," he sighed, holding up twisted fingers. "Real good."

"So how'd you end up here?"

"People lost their farms and such with the damnable Depression. Moved away. Business fell off. I left town to find some work to keep our—my—dream alive, and when I came back she was gone."

Norman nodded and winced at the tired man's pain. He understood. "You just found your house empty?" he probed.

"Yep. Gone off with the first man who offered her some excitement from the dreary life with old Skully, I suppose. Serves me right for being glad the first man she loved was dead. Serves me right, I suppose. Oh, but she was a looker . . . a real dame, yes sir. A real pleasin' woman. Better than I suppose should have me for a husband. So here I am. A wanderin' fool."

Norman perceived the man differently now. He had a life. Gone bad, but a life.

He loved Mary Jane but he'd never let a

woman own his heart that it hurt so bad he'd go off and give up on everything. No sir. He was in pain but no fool. And he'd never be glad the man she loved was dead just to have her. No way. He wasn't judging the man, just saw no fight in him.

"Got my kids though. She lets me see them two times a year. That's where I'm headed now. Amarillo, Texas. Got me some new clothes, some razors, cologne. I aim on looking good for them and makin' sure they know their daddy loves them."

Norman felt for the poor man's luck.

"You were right kind to give me this. I thought there was somethin' better in you than you first showed," he offered, holding up Norman's gift. "I like Spam. Lasts forever it seems. Somebody ought to get a medal for figuring out how to can this stuff. Want a sandwich?"

Norman shook his head. "No, thanks. Sorry, Mr. Skully, for your bad luck. And sorry how I behaved. I had no right."

"So it's a woman, eh?" he spit back as he twisted the lid back with the tiny key made for it.

"Yeah."

"Well, it don't get no better, sorry to say.

Not unless you find someone to fill up the hole in yer heart. Hope ya can."

Norman smiled politely and grimaced as he turned away.

"Needles Town comin' up, then we cross the Colorado River. Guess we'll make good time this trip. Where'd you punch yer ticket for?"

He answered slow. Deliberate.

"Home."

"Mr. Skully?" Norman called above the clickity-clack of hundreds of freight car wheels turning in unison against the iron rails. "Mr. Skully?"

The slumbering man, slumped against the side of the car, finally stirred. "What is it? We there?" he stammered as he jolted the sleep away with side to side shakes of his head. "You still here?"

"Still here."

"What you wake me for? I was dreamin' real nice."

"Sorry."

"Well, get on with it. You woke me, now make somethin' of it."

"I thought you'd like a drink. Got some bottled Cokes in my bag."

"No booze?" the old rail rider snorted eagerly.

"Sorry. I don't drink."

"Well, best you don't get started. Give me one of them," he directed. He caught it in his lap as Norman tossed it gently.

Skully opened the bottle by wedging the cap against the edge of a metal brace on the boxcar wall and popping at the top quickly with the palm of his hand. "Ahh," he slurped, adding a satisfied belch when he had drained the glass bottle. "I like Pepsi-Cola better," he said. "But this will do."

Norman smiled and nodded. He didn't know how to begin, but he wanted someone else's thoughts on what was troubling him; even a railroad-riding bum's thoughts would be better than the solitary confinement he found his mind locked into.

With nowhere to go with his pain and no one to tell it to, Skully at least offered someone to voice it out loud to.

"So is Skully your last name?"

The old traveler took the cap off his head, revealing baldness. He leaned down to show the top. "Got this hairdo compliments of the U.S. Army in World War One. A gas attack in the trenches in France was all it took. Lost my hair. Never grew back. The other men said I looked like a skull with skin and eyeballs. Not too flattering. They all began calling me 'Skully' and it stuck."

"So what is your Christian name?"

"James Benson Scally, at your service."

"So you never grew your hair back?"

"Nope. Kind of convenient really, if you stop to think about it. Not like that thick mop of yours." He pointed. "No lice problems, no need to wash it with soaps and such. Real convenient."

"So you were saying about your wife leaving you. You want to talk about it?" Norman probed.

"Do you?" he returned.

"Well, I was wondering why you just didn't go after the guy who stole your woman and all. How you live with the anger and such."

"It's a fool who gives anger and a fool who gets anger. Anger is good for killin'—like war. But that's about it."

"You mean losing her didn't make you boil?"

"Sure it did."

"Did you ever get over it?"

"Nope. Just dealt with it. I guess love's imprint is written so deeply in the heart that a man would have to have surgery to dig it out. It aches . . . oh it aches, yes sir. But I got to be the one right with God. I didn't cheat nobody, didn't run off on her. I just keep rememberin' that if I lived in a perfect world, she wouldn't have hurt me so. Then I leave it be."

"Hmmm."

"You're hurtin' bad, aren't ya, boy?"

"Appears so. I can't get over caring, wanting her. I never told anyone about it." Norman tossed his Coke bottle off into the night. "She loved me first, then my galdarned brother. A woman like that ain't worth it but I can't seem to get her off my mind."

"She burnt it into ya. I know that feelin'," Skully offered.

"So what did you do?"

"I drank booze first. I'm no drunk, but I've been known to forget my problems too many days in a row. I can stop. Most folks can't. But I found it still hurt when I come to my senses."

"Then?" Norman prodded.

"Worked any job I could as far away as I could from my former life. I didn't care if I lived or died. There was nothin' to go home to. Nothin' mattered anymore."

"So that's where you're at?"

"Yep. Except, my kids. I was forgettin' that I had them precious gems. Now they matter. Yes, sir. Oh, she's a changed woman and I don't feel nothin' for the woman she is today, but that gal I first loved . . . no sir, I don't think no man can get over the gal he first loved. Romantic fools is what we are."

"Yep. Fools. Darned fools."

"Just remember. A fool stays angry, except you want to kill someone. Killin' is for war, boy. You go after that girl or back away and leave it be. Nothin' in between will make ya feel better. One or the other. That's about all I got to say. Got another Coke?"

Norman threw him his last bottle. He'd resupply himself next train depot stop. Come morning they'd be near Phoenix. He might as well sleep on the advice from the migrant philosopher Skully.

Anger was eating him alive. He hated how it got between him and Lucian. He wondered if he could just let go. Just leave it be, as the old man suggested. *One or the other*, Skully said. Maybe he could give Lucian the chance to trade with him, be angry for a while. Maybe he could win her somehow, get even. Let Lucian taste some of his own medicine for a change.

That kiss was something else, he thought. She felt it. He was sure of it.

Like fire, he thought sullenly.

It was as electric as surges through a high voltage power line. *No way she could deny that.*

She had to see another side of him, that was all. Lucian was having his chance for now. Next leave, he'd find his way back to L.A. in uniform. This time he'd be direct. Lay out all his plans, everything that would make a girl happy. He'd ask for one more kiss. She'd have to make up her mind. Then he'd leave it be. But not until then.

CHAPTER 20

It had been three months since the two brothers had parted ways. Fort Bliss, Texas had been home to Norman long enough now. He was eager to get back to working the Santa Fe line in Albuquerque. It was close enough to visit Warm Springs, and work out the details for the small plot of land, the abandoned Dearborn place. Then he'd head on out to L.A. and give Mary Jane an offer Lucian couldn't touch.

He'd always wanted to be a "cowboy" and when he joined the New Mexico outfit it was U.S. Cavalry, one of the last in the country. Playing cavalry with the New Mexico 111th was the most fun Norman had ever had in his life. Like cowboys and Indians, the weekend soldiers played their part in the Southwest army post. They were like boys chasing around the New Mexican and Texas desert on horseback, imagining the glory days of the U.S. Cavalry.

Nearly one-third of the troop was Native American and Mexican-American. A mix of work-day occupations, the guardsmen were ranch hands, college boys looking for adventure, business owners, high school students, and anyone looking for some extra money each month.

Now the 111th was being disengaged from their role as horseback riding infantry and being converted by order of the regular army to "coastal battery" anti-aircraft units. National Guard units across the country were being "federalized" to meet the growing menace of the German and Japanese military machines in Europe and Asia.

"Craziest thing I ever heard, Norm. There ain't no 'coast' in New Mexico. The whole Mexican aircorp ain't got three planes. What's the Nazis gonna do? Maybe send their Luftwaffe over here to the Mexico side and bomb what? A bunch of sagebrush, jack rabbits, haciendas maybe?"

"Well, Private First Class Johnny Mead, it appears that it falls upon me as your corporal to inform you that 'coastal' means we'd be shipped to the 'coast.' I've been there. Hope to shout it's L.A. Got a girl there," Norman boasted.

"A girl, huh? How's come you never told me?" Mead grinned. "Got a picture?" the cousin asked.

"Nope. Lost it," he lied.

"So you getting married to her? Asked her or something?"

He changed the subject. "Got inspection and then after that I'm headin' out West to ask her."

"Man that's swell Norman. Really swell!" Johnny congratulated with a solid slap on the back. "So you think they'd move the whole New Mexico Guard to California?"

"I don't know. Maybe the Gulf Coast, maybe the East Coast. But being out West, with the Japs acting up in the Pacific, I'd guess the West Coast. Hey, maybe even Hawaii." Norman brightened. "Wouldn't that be something?"

The two soldiers polished their boots, and

readied for inspection. "So what are you doing, Johnny? Goin' home? Back to the job?" Norman spoke up as he brushed at his boots.

"I dunno, Norm. Pop wants me back at the ranch outside of town here. I got an itch to travel. With this Guard money I figure I'd last a month, maybe go see California like you did. Ride the rails for free, hang out at the beach, see San Francisco. I hear the girls there are really somethin'.'"

"Yeah. Well, we got to be back here in a month. Maybe that would be about right, a trip for a month. I hear rumors of a long bivouac after we get back. Some training before being called up permanently."

"Called up? They wouldn't call us up unless there was a war or somethin', right?"

"They can do anything they want. Since we got the highest scores in the whole darned army at anti-aircraft battery tests— and the Regulars, those career-lifer army pals of ours, aren't too happy about it— maybe the army would send us out somewheres, just to make sure we are ready."

"You think the Germans would attack us?"

"I'm thinkin' from what I'm hearin' that the army is up to its eyeballs in trying to figure out how to protect all the islands we got out in the Pacific. There's Hawaii, Guam, some-place called Wake, and the Philippines. The Philippines are the most threatened now with the Japanese attacking all around it."

"Where's the Philippines?" Johnny posed innocently.

"A thousand islands or so with a bunch of army, navy, and aircorp bases out by Aus-tralia somewhere. Guess we have been pro-tecting them people since we won the islands from Spain in the 1898 war."

"Hey, Norm. Lookie there." Mead grinned, pointing toward the barracks door. "If it ain't dear old cousin—"

"Lucian! What the blazes you doin' here? Thought you was going to go to USC. Last I heard." Norman smiled, letting go of his boots. Angry memories had melted away. He ran to greet him.

"How ya doin', brother?" he drawled, a wad of tobacco wedged in his cheek. "The army treating you boys good?" he asked as he set his duffel bag on the barracks floor.

"You aren't . . . ?" Norman questioned, in-specting him up and down.

"Yep. Just got my new assignment. Head-quarter's Battery. Did my basic training at

Fort Sill. Guess they don't ride horses here no more," he said, opening his arms for Norman. They embraced and laughed loudly.

"Lucian the cowboy? So that's why we got changed from cavalry. They heard you was comin'! Haaa!" he bellowed, still not believing Lucian stood before him. "Well what does Pa think?" Norman asked, happy to see his brother. "You hear from him?"

"Sure did. Pa likes the idea of us bein' together, considerin' the way things are. When I told him I was joinin' up, it made him proud, real happy. He's gettin' along fine. Guess he wore old Harry out. But he's got a couple of young boys helpin' him out some.

"Just came from there. Decided to take my earnings and put them in the bank. Gave Pa the right to withdraw 'em if he needed. Figured the National Guard pay would be workin' out good for now, with the way things are," Lucian finished.

Norman backed away and allowed Lucian to follow him to his bunk. Memory. Thoughts of Mary Jane. Wondering how to broach the subject swept over him, uninvited, unwanted. "Why didn't you say something, write me about you joining up?" he asked.

"I wanted to surprise you." He smiled.

"Well look at them stripes," Lucian added. "How ya doin', Johnny? Where's cousin Tom?" he asked, thrusting his hand forward for a hearty handshake.

"He broke his leg. Got a discharge. Just as well. He was a lousy soldier," Johnny Mead laughed good-naturedly. "Sure is good to see you, Lucian."

"You think I'll be a good soldier?" Lucian asked, looking for a place to spit.

"You won't make it to payday," Norman laughed. "And you better not let your platoon sergeant see you chewin' that stuff in the barracks or you'll be up 'til dawn the next day scrubbing floors with a toothbrush and lye soap."

"I'll make it to payday, brother. I'll make it just fine. Where . . . ?" He looked for someplace to get rid of the chew.

"Over there," he pointed out, as he stowed the rest of his gear.

"The latrine?"

"Yeah. And show some class. Flush real good, will ya, Lucian?" He grinned. "We don't want to pay for your foul up."

Lucian followed the instruction. "Norm, I best be goin' over to the training barracks. Guess we'll be learnin' how to shoot down airplanes." He grinned with his arms extended. "Just thought I'd say howdy. Let you know . . ." He stopped and searched for the right words to complete his thoughts.

"Johnny, could you excuse us. We need a word. In private," Norman asked.

"Sure thing Norm. Lucian." He nodded. "See you real soon. Hope you like push-ups," he laughed, slapping Lucian on the shoulder as he passed by and out of the barracks.

"Go ahead. Say what you're gonna say, Lucian."

"I'm real sorry, Norm, about how things turned out."

"Well, I've cooled off some," he returned.

"Well, I'm glad. Real glad. Part of this, me bein' here and all is because of all this war talk, and part of it is to be near home. I guessed you were right about home," Lucian said.

"Okay, Lucian. But what about Mary Jane?" Norman asked directly as he stowed his duffel bag at the foot of his bunk.

"She's fine," he replied truthfully. "Nothing much happening between us," he added nervously. A lie.

"Nothing?" Norman quizzed, trying to hide his interest.

"Not married or nothin'," Lucian responded, knowing he couldn't tell Norman how he'd asked her to marry him before leaving California. Knowing that she would be traveling home to Warm Springs to take care of her ailing granddad, and knowing she'd probably say yes by the time he got there.

"So how is she?"

"Fine. Goin' home next month. Finishin' up her schooling and then gonna take care of old man Harrison for the summer."

Norman's heart pulsated to a new beat. Sadness fled as soon as he had seen Lucian. He knew that something had to be behind it. Maybe Mary Jane had seen through Lucian. Had realized the substance of who he, Norman, really was.

CHAPTER 21

One Month Later, Albuquerque,
New Mexico

At a small railroad station in the recovering farmland of southern Oklahoma waited the girl, his pa, the grave of his mother, home. He had been energized just at the thought of her. But now those thoughts were once again mixed with anger, confusion.

He strained under the weight of each gunny sack of dried pintos, throwing one after another over his shoulders and neatly stacking them on a warehouse pallet. He was confused. A new twist threatened his plan of happiness.

He'd never gotten back to Los Angeles as he'd hoped. Mary Jane had left too soon for Warm Springs for that. He'd gone home after Guard training to look her up. She was courteous, smiled. He had given her something to think about with that trip. But then Lucian showed up.

He didn't want to push too hard. She was confused enough. He could see that. He decided to give her time, a breather, be a gentleman. He had written to her twice, and she replied to both letters. Although not romantic, he believed there was something there until now. After all, she had signed them: *Love, Mary Jane.*

It hurts too much to be in love, he concluded, throwing one burlap sack after another on the pile, now higher than his own head.

How could Lucian do this to me? he quietly questioned over and over again. They had always counted on each other during the tough times of the thirties. That made this all the more difficult. His old anger that had settled down was all stirred up again.

Skully the railroad bum had said, "Let it go." *How?* He questioned over and over in a private mental battle for peace of mind.

Norman could see her standing on the railroad platform in Warm Springs just one month ago. He had always been polite, a bit held back on his true feelings. He never really believed she showed serious interest in his brother. Lucian just wasn't that committed. He had asked his brother, "Are you in love with her, Lucian?" He had replied, "Sure, she's a great girl." That was no commitment. He was just foolin' around with her feelings.

She had smiled at him, left hints, an extra squeeze on his hand when he came on back to Albuquerque. She even said, "Norman, you are the greatest," and touched his cheek softly when he left her standing there at the depot.

This time, this visit home, he would have asked her, would have overcome his shyness, his reserve, if Lucian hadn't shown up unexpectedly.

How could Lucian do it? He asked himself again as he threw one bag atop the next. Anger surged into every toss of the filled burlap sacks. He had to get rid of it. But this!

"Norman." He heard his name called from the dock. "Norman!" Lucian yelled louder.

"What do you want?" he barked back.

Lucian stood at the massive sliding warehouse door. "I want to clear something up."

"Leave me be."

"I can't do that."

"I don't want to talk about it."

"I never said I wouldn't ask her," Lucian returned sharply.

"You understood how I felt," Norman challenged.

"I can't help how you felt. What about my feelings?"

Silence.

"You'll get over it. You always do," Lucian consoled him.

"Don't be so sure!" Norman shot back with a grunt as he threw the last hundred pound sack of dried pintos bound for the market on the pallet.

"Stop worryin' about it then. She hasn't exactly said yes to me. Maybe she won't, then what will you do?" He lied. Lucian knew she had already decided, that they were engaged to be married upon his return home this week.

Norman glared as he reached for his time

card, punching it through the clock one final time before they both would return to the country train depot in Warm Springs. They had exactly one week of leave time before their National Guard unit went on active duty.

Lucian stood in front of Norman as he tried to pass by him at the warehouse door that led to the loading dock.

"Don't mess with me right now," Norman said, pushing him aside.

Lucian quickly put himself in front of him again.

"Lucian, I'm warning you . . ."

"Let's get this straight. I didn't mean to fall for her like I did. She likes you—we both know that. Hey, we do look exactly alike, you know. You just didn't move fast enough. And I . . . well, how was I supposed to know?"

"You knew," Norman said as he shifted his feet to get by his brother who was backing up with his every step.

"There are plenty of girls out there. You just got to understand."

"When hell freezes over I will," Norman groused as he side-stepped his twin and made his way to the depot loading dock office to turn in his card for his final paycheck.

Lucian was on the platform outside the door waiting with his hand outstretched. "I won't bring it up again. Let's shake on it."

The sun was hot. With Norman's last shift at the railroad loading dock just ending, he was in the mood for a shower, some hot food at Frankie's Depot Grill, but not some lame effort on Lucian's part to smooth things over.

Besides, he needed an aspirin for a headache his heavy thinking caused. He had never been so restless, sleepless. Perhaps that was the cause of the headache, but only God knew that heartache was worse.

"Do you love her, Lucian?" Norman asked bluntly, face to face.

"Well, yeah. Of course," he replied, caught off guard by the question.

"No—I mean really love her—deeply love her. No passing fling?"

"Sure," Lucian responded.

"See!" Norman shot back angrily. "There you go! That's the difference between you and me. I'm committed and you're not!" he accused, jabbing a finger into his brother's chest. "I'm what she needs! Not you!" he shouted, and pushed his brother aside as he headed down the steps and to the time clock to punch out for the final time.

Lucian jumped off the dock and ran to catch up with him.

The only other girl Norman ever admired even close to Mary Jane worked at the Grill. Luisa was her name. She didn't do to him what Mary Jane did, but Luisa and her pitch black hair and smiling brown eyes somehow helped him to forget about the blonde when she came around to his table. Maybe it was time to notice her, give in to Lucian's winning of Mary Jane. Look somewhere else.

Lucian's graveyard shift left him fresh, full of energy. *He never seems to suffer,* Norman thought to himself as he stormed forward with Lucian on his heels.

"It's gonna be a long trip in that boxcar back to Warm Springs tonight. I'd like you to just accept what I've said and think it," Lucian voiced from behind with hand outstretched again.

Norman needed some time. He didn't want Lucian to see him roll over as easy as that. "Buy me dinner, an ice cold Coke, and I'll think on it," he finally replied with his back still turned to his brother in a reluctant direction toward reconciliation. "I haven't changed my mind. But I don't want to talk about it anymore, either."

"I'm sorry," Lucian offered, seemingly genuine and sincere.

"Yeah. Me too," Norman replied, grabbing his duffel bag as they headed off the dock to the diner a block away.

"Here," Lucian said, taking the bag from his brother. "I'll take this over to the Guard armory with my stuff. Lieutenant Kerns let me use a jeep. Why don't you go ahead and order? I'll be back in thirty minutes and pick up the bill and we'll swing on back to the armory to shower, rest, and collect our stuff before heading out tonight."

"Hope these regular army guys know . . ." Norman's voice drifted off plaintively as he sought for a way to stay away from the subject of Mary Jane, his disappointment.

"Know what?"

"Know what they're doing. We're weekend soldiers. We've just about got things paid off back home, and—"

"And we're together," Lucian cut in. "We're a team. Besides, active duty means more pay, free food, a place to bed down. We'll just get the station and the land paid off all the faster by holding onto the money. Besides, the Philippines can't be that bad."

"No one says it's the Philippines we're headed to," Norman countered.

"Scuttlebutt at Headquarters Battery," Lucian responded. "I guess whatever happens at least we'll have the money to do the dream Pa always wanted for us."

"Funny how interested you are in Warm Springs, the station and such, all the sudden. Anyway, it's a long way from Warm Springs, some ten thousand miles to be exact, and the Japs aren't exactly friendly these days—if it is the Philippines."

"It'll never happen. They'd be suicidal to attack any U.S. military base in the Pacific. Be back in a jiff. And I want to see a smile," Lucian called out as he threw the duffel bag in the back of the jeep and jumped into the driver's seat. He spit his chewing tobacco out and offered Norman a stained, toothy grin.

Smile, Norman thought, as he shook his head. They'd been best friends as much as brothers. During all the years of the Great Depression they'd watched out for each other.

Lucian even followed him into the Guard

for the extra pay and the free place to sleep at night while working the docks on the Santa Fe line.

"Smile," he huffed. Why'd Mary Jane have to show up anyway? As long as she had been out West, in California with her folks, Lucian hadn't been able to touch her. He'd forgotten her for the next blonde who'd come along. Completely forgotten her. It complicated things, her coming home— complicated everything.

CHAPTER 22

"Remember that fella from Minnesota who worked with us out on the Santa Fe docks in Ventura, the summer of forty?" Lucian probed, seeking to break the monotonous clickity-clack rhythm of the rails meeting boxcar wheels. "What was his name?"

"Al Handy," Norman responded sleepily from the opposite corner of the empty rail car.

"Yeah, big Al," Lucian chuckled. "He was a real card, a real joker."

No response.

"Remember how the trainloads of oranges would come in piled high up the sides of the cars and make a mound—seemed like hundreds of those cars we must have unloaded that season."

"Yep," Norman snorted.

"Remember how Al always took a bite out of the first orange he'd toss into the crates on the dock and tell us whether they'd be juicin' oranges or eatin' ones?" Lucian laughed. "This one time I tossed a wormy one and said, 'Hey Al, try this one.'" Lucian laughed in a dialogue with himself as the train clanked on north toward Oklahoma and their getting off point, the town of Redemption. From there they'd hitch a car ride up to Warm Springs.

"Well jus' so happens I no sooner say the word than he bites into this particularly ripe juicy one I tossed to him, and smiles this big grin with a mouthful of orange pulp, 'Juice,' he says as it dripped out the corners of his mouth. 'Somethin' strange in this one,' he says as he spits the pulp out and sees the fat remains of a fruit worm on the concrete. He looks at me like I had put it there or somethin'. I tell ya, Norm, I never had such a good laugh. Then he started throwing oranges. I threw back, then he chased me a mile before givin' up. Remember?" Lucian smiled.

"Yeah, I remember. Almost got you and Al fired."

"Those were good times. Big Al—I hear he joined the marines. He was always jealous of the marines getting the girls in San Diego. Yes sir, pretty place that California coast all dotted with them orange groves and such."

"Mighty pretty," Norman sighed. He nodded off to the rhythm of the steel wheels working turn after methodical turn against the rail. The whistle blowing from the engineer warned against any one crossing the tracks up ahead.

"Norman," Lucian tried. "Norm, I need to tell you something," he voiced a little louder. Lucian considered the silence and gazed upon the brother who had been so true to him, the family. Whenever he needed Norman, he had been there.

He felt the lie was justified, the half-truth about him and Mary Jane. He needed some time to figure out how to tell him. To work up the courage to get straight out with it.

There was a ceremony going to happen this weekend. At a small church just this side of Warm Springs. He hadn't purchased a ring yet for Mary Jane, but something would work out.

He'd like Norman to be the best man, to carry the ring for him. He'd like it with all his heart for things to be square, right, even, between them.

He'd make his vows this weekend with the woman they both loved. The bond between him and Norman would be stronger or weaker as a result of what he was about to do.

It would all take place in the church and he hoped that God would be there, witnessing for Norman that he didn't mean to hurt him. He really was a changed man, more serious, ready to settle down. He needed his brother to be there for him.

He looked upon his sleeping twin and wished he could change or fix his lies before Norman felt hurt too deeply. He now could only pray for God to be there at the wedding, give Norman peace. Be in Redemption with them.

CHAPTER 23

All who were left in the town and countryside surrounding Warm Springs were in attendance. J. D. Briggs, Pastor of the Country Church in Redemption, began.

"Dearly beloved, we are gathered this day to witness the marriage of two of our own, Mary Jane Harrison and Lucian Parker. This is a joyous occasion . . ." Norman tuned out the words of the pastor as he stared into the chapel's stained-glass window above the altar.

"Joyous" hit Norman harder than a truckload of bricks could hit a man buried ten feet deep in them. He lost all regard for where he was, and what he was doing as he sat in the pew in the front row, witnessing his brother taking from him the only woman who had ever meant anything to him.

"The Bible teaches that whatever God shall bring together no man should put asunder. It also teaches that this union should be until death, meaning nothing should stop them except the final breath of life. Lucian and Mary Jane, I counsel you to honor each other, trust each other, and let no woman, Lucian, and no man, Mary Jane, come between you—ever. Can you both agree to make this promise?"

"Yes," Lucian offered, smiling into the eyes of Mary Jane.

"Yes," she added with a hint of nervousness, aware of Norman's heated anger for his brother. She tried not to let it affect her poise.

"Lucian Parker, do you take Mary Jane Harrison in the holy bonds of matrimony to love, cherish, to have and to hold, in sickness and in health, in poverty or in wealth, and under all circumstances such as life may offer as your legally and lawfully wedded wife until death do you part?"

"I do."

"Mary Jane Harrison, do you take Lucian Parker in the holy bonds of matrimony to love, cherish, to have and to hold, in sickness and in health, in poverty or in wealth, and under all circumstances such as life may offer as your legally and lawfully wedded husband until death do you part?"

"I do."

"Then according to the power vested in me by the church and the State of Oklahoma I pronounce you man and wife. Lucian, you may kiss the bride."

Norman closed his eyes, squinting against the heat building up in them. His fists closed as if squeezing the life from some small unidentifiable insect or animal—rage filled him, turning his fists white then red and back to white.

He looked at his finger where a ring had been. The one Pa had given him to pass on, the one coming from his mother's side of the family, the one with the family motto engraved on it. His pa had given it to him last year deciding the more serious Norman would probably marry first. Then days ago he had asked Norman if he could offer it to Lucian, being they didn't have a ring for him and Mary Jane wasn't fixed to buy him one.

Norman couldn't leave the ceremony but he couldn't stay much longer. The small chapel filled with townsfolk drowned out his temper-congested mind with happy cheers and applause, oblivious and unaware to the breaking of his heart and the destruction of so many dreams.

"Lucian, you and Mary Jane may exchange the rings."

Those words fell hard on Norman's ears and he held his composure out of duty and respect.

The happy couple turned and smiled toward the crowd who now thronged them with hugs, well wishes, and cheers. Lucian in his army uniform and Mary Jane in a gown fit for a princess were being regaled with all the pleasure and approval a small town could afford.

Jason looked back at his son Norman and discerned the pain. He wished he could fix it for his boys. His was a mixture of joy and sadness. *Identical twins could do that to a man*, he thought.

A small band began to play as Norman shuffled through the crowded chapel to the exit and headed for the highway. Crossing the road he stuck out his thumb and caught the first passing car.

"Where to, soldier?" the middle-aged driver asked with a smile.

The sounds of festivity, laughter, and Norman's imagination of his brother touching the woman he loved was more than his mind could cope with. He had to get away as fast as he could from Redemption, swearing he wouldn't come back, nor step foot in the house of God which had betrayed every sacred emotion he had.

"I say, where to, soldier?" the man asked again as Norman sat, staring straight ahead, caught in the vision of overwhelming loss.

"Huh? Oh, yeah. Home. I'm going home."

"Where's home?"

"Warm Springs."

"Okay, then. Here we go. Looks like quite a gathering at the church. You must be in a hurry to leave a party like that," the man offered.

"Yes. Yes. A hurry. I am. I am in a hurry. To leave. Yes sir. Shipping out."

"You don't say. Where to, young man?"

"Only God knows."

* * *

The next day burned hot and scorched the land around Warm Springs like a furnace turns black coal to fiery red then white powdery dust. Forty days straight without a letup in summer heat and the land looked all the worse for it. Dry stubble for shrubs and burned yellow field grass.

There was no mercy from Mother Nature and the fireball in the sky showed no compassion this day as Norman stoked the fire even hotter than hell—or so it seemed to him—readying the train with his father to take her down to Redemption, and there pick up the new married couple for their final destination, Albuquerque, New Mexico.

His pa was busy preparing the caboose for them to have a little privacy in, a honeymoon car. Norman couldn't bear the thoughts coursing through his mind as he shoveled coal from the tender into the fire. He had to keep his mind off it somehow, endure the trip, be indifferent.

His body was soaked with perspiration that also dripped from his brow like rain. He couldn't talk to anyone. Not his pa, not old man Harry, and certainly not to God. He'd already trusted God—that didn't seem to do any good. He needed to get away but there was nowhere to run.

Cursing under his breath, curses mixed with love and hate, jealousy and rage, and strange thoughts of wishing the two people he loved more than life, Lucian and Mary Jane, the best, tormented him.

"Norman! We still need to fill the tanker car. I'll take over. You go get changed. Hook up the hose and get some fresh clothes. And put some water on you before you take to heat exhaustion," his father called from the bottom steps of the engine compartment. The roar of the fire, and Norman's own inquietude had shut off his father's voice.

"I say, Norman!" Jason yelled again, cupping his hands as he stepped up into the engine compartment, grabbing his son's soaked shirt sleeve. "Norman. Norman, son. Slow down. We got the fire up. Now go cool off. Fill the tanker."

He nodded and climbed down to the landing. Dispassionate now, he stared at the planks. Planks on the dock were warped from the sun, so hot they were popping from the nails holding them to the floor joists. He reached down to a pickax that had fallen off one of the cars and onto the deck. He walked a few paces toward the water hoses under a boiling heat that seemed to evaporate the salty wetness from him. He stopped and looked at the pickax.

"No!" His voice roared as he flung it downward into the planks nearest his feet. He swung it over and over again until he had fractured the plank and then sunk to his knees sobbing—a child's cry, something he didn't, couldn't do until now.

"God?" he squeaked from a closed throat, parched from the heat and emotion gripping it. "I never wanted much," he followed. "Where did you go? And look at my pa . . . ," he cried upward in desperation. "My heart, my guts, my mind, it's all crazy. Sick and crazy," he cried, kneeling over the hole he had made in the boardwalk.

After a few moments he arose, composed as suddenly as he had fallen apart—mechanically composed with a job to do. He stripped to his shorts, showered himself with soothing water first, then connected the hose to the tanker. He looked at the ruptured plank, knowing he couldn't leave something broken. Going to the shed he grabbed a pair of overalls, no shirt, no shoes yet, found the hand saw and a spare board and cut. He cut, hammered, and fit it into place. A reminder of the heat he felt, the patch served its purpose. An outlet to madness, a fire in the mind so hot nothing on earth was made to put it out.

"Anger is for killin', for war." The rail bum Skully had been the only one to give him any advice worth heeding.

He secretly hoped for war now, a reason to shoot at, kill someone. He believed in no one but himself. God had certainly not rescued his poor fevered senses. Where was God for his pa? Off in the cosmos while his mama died from a twister. It was something God could have fixed if he had the mind to.

And no man could counsel him to help make meaning of the heart that quaked hard and bad like an angry charging bull. A bull, not knowing which way to turn to fight the tormenters surrounding him, at least would mercifully be dead sooner than he. If he died in a war, so what?

"I swear, if Lucian ever breaks her heart, I'll be there. I'll make it right. I swear," he muttered in a new and calm resolve.

"Norman! Gear up. We ready with the water?" he heard his father's voice call out from the engine compartment.

He checked the tank. Full. Disconnecting the hose, he gave himself another strong dousing, swallowing as he did. Grabbing his shoes, he sat. Pulling them on, he examined his patch work on the loading dock. "Good fit," he congratulated himself with ambivalence, stringing his boots snugly.

The sun mocked his attempts at cooling down. He spat out the bad taste in his mouth onto the patch, got up, and squinted, wondering if he would ever return here again.

"Son? We ready yet?"

"It's done," he yelled back. "Done, Pa. All done."

CHAPTER 24

The 200th Coastal Artillery, New Mexico National Guard, had been federalized. The orders were in. "Undisclosed destination. Pacific training exercise. One year duration." The regiment was packed and ready to board trains headed for San Francisco.

New draftees combined with doctors, lawyers, cowboys, rail hands, college students, high school graduates, shopkeepers, Native Americans—mostly New Mexicans, with a few Oklahomans, Texans—and even a boy from Indiana looking for adventure. Bunched together, full of bravado, they were being cheered by the adoring friends, relatives, and fellow New Mexicans as the band played on. The 200th was ready to ship out to the west coast.

"Johnny! You seen Norman?" Lucian called above the noise.

"Nope. Last I saw him was at reveille. Said he had some business to do. Haven't seen him since."

"He's got me nervous. I've got to get on over to Headquarters battery but I need to see him before we ship out."

"I'll tell him you're looking for him. You two got in a fight? Something like that?"

"Something like that."

"You married his girl. I mean, he told me. Well, you know. He's pretty sore. Why don't you just leave him be? He'll come around. He's probably hiding out in one of them freight cars. You know Norm."

"Yeah, I know Norman," Lucian agreed. "If you see him, tell him I'm lookin' for him."

"Sure thing, Lucian. You take care. We'll see you along the way. Don't you worry. Norman, with the help of the good Lord, will come out of it. I'll watch him. Don't you worry none."

"Thanks Johnny. I'll be getting on back to my battery."

"Say, what are you guys shootin'? I mean what guns you all experts in?"

"Fifty calibers."

"They get 'em all loaded? Some of our stuff is still missin'. We're shootin' them thirty-seven millimeter artillery pieces with the new-fangled scopes, range finders that take a scientist to figure out. Maybe Norm is on the hunt."

"Yeah. Maybe so," Lucian agreed.

Lucian mingled with a few of his friends from the regiment, hoping to catch a glimpse of his brother. It worried him. He had wanted Norman's blessing. He cursed himself for the trouble it all turned out to be, but mixed in those feelings was a bliss he never had known existed.

The honeymoon wasn't much, two nights alone in a rented room in Redemption, then the train ride into Albuquerque, two nights more, and then Mary Jane returned with his pa, Harry, and the government load old man Monroe had contracted with him to take into Amarillo on his way back.

He couldn't look Norman in the eye. It hurt too much. He, Lucian, had taken the girl that had Norman twisted and wound up into a finely tensed spring, and then there was the ring. He had to have a ring for the wedding, but he didn't need to keep it.

Lucian felt like a no-good jerk, stripping the ring with the inscribed family motto off the finger of his twin brother. He wanted badly to make up, do something, be like old times when they would die for each other. There was never a dull moment growing up with Norman along the rail lines. Although he'd been the playful one, always able to bring reserved Norman into the fun he'd make up for them, Norman helped keep him in line.

Meeting Mary Jane, then marrying her, put the two brothers into a hellish tailspin. He couldn't deny his heart. He loved that girl like a heat-crazed man dying for a drink. He drank from a well of love he couldn't have imagined, and left Norman hanging out to dry. They had shared everything, but this was where the best of brothers and friends drew the line.

He kicked at the dirt, wondering if he was his brother's keeper or his brother's enemy. One thing he knew for sure. He'd look out for Norman, make it up somehow. He was going to do right by him.

He spit out a cheek full of tobacco juice away from the crowd and looked up.

"I'll be," he said, smiling, stunned. He shook his head and rubbed at his eyes. "Norman?" he mouthed with a questioning look. "I'll be a son-of-a-gun." He grinned, watching his brother and the young woman.

CHAPTER 25

Mary Jane settled into a support role for her grandfather, who was beginning to act his age. He had slowed and wasn't the help he had wanted to be for Jason Parker and the shortline out of Warm Springs.

She had never imagined returning here, not to a dull boring life in a town that couldn't boast of a minimal social environment. Not a church, not a theater, not more than three seats at the soda fountain at Kelly's Drugs.

Marriage meant something though, and family needs meant she'd be obliged to care for Grandpa Harry and equally for the lonely father of the man—men—she loved.

She considered the thought. She was guilty of the unintended heartbreak of her new husband's equally handsome brother, Norman. *I could have been happy married to either*, she contemplated. What a mess I caused, she mused, biting at her lower lip. *I should have said no to Lucian and could have avoided hurting Norman.*

Love has its own set of rules, though. She knew Norman couldn't understand any better than she why she could feel so differently about men who looked identical. How some chemistry of the heart worked for one in one way and for the other in another way made no sense at all. There was chemistry for both of them, just different.

She felt guilty of the crime of responding too well to the accidental kiss that day at the café in Santa Monica. There was absolutely no difference in the passion she felt kissing Norman while she thought she was kissing Lucian. *Yes, I could have been happy with Norman too,* she posed silently to her worried mind.

The heart has a mind of its own, she concluded. What was she to do? Deny her stronger feelings for Lucian? Maybe it was the fun way he had about him, the boyishness over the more sober and serious Norman. Maybe that was why she was attracted differently to him.

Let it go, another voice inside her urged. There was danger in playing with the mind too much. "Follow your heart, obey God, and let the rest sort itself out," her father had wisely counseled back in California the day before she came back to Warm Springs. Her kin were practical and devoted people. That was what she needed to be now.

She prayed a real prayer today. Not the daily ritual type where you say the same things, ask for the same things, like having a check-off list between you and the Almighty.

No. Today's was a real prayer.

She looked over at tired Grandpa Harrison. He slept in the easy chair as soundly as a worn out puppy from too much play. He had loved the idea of working with Jason Parker on the shortline.

The prayer she said today lingered in her mind like a pleasant memory. It was simple really. She had asked for strength and courage to give more than to receive. This place and Lucian's deployment to some unknown destination meant she would have to forego any self-centered wants.

So she prayed to find the way to become *selfless*, a servant to these two men at home that meant so much to her and to her two men abroad. Funny, she was only married to one of them, but felt they were both "her men."

Perhaps that would change when Lucian returned and Norman found someone. Perhaps Mr. Parker, her father-in-law, would find a widow or such to help him in his loneliness too. Grandpa would always have her until he was gone.

She knelt by the sofa while the old man slumbered, and supplicated a God she had barely begun to understand, petitioning for patience, understanding, and for the safe return of her beloved Lucian . . . and Norman.

CHAPTER 26

August 1941, U.S.S. Coolidge

"I don't suppose we'll all get to see these shores again." A deeply pensive Johnny Mead spoke soberly as he and Norman leaned against the rail. The converted luxury liner, now troop ship, was headed past the Golden Gate bridge to open sea.

"San Francisco sure is a pretty sight. I guess seeing the country from this view makes it all real. It's been like playing army up until now," Lucian spoke up. He came from behind them unexpectedly.

"Didn't think you'd ever show up," Norman

responded, moving aside, making room for his brother. "Johnny here thinks we are going to lose some men. He's a bit touchy about them Japs out in China."

"All I said is I guess some of the boys won't make it back. I don't know why I feel that way. I just do. That's all," Johnny answered defensively.

"I'm goin' back, cousin. This is a one-year vacation. No Japs are gonna attack American bases. They aren't that stupid." He turned to Norman. "So you gonna write Luisa back in Albuquerque? That was some kissin' goin' on at the depot as we loaded the train. I was lookin' all over for you, then bingo! There's my brother with the prettiest señorita in Albuquerque in his arms." Lucian smiled, changing the subject.

"Yeah, I suppose. She is a pretty woman," he answered, trying to convince himself that he'd put Mary Jane out of his heart. "Look at that skyline, will ya? And those rolling hills. It almost makes a man forget about Warm Springs," he said wistfully. "You got California right all along, brother," Norman added.

"I guess we'll be seein' it about this time next year. Sure is a lot of water out there.

Wonder how Pa is gonna make out. He turns fifty next year, you know. Sure is inconvenient, this training deployment," Lucian observed.

"Not much he can do but make out. He's a tough old bird. He's got them two young boys, Jimmy and Hank from Kelly's, the drug store man. Those Kelly boys are eager to get out of town. I imagine they can shovel coal, load cars, handle the boiler tank as good as you and me with a bit of motivation."

"Still, with Mama gone. It's a sad sight, I'll tell ya, Norm. Sure glad I went back home. Sure glad I did," Lucian said, thinking about his bride. He was comforted knowing she was there in Warm Springs for moral support to his pa. He was glad to see Norman getting over the anger, the jealousy, though he supposed he wouldn've felt the same.

"So is Luisa a good kisser? I mean back at the station in Albuquerque, you two really had something going?" Lucian quizzed, breaking the silence.

"As good as Mary Jane, I suppose," he replied.

"Hey, what do you mean by that?"

"Just what I said."

"How would you know?"

"How do you know I don't?" he dug back.

Silence.

"Well boys, I think that was mess call. Chow lines are formin'. Do I have to eat your share?" Johnny had been silent, casually taking in the brotherly exchange until now.

"Come on." Lucian nodded.

"I'll be along. Save me some," Norman replied quietly. "I want to think."

They left him there to ponder the California shoreline, now disappearing from the stern of the *Coolidge*. It was August 1941 and by August 1942 he'd be back watching an anxious Lucian see this shoreline come into view. He was glad he was moving away from the pain—as far as the army would send him was fine by him. One year might do it, might help him forget his brother's wife.

He had a picture of Luisa with him and she promised to write. He could eat in the mess hall, save his money, and marry her when he got home. He could love her. He'd just be as cold as ice in the company of Lucian and Mary Jane. Guess he'd leave Warm Springs to them, maybe give them the Dearborn spread he bought with his Santa Fe earnings as a late wedding gift.

He'd move on out to New Mexico and make a new life. One year reinforcing some army outpost in the Pacific should help him make up his mind.

If the Japs ever attacked, if there ever was a war, he wasn't going to hold anything back. He didn't care enough about returning, not yet. Not that he had a death wish, just that whatever the pain was that lay ahead, it couldn't possibly do to him what the girl from Warm Springs had done.

They don't make torture like that, he considered. *They surely don't.*

CHAPTER 27

Present day, Warm Springs, Oklahoma

Seventy-nine-year-old Lucian Parker covered years in minutes as he kicked at a knot in the creaky boards of the antiquated loading dock. The fiery noon sun baked the hardwood planks hot and white if left to themselves. It did the same to just about everything in this part of the country if left without tending to. Lucian must have applied a thousand gallons of linseed oil over the years to condition them—keep them from rotting away.

Time for another coat, he thought to himself. The sun sweltered just like it did that day he and his brother had left from here for war so many years ago. There was never any forgetting that day.

Yes sir, the same fireball in the sky looked down on me on this very loading dock— shone on my dear brother, too. Funny how it goes. The sun—just like an old reliable friend. Maybe it knew who he really was, had been, he mused.

Odd that he should think that way. The sun had about killed him in the Philippines. *That was then*, he thought.

It was his heritage to keep this small train station alive. Alive and telling its silent tale of the past glory days when train tracks meant survival because of a shortline rail to the outside world. At least the world outside this part of Oklahoma territory.

The surviving brother pondered on what that meant now, and he felt the same pangs of guilt that had dogged him every hour of every day since the end of the war fifty-five years ago.

Lucian Parker paced the planks today like a man looking for a precious lost coin hidden somewhere in the grains of the noisy squeaking timbers, or wedged between the heaviness of the joints that made up Warm Springs' nearly one-hundred-year-old train depot loading dock.

It was a shortline railroad because the sixty-five-mile track was a one-way rail run connecting the farming community with the mainline to the south.

Shortline, he contemplated as he paced, waiting impatiently for his sweetheart to arrive so they could take the original 1907 Baldwin steam locomotive down the line to Redemption. *Switchman too*, he laughed self-consciously.

He stopped and looked quizzically at a design in the grains of wood beneath his feet. He remembered this spot! It had been patched the day they both shipped out to join their National Guard unit down in New Mexico. They had been home for one week and needed to get back. *It was the honeymoon train ride*, he winced.

Norman had put a pickax through the plank in anger, he said silently to himself. *Norman*, he whispered reverently as if he could bring him to life, stand him before him this very day and speak to him somehow.

Funny how it goes. It seemed like yester-

day and his life passed before him as if it
were a dream.

Norman.

Lucian.

Twins.

The same, yet so separated from each
other by time. Time was now a blur. All a
blur of events running together in a string. A
string of memories so jumbled with the fateful days of war—as if the war had defined
him and everything before or after it. And
then there was Mary Jane. Indeed, they
both had loved her.

But the events of those days did feel like
yesterday to him now. The anger between
them on that day had been sharp and hot.
The anger between the brothers was dead
now, though. As dead as the wood he
walked upon. Salty moisture found its way
to his lips.

His age-spotted hand swiped at his eyes
as he blinked away the watery mirage. *I
loved him*, he whispered in a deep and reflective voice to the repaired patch on the
wooden boarding platform, as if he could redeem the day from the bitterness that had
spilled over there so many years ago. "*I

loved him!" he announced convincingly to the fireball glaring down upon him.

He and Mary Jane would go to Redemption now, make a stop to pick some folks up for the ride on this final train run into Albuquerque as soon as she arrived from the ranch house.

They'd present the old steamer to the local railroad museum and park as a gift from the family. From there they'd head to the Philippines, but his mind would linger for a while in 1941.

He stared at the spot where the pickax had angrily landed on the platform. It dissolved into that very hot day. A day that he confronted his pain. Pain and emotion that had been pent up inside him setting up this whole chain of events he had lived.

Dear God in heaven, I loved him like life itself. His moist eyes reflected thoughtfully, ardently, as he gazed toward the noonday sun overhead. He hoped he had done honor to his brother . . . to his name.

CHAPTER 28

Present day, Manila City, the Philippines

The jet landed in Manila a little more than one week from the day he had paced the Warm Springs loading dock. One week is all it took to get there, yet he had let so much time go by.

It was the first time Lucian Parker had returned to the Philippines since the end of World War II. He always meant to come here, it's just that he was always so busy with raising the family, the ranch, the depot, the myriad other things that kept a man preoccupied. And if he did come, then he knew he would be making a commitment to something that could change his life and that of his Mary Jane.

He wasn't sure he was ready for that, until now. Besides, he would have to remember many events that he would just as soon leave buried—forgotten. Mary Jane had probed once or twice, right after the war, but he couldn't talk about it. He begged her not to remind him of his three years in hell. There were just no words that could be formed. None sufficient to describe it all. It caused too many painful memories of death, anger, jealousy, rage. She had honored his request for all these years.

And he had always lacked a certain quality his brother had been full of. Coming here would remind him of that. He wished he had more confidence in himself and what Mary Jane felt for him, but he lacked it—plain and simple. That was a weakness that he just couldn't live with anymore. His lack of confidence. Especially in himself, and the feelings of wronging his brother so long ago.

So he was here at long last. But he forgot the new stone grave marker, a white stone marker to replace the one there. He had it made for this occasion. No matter. The shipping company said it would arrive within days on another flight. He would have to make arrangements with the caretakers of the cemetery. Then it would all be right.

The marker he had fashioned and gotten permission to place at his brother's burial site would reveal the truth. It would say all there was to say. The names, places, events . . . the brotherhood that was and is shared by twins.

A much older man now, he hurried through the U.S. military cemetery outside of Manila. He was a man with a mission. With gaze wide, blinking away the stinging wetness that caused the whiteness of his eyes to redden, he rubbed the teeming moisture with the back of a time wrinkled hand, reading each tropically fungus-covered grave marker as he did.

"F-125. This is row 'F.' I've got to find plot 125," he said aloud as his wife struggled to keep up with him. Row after row of white crosses bore names and symbols of men who once were young and filled with dreams. He had known so many of them.

"Lucian," she called out. "You've passed it. It's the other way," she yelled, cupping her hands to her mouth.

"Oh," he mumbled as he quickly turned about and started with the same urgency in the opposite direction.

His wife watched him as he passed her by, seemingly oblivious to the fact that she was even there. She had never seen him like this, although she should have known visiting this place would make him almost crazy with grief. He had loved his brother so.

"I'm back. I've come back, brother," he whispered with deep respect as he hurriedly made his way to grave marker 125. He stopped. Legs frozen stiff. His hand moved mechanically to his trademark, and new for this occasion, dark brown fedora, removing it from his head and placing it over his rapid, rhythmic heartbeat.

It was 1945 suddenly and he was twenty-five years old. A sudden chill swept through him. His head bent, immobile in one direction—toward the white cross. He gently swept his fingers across the fungus-covered grave marker seeking to erase the name, as if he could bring his brother back.

The spot was soon cleansed by the intermittent moisture from the sky mixing with his own tears. This was a far more emotion-laden moment than he ever could have imagined. He had never allowed Mary Jane to see this side of him. Now he couldn't stop. The dam bursting inside his soul crumbled to the power of the salty emotion welling in his eyes and he couldn't plug the hole.

Now bent with age, he watched as the drops fell against the simple stone marker. Then they would stop. He knelt next to it, moving his hand over each word gently, reverently, as if in touching the words he could bring them to life. He whispered them aloud again and again:

Captain Norman B. Parker,
200th Coastal Artillery USA.
Born April 6, 1921.
Died from wounds March 15, 1945.
"Greater love has no man than this."

"Lucian? Lucian," Mary Jane called softly, sweetly. "You've been here an hour now. Shouldn't we be going?" She had remained in the car until now giving him the time he needed to be alone.

"Can we come back tomorrow?" he asked as a small child would, seeking permission from the adult directing his life.

"Of course, dear. But the heat and all. I'm afraid . . ."

"You don't understand," he whispered as he stood up and took in a deep breath of the humid, sultry Philippine air. "You can't understand," he said, emotionally struck by the thoughts coursing through his tired mind as he wiped the last drop of moisture from his eyes.

"Yes, I can. I can understand, Lucian," she responded sweetly.

"No. I'm afraid you cannot! No one can. No one," he insisted, taking one final grieving glance for the day at the tombstone. Putting his arm around her and walking slowly toward their chauffeur-driven car he repeated the dictum: "No one can understand."

CHAPTER 29

Lucian Parker sat on the edge of the bed at the historic Manila Hotel near the port and just outside the Inturmuros section of Manila. He had been in this hotel once before, when war broke out. It was here he was promoted in rank, along with his brother in December 1941.

He had reserved this room for this occasion. One thousand and eight hundred dollars per night. The MacArthur Suite was a special suite of rooms very few had seen before the war. It had been the famous general's home—his family's residence when he served as commander of the American armed forces in Southeast Asia. Now it was available for anyone, at the right price.

He couldn't sleep. Not now. This was the moment he should have lived—should have been done with—years before. He sat there pondering what he would say to Mary Jane when she awoke. Why he had been willing to live since the war without making the issue plain—the truth known to Mary Jane, he didn't understand himself. He guessed he would have to relive it once more this night, make sure he identified his reasons for doing things the way he had.

Although the neon lights of Manila's downtown district ignited the streets with their fiery red hues, the night sky had turned an ominous black with the monsoon clouds sweeping over the large island.

The monsoons, he whispered to himself. Monsoons that spent their tropically charged moisture on so many paved roads and busy intersections that didn't exist fifty-five years earlier. The monsoon didn't stop the city—it never had.

The damp, hot, humid wetness that he once had counted on for survival during the war—to quench his thirst, to bathe in—it reminded him that some things can never be changed.

But he had changed. He was Lucian Parker, heart and soul, *wasn't he*? He had confided to another person once after the war and had promised to take care of the nagging burden. But insecurities are hard to conquer, he reckoned.

He frequently would make a commitment to make things right to the minister up the road from Warm Springs. Pastor J. D. Briggs was his name. Dead now, his son Jeffrey B. was at the pulpit. J. D. had been a good listener, Lucian remembered; a good friend, too.

He wasn't sure if the son knew his secret. Maybe he should have told him as well. But he remembered those Sunday conversations on the steps of the church porch in Redemption, a town about the size of Warm Springs.

"I've lived the best I can. Do you think it's enough?"

"You know I do, Brother Lucian. When you gonna stop this guilt trip and tell Mary Jane and get on with it?"

"Soon," he would answer. "Soon."

Redemption, he said silently to himself as he bowed his head and gazed intently as if in so doing he would discover the thing on the floor—the thing he had lost so long ago.

And the promise he would make to Pastor Briggs made him feel he had halfway accomplished just that—an expiation of sorts, a deliverance from his guilt. The word "soon" was used a lot over a fifty-five year period of time.

"You can't fool the man in the mirror," his pa, Jason W. Parker, used to tell the two of them when they were just boys growing up first along the rails near Tulsa, then in the whistle-stop railroad station in Warm Springs. Of course, for Lucian Parker, the words truly had a double meaning.

He was not able to put it off any longer. Not now. No matter what a man, or a woman for that matter, does to slow the aging process, the mirror pretty soon gets through. Oh sure, the man staring into the mirror feels like a twenty-year-old inside. "That's the magic of this thing we call life, I suppose," Jason Parker had added once when Norman and Lucian last saw their father with shaving mug and brush in hand before they left for the war.

"But living a lie doesn't make it truer just because you lived it longer," Jason reminded them both. "Be true to the man in the mirror. I'm mighty proud of you boys."

He had been true to the name—he was sure of it. At least he had been true to the *Parker* part, by giving that name the best he had inside of him.

But he had failed Norman. And that was what Lucian really stared at each day when he looked into his mirror—a lie lived just a little longer.

He considered the woman he loved so dearly. Mary Jane was sound asleep. She would chastise him for not getting any rest. But no matter how tired his body was, his mind was alert to this day. It was a day that could destroy everything he had come to regard as important if Mary Jane didn't handle it well.

She was such a fragile flower. He loved that quality, *the fragility, the utter feminine tenderness*, he thought to himself as he turned to gaze once more on her serene repose.

The air-conditioning reminded him that in hours to come he would greet a morning filled with steamy vapors in a lush green land made up of hundreds of tropical islands and millions of struggling people who didn't share, and never would, the comforts of life he was able to give to his beloved "Missy," as he often tenderly called her.

He was anxious to go back, for the second and final visit, to the American cemetery and there spend some final moments at the fifty-five-year-old resting place of his twin brother wounded in action on that day in 1945. He had to go there and talk it out. Make sure he'd done all he could. And as much as Mary Jane meant to him, he needed to actually talk, be alone, just hear himself voice the words aloud, relive the story—just this once since the war—and then it would all be done. Once he had, he then could offer no more. It would have to be enough.

He questioned himself as he walked from the softness of the mattress to a rigid but elegantly padded lounge chair situated near the balcony and the sliding glass windows that gave view to the teeming port city below.

The man from Warm Springs had come back to face the war that had been buried so long. *Who was the man? What was he made of?* He queried himself in soliloquies only the sleepless ever know.

CHAPTER 30

The night's veil had turned the steady rain to a mere drizzle as the lightning disappeared on the eastern horizon, and with it the monsoon downpour. Breaking through the fragmenting cumulus, a full moon illuminated the cleansed city. He had reminisced long enough. It was time for action now.

Humidity lingered in the air, and the very definable scent of Philippine life and tropical foliage mixed with moisture drew him into a reverie he couldn't dispel. It reminded him of their last, final, desperate day together—the brothers' battle for survival during the war and freedom from the Japanese prison camp and the final train run when he finally rejoined his brother.

He got up slowly from the easy chair that faced the balcony overlooking the sleepless city and approached his beloved Missy. She was sound asleep from the travel, the worry, and age catching up with her. He caressed her cheek softly with the tenderness of a father to a child and then kissed it. If she stirred—awoke—he wouldn't leave her. If she did not, then he would leave a note and go to the place that might heal his broken spirit.

He scribbled a note:

Darling,
I will be with Norman. I couldn't rest. See you when the shadows flee. Don't worry. It isn't the first time I stayed out all night in the Philippines.

Love you darling,
Lucian

He taped it to the bathroom mirror and, grabbing his overcoat, slipped quietly from the hotel room.

CHAPTER 31

Lucian, normally wearing his fedora, wore instead for this occasion a blue baseball cap with the name of his outfit emblazoned upon it: 200TH COASTAL ARTILLERY, NEW MEXICO NATIONAL GUARD.

An Oklahoman, he was proud of his unit, his cousins, and his friends from the state of New Mexico that he had adopted as his second home. Although he never talked about the war, and didn't go to reunions for fear of what memories might do, he was proud of his men, brethren all, and the fighting spirit they had shown during the war and imprisonment of more than fifty years before.

He had had this hat made up for this trip. He also carried with him something more powerful in its symbolism and meaning than anyone could possibly know. Around his neck was the dangling set of dog tags he had worn from the beginning of his military training at Fort Bliss until right before leaving Manila when his war ended. They seemed to possess a magical potion for his spirit. They were his true identity clanking like train wheels do against a track—connecting him and moving him closer to his beloved brother.

When he reached the covered hotel portico, a Filipino concierge asked him if he needed a cab. He nodded. The youthful man smiled and waved to a waiting yellow sedan. Lucian fixed his eyes upon the young man who promptly opened the door for him.

"I know you, don't I?" he asked before stepping into the backseat. The boy looked so familiar to him.

"No, sir."

"Well then. Here you go," Lucian said, fumbling for a five dollar bill and handing it to him.

"Thank you, sir. Sir, if you don't mind me asking, you were a fighter for the Filipinos in the big war? I see your hat." He smiled, pointing to Lucian's cap.

"Yes," he replied, door ajar, but seated now.

"I want to thank you for your service to my people and country. My grandfather spoke much of you Americans. He was a fighter too." The young man stood back and saluted happily to the old veteran.

Lucian returned the salute. He had never been thanked since that same day he finally reached his brother after the firefight to rescue the fellow prisoners of Cabanatuan. He had supposed the Filipinos were grateful, but he had not been certain, had never been saluted or thanked directly.

"Thank you, young man," he muttered. Lucian sat in the backseat of the cab, lost in memory. In his mind's eye he saw another young Filipino who had sacrificed his life for him and his brother the same day they were wounded during the escape.

A good man, he whispered as the driver patiently waited for instructions. *Manuelito, if I could only tell you . . .* , he muttered under his breath.

His mind busily drifted through time as it had every waking hour for days now. Every young Filipino now reminded him of his World War II guerilla friend, Manuelito Salazar.

"Where to?" the cab driver asked.

"American Military Cemetery."

"This time of night? Maybe it's not open."

"Then I will pay you to drive me there and back," he answered.

"Okay, Joe. I do it. You have friends buried there from the war?"

"Yes. Many friends. Too many."

"Where you from, Joe?" the driver asked, looking into the mirror at the old veteran.

"Fort Stotsenberg, then Bataan, then Camp O'Donnell, and finally Cabanatuan. In the mountains with the guerillas too."

"No! You a prisoner of war of the Japs?"

"Sorry to say."

"What state you from, Joe?"

Lucian Parker hadn't been called "Joe" in five decades. The kids, the men especially, had referred to all American military men as "Joe."

"Oklahoma. But I fought with the New Mexico National Guard."

The cab driver offered a suddenly sullen, serious gaze into the eyes of the man in the backseat through his rearview mirror. There was silence for some time as they drove through the city to the cemetery.

"So you know Cabanatuan. Santa Rosa, too?" the driver finally quizzed, anxious to know more about the American.

"My brother and I drove the train before the Japs invaded. Then my twin, he drove the Jap train past Santa Rosa and back here to Manila, with supplies and such. Did as much damage as I could. Got our boys all the food he could sneak in, too." He smiled with a memory-filled sense of satisfaction.

The cab driver's eyes raised as he inspected his rider carefully in the rearview mirror. "I got family in Santa Rosa. A house there. My sister lives in it. I was born in Santa Rosa. They help many American fighters. I was born just after the war. My father died helping Americans after escape from Cabanatuan."

The driver's heart raced strangely. The cabby searched the man's face for a response to the bait in the words he had offered. This man had been, at the very least, in the same places, at some of the same times as his deceased father.

"Lots of Filipinos died at Cabanatuan,

Camp O'Donnell . . . it was a cryin' shame, a real cryin' shame. I'm sorry."

"My family still keeps photo of Americans there. Not all Filipinos seem grateful, but many still are. Especially around here in Luzon. Too many Americans and Filipinos fight and die together to forget."

"Good. That makes me glad. They shouldn't forget. No one should," Lucian replied as he peered out the rain-streaked window at the buildings now flying past. They were on the outskirts of the city where the seventeen thousand graves lay quietly in testimony to sacrifices made by young men.

"Hey, maybe you knew my father," the curious cabby finally offered.

"Maybe so," Lucian replied, dryly. His mind was on other things, other events as he rolled the window down to get some moist night air. "It all comes back to me now," he whispered.

"I don't hear you. You say what?"

"Nothing."

More silence absorbed the sound of tires on wet asphalt. The rain had cleared from the sky completely. The driver rolled his window down for fresh air.

"So why you go to cemetery so late? Not scared of ghosts?" The driver smiled.

"Just of my own making," Lucian mumbled back.

"But you can't stay all night. Maybe you want me to bring you right back?"

"Maybe."

"Here it comes. Looks like you can go in. Maybe you want me to stay? I can give you good rate. War veteran rate."

"I'll pay you a U.S.A. rate for overtime. Let's say fifteen an hour times two? Thirty total per hour, ghosts or no ghosts."

"You got it, Joe!" The cabby smiled as he brought the car to a slow five miles per hour. "Which way we go?"

Lucian pointed to a tall palm tree he had noticed marking the row. The driver pulled alongside the shoulder where the pavement ended and grass began.

Lucian grabbed his raincoat as he opened the car door. Looking to the driver to tell him to wait, he drew back suddenly from the man, uneasy, stunned. Clearing his eyes with the backs of his hands, looking intently at the Filipino again with only the illumination of a full moon to help him, he appeared surprised, startled.

The driver opened the door and got out. "What's wrong, Joe?"

"You!"

"Me?" the Filipino said, approaching him.

A full two heads shorter than Lucian, his dark but friendly Filipino eyes gave way to a sense of familiarity. A part to his full head of hair and a certain boyishness for someone at least fifty years old reminded Lucian of another time here in Luzon.

"You! You're Salazar! Manuelito Salazar!" Lucian pronounced, incredulous himself of the fact. He drew himself closer to the man now standing in the halo of a luminous moon. "It was a night like this, Manuelito. Right after the raid on Cabanatuan. *Remember?"*

The Filipino returned the piercing gaze of the American caught up in his own history with a smile. His eyes moistened and uncommon emotions seized him. *"Señor Parker . . . You are Señor Parker?"*

"Sí," replied Lucian with a juvenile innocence and eagerness to hug, shake hands, do something.

"My father was Manuelito. I am his son Vincente. Vincente Salazar. You are the man in the photo . . . *Sí?"*

"Photo? The one the little girl took behind the house in Santa Rosa?"

"My older sister."

"I am the man." The two men embraced unashamedly.

"Manuelito," Lucian offered with a cracking voice. He fixed his gaze upon the diminutive Filipino as if searching through him to some other place and time.

"My father, Señor Parker—he is . . ." he tried to finish.

"Manuelito . . . I never told you . . . I didn't get the chance to say . . ." He brushed at the water flooding his eyes. *"To say thank you!"*

CHAPTER 32

Mary Jane possessed secrets of her own. She was married to Lucian. Lucian and Norman went to war. Lucian came back. He had changed some. War can do that to people. But he said he was Lucian. Was she supposed to question that? There were times she could have sworn . . . but no, she always believed that this was her Lucian.

They had been married but a few short days before he shipped out. With the exception of one year as a child in the schoolhouse at Redemption, she had known the brothers little more than two years upon marrying Lucian. Just one of the twins came home from the war. It had to be Lucian. He had said so. Why shouldn't she believe him? She had him back. Nothing else mattered.

Hearing the hotel room door close behind him as he left had filled her eyes with moisture, brought on more frequently now. There was unusual emotion between them lately. Lucian was ill but wouldn't divulge what the doctor had told him, only that he needed another checkup when they returned home. But she sensed it was serious, probably even life threatening, to bring Lucian to the point of revisiting all his war memories.

She had never seen him shed tears, become as drawn out in turmoil as in this past month. But then he had buried the war, had asked her to never bring it up. He had shut it out for so long. Perhaps opening that door to those memories for the first time let the deep, uncontrollable emotions surface. And perhaps that was natural after all, she posed to herself in silence.

But now she faced her own struggle with the past. She hadn't meant to deceive him, to allow him to deceive himself. Why couldn't she just hold her arms open and say what her heart and mind knew to be true? Instead she embraced something she desperately wanted to believe.

The trouble was, the longer they had lived the ruse the easier it was to believe. And somehow she even thought it had its own life. Lucian was Lucian, Norman was Norman, just like before the war. The man who kissed her, loved her, was the man she married. That was that.

But nagging in the background was the thought . . . *No!* She would not allow herself to finish the thought. She never had.

She arose and wiped at the streams of dampness on her cheeks with the palms of a wrinkled hand. She held them up and looked at them thoughtfully, wondering how they had gotten that way. She was nineteen but days ago, or so it seemed.

She walked to the bathroom and stared at the note taped to the mirror. She didn't have to focus her eyes or get her reading glasses. She knew where her sweetheart of fifty-five years had gone. He was where he should be and there was no stopping that man once he made his mind up. Both brothers were just as stubborn. Now both Lucian and Norman needed to be alone together, even at this hour.

She closed her eyes and mouthed a simple plea: *"Dear God, Please allow me the courage to talk to him. To tell my beloved that I am so very sorry. Please forgive me for the falsehood I have built and the pain I have caused my sweetheart. Give me strength, oh Lord."*

She wiped at her eyes and went to the dresser and pulled out the well-worn envelope marked *April 25, 1945*. It had been a letter from her to her newly-returned-from-war husband. She never had the will or courage to give it to him when he returned to the States. He wouldn't talk about the war, the past, or the death of his brother. It simply made it all the harder to give it to him.

She knew what she must do. The night would be given to her darling lover to do what he had to do in reconciliation with his brother. The morning would be given to her to do what she should have done fifty-five years ago.

CHAPTER 33

The American and Filipino stood respectfully before the marker, a white cross illuminated by a full moon. Lucian took his coat off and laid it upon the uncut grass to shield him from its moisture. He sat upon it and brushed at the wetness upon the fungus-blackened cross of his brother's grave.

"I couldn't sleep," he said quietly.

"I understand, Señor Parker."

He eyed his new Filipino friend as if looking through him. "You are your father to me this night. Now I know . . ." His voice trailed off plaintively. "I thought I was . . . and you were . . . Now I know," he repeated softly.

"Know what, Señor Parker?"

"This is how it should end. You want to sit? Maybe I could tell you more," he offered as one gentleman would a chair to another.

"No, thanks. Maybe I should leave you alone?"

"I suppose so. I could tell you some real stories, stories of our fight to survive, how we almost made it back. We'd all be alive today if . . . Manuelito, my brother, and me, that is." Lucian stumbled with his words and again quietly voiced, "if . . . ," leaving it at that.

"I go get my poncho. In the trunk. If you know some things about my father, maybe you share them. That would maybe never happen again."

"Maybe. I want to talk tonight, though. I surely do," the man from Warm Springs replied.

Vincente returned and spread his poncho on the ground. "I never spend time at cemeteries. Too spooky. Your stories better be good." He grinned.

"Well, good or not, they are about us—my brother, your father, and me. You still want to hear?"

The Filipino nodded. "Can the dead hear us, you think?"

He sighed, head bent toward the headstone of his twin brother's resting place. "I hope so," he breathed.

"It was before the war. I was angry as hell at my brother for something he had done. Riding the rails home from Los Angeles to National Guard training at Fort Bliss, Texas, I met a stranger. His name was Skully. I was pretty angry. Angry at my brother."

He went on to tell the younger Filipino about the rail bum who had wisely given him a gift of understanding how to direct his anger. Then he explained all that had happened between himself and his brother that brought them to join the New Mexico National Guard and finally find themselves in the Philippines in 1941.

CHAPTER 34

September 1941, Manila, the Philippines

After eight weeks at sea the men of the 200th Coastal Artillery had landed in a verdant tropical garden city of wide avenues lined with palm trees. It was a stark contrast to earth-colored New Mexico and other parts of the country they had known.

"Look at them pretty señoritas will ya? Man, if we haven't landed in paradise. I've never seen so much green mixed with so many contented people in all my life. Sure got more green than all of New Mexico," Johnny Mead remarked as they rode through Manila in the back of the carriers forming a long column for their new assignment.

"Sure does, cousin," Norman replied. "Wonder how Lucian's doing," he added.

"He'll be ahead of us with the HQ Battery. I saw them taking off and loading the fifty-calibers first. They'll be waitin' at that Fort—what's its name?" Johnny asked.

"Stotsenberg. Fort Stotsenberg. Next door to Clark Airfield where they got a bunch of them P-40 fighter planes and B-17 bombers they want us to protect," Norman answered dryly.

"Yeah. Anyway, it's a few miles up the road north, they say. Maybe an hour, one fella who's already been and back says."

"Guess so," Norman replied, eyeing the steam engine pulling out from the station off to their right. "We ought to get our regiment one of them," he pointed.

"One of what?" Johnny Mead asked.

"One of them," he grunted and pointed. Wouldn't need fifty trucks. Just one of them babies and maybe ten boxcars, some trucks for loading and unloading is all."

"Yeah, I guess you'd like that."

"You bet I'd like to run one. I'll bet I could

make that iron horse purr. They ought to take better care. Look at the rust on the boiler. One of these days she's gonna bust wide open. Get somebody killed."

"Say, you guys . . ." Johnny started in his friendly talkative way with the other men riding in the back of the army duce-and-a-half. "What do ya think of them Filipinos?"

"Who?" Julio Martinez from Gallup questioned as he looked in the direction Johnny pointed. "Those are women, knothead! Women are *Filipinas. Filipinos* are men. Get the *'a'* and *'o'* right. Put an 'a' on the end for women, an 'o' for the men. Good thing I'm along with you, *hombres*," he laughed, shaking his head.

"Look! They're waving at us," Johnny added gleefully, shouting and whistling. "Viva *las* Filipinos!" Johnny shouted, hands cupped to his mouth.

Martinez and the other Spanish-speaking New Mexicans roared loudly at the innocence of the ignorant white boy's mix-and-match efforts. Norman grinned.

Norman's mind wandered as they passed through the ample palm tree-lined boulevards of the Philippine port and capital. Filipino natives, mestizos, Spaniards, Orientals,

Europeans, Americans, all seemed to mix and blend easily as the business of commerce was carried on in a careful sort of drowsiness.

Colorful *pambusco* buses full of riders from all classes, horse-drawn *calesas*, the newest Packards driven by business elites, chauffeured limos, and old pieced-together clunkers from the early 1900s mingled freely together, adding a managed sense of disorder to the laid-back rhythm of the city. Any hint of a war was belied by the languid yet prosperous scene.

They were soon on the outskirts of Manila, a long caravan of men and equipment ten thousand miles from the dry Southwest and home. They passed through the narrower streets of the Inturmuros, a three-century-old fortress port city built by the Spaniards to ward off pirates during colonial times.

The army seemed to enjoy offering the citizens any parade they could to add a sense of stability absent from the rest of Southeast Asia. The Japanese warlords had been stepping up their collection of conquered lands, and anyone familiar with maps could see the Philippines lay in the path of conquering Australia, if the Japanese had a mind to do it.

It was good to get away from the bad feelings that had lingered so long back home, Norman thought. The hard feelings against Lucian and feeling his heart crushed and losing purpose was washing away with this new adventure. He wanted to be glad for Lucian's sake. He would get a year to put Mary Jane's face out of his mind and try to replace the image with that of the pretty and fair-skinned Mexican-American girl, Luisa.

"WELCOME TO FORT STOTSENBERG," the sign read as the first trucks arrived near dusk at the sprawling compound. From Lucian's vantage point he could see nothing worth defending, just a pleasant, easy-going army camp full of neat barracks, a few Quonset huts, and some near naked Negrito natives ambling by.

His first order of business was to try a transfer again. He felt the need to look out for Norman. He had always felt his twin was the more innocent one, the less worldly. And though exactly the same in age, looks, and background, he, Lucian, had so often played the part of *older* brother.

The 200th was a pretty easy-going outfit as the army went. Officers mingled easily with the enlisted men, and the men respected them for it. Everyone pulled together. The Parkers weren't the only family members in the regiment, either. There was a father and son, several cousins, and brothers, although the Parkers were the only identical twins. These men were all family and extremely motivated to be the best.

"I want those fifty-caliber machine gun crates and that ammo dispersed immediately," the platoon staff sergeant bellowed at Lucian and his crew as they unloaded the equipment from the back of the truck. "I'll be back in thirty minutes with our orders and location, and then you'll stow your personal gear in the barracks."

"Hey . . . Psst, Parker," Bogan, the Navajo private in the crew called. "Stand back real careful like." He took out a long shiny new *bolo* knife from his pack—a native Filipino *bolo* knife he had purchased earlier in the day from a street vendor in Manila.

"What?" Lucian questioned. He looked around him to see the frozen expressions of six men staring down toward his feet in the ankle-deep grass.

Woosh! The sound of the blade sliced through the air as the knife flew effortlessly from Bogan's hand, pinning the head of a ten-foot python to the ground.

Lucian stood there frozen stiff, legs spread, snake stuck to the ground between them, as he realized how close he had come to a different kind of danger his first night in the new country.

Bogan picked up the snake by the neck as it still writhed. "Killed me a lot of rattlers in my day, but this beats 'em all. This snake's skin would bring me a small fortune back home. Think I'll keep him."

The gun crew gathered around, jokingly congratulating Lucian on not becoming dinner.

"This ain't Kansas anymore," laughed Martin.

"Yeah. That mother of all snakes would've eaten Parker and Toto too!" Jensen ribbed.

"Yeah, but they say there's another one in the outfit that looks just like Private Parker here."

"What, the snake or Parker?" Bogan asked dryly to loud whoops and laughter.

"Now if one of us here had been eaten,

that wouldn't be right. But Parker has a replacement!" Martinez chimed in.

"That's a helluva smart snake, knowing he had a choice of twins for dinner. What a shame." Bogan smiled as he held his prize up for others to see. Together they manhandled the snake and carried it out to the passing trucks entering the gate. "Welcome to Fort Stotsenberg," they howled as each wide-eyed load of entering soldiers stared in amazement at the bulky snake.

Lucian thought about the light moment, the teasing. They were right. He could be replaced. Norman could play him, he could play Norman. They could keep up the confusion all they wanted. It could come in handy someday.

CHAPTER 35

December 8, 1941, the Philippines

"We're at war!" Johnny Mead shouted. "Hey you guys! No joke! The Japs. They've gone and done it. They attacked Hawaii. Just heard on the radio."

"So maybe there is another radio joker like that guy who created the Martian invasion back in the thirties. Who was that guy?" Tom Stinson asked.

"Orson Welles," Julio Martinez yelled, lounging on a cot reading a comic book.

"Yeah, well, anyway, he got the whole country tuning in to his show. Got everybody all riled up," Stinson yawned. "It's too early in the morning for a war anyway," he chuckled, falling back into his bunk.

"Norm, I just heard it in the mess hall. Where's the radio? Who's got the damn radio?" Johnny repeated in a voice wound tight with urgency.

"That's our radio over in the mess hall. Cory Martin took it over last night for background music during the poker game," Hank Chambers offered. "I say we go over there and get it back," he complained and dashed out the barracks to retrieve the squad's personal radio.

Norman inspected Johnny carefully to detect any trace of a practical joke.

"I'm not kiddin', Norm. Come on."

"Well hell-fire, you guys are all bent out of shape for nothing," Stinson groused, pulling his trousers up and slipping into his boots to follow the others.

"You fellas get to your stations pronto," Platoon Sergeant Winters called above the bustle of men scrambling in all directions. "And go back in there and grab your damn rifles and helmets first! We just might be at war! I'm headed to the CO's hut to check this out. Move!"

"I gotta find Lucian," Norman called out to his cousin. "He's just across the way. Cover for me until I get back!"

The hundred yard run put him into a sandbagged emplacement protecting the .50-caliber machine gun Lucian and two other men handled.

"Anybody seen my brother?" he called above the excited noise coming from the command hut nearby.

"He went to Manila yesterday. Took a ride with Sergeant Riley for some more supplies," the Native American, Jimmy Bogan answered.

"When you see him, tell him I'm at my gun," Norman called above the noise of aircraft engines warming up.

"Sure thing, Norm," called back the friendly Bogan as he calmly loaded the ammunition box onto the heavy machine gun.

He ran in the direction of the company command hut. Formalities were being overlooked. The spirit of the 200th Coastal Artillery was high. Officers and enlisted men surrounded a table set in the center of the room. He figured he could ask a favor of Lieutenant Kerns, Lucian's platoon commander.

"What are you doing over here, Norman? I already got one of you Parker brothers to worry about," Kerns turned his head as he sat at a table with the company commander and staff officers listening to a radio broadcast.

"Sorry, sir. It's Lucian and . . ."

"Yeah, I know. I sent him down to Manila yesterday to get us some extra parts and ammo for the guns. Good thing too. Listen to this," he said, adjusting the table radio to KMZH, the powerful English-speaking station broadcasting from Manila.

"That radio guy in Manila, Don Bell, was just giving an update on the rumor of Japs bombing Pearl Harbor," interjected one of the men standing next to Norman.

Static played noisily as the lieutenant adjusted the tuning knob. The room filled with eager soldiers wanting to hear confirmation of the rumor. It was still December 7, Sunday in Hawaii, but Monday morning December 8 in the Philippines. The announcer's voice suddenly surged from the static:

This is Don Bell at KMZH with a breaking news flash from our sister station in Honolulu. I am listening to reports at this very in-

stant as they are relayed to me. This is what I am hearing:

The Japanese fighters and dive bombers have finally cleared the skies over the island of Oahu. Extensive damage to ships on battleship row. Several sunk. Most ships on fire or damaged.

It isn't clear whether another wave of enemy planes is to be expected or if the Japanese plan an invasion. The scene is one of complete and utter chaos. No one is waiting for orders as they fight the burning flames on ships, planes, barracks, buildings, docks, and rescue men and women trapped in the rubble.

Hickam Field bombed. Planes destroyed on the ground. Dozens on fire. Death and destruction, smoke and explosions as we speak. General panic as civilians are just realizing that this was no naval exercise or accident.

The people are in stunned disbelief to know Japanese aircraft have attacked in waves a territory of the United States. Sirens, ambulances, general mayhem, as rescue efforts organize and the realization sets in that this is war! Thousands perhaps dead and injured in preliminary estimates as reports coming in that one or more entire battleships with full crew have been sunk!

Wait, here we go. Our source tells us the battleships Arizona, California, West Virginia heavily damaged or sunk! The carriers were at sea. No carriers hit. Destroyers, cruisers badly damaged.

Our communication line to Honolulu just went dead. I'm sure this is only a temporary delay in transmission.

I'm Don Bell. Let's get prepared, Manila! Looks like we'll be next! We'll be back with more news on this shocking story of war waged against the United States in the Pacific in just a moment.

The room was thick with silence except for the static from the radio set. The lieutenant was playing with the dial hoping to pick up some more broadcasts as Captain Jenkins radioed battalion headquarters at Fort Stotsenberg for confirmation.

"That guy Bell is playing mind games with us. He's a hot head. Always spoutin' off about the Japs. The Japs this and the Japs that. It's a hoax," one of the sergeants said.

"I wouldn't be so sure about that, Bill," another guardsman answered. "If they wipe out the fleet in the Pacific, we're goners and them Nips know it."

"Ah, bull! That radio guy in Manila is just pulling our leg. Gettin' everybody to listen so they can sell more ads. I got a business back in Demming. That's exactly how to get people tuned in," added another soldier.

"That's right. Besides, how could the Japs get so close to Hawaii without being spotted?" the sergeant reassured himself.

Norman tapped Lieutenant Kerns to get his attention. "Sir, I'd like permission to speak with you."

"Not right now, Corporal. Get back to your unit," he answered, agitated, with his interest clearly focused on the small tabletop radio.

Norman broke away from the crowd gathered at the table and ran back across the field to his 37-mm anti-aircraft gun.

"You think this is for real, Norm?" Johnny asked excitedly, as he strapped his washbasin-style helmet on.

"I can't say. I heard a radio over in the command hut across the way. The radio guy is all excited saying Pearl Harbor's been bombed, ships sunk, sneak attack, thousands dead . . . I don't know. I'm sure worried about Lucian. I know what he and Riley are up to."

"Yeah, what's that?"

"He and Sergeant Riley from HQ Battery have got some trading going one with men from the 60th Coastal Artillery on Corregidor. Seems they want some guns and parts and we want some from them. Shipments on parts down at the Quartermaster's in Manila got all goofed up. We can't fire some of the three-inch guns and they can't fire some of their thirty-seven millimeters."

"Where the heck is Corregidor?"

"It's out in Manila Bay. And if he gets caught out there, he might not be able to get back. If the Japs attack, well, I'd rather be where I can keep an eye on him, look out for him."

"He's a big boy, Norm."

"Yeah, well I promised my pa I'd bring him back, look out for him."

"I suppose my Uncle Jason, your daddy, made Lucian make the same promise. You just don't know it."

"Suppose so."

"Okay, boys," the sergeant yelled. "It's official for now. Dig in. Get ready for a war.

Keep your eyes peeled and helmets on. This is what we trained for."

Norman thought he'd lost his religion at the church in Redemption that day six months ago, the day his love was taken by his brother. He felt anxious now, wondering how to protect his twin.

He prayed. He silently offered a petition, the first one in months, for Lucian's safety, and wondered why it had to come to this to see what really mattered most.

CHAPTER 36

"Look at the waves of navy fighters coming over. Some big exercise going on, you suppose?" Lucian drawled, with the first chewing tobacco he'd had in months wedged in his cheek.

"Thought you said you gave that stuff up," deep-voiced Sergeant Riley answered. They both gazed intently at the plane-filled sky as the sun climbed to midmorning over the teeming port city of Manila.

"I gave it up for Mary Jane. But she isn't here, so might as well enjoy some vice." He grinned. "So you suppose they're navy planes or army aircorp?" he asked again as they both watched intently from the bow of the small navy patrol boat that had taken them to Corregidor and was on its return run across Manila Bay.

"Looks like they're headed right smack over Manila," Riley answered. "Maybe some Military Day parade. Showin' off for General MacArthur's birthday or another bigwig maybe?"

"Could be. What's that stuff they're dropping? If it's a celebration, why haven't we heard about it? Look." Lucian pointed to the tiny falling objects still miles away from their position in the bay.

"Can't make it out from here. Mighty curious, like floating black dots," answered the rough voice of Sergeant Riley.

The sound of sailors shouting commands and racking the deck guns, readying them for action, alerted the two soldiers that something was wrong with the planes. Clouds of dust and faint explosions were now rising from the city they sped toward.

"Those are Jap bombers!" the ensign at the controls, with binoculars in hand, yelled. "Meatball markings all over 'em! Grab a rifle!" he yelled, directing Lucian and Riley to a gun rack.

"Japs?" Lucian questioned as they both quickly perceived the war game they had been playing in the Philippines with the National Guard suddenly was real. "The Japs are nuts! They can't attack the U.S. and get away with it," Lucian called to Riley as an innocent trusting boy would, stunned by the sudden appearance of an unsuspected bully.

"Here!" Riley returned tossing a .30-caliber navy carbine to Lucian. "And you'll need these," he added, sliding some ammunition clips across the deck to him.

Salty spray moistened the deck as they sped in the direction of the unprecedented spectacle—waves of Japanese planes dropping death upon the peaceful sleepy port city in broad daylight.

"Arrogant SOBs," Riley spit as he focused on the sight.

To Lucian it all seemed unreal, some ruse, a game, spoiling the army vacation he had planned would end in twelve months so he could return to Mary Jane and begin his new life. He thought of Norman back at the fort, what might be going through his head right now.

Their small speeding craft was an unnoticed speck of navy gray on white foaming breakers in the blue Manila Bay as they approached the sound of confusion on the looming shoreline.

"They're after the ammunition dumps. There goes one!" the ensign called out as a fireball shot skyward from the docks. "The storage, fuels, ammo, big ships, gun emplacements. That's what they'll go for first. We'll head for Manila North Harbor and the shoreline away from the stuff they'll be bombing down south here," he yelled above the engine noise.

"Keep an eye out for fighter planes," called a sailor on the bow gun behind him to the two soldiers crouched on either side of him.

"Say, Riley. Think these carbines can hit a plane?" Lucian called out.

"If it's sittin' still, I suppose," he answered dryly.

"How do ya lead a plane that's going two hundred miles an hour?" he called back.

"Real fast," Riley replied with a wink.

Lucian sought to discover the bravado and carefree composure of his movie heroes who handled danger so well. He wondered if the tough Riley, an amateur boxer and cowboy back home, was afraid. He had swaggered into more barroom brawls than any man in the regiment he'd ever seen.

Lucian wiped thoughtfully at the perspiration beading on his brow. *Was Norman under attack at Clark Airfield? Was he in danger?* His own crew, with Jimmy Bogan, would be handling the .50-caliber machine guns without him. *Any deaths among his friends?*

No, the Japs would have to tangle with the P-40 fighter planes at Clark. The planes would all be in the air mixing up the skies in dog fights, he supposed. That would make it hard for the guys on the ground to even be in the fight for fear of knocking one of their own planes out of the sky.

The aerial action seemed unreal, movielike. The billowing smoke, the exploding docks before him were a new scene his mind tried to grasp, as he alternately focused upon the planes now clearly marked with a red ball on each wing.

A transport ship exploded into a fiery cloud of confusion and he could see specks, forms of men, leaping from its deck into the water, which also caught fire.

"Radio from Manila says the Nips attacked Pearl Harbor earlier today. It's war, boys!" the ensign confirmed as his radio operator continued relaying messages. "Hold on!" he screamed as he added throttle to gain speed and began jumping the small ship from side to side in an evasive maneuver.

"Jap fighters," pointed out the sailor strapped in and manning the big .50-caliber gun on the stern of the patrol boat.

"They see us, you think?" Lucian called across the bow of the craft to Riley who occupied a position opposite him.

"I don't think they are after small stuff. Still . . . I don't think so. No, they're protecting the bombers and strafing the docks," the sergeant answered.

"How far away are those Jap planes over there?" Lucian yelled back.

"A mile maybe," he answered.

The navy ensign at the controls zigzagged wildly as the plywood PT boat raced toward a shoreline above Manila and away from the attacking enemy planes.

"Ensign Murphy!" one of the gunners warned. A Japanese fighter made a low pass over them and then circled back.

"Okay, boys! Hold on. Fire when he's in

range!" the youthful ensign shouted at the top of his lungs.

The fighter came upon them in an arrogant show of confidence, attacking head-on when he could easily have used the sun to shield him or could have attacked from the rear.

Lucian looked wide-eyed to Sergeant Riley who steadied his carbine with the eye of a man determined to pick off a running jackrabbit at one hundred yards. Lucian turned toward the lone Jap plane, imitating him.

The deck-mounted machine guns opened up from both bow and stern as the ensign at the helm guided the boat in wide sweeping turns to avoid direct fire from the enemy plane.

Lucian tensed, felt the surreal danger of the moment. The rapid rattle from guns was deafening. The aircraft was within range to make out the face of the determined pilot as he sought to angle into the swerving craft.

The Japanese Mitsubishi fighter plane, a Zero, spat bullets, splashing in the water toward them. The boat's crew had the advantage of evasive maneuvering out of the line of fire. Added to the advantage were two lethal .50-calibers and two angry New-

Mexican guardsmen with carbines trained on one lone and overly confident Zero pilot. Altogether the playing field was leveled.

Lucian poured his fire into the cockpit along with the other men as the plane made a low and unsuccessful pass overhead. As if in slow motion, he watched blood explode in the canopy and the plane arching wildly, first up and then straight down, crashing into Manila Bay behind them as they sped on.

"Whoo-hoo! Take that Tojo!" Lucian exultantly screamed with the cheers of the crew. The ensign grinned widely as he continued his course for the safety of shore.

"Keep your eyes open. It ain't over," the ensign called out.

Lucian experienced a feeling of high euphoria. Riley rolled over to him and offered a congratulatory smack on the back. "We're killers now." He smiled.

"Yeah," Lucian observed. It seemed little more than a violent game for several moments. They were untouched, unfazed. The bombing was distant, and except for the enemy pilot he hadn't seen anyone dead, anything destroyed.

No, this was as fun as a shooting gallery, he thought. It was like back home in the penny arcade. Picking off targets and scoring the victory. No one really died in the shooting gallery and he sensed all that was happening as dreamlike.

The entire crew celebrated and swelled with an eager anticipation for another go at the enemy as they scouted the sky above and beyond them.

"You hit the beach by those palms. That small boat dock over there. Grab your gear and then hightail for the bushes beyond that nipa hut!" the ensign yelled. "And take those rifles, with some extra ammo! As soon as your feet hit that dock, we're out of here! You guys copy that?"

"Roger. We copy," Riley yelled back above the patrol boats' diesel engines and the immediate background noise of warfare. He turned to Lucian. "Where's that sight, the range-finder for the thirty-seven millimeter gun we got from those boys on Corregidor?"

"In the gunnysack with the other gear."

"You grab it. I'll take the carbines, and some of the small caliber ammo," he pointed out.

"What about the crate of fifty-caliber stuff we were supposed to take back to Clark with us?"

"It stays, Parker. Those guys gave us carbines. They get the ammo. Unless you figure you can handle it on your back at a dead run."

Gloomy black plumes of smoke and fiery explosions now became real, not some distant mirage. With their slowing approach to the shore everything about this surprise attack was disturbingly clear. They weren't going home anytime soon. They'd continue under attack and now would be fighting for their lives.

The first wave of Mitsubishi bombers and fighter planes had disappeared and now the wail of sirens, the sounds of victims stunned by the attack's interruption of the placid Filipino morning filled the air. Vehicles on fire, screams of people missing their family members, military scrambling to rescue comrades, put out fires, make some order from chaos, was all too apparent. So too were bodies lying in the streets, amid the rubble, dazed walking-wounded, the stunned look of horror on the faces of people unprepared for war.

Hitting up against the small pier, the two soldiers waved a "thanks" to their navy friends and jumped from the craft to the dock, dashing the fifty yards to the beach. Putting the engines in reverse, the patrol boat was quickly on its way to take part in the war from their base at Corregidor. The closest vegetation offering a sense of camouflage became the two soldiers' first stop so they could gather their senses.

"What's next?" Lucian asked, exhaling heavily, excitedly, from the run.

Both men looked around and could see that from the shore where they crouched they were at least one hundred yards north of the closest buildings and the chaos engulfing this part of Manila.

"We get back to our post at Clark Field pronto. Let's go." Sergeant Riley waved as he led the way.

CHAPTER 37

December 7, 1941, Warm Springs, Oklahoma

Townspeople gathered around the depot at Warm Springs. Jason Parker had blown the shrill whistle five times signaling "emergency," which was an agreed form of getting the attention of the entire town.

In cars, trucks, and on foot they came to see what the commotion was. A fire? Word of a disaster in Redemption—needing the efforts from the men and women of Warm Springs? They gathered, excited and anxious on the shortline loading dock. Most had returned from afternoon church.

"Gather 'round. Everybody gather around," urged Jason, who not only ran the train but served as the town fire marshall. "I've got some bad news. The worst possible news. Best we all listen to this together. The United States has been attacked by Japan."

"If this is some kind of joke, Mr. Parker . . ." Ben Potts, a farmer, shouted from the back of the crowd.

Mary Jane held her hand to her mouth. Her face flushed with panic. Her heart picked up its beat to a race, accompanied by a sudden grip of nausea. She was sure Jason Parker was not a practical joker. Her heart pounded to a fear beating inside her mind, an instantaneous perception that Lucian and Norman would be fighting and not coming home anytime soon.

"Listen up. Everybody listen and be quiet please!" he shouted. The sudden chattering and challenging built to a roar of questions all at once.

"Hush! Now just hush!" he shouted as he stood on a crate in the center of the crowd. "I just heard the news on the radio. This is no joke. Pearl Harbor has just been attacked by Japanese planes and they sank most of our navy ships."

"Where the Sam-hell is Pearl Harbor?" Ben shouted back.

"Hawaii, Ben. Hawaii. That's American territory. Listen up. I've got a radio inside. If we'll all file in real peaceful-like, take up benches, and hush, they say the reports will be updated every hour. Now come on in and let's hear this together."

Jason could see the uneasiness, the moisture in Mary Jane's eyes. They were his boys out there too. She rushed to his side embracing him tightly, fearful. He returned the embrace and guided her into the small passenger station and loading room.

Pulling up two chairs to the table near the radio, he turned up the volume and made sure Mary Jane was right beside him. Others gathered closely. The room was filled to overflowing as all the townsfolk seemed to hold a collective breath of anticipation.

This is CBS News with the latest on the un-provoked Japanese attack this morning at dawn in the Hawaiian Islands. At 7:55 A.M. Hawaii time, waves of unidentified planes be-gan to appear over the skies of Oahu. By the time radar had communicated the arrival of unidentified aircraft it was too late. Groups of enemy torpedo-bomber planes coordinated their attacks on Ford Island Naval Base, the area known as Battleship Row and Pearl Harbor Naval Station, army bases and air-fields at Scofield, Wheeler, and Hickam Field, Ewa Marine Base, Kaneohe Naval Air Station, Bellows Field, and John Rodgers Airport.

At this time it is known that the seven bat-tleships anchored in the harbor were the Arizona, West Virginia, Nevada, Utah, Ten-nessee, Oklahoma, *and* California. *All have been seriously damaged or sunk with high losses in killed and wounded. An unspecified number of destroyers, cruisers, and other na-val craft have been sunk or severely dam-aged during the raid that lasted nearly two hours.*

It is not known how many of our aircraft have been destroyed but the number may be as high as one half of the estimated four hun-dred aircraft located on the island of Oahu. Our forces are credited with bringing down twenty-nine of the attacking enemy aircraft. The clouds of war still hang low over the scarred remains of ships, barracks, burned fighters, and bombers all across the island of Oahu.

Casualty estimates range in the thousands.

Hold on . . .

. . . it appears we have some additional breaking news . . . this just in . . . It is now confirmed that the Japanese military has conducted air strikes against targets in the Philippines at Manila, and various U.S. army airfields, as well as naval facilities and ships stationed in the port city of Manila. For more on this breaking development stay tuned to your CBS radio station.

The sounds from the radio were drowned out by the excited and emotional chatter among the more than one hundred townsfolk filling the small rail station. Jason looked into the eyes of his daughter-in-law and read the same fear and uncertainty that filled his own heart.

He had lost the love of his life little more than a year before. His only children, twin sons, were no doubt engaged in the defense of the U.S. military bases as they sat there trying to comprehend what had suddenly happened to their world.

"We had such good plans, such happy plans for our boys," Jason finally spoke to Mary Jane as she struggled for self-control. His composure was lost as she threw her arms around his neck.

"What do we do, Mr. Parker?" she cried. "I'm afraid. What do we do?"

Several faithful church people from the community had already gone to their knees. One after another followed until a quiet fell upon the crowd.

A voice arose from the back of the room. It was a voice recognized as the oldest resident of the small Oklahoma town.

Harry Harrison had found his way from his bed to be with his townsfolk and granddaughter in this moment of trial.

With respect for the man who had two sons in the battle, and a granddaughter whose husband was one of them, the not-so-devout old man Harrison began:

"Almighty and gracious Father of all . . ."

CHAPTER 38

Morning, December 8, 1941,
the Philippines

Fort Stotsenberg and Clark Airfield sat side by side. Most soldiers weren't even on duty yet. It was a casual day with some on and some off. Pearl Harbor was still a rumor this morning, unconfirmed, like so many rumors which swirled through the fort and didn't come to pass.

It wasn't more than two hundred feet from Norman's position that his first sergeant stood out in the open near runway number one as fighter planes warmed their engines, readying for flight orders.

Waves of planes appeared in the distance. All gunners held off, unsure whose they were. Some said they were new B-17's from the States, reinforcements. Others thought they were planes from some of the other Luzon airfields on maneuvers.

No alert, no sirens, no advance words explaining what or whose these planes were until it became suddenly clear. They were bombers and curious black dots started falling from them. Some men started ignorantly running toward them, thinking they were parachuting packages. Others stood there, gazing intently at the sight.

A whistling sound followed the falling objects. New to the inexperienced soldiers the whistling was followed by a thudding of earth-shaking explosions raining in a direct and advancing line from north to south as if someone had set off dynamite charges every ten feet and was pushing the plunger every two seconds.

Eardrum shattering blasts in rapid succession burst from the earth, throwing tons of debris, shards of hot screaming metal, fire, and smoke as each explosion marched from one end of the field to the other. The enemy bombers flew over, taking the Americans by complete surprise.

Norman stood temporarily transfixed at the new sights and sounds along with everyone else at Clark Airfield. *Boom, boom, boom, boom, boom, boom* . . . The steady stream of explosions advanced. He watched as a crew chief for a nearby B-17 was standing, squinting into the sun, trying to make out the markings on the planes one minute, simply disappearing in a bomb blast the next, disintegrated, as if he had never been standing there at all.

Now the sirens, shouts, screams of the suddenly wounded, exploding P-40 fighter aircraft with pilots in them on the ground, others taking off and being caught in the bombing, created instantaneous mayhem and destruction. A placid, sultry Philippine afternoon had been transformed in an instant to a fiery inferno.

Transfixed no more, Norman, Johnny, and the others scrambled into their gun emplacements and put them into action.

"Open fire!" Norman yelled at the top of his lungs amid sounds of bomb explosions, machine-gun fire from strafing enemy planes, and their own anti-aircraft guns be-ing fired for the first time since the 200th Coastal Artillery had arrived in the Philip-pines.

"Lead him. Thata boy, Johnny. Come on, you got him now!" he encouraged as he loaded while the younger cousin sitting in the swivel chair of the 37-mm artillery piece sighted the oncoming Japanese Zero.

Clark Airfield had been totally taken by surprise. Saboteurs had taken out the phone lines the night before, and though scout planes had tried to warn the base, it had been too little, too late. Its P-40 fighter planes and B-17 bombers were still sitting, waiting—warming up engines—for orders to take to the skies.

General MacArthur's headquarters staff, with nine hours notice of the sneak attack by the Japanese on Pearl Harbor, had failed to order the B-17s and P-40 squadrons into the air. Now they were being obliterated on the ground. Like rows of ducks in a shooting gallery, the flight lines were put to the torch of enemy bombs and heavy machine-gun fire. It couldn't have been easier for the Jap-anese.

Pilots rushing out of the mess hall to their

planes were shredded to pieces like so many puppets shook loose from their strings. Their bodies appeared shaken and torn to bits by dogs of war at play.

Planes that weren't on fire or destroyed on the ground and had gotten off into the air were now engaged in dog fights near or over the field itself, making it harder for the men firing their weapons from the ground to avoid hitting some of their own.

"I think I got him, Norm. Yeah I did! Look at the smoke coming out of him," Johnny Mead hollered excitedly. "He's going down! Definitely!" the eighteen-year-old from New Mexico exclaimed triumphantly.

"Come on. Here comes more trouble. Keep blasting those Japs! Fire at the red dots, the meatball markings!" he shouted to Johnny. Norman hurriedly loaded, aided by the efforts of Private Bob Cory who was running back and forth, distributing ammunition along the line of gun emplacements with Stiles and Stinson.

"Good Lord, Oh! No! No! No!" Norman shouted as he waved at the men running toward their emplacement. Guns blazing, the approaching Jap Zero was tearing up the earth and headed directly for the three men who were valiantly trying to keep the ammo spread out. "Cory!"

He waved for him to get down as Stiles and Stinson dived into a nearby ditch. A terrified expression crossed the face of the young high school graduate from Santa Fe as bullets ripped into his back, tossing his body forward like a rag doll being flung and discarded to the ground.

"Get that Jap SOB, Johnny. Get him!" he screamed as he pulled a Browning automatic rifle up to his shoulder and unloaded it into the speeding Jap fighter. The fighter pitched. It was close enough for Norman and Johnny to hear the sounds of the heavy slugs tearing into its aluminum skin with a *thump, thump, thump,* as it rolled over their heads and crashed into the jungle a half mile beyond them.

"I'm going out for him," Norman called as Stiles and Stinson dove into the emplacement with more ammunition. "Keep firing!"

He ran the few yards to the crumpled body and scooped the lifeless boy up. He sprinted in a furious run toward the aid station, which was now under attack.

Turning back he ran for the nearest ditch. "Medic!" he screamed. He no sooner laid the boy down than he jumped back, gasping for air, vomiting uncontrollably at the ghastly sight of the headless body torn to a bloody pulp by the Jap Zero's guns.

Horror swept through him in violent waves of nausea. Scrambling to his feet, spitting vomit as he went, he found himself on the other side of the field at Lucian's gun emplacement.

Private Jimmy Bogan was firing fast and ferociously from the last box of ammo loaded by a man now flailing his arms and legs, gasping for air, rolling on the ground in panic. Blood oozed from his wounded throat.

"Who is this guy?" Norman, still shaken, asked, trying to console him, putting his hand helplessly to the young man's throat.

"A pilot, I think. Saw him scramble over here from his burning plane. Load for me, Parker! Come on! Don't stand there! Load! He's a dead man!" Bogan screamed above the cacophony of firing, explosions, planes falling in twisted agony from the sky.

He mechanically loaded for the angry Native American and watched as if in slow motion the entire scene of war was being played out by others on a giant panoramic screen. He momentarily looked down at the man who would have been Lucian had his brother not gone off to run errands for the company to Corregidor.

Limp and lifeless now, the gurgling stopped as the wide-eyed and deathly still young pilot lay bloody, facing the sky. An expression of shocked amazement that he had been killed seemed frozen on his face, in his open eyes.

The firing continued and he wondered if Lucian would find him dead too. So soon. In an instant the thought crossed his mind that it would at least ease one thing, should it happen.

He saw the face of Mary Jane and knew his torment would finally end and his brother could also be at peace. The thought caused him to well in anger and recklessly stand above the emplacement with his .45 automatic pistol and fire, along with Bogan's firing, at the oncoming plane.

"Come on you lousy sons-a-bitches! Come on!" he screamed, emptying his weapon into the sky.

Seeing the nearest other .50-caliber machine-gun crew all dead or wounded, he abandoned Bogan and sprinted across the open field. Rocked by shrapnel, explosions, ignoring the mad scream of diving Japanese fighters, he pushed aside a dead man and put himself behind the gun firing furiously, screaming obscenities at the attackers in the air.

"Come on and get me! Come on! That's it! Here I am!" he hollered at the top of his lungs as he dueled with a fighter diving directly for him.

The rail bum Skully had been right. He had taught him a valuable lesson. *"A fool stays angry except when you want to kill someone. Killin' is for war, boy."*

Lucian and Sergeant Riley had hitched a ride up the main highway with a soldier in a jeep also trying to make his way back to his outfit at Clark Airfield.

The first wave of Japanese planes had disappeared from Manila Bay. Now he and Sergeant Riley swerved in and out of the burning wreckage that occupied parts of the highway.

"Hey, look!" Lucian called to the driver who was slowing down at a railroad crossing. Coming to a stop, he jumped out, followed by Riley as some Filipinos were shouting frantically to others down the rail line for help.

They were removing the bodies of the engineer and fireman from the cabin of the tired-looking steam locomotive that had been attacked moments before by a Japanese fighter plane. The Filipinos lay the two lifeless bodies down carefully to one side of the tracks in foot-high elephant grass and ran back to look the engine compartment over.

Blood soaked the floor and flesh and bone fragments splattered across the controls. The Filipino train crew looked on in shocked stupor, unable to comprehend how to handle this ghastly and sudden turn of events in their work day.

"Hey, get that bucket!" Lucian pointed to one of the Filipinos. Lucian's years of experience in railroading took over.

A metal bucket hung from a rack behind the compartment over the coal car. "Put some water in it. Here, give it to me!" He motioned, agitated at their inaction.

He looked around him and went for the nearest ditch carrying rain run-off that now sat stagnant and squirming with mosquito larvae. Filling it, he yelled at the Filipinos to get out of the way as he doused the compartment, washing the blood from one side out the other. "Go get more!" he commanded as he stepped up into the engine compartment and took control of the train. He began to methodically check the gauges, boiler pressure, fuel, throttle, brake, oil . . . "Riley. What do you say we take this train north, as close as we can get to Clark Airfield?"

The stunned sergeant grunted approval and handed him the filled bucket of brown putrid water, alive with disease, which Lucian liberally splashed over the bloodied seat, controls, cleaning the evidence of death off best he could.

They stood by as the Filipinos talked excitedly to each other in Tagalog about what had just happened. No one seemed to be the leader of the group. Military vehicles started up the road toward them and a general gridlock had begun to form on the road where the train sat blocking the only crossing for miles.

"Hey, you! Come here!" Lucian ordered to one of the more talkative of the Filipino crew. "You speak English?"

"Yes. I speak real good English," he replied proudly.

"Who's in charge here?"

"Those dead guys," he said, pointing to the two bodies lying in the grass.

"Where is this train headed?"

"San Fernando, then loading supplies to trucks for army bases. But how we to get the train moving again and not block the main road from Manila to north? You know how to drive?"

"Yeah. Do you?"

"No, Joe. We are all new. This is our first day. Others ran away that maybe know something."

"Tell 'em we're taking over," Sergeant Riley yelled grabbing the two carbines from the jeep. "Let's fire this up. Show me what to do, Lucian," he called above the noise and waved off the jeep driver who scurried around the train and up and over the tracks to keep heading north.

"You ride with me," Lucian said to the diminutive Filipino. "Tell your pals we're heading to San Fernando. Tell them to take over where they left off. Come on," he said, extending his hand downward to help the young man up. "What's your name?"

"Manuelito Salazar, at your service."

CHAPTER 39

Jason Parker came early to the small home on Main Street. The entire town, and country, for that matter, were gathering in each home around radio sets to hear what the president of the United States would tell Congress this day after Pearl Harbor.

Japan had attacked, decided on warfare against the sleeping giant America. *Japan and Germany are allies*, he muttered to himself as he opened the gate. This could only mean one thing. War. War on a worldwide scale.

A second war involving all the powerful nations in little over twenty years! he brooded silently to himself as he knocked on the front door. *My boys*, he groaned inwardly.

"Good morning, Jason," Harry coughed, cracking the door open to a cold December chill.

"I wish I could say it was a good morning, Harry. I'm afraid I can't."

"Well, habit is hard to break, I guess. So, bad morning it is. What a damnable shame. A cryin' shame. Millions are gonna die in this one, Jason. You remember the last one, don't ya?"

He shook his head in sad confirmation of the estimate. Some twenty-five million people had died in World War I a mere twenty-three years earlier.

"Hello, Mr. Parker," Mary Jane offered, coming from the kitchen with coffee for both men.

"Thank you, granddaughter," Harry said. "Please sit, Jason." He pointed to the sofa. Jason thanked Mary Jane and warmed his hands with the coffee mug as he sunk into the comfortably worn cushions.

Mary Jane adjusted the dial on her Zenith table radio. The news had been on around the clock, repeating the same statistics over and over again; confirming their worst nightmares. The Philippines were under siege from the air and the landing of Japanese army troops was expected any time.

There was no way to know the fate of their loved ones. Chaos reigned. The army couldn't tell them. And even if mail got out of the Philippines it would be weeks, possibly a month, before Lucian or Norman would be able to get word out on their condition.

"I guess there's nothing we can do," Mary Jane voiced, breaking the stony silence.

"Pray, daughter," Jason answered. "And *keep the faith*. It's something we said to each other all the years I was married to Mrs. Parker. 'Keep the faith' meant something to her family and so we always said it too. Hope the boys know we're in this with them," he offered in a low emotionless voice.

"I'm going to get better, Jason. I'll be able to get back to helpin' you on the shortline soon," Harry announced optimistically.

"You just take care of yourself, Harry. I can't afford you to worry about it. Take good care of Mary Jane here. For Lucian. It's all I ask of you."

They sat in quiet, sipping the coffee mechanically. Mary Jane brought out a tray filled with hot slices of homemade bread and jam. It was something to do. Waiting to hear any item that could reveal the conditions of their troops in the Philippines was all they could be bothered with. The radio repeated the same news every hour, occasionally offering updated casualty numbers of the dead and wounded at Pearl Harbor.

Like the day after a funeral, they offered consolation to each other. They repeated in as many ways as they could their favorite speculations on how God would protect and take care of their boys. Jason offered that the boys were in good hands under the experienced command of General Douglas MacArthur. Maybe they'd give the Japanese such a hard time they'd think twice and back off any invasion, he suggested.

Mary Jane thought they would be evacuated by the navy.

"No," Harry replied. "It ain't that easy. They'd have to fight. Sure there will be reinforcements, but they sure enough have to stop the Japanese in their tracks," he voiced firmly.

The radio announcer abruptly caught their

attention, derailing their banter and specu-
lation:

*Ladies and gentlemen. It is reported that
President Franklin D. Roosevelt has entered
the Capitol building and is preparing to
address Congress. We are interrupting this
program to broadcast that speech. Please
stand by.*

They sat erect in eager anticipation. Suddenly the air changed to one of anxiety for
what the most powerful man in the world
would say regarding the state of affairs between the United States and Japan. As
much as anyone, this solitary man held the
destiny of the Parker boys and all the other
soldiers in his hands. The announcer returned.

*To all our CBS radio listeners. The president
of the United States will now address the
combined houses of Congress. We are
switching to our Washington, D.C. radio
broadcast. Stand by . . .*

Jason Parker approached the table radio
as if he were in the presence of an actual

person. Mary Jane followed while Harry contented himself to close his eyes and rest back into his easy chair.

"It's the president, alright," Jason whispered respectfully as he turned the volume up.

Yesterday, December seventh, 1941, a date which will live in infamy, the United States of America was suddenly and deliberately attacked by the naval and air forces of the Empire of Japan.

The United States was at peace with that nation and, at the solicitation of Japan, was still in conversation with its government and its Emperor looking toward the maintenance of peace in the Pacific. Instead, one hour after Japanese air squadrons had commenced bombing in Oahu, the Japanese ambassador to the United States and his colleague delivered to the Secretary of State a formal reply to a recent American message. While this reply stated that it seemed useless to continue the existing diplomatic relations, it contained no threat or hint of war or armed attack.

It will be recorded that the distance of Hawaii from Japan makes it obvious that the attack was deliberately planned many days or even weeks ago. During the intervening time, the Japanese government has deliberately sought to deceive the United States by false statement and expressions of hope for continued peace.

The attack yesterday on the Hawaiian Islands has caused severe damage to American naval and military forces. Very many American lives have been lost. In addition, American ships have been reported torpedoed on the high seas between San Francisco and Honolulu.

Yesterday the Japanese government also launched an attack against Malaya. Last night Japanese forces attacked Hong Kong. Last night Japanese forces attacked Guam. Last night Japanese forces attacked the Philippine Islands. Last night the Japanese attacked Wake Island. This morning Japanese attacked Midway Island.

Japan has, therefore, undertaken a surprise offensive extending throughout the Pacific area. The facts of yesterday speak for themselves. The people of the United States have already formed their opinions and well understand the implications to the very life and safety of our nation.

As Commander-in-Chief of the Army and

Navy, I have directed that all measures be taken for our defense.

Always we will remember the character of the onslaught against us. No matter how long it may take us to overcome this premeditated invasion, the American people in their righteous might will win through to absolute victory.

I believe I interpret the will of the Congress and of the people when I assert that we will not only defend ourselves to the uttermost but will make very certain that this form of treachery shall never endanger us again.

Hostilities exist. There is no blinking at the fact that our people, our territory, and our interests are in grave danger.

With confidence in our armed forces—with the unbounded determination of our people— we will gain the inevitable triumph—so help us God.

I ask that the Congress declare that since the unprovoked and dastardly attack by Japan on Sunday, December seventh, a state of war has existed between the United States and the Japanese Empire.

Tears streaming down her face, Mary Jane reached across the table for Jason's trembling hands. He was playing with the dial as if he could rewind the speech. With his first-hand knowledge of war—what the killing fields where his boys were could become—he reached suddenly for the tender young lady coming to him for wisdom and reassurance. In silence he held her tight and allowed her to vent the tears.

Reassurance? He offered none.

Lucian had barely returned to the destroyed airfield when he found his brother standing next to one of the radios that had survived the attack of the day before.

"Well! You are a sight for sore eyes!" Norman shouted, running over to his brother who appeared suddenly in the doorway.

"You're a mess, too," Lucian laughed, happy to see his twin alive. "We made it, thank God!"

They embraced.

"I wonder if Pa and Mary Jane are listening," Lucian thought aloud, pointing to the radio set and the gathered men.

"Will you two go celebrate somewhere else?" shouted an angry soldier. "This is the president."

"They're listening," Norman assured Lucian in a whisper. "Come on."

They stood outside the hut in silence during the brief Roosevelt speech. "We aren't going home for a long time, Lucian," Norman observed first as the hut filled with the soldier's thick silence.

"Yeah, I know."

They left the gathering at the radio, men wanting more news about what it would mean to them in the Philippines. Both brothers' eyes turned to the sky and searched it, listening while they made their way back to their combat positions.

"I rode a train into town a bit yonder."

"No way!" Norman responded.

"Not only rode it, I drove it. A Baldwin. Just like home. I couldn't believe my eyes! Seems the Filipino government took over the train-running from American authorities some time back. And they got American turn-of-the-century steamers all over the place down here."

"Get out of here! You're pullin' my leg," Norman replied, incredulous.

"Yep. On our way back from Manila. Bombs were fallin' just about like here, I suppose. There was this old steamer train, a bit older than ours back home, I suppose. It was blocking the main exit north, the highway, so I took it over."

"Just like that?"

"Well the engineer was dead, the fireman too. I taught Riley real quick and met a little Filipino, last name of Salazar. He was eager to learn and help out, so here I am. With a trainload of ammo to boot."

Norman shook his head, amazed at his brother's good fortune and the fact that the train had not been attacked a second time.

"You didn't have to join up with this outfit, Lucian. You could have still been home with Mary Jane. You'd be getting drafted right now, but you wouldn't be stuck here. Why did you do it?" Norman probed.

"The extra pay, I guess. Getting married and all."

"No, really," he asked again.

"I was worried about you. How you were gonna handle things, you know with me and Mary Jane. Down deep I knew I had hurt you, Norm. I didn't want that. Besides, I'm your twin. You're not supposed to go off and fight without me. We got to look out for each other."

Norman smiled. It pleased him to know

Lucian had some feeling underneath all the layers of bravado and easy living. "I suppose there's only one thing we can do now," Norman replied as he stopped his brother and put his hands on his shoulders.

Lucian held up the ring on his left hand. Three engraved letters suggested what they would have to do. Now it was a matter of enduring it well.

Norman threw his arms around his twin and held him tightly. "I'm so glad to see you, brother. Man, I was afraid I'd lose you."

Lucian squeezed back. "Me, too. Come on. Let's see what Johnny and the rest of them are up to. I don't suppose the Japs have surrendered yet."

"Don't suppose so." Norman smiled, happy to see his twin safe, as they hurried to their fighting positions.

CHAPTER 40

"It appears after days of bombing and with the destruction of Clark Airfield and virtually all the army aircraft being destroyed on the ground by the Japanese, that our military planners have surrendered the air to the enemy," the independent station from Manila declared.

"Expect the Japanese to continue their methodically planned attack stratagem so well-played out across the Pacific, in China, Manchuria, and elsewhere. Bomb, then invade. They are known for the cruelest barbarisms elsewhere. We can expect no

different here," the announcer declared in his monologue.

"Even now their agents are scouting the countryside, sizing up our military defense on Luzon. Rumor has it that General Mac-Arthur will declare Manila an 'open city.' He plans to allow the Japanese to walk right in and take over without a fight!" the radio man continued in his tirade aimed at the military and their lack of preparedness.

"And you can be sure that while reinforcements are talked about, the Pacific fleet coming to the rescue, that it is a stream of hogwash being tossed around the rumor-mill by well placed military brass in an attempt to keep us all calm," he continued.

"My sources back in the States confirm that there are no shipments being readied for our rescue. There are no ships steaming this way to intercept the Japanese. They are too busy recovering from almost total destruction at Pearl Harbor!

"Besides that, my sources say that America continues supplying Britain with war material at an unprecedented rate. It looks like we are being left to ourselves, folks. We'd better prepare for a long and deadly siege!" He ended the broadcast with a barb directed

at General MacArthur and his planners, saying he expected to be shut down and off the air for it.

"He probably will be shut down," Norman concluded to the gathered group of soldiers.

"I think the guy's right," Bogan declared. "They aren't sending the cavalry. Hell, if they had to federalize us, the National Guard, it means there isn't anyone else to send."

Silence. They could read each other's minds. The well-educated Navajo from Shiprock made a lot of sense. America was totally unprepared for a major war in the Pacific, let alone Europe. And now Germany, being an ally of Japan, would declare war on the United States. The world had never seen a war spread out over all its continents before.

"Well, we all knew this would happen. Down deep, I mean. The peace couldn't last no matter what anyone said about the United States being too big, too tough for Japan. All they had to do is what they did. Clobber us while we were sleeping. If we don't wake up and gear up we'll have to give in to what they want," the lieutenant, a college-educated man, deduced.

Lucian had been taking it in, chewing his

last wad of tobacco, spitting outside from where he stood listening, leaning up against the window opening to the bamboo nipa hut the battery had taken over. "MacArthur says reinforcement troops are on the way even now. Washington told him so. Food and ammo too."

"Washington? You believe because it comes from Washington?" another soldier bit back.

Lucian shrugged and spit.

"They won't let us down," Johnny Mead offered with boyish faith.

"That's my boy," Lucian pointed out with pride.

He, Norman, and Johnny Mead were finally together. A transfer was pushed on their insistence that they were sticking together. The captain of each battery gave in, realizing that the brotherhood throughout the units was more important to cohesiveness than any regulation. Besides, they were all family and knew the importance of it. They'd be better fighting together than apart, they reasoned.

"We got our orders," Lieutenant Kerns spoke up after receiving a call from the Regimental HQ. "We're becoming part of a new regiment. The first new regiment to be formed during the war.

"Called the 515th, we are going to protect Manila. Seems they don't have any anti-aircraft to speak of. In additional to that, we are getting some new half-tracks with 75-mm cannons. The following are going to get the privilege of figuring out how they work. Crews of three. Listen up," he shouted above the grumbling.

"Parker brothers and Mead, crew one. Bogan, Stiles, Stinson, crew number two." He proceeded with names until all crews were formed.

"Let's pack up. We're moving out at sunset on a 'lights out' seventy-five mile drive to Manila. One man packs and rotates with the others in the crew. I want everyone not packing to man your former gun emplacements. We're under threat anytime for more Jap bombers."

"How do ya like that, Johnny, Norm? We're fighting together. We'll be invincible!" Lucian smiled, slapping them on the back as they jogged to their weapons. "You go first, Johnny. Find out which truck we're supposed to load up. Go on," Lucian ordered.

"I thought I was the one with the stripes."

Norman pointed to his shoulder, clearly showing off the two rows.

"Small detail. I hear they are gonna make me sergeant for the one semester of ROTC at USC," he teased, landing an elbow in his brother's side. "Come on. We got some gear to get together."

Norman wondered what they were thinking about at home. *Do they know the danger we are in? Do they know we are alive? Of course not. How could they know*? He wondered just for a second how Mary Jane would feel if one of them didn't return. He dismissed the thought—it was unworthy of him. He couldn't think that way. She was Lucian's.

He tried to think on the fair-skinned and beautiful Luisa, but his mind drew a blank. He wanted to force his heart into loving her. She was worth loving. He'd received a letter each week from her. She surely would make a marvelous wife and mother for his children. She was beautiful in every way.

But his mind drew a blank. The only face he could make out clearly was of a girl he couldn't talk about, shouldn't think about, couldn't have.

CHAPTER 41

Three days later, December 11, 1941,
the Philippines

Refugees from the bombing in Manila choked the highway north out of the city. The Japanese landed south on the island of Luzon and rumor had it that they had landed on the north shore as well.

"Lucky the Japs aren't bombing this highway tonight," Johnny Mead observed as the three of them made their way in "lights out" against the steady stream of civilians leaving the port and capital city.

"You think they know something we don't know?" Lucian grinned at his brother.

"What's so funny?" Norman replied. "This isn't funny."

"Just seems to me that when people leave a city like this it offers little reason to protect it. Who's gonna be there but us military? The Japs would just love that. Comin' from the south, north, and blockading the port form the sea. I hear the navy up and left."

"Cowards," Norman grumbled.

"Darn right. It ain't right to leave us here like this. If those folks are heading for the hills, seems we should clear our stuff out of Manila and do the same."

"We got to fight, 'em, cousin. Stand our ground," the younger man said.

"Johnny, you are a true patriot," Lucian answered.

"True-blue through and through," the eighteen-year-old proudly replied.

"Well, I figure MacArthur will have us make a stand all right," Norman added to the banter. "Then we'll take everything out of the warehouse we can and make a stand some-where else until reinforcements arrive."

"Probably why the navy left. To go get

'em. Right?" Lucian furthered the conversation with a touch of hope.

"Right," Johnny blurted out. "They won't leave us high and dry. No sir."

The night dragged on as the column of trucks and scout cars, towing the artillery pieces and equipment of the newly created 515th Coast Artillery made their way at a snail's pace south from Fort Stotsenberg and Clark Airfield toward their new battle assignments.

"No fighter cover. Sure would be nice to have fighter cover," Norman suggested.

"That's the first thing MacArthur better get us. This stuff of being sitting ducks for the Jap bombers who fly five thousand feet above our gun range is getting old."

"They're probably on their way now," Johnny Mead chimed in optimistically. "Probably headed here from Australia as we speak."

"Hey, lookie there," Lucian said, pointing. "We're close now. Even pitch black outside I can recognize this place. This is the crossing where I picked up that old locomotive."

"No foolin'?" Norman replied, trying to make out the scenes off the jammed road.

A jeep came up alongside. Lieutenant Kerns pointed out a location and told the men to pull off on the next side street. It led to a warehouse located in a densely forested field. Lights were still out. Each truck followed and relied on the dim outline of the truck tailgate immediately ahead of him.

They crept along another hundred yards and made an exit to the left through civilian carts, *calesas*—horse-drawn carriages— and every so often a Pambusco bus filled with people, belongings, chickens, pigs . . . Two Filipinos with *carabao*-drawn carts stubbornly refused to move for each other, blocking the exit for the American convoy.

"What's troublin' you boys?" Lucian asked, jumping out of their stopped truck.

"He stole my chairs. They fall off my cart and he picks them up and keeps them," one said, pointing angrily at the other.

"Says who?" demanded the accused Filipino. "You gave these to me at Intermuros. Why you lie like this?"

"What you mean lie? I never said that. You the one who lies!" the accuser returned defiantly.

Lucian walked calmly over to the chairs held by one of the women. A baby in her arms was crying. "Give me those," he said, irritated. Yanking one of them from her grip he lifted it over his head, tossing it into the back of the truck. He took the other and did the same.

"They're mine now. Here's twenty pesos. Ten each," he announced. "Take it or leave it," he reiterated sharply. "Now move before I run over those carts of yours. When I get back in the truck we are headed in your direction."

The two men grumbled, took the money, and began to move.

"Thought I was gonna have to get violent for a minute there." Lucian smiled at Norman as he got back in the truck. They lurched the truck forward and startled the battling Filipinos who whipped at the water buffalo to get the carts moving.

Dimly outlined by a half-moon breaking from clouds, Norman drove toward a waving figure near the building partially hidden by jungle growth.

"You men grab your gear and hightail it to a clearing about fifty yards behind that building. Now hide your truck from the air. Pull that truck into the bushes over there. Everyone camouflages their own," Lieutenant

Kerns ordered. "Keep your sidearms ready. We don't know if Jap saboteurs are mingling in this area or not. But they've made their presence in Manila known."

They followed instructions, met at the rear, and found their newly assigned vehicle—a half-track with tank treads—with a machine gun mounted on a moving turret and a 75-mm self-propelled cannon good for close range fighting.

"From here, men, you will be spread out to all hell and gone. We have no communications equipment to speak of. You'll be supporting whoever, whenever you get a command from a superior officer. My job will be to inform you the best I can. To keep you on my maps and communicate by runner and when practical through the other units in the field you may be assigned temporary duty with." The lieutenant paused. "This is a helluva way to fight a war. I know you men would prefer to stick together, but we have our orders."

Assignments were given. Norman commanded the half-track with Lucian and Johnny manning the guns.

"You think you can drive this thing?"

"It's got tracks," Norman replied, smiling

as he worked the gears while playing with the ignition.

"It's not a locomotive . . . you actually have to steer the thing, Norm," Lucian drawled as he worked cosmoline off the guns.

"You watch. I'll be the best darn driver in this outfit," he replied.

"Whoever thought of putting this gooey stuff in gun barrels and breaches, and smothering firing mechanisms with it ought to be courtmartialed and given a sentence to clean cosmoline off guns for the rest of his life," Lucian protested as he struggled at wiping the petroleum-based goo off the guns without enough rags. "How the heck are we supposed to fire these things?" he complained.

"The lieutenant dropped off this here map. Oh, and here's a pile of rags he handed me for that cosmoline stuff. Looks like you boys are back in the train business," Johnny offered as he came from the darkness where he had been called by Lieutenant Kerns. "Lookie here," he said, pointing, unfolding the map on the ground. He pulled his Zippo cigarette lighter out and began to strike at it.

"Cover that thing! No lights!" Norman

scolded. He put his poncho over the map and the three ducked under to safely use the lighter and take a look at their assignment.

"Train depot outside Intermuros," Lucian said excitedly.

"Where's Intermuros?" Norman asked.

"Here," he pointed, "it's the walled city area on the map with narrow streets. Old part of town. By the docks. I passed through it on my way to Corregidor a few days ago. We'll be outside on the tracks right here at this point."

"I guess Kerns knew we'd feel at home on the railroad." Norman smiled.

"Yep. Looks like we got a sweet assignment, boys. All the stuff being shipped back and forth. We'll be in fine shape. Let's go." Lucian folded the map and handed it to Norman. "Tank commander, sir? Your map," he laughed.

Norman beamed. "Come on, Johnny. This is a good omen. It's like going home."

"So do you think we will be hearing from the army?" Mary Jane asked Jason Parker as she set the table. Jason was a permanent guest for dinner now that he was all alone.

He shook his head. "It takes weeks in all

the confusion to sort things out, darling. I was in the first war, 1918. The National Guard from Kansas. I was there one week when we were sent to the front and I was wounded within one hour of our first fight with the Germans. Just seriously enough to get out, get a disability.

"So I didn't see much of the war. But I was nearly back to the States before my family heard a word about it. I don't know if you knew this, but I was married too. My wife, Maria Linda, had our boys while I was over there in France. I can tell ya from experience, Lucian is as concerned about you being worried over him as you are about him being safe."

"Well, I can't help it. I think about both of them, you know. Do you think that's strange, Mr. Parker?"

"No. I don't believe you can think about one without considerin' the other. I know I can't. Mother never could either."

"I'll turn up the radio," Harry said with a slight cough. "This winter sure has me feelin' low," he said as he ambled from his easy chair to the Zenith radio set on an end table by the sofa. "I do look forward to some of that chicken broth to ease this chest pain I'm feelin'," he added as he went to his chair at the table.

"Grandpa, you need to get to Redemption and have Doc Willis take a look and listen to those lungs of yours," Mary Jane counseled lovingly but with sternness.

"Nonsense. Nothing like good food and workin' through a bout with a little cold that fixes a man," he responded, coughing with a wave of his hand.

"She's right, Harry. I'd be glad to run you on down there tomorrow with a load of lumber I'm takin' for the Johnsons to the mill. Seems the demand for pine has picked up all the sudden like."

"Guess I know who to call for the right size pine box," Harry chuckled.

"Grandpa, you knock that off!" Mary Jane scolded.

"Seems to me if you are callin' for a pine box, you'd have a right hard time gettin' through, if you were already *dead* set on needin' one," Jason added with a grin, then a hearty laugh.

"Haaa! That was real fine. Mighty good," Harry offered loudly, happily at the man-style jest.

Mary Jane frowned. "You men!" she

scolded as she turned to the kitchen to bring the soup and bread.

"Offer grace, will you please, granddaughter," Harry asked weakly as he sipped from a glass of water.

"Yes, grandpa," she replied grabbing at both men's hands.

"*Almighty God our Father. We give thee thanks for this daily bread and all that has been so generously provided to this home. We pray for our boys in the war...*" She stumbled on her words. "*Bless them, oh Father, to have food, shelter, and protection from the enemy. Give them strength. Give them our love.*" She paused. "*Bring them home to us. We pray this offering of thanks and put all things into thy caring hands, in Jesus' name. Amen.*" Breaking her grip she wiped at her eyes then excused herself to the kitchen.

"Our boys," Jason whispered, staring into his bowl as if something there could answer the question gnawing at his mind too. Mary Jane returned with bowls of hot baked rolls, feigning cheerfulness.

"Thank you, granddaughter. Now for the grub." Harry pointed to the chicken soup and rolls with a handkerchief covering his chronic cough.

They ate quietly as the news of war offered dark tales of increased damage to Manila, bombings, and now the first landings of Japanese troops on Luzon.

Mary Jane could read her father-in-law's mind as he clenched his fists, struggled to eat, stirring the soup in circles with his spoon as he listened intently to the CBS news reports.

Jason's eyes watered at the thought of his gentle sons suddenly being forced into manhood, danger. "War's no damn good. It's no damn good," he finally declared, getting up to leave the room for some brisk December air. "I'll see ya all in the mornin'."

"He'll be okay, sweetheart. Just give him time." Harry patted his granddaughter's hand.

She shook her head knowingly as she struggled for composure. She had to be strong for Lucian and Norman's father and for herself.

"I just think I'll retire early," Harry said with a raspiness to his voice, an unsteady breathing. "You get me up early. I think I'll take that ride into Redemption tomorrow with Jason to see the doc."

Mary Jane smiled and gave him a kiss and wondered how to comfort her father-in-law with the faith she knew she had to muster up. Then she would retire and try to get through one more day. *Just one day at a time*, her mother would tell her whenever she had gotten to worrying about something. *God just gives one day for us to live*, she could hear her counsel.

Morning came with a deathly chill spreading across the plains states. She had not wanted to cause her grandfather any discomfort on such a cold day and had decided to call Doc Willis to see if he was making house calls up Warm Springs ways.

She went to his room. *He must have finally gotten some relief*, she thought at the stillness coming from his slumber. She left him alone and greeted Jason Parker at the door.

"Welcome. Come on in. I wasn't expecting you this early, Mr. Parker," she said politely.

"Well, I guess you would like to see what I got," he smiled.

He held a cablegram out to her.

She excitedly read it.

Dear Pa,

This will have to be short. Me and Lucian and cousin Johnny Mead are fighting this war together. All is well. Found a military unit handling these cables. Assigned to guard a train in Manila. Safe. Well armed. Looking out for each other. Tell Mary Jane Lucian sends love. Me too to all. Norman.

"Now how about that?" Jason beamed.

"Oh!" Mary Jane squealed delightedly. "Oh! I've got to tell Grandpa," she said, running down the hallway calling him in childlike excitement.

Jason stood there, thankful to God for word from his sons. He should have known, as resourceful as they were, they would find a way to get word out. *Proud, yes sir mighty proud*, he thought to himself. And relieved.

"Mr. Parker!" Mary Jane screamed in a shrill, alarmed voice from the bedroom. "Oh, Mr. Parker he won't wake up! Wake up Grandpa! Don't! Oh, no!" she cried as Jason dashed down the hall and entered the room. She was kneeling with her head on her grandfather's chest, trying to discern a heartbeat. "Is he . . . ?" Her watering eyes begged as she crumpled to the floor beside him.

Jason picked her up gently and took a look, felt for pulse, opened his eyelids. He listened for a breath, heartbeat. He turned to her and put his arms around her as she fell into them, sobbing.

"He's gone. Real peaceful. Real happy. A real saint of a man. I'm sorry, Mary Jane."

CHAPTER 42

Norman was glad he had sent the cable. He didn't have time to go tell Lucian about his discovery. He had been sent into the army headquarters, the Hotel Manila in the Intermuros section of town with Lieutenant Kerns and found the sergeant handling cables, willing to take ten dollars for the short telegram.

He was called by Kerns to go with him to check out the possibility of handling the train schedules for army deployment of munitions and equipment to rear areas in the event of an evacuation from Manila.

"Seems someone looked over our records

and saw your work history on the railroads for the Santa Fe. Must have impressed someone to have us here in MacArthur's HQ."

A siren sounded as bombs started falling in the distance. The artillery outside fired protecting bursts into the sky. Norman and Lieutenant Kerns followed staff as the headquarters was quickly evacuated to makeshift bomb shelters.

"We ought to go out there and help those boys. They're from the 515th," Kerns said as they sat through the blasts that appeared to be blocks away. "I don't fancy sittin' here waitin' for a bomb to hit me. What do you say, Parker? We in this war?"

"You go, I go," Norman replied, washbasin helmet strapped firmly around his chin, Colt .45 strapped to his waist.

"Let's go, Corporal Parker," Kerns whispered and waved his hand for Norman to follow.

They ran from the safety of the shelter to the front of the building, pulled their weapons from the jeep parked in an alley, and then headed for the sandbagged 37-mm gun firing at the bombers overhead.

"Howdy do, Lieutenant," said a smiling

New Mexico guardsman noticing the familiar New Mexico Guard shoulder patch on the two newcomers. "Welcome to the war." He grinned.

"Good to be with you boys too!" Kerns shouted back. "Here," he said handing the ammo over to the gunners as Norman began transferring it from a nearby bunker.

Lucian and Johnny manned their guns at the train depot as the train left for a side-rail and camouflaged shelter. No sign of fighter planes. The bombers seemingly passing over the depot as a target on this day left them anxious, but not firing yet.

"Wonder how Norm's doing in all that stuff." Lucian nodded nervously toward the downtown district and the waterfront. "Can't see how a man comes out from underneath all that, but they do every time," he noted with a hopeful sigh.

"He'll be fine. We aren't gonna get it," Johnny assured him. "Maybe some other guys, but not us," he added, certain of his youthful immortality.

"Bombs don't play favorites," Lucian replied.

"Just the same. It ain't our time," the young man responded.

"I like your attitude, Johnny."

"Sure. Anytime, Lucian. You know how to drive this thing?"

"Sure do. Went over it with Norm for about fifteen minutes. Think we ought to give her a go?"

"Maybe," Johnny replied anxiously, suddenly not so sure of himself as bombs began to hit a mile closer.

"Here we go," Lucian shouted as he cranked the engine over. "Just like a tractor, more than likely. At least it has front wheels," he said as he lurched forward with a jolt, then hit the brakes just as hard.

"Hey!" Johnny called. "Careful! I about set this gun off!"

"Take your hand off the trigger!" Lucian shouted back as he put it in reverse.

"Bombs are sure fallin' closer," the young man shouted down to Lucian.

"Here we go," he called back and sent the half-track into full speed forward in the direction of the camouflaged trains. "I kinda like this," he yelled up to his cousin with a smile.

The young man replied with a look of controlled terror.

"The General saw what you two boys did," a major from MacArthur's headquarter's staff said approaching Lieutenant Kerns. "He wants to know your names, rank, and unit."

"Lieutenant Jeremiah Kerns, newly formed 515th Coast Artillery, New Mexico National Guard."

"Norman Parker, sir. Corporal, same unit, sir."

"Hmmm. Not even regular army. The General is going to appreciate this." He smiled. "You boys were outstanding. That's the kind of fighting spirit this army needs to keep Manila and the island from falling to the Japs. Both of you are to be commended. I am instructed to inform you that each of you are to be elevated in rank effectively immediately. You will both be receiving citations and I wouldn't be surprised about medals as well. Congratulations Captain Kerns. Congratulations Lieutenant Parker."

"But sir, I'm just a Corporal and . . ."

"Are you being ungrateful to General MacArthur, son?"

"Well no, sir, but see, I . . ." Kerns looked on with a wide grin of appreciation for the spot Norman had just been put in.

"Well then, you were a non-commissioned officer. That's what corporals and sergeants are. You have received a battlefield commission to replace this man Captain Kerns here. You doubt your abilities?"

"No sir, it's just that I guess I should be a sergeant first and my brother see, he fights with me and he's a private. And . . ."

"Captain Kerns. What's the name of this man's brother?"

"Private Lucian Parker, sir," the new captain replied.

"Fine. Private Parker is to be made a sergeant. See to the paperwork. Sergeant!" the major called to a staff member cleaning the debris from his desk. "I want you to get all the information down regarding these men. They are being promoted in rank. Fill out the papers and get them to me immediately." He turned back to the two New Mexican guardsmen. "You men will fill the sergeant in on our conversation. I must get back to the general. That will be all."

"Yes, sir," Kerns saluted.

"Yes, sir," Norman added with a salute.

"Oh, and Lieutenant Parker?" the major asked. "What's your specialty?"

"Well, all the guns in our outfit, really, sir. I'm here on some matter about running a train schedule for the army though, sir."

"Fine. You and your gun crew are now to be assigned to headquarters' staff. Captain Kerns, I assume you are here on the same matter?" the major inquired.

"Yes, sir. I was ordered to bring Corporal . . . I mean Lieutenant Parker here."

"Well, you have real fighting spirit. Let's see what we can do for you. We need more of that spirit on this staff. These men have had it too cushy. Thank you, gentlemen."

"Thank you, sir," they both replied.

"Well. Life sure can offer its surprises, wouldn't you say, Parker?" Kerns smiled.

"Yes, sir, I'd say so. I still can't see why, I mean this seems too much, too unreal for just doing our job. Heck sir, I just didn't want a bomb falling on me without fighting back. I'm not so brave. I just don't like sitting around, that's all."

"Funny how we all see things different. I'm sure even you and your brother Lucian have seen the same thing different on occasions."

"Oh yes, sir. That we have. That we surely have."

CHAPTER 43

"It doesn't seem much like Christmas, does it Mary Jane?" Jason Parker said as he wiped his face with a napkin. "It was a fine meal though."

"Thank you," she said somberly. "No, it does not feel like Christmas. I can't believe how suddenly events can make everything so topsy-turvy. One day life is good, the sun is shining, we're laughing and singing, the next . . ." She shook her head sadly. "The next day the ones we love are gone. Just gone."

"Sure does make one stop and think," Jason sighed.

"Surely does. That it does," she returned quietly.

"Sounds like our boys are holdin' up real good. Real safe compared to others. To think they are on General MacArthur's staff. Running the trains and such." Jason tried to lighten the mood.

"I keep thanking God that they can send these cablegrams every week. That is mighty comforting. I don't know how the families of the other boys do it without hearing from them. I only hope they will be able to stay assigned with General MacArthur's headquarters staff, keep close to that machine that sends these," she offered, holding the several cablegrams up.

"I do as well. It sure is a blessin'. I'll have to get back to the trains tomorrow."

"I'm glad you got those boys working with you, Mr. Parker."

"Me too, dear. Boys is about all that will be left. That and older men over thirty. The draft will take our young men away. Well, I guess I better be goin'. Sure you're okay alone here? Patty at the corner store says she'll come and stay with ya if you need company nights. I know with Harry gone and all, well, it sure must be lonesome."

"Thank you kindly. I do appreciate it. When things settle down a bit I may board this place up and head on back to Los Angeles. I still have a job offer there. Parents are there and all, too."

"I surely will miss ya if you do. I surely will," Jason Parker said, shaking his head in anticipation of ending up in Warm Springs totally alone.

She embraced him warmly at the door. "I'm not leaving yet. Don't worry none. I will need some time is all. Let's be happy for the boys. I surely do love them both."

Jason nodded, stopped, then turned to face her. "Mary Jane. I know this is none of my business, but if you wouldn't have run into my son Lucian, and knowin' how Norman feels and all, would you have married Norman if he had asked?"

She smiled, blushed, and blinked at the sudden moisture to her eyes. "I feel so ashamed," she said as a solitary tear streamed down her face. "Yes. I would have married him. Yes. I love both your sons, Mr. Parker. I hope you don't think . . ."

He put his arms around her and kissed her forehead. "Thank you, daughter. You know he loved you too. It sure hurt both my

JAMES MICHAEL PRATT

boys to love the same woman, but I can't see how they could've done anything else."

She held him tightly and wept unashamedly. "This is so hard, isn't it?" she struggled to say.

His eyes glistened as he headed out the door for a very silent Christmas night alone at the depot. "It surely is hard. Harder than all my life put together. It surely is."

"I wonder what Pa is doin' tonight?" Norman remarked as they watched the sky from their position atop the half-track outside the train station.

"He's at Mary Jane's, no doubt. Sure is hard to imagine that place without Harry. Sure glad they were able to get that cable through to tell us about things and such."

"Surely must be hard. I miss the old guy. Poor Pa, what with Mama gone, Mary Jane talkin' about leavin' too. Don't suppose we will be back anytime soon," Norman replied.

"I'm not so worried about Mary Jane now that she's hearing from us. I worry about Pa though, bein' alone and such. Must just about kill him between runnin' that steam engine alone and sleepin' alone in that cold depot. I always thought we'd get the house rebuilt before we left for somewheres. Can't be Christmas without Mama."

"Nope," Norman agreed.

"I sure do miss Albuquerque in the winter. Sometimes we get that light snowfall, ya know? Me and the boys would always head up to the hills and do some sleddin'. Turkey cookin' in the stove. Mama's homemade pies. No, sir. This does not seem like Christmas," complained Johnny.

"Well, Sergeant Parker?"

"Yes, sir, Lieutenant Parker, sir."

"I'm gonna visit the latrine. Please do not allow the Japs to drop any bombs while I'm gone."

"Could be comical." Johnny grinned.

"Corporal Mead, you keep your eyes in the sky and shoot down the first bomber who feels inclined to interrupt my solitude," Norman commanded as he jumped to the ground from the half-track.

"Yes, sir." He smirked, offering some unheard words that both he and Lucian quietly enjoyed.

"Here they come! Ah, horse collar!" Norman protested, offering a string of military-learned expletives as he darted back to the half-track positioned behind the fortresslike thick walls of the Intermuros. Well within sight of the abandoned station he yelled to Lucian, "Open fire! They aren't gonna get my train depot!"

"Some Christmas party!" Johnny yelled above the firing of his recently mounted .50-caliber replacing the smaller caliber machine gun the half-track came with.

"Fireworks and all!" Norman hollered as he started helping feed ammunition to both his brother and cousin.

"We best keep this a moving target rather than a sittin' one," Lucian called above the din of explosions.

Norman put the half-track into gear and rolled along the wall making it harder to hit, giving some protection to the crew as they fired just over the thick wall surrounding the old city at the oncoming fighters.

"Merry Christmas you lousy Nip!" Lucian cried as both he and his cousin dueled point blank with an incoming fighter following the half-track. Tracers from the Jap Zero spit up the moist soil in their direction as the vehicle retreated.

"Take that home to the emperor!" Lucian shouted as the wing of the fighter crumbled under the barrage of 75-mm cannon and machine-gun fire from the armored car.

The enemy plane cartwheeled and exploded into the train depot a kilometer beyond them.

"No! You lousy no good for nothin'!" Norman shouted, raising himself from his driver's seat to witness the spectacle.

"Well, we did kill the Nip," Lucian apologized. "You could at least say thank you," he added.

"Ah hell, Lucian. Couldn't you have shot his other wing off?" Norman replied, annoyed. "There are fields all around the depot. This is my depot!"

"That's war," Johnny added as the skies developed the stillness that had enveloped them just moments before the sudden and furious air raid.

"Wave number one. They are just saying, 'Merry Christmas' with that one. I'm sure they aren't done. Let's go check the depot and warehouses."

They were greeted with a devastating sight of body parts, gun emplacements blown apart on the other side of the station, and the warehouse on fire. "Some of the boys didn't make it out of here it appears," Lucian offered dryly.

"Glad we got that last load of ammo out. A helluva lousy way to go," Norman sighed as they jumped down from the half-track to run to the aid of a Filipino struggling to remove a fellow train station worker from the wreckage of the burning depot.

"Lookie there, Lucian. That Jap pilot is still alive!" Johnny called out as he turned to see a shaken fighter pilot try to upholster his sidearm and get out of the mangled cockpit of his wrecked Zero.

"He ain't no more!" Norman declared as he walked toward the broken plane and turned his own army Colt .45 on the shaken, struggling enemy pilot.

Pop, pop, pop, pop, pop, pop, pop . . . Norman rapidly pulled the trigger and unloaded his entire ammo clip on the man.

"He surely ain't no more. Merry damn Christmas to you, Mr. Tojo," he spit out angrily, unashamed.

Norman had just killed with hate and for a moment he was glad. It wasn't good enough for the Japs to start the darn war, he thought. *This guy just wrecked my station and was going to take the whole family out, too. Thank you too, Mr. Skully,* he thought.

"Hey lookie here." Johnny smiled, holding a Japanese rising-sun flag up victoriously. "And a real Jap officer pistol, too!" he exulted as he picked through the mangled wreckage, pushing the corpse aside.

Lucian was stunned at the coldness with which his brother had just killed the enemy flyer. Not that it was wrong, just that it was different. This was face-up close and Norman did it with no more emotion than shooting a jackrabbit.

"What are you lookin' at?" Norman asked as he reloaded a new clip into his .45 and holstered it.

"Something different. Something surely different, Norm." Lucian checked out the injured Filipino while Johnny ambled back from the wreckage with his war souvenirs from the dead pilot.

"I know you, don't I?" Lucian asked the Filipino.

"Sí. You are the Americano who drives the train that first day of the war when we get the engineer killed." The small man smiled. "I am Manuel. My friends call me Manuelito. Manuelito Salazar. Remember?"

"Yeah. Yeah. Hey, Norm. This is the guy I told you about. The little Filipino who became my fireman from Manila up to Fort Stotsenberg."

"Oh, yeah. I heard about you. Well, let's get this injured man some medical help before he dies on us and find the best place we can to spend the remainder of Christmas."

The little Filipino chatted excitedly as he helped his injured friend to the half-track. "I want to fight, help, maybe work with you Americanos?"

Lucian looked at Norman and shrugged his shoulders.

"Where's your train engineer?" Norman asked him.

"Right here." The Filipino pointed to the man lying near death on the floor of the fast-moving vehicle with Johnny at the controls.

"Seems all you do is hang around dead train engineers," Lucian offered in a morose jest.

"Well, he ain't your engineer no more. You are." Norman pointed to him with a gentle jab to his chest. "Lucian, let's go see what we can do about getting this man some training. Maybe we can help Captain Kerns see the need for us Oklahoma boys to take this thing over now. We have been pulling double duty as gunners and loading schedulers for this army pullout long enough. Time to run the train," he said.

"Amen to that Lieutenant, sir." Lucian grinned.

They raced through blacked out streets, over rubble, around ruins, bodies, to the aid station and army HQ in the Inturmuros and a change of assignment.

CHAPTER 44

Present Day, American Military Cemetery, Manila

"So that is how my father becomes friends with you and your brother, Señor Parker?" Vincente Salazar asked after the hour of storytelling that had kept him totally engaged in the reminiscences of the weary man from Warm Springs.

"Yes, that is how it was. Your father was a good man, and in spite of the hell raging around us in the war, it was easy to see he had a happy nature about him. Real likable, hard worker, loyal. You couldn't find anyone more loyal than your father. No sir," Lucian acknowledged.

"Cemeteries always scare me. I can tell you, Señor Parker, this is strange, me finding you and us being here tonight. My mother never remarry no other man. She loved my father and her last words were his name. You believe that?"

"Yes. Certainly I do. I can hardly believe myself that I could meet the son of my loyal wartime friend. Somehow I feel like Manuelito is watching, maybe my brother too. We are all back together again tonight," he sighed, tired from the hours of sleeplessness the thoughts of this day brought.

"Over there, about ten rows is the grave of another relative of mine. Johnny Mead. Brutally killed. Just eighteen years old too. I do believe God maybe heard my prayer and sent you to be with me tonight."

"I don't go to mass much you know. But I believe God does strange things," Vincente Salazar agreed.

"Yes he does. But no more stranger than men do, Vincente. No, maybe men do stranger things, things they know they shouldn't, but they stubbornly go ahead anyway."

"What you mean?"

"Well the whole cotton pickin' war for one was a nightmare; strange coincidences marked by terrifying moments one minute, punctuated by humor the next. Killing a man and feeling no remorse, then eating off his plate. That kind of stuff is curious. Only war could provide so many freak, crazy, out-of-the-ordinary events. Things no man would do in normal life."

"Maybe true," the Filipino agreed.

"Absolutely true. Do you think any man in his right mind would intentionally risk his life for someone else when he knew it was sure death? Suicidal? Oh, the stories I could tell you. All strange but true. Hating and killing one minute and yet out of those events is born also some of the greatest heroics and virtues a man can have or do."

"Like what?"

"Like love."

"Everybody knows about love. No, Señor Parker?" replied the diminutive fiftyish Filipino who looked half that age.

"No, my friend, Vincente Salazar." Lucian picked himself up from the poncho spread on the ground and stretched his tired back. "Not everyone knows about love. Men and women die never understanding it."

Looking up into the clear but moonlit sky he noticed the stars were far brighter here on the outskirts than in the city. He could see a dancing light it seemed. Streaks of lights moving from side to side, pulsating. They mesmerized him, the way an air raid would back then. "Do you see those strange lights in the sky?" he asked his Filipino companion.

"Sí, of course, Señor Parker. Those are searchlights from the waterfront. They use them for restaurants now. Making advertisements. You know. Stuff like that."

"Oh. Not many of them where I come from. None to be exact." He chuckled at his lack of judgment. But they seemed to have him transfixed, hypnotized. They took him back to other Manila nights full of terror and of brotherhood.

"No one knows love like a man fighting for his brother, his family, and country. And," he interjected into the silence, "for the girl he loved."

Vincente waited patiently for the old man to go on with the story wherever he would.

He sat down. "Now your father and me, we became real friends on those train runs out of Manila in the final days before our surrender. Yes, sir, right good friends."

CHAPTER 45

January 1942, Retreat to Bataan

"Manuelito! Come here fast!" Lucian yelled. "Johnny, you go and lock and load the .50-caliber and get the half-track over here! Pronto!"

"Lucian!" Norman called, panting heavily from the dead-run he had been on from Clark Airfield nearby. He called out again above the noise and pandemonium caused by hundreds of soldiers and their machines scurrying over the destroyed army airfield and its neighboring army base, Fort Stotsenberg.

The Japanese had just launched an artillery barrage hitting the American bases. The front lines, just miles away, were reducing daily. Now it was a matter of the remaining U.S. military and Filipino forces holding out long enough to get all the men and supplies they could into the Bataan Peninsula. There they intended to hang on until promised reinforcements from the United States arrived.

"Lucian! Thank the good Lord—you're okay. I thought I was a gonner. Where's Johnny? He okay?"

"Yeah. He's fine. Those stubborn Filipino railroad bureaucrats won't turn the rails over to us. I did the best I could. Showed them MacArthur's orders and everything. I think we're just going to have to steal a train."

"Steal a train, Señor Parker?" Manuelito asked, incredulous. He had just finished loading a truck with supplies from a storage room at a destroyed barracks building for transfer to the railroad at Capas junction, a few kilometers outside the fort and airfield.

"That's right," Lucian observed. "Those Filipino authorities don't want the train destroyed. They think if they're in control the Japs won't bomb it, or some galdarned thing. They are actually waiting for the Japs to arrive and take over and want to be in good with them.

"I should have shot them on the spot but the general and his staff wouldn't like it. But that was all that stopped me from tying those guys up and setting them out under that incoming Jap artillery."

"Lucian. We don't have much more time. There is no way we are going to get all we could have. I just came from warehouses three and four," Norman panted, still out of breath.

"Yeah those regular army fellas who wouldn't release the stuff two weeks ago with the paperwork from MacArthur's HQ just verified," Norman continued. "We're cleared to load as much as we want, but now those birdbrains are going to have to destroy tons of rice, other food, and ammunition so the Japs don't get it. The galdarned fools!"

"A lot of people are going to die because of paperwork, I'm afraid," Lucian observed. "We should have just taken it that night when we had the whole platoon up here with the trucks empty. Now its just the four of us."

"Norm, we're gonna have to take the train by force."

"Fine. Tell me your plan."

"Well you're the lieutenant. But this is my idea. Manuelito here is gonna be our hostage. We are gonna put him in the cab at gunpoint while Johnny aims the .50-caliber gun at the railroad director's office. You will fire a warning burst with the 75-mm cannon. Destroy something, a palm tree maybe, so they know we mean business. I'll take Manuelito with a pistol to his head and . . ."

Manuelito turned pale. "You wouldn't shoot me, would you, Señor Lucian?"

"Only if you turn traitor," Lucian responded with a polite smile. For this plan to work he needed to have Manuelito fearful, exhibit it, be in doubt.

"No worry with me," Manuelito responded with a hard swallow.

"Okay, Lucian. But look. We need to be able to do this *pronto*. The side rails to warehouses three and four haven't been hit by artillery or bombs yet, so we can go ahead and get the train over there. But we got to do it quick."

"Done deal. Manuelito?" Lucian smiled as he pulled his Colt .45 from his holster.

"Don't use it. Okay, Lucian?" the diminutive Filipino smiled nervously using first names now. "You're kidding, right?"

"Don't make me use it," he replied as he pulled him under his arm. "Don't worry," he whispered, holstering it. "Just don't panic." He grinned.

"What we are doing now means there is no turning back. We have to be ready to kill if we take hostages." Norman winked at Manuelito. "I don't mean you, but your bosses better not get in my way. I got a starving platoon I was just put in command of down in Bataan. We are infantry now. I will kill to keep them alive," he said, staring directly in the eyes of the smaller man. "You tell them in Tagalog that we mean business."

"I understand," Manuelito observed. "You two brothers are very difficult Americanos." He laughed, suddenly relaxing as he understood their intent. "I am *cien por ciento*, one hundred percent, with you. I am ready to fight too," he pledged.

Lucian saluted his brother in mock respect for military authority. "Lieutenant, let's go get the stuff."

CHAPTER 46

"Pull that whistle again, Norm!" Lucian growled. "That damn oxcart better be movin' off the tracks. I got a load of ammo and food supplies and the Japs are eight hours behind us!"

The urgent sound of train and whistle didn't budge the carabao as the distraught farmer ran for safety and watched his animal swept aside like cow dung.

"That would have made mighty fine steaks. Don't you think, Manuelito?" Norman called above the noise of engine, steam, and fire as the young Filipino shoveled coal furiously with Lucian to keep the boiler hot.

"What you say?" he called back.

"Nothin'."

The train was suddenly protected by as many P-40 fighter planes that the army had left and could spare. From Clark Airfield and Fort Stotsenberg to Manila seventy-five miles south, stores of supplies were either being transferred or destroyed.

The entire city of Manila had been evacuated days earlier on December thirtieth, and piles of supplies at Rizal Stadium and other locations were being left behind to either be destroyed or fall into the hands of the Japanese. Too much fell into their hands when the Japanese occupied the city on January second, 1942.

Now the enemy was cornering the Americans and Filipino defenders in central Luzon. Their retreat was already decided by MacArthur's War Plan Orange. The plan called for retreat into the ample and mountainous Bataan Peninsula. They were to hold out until reinforcements and supplies reached them, but not surrender the island of Luzon.

A fine plan on paper. But one hundred thousand hungry and diseased men without enough ammunition to fight, and all because of inadequate and poorly prepared military authority, did not a good defense make. Adding the thousands of homeless fleeing Filipino civilians to that and it was a mess that only guns could solve.

Part of the fault for not getting the supplies shipped in time to Bataan was the army's doing. Too much bureaucracy, paperwork, and authorizations by order-following regular army staffers who never fired a gun at the enemy but could shoot down common sense in a New York minute.

"This train and its cargo are being appropriated by special military authority," Lucian had called out to the Filipinos at the train station.

Parker authority to be exact. Corporal Johnny Mead had manned the half-track mounted machine gun and persuaded the Filipino engineers, who had not been persuaded by normal military bureaucratic means, to turn the train over to the new American authority. Manuelito, the only Filipino conspirator, acted as if he would be shot as well if his friends in the train office didn't obey.

"Funny how guns work, Norm," Lucian shouted. "Paperwork gets us into war, acts of Congress and such, generals signing some order, and then guns get us out. You suppose we'd still be arguin' back there with them Filipino train fellas in Capas?"

"Suppose so, brother. I'll bet you they don't argue with the Japs when they pull into town," Norman yelled. "You know, Lucian. I got this idea. I see this whole darn thing unraveling and us being trapped or captured by the Japs some day soon."

"Don't talk like that."

"I don't like to but it's a sight better to be prepared, after what we've seen. Don't you think?" Norman shot back above the fiery noise in the engine compartment.

"I surely do, brother. What's your great idea?"

"We got a lot of canned goods, see? I figure we are going to back ourselves up against the sea down in the tip of Bataan before any reinforcements arrive. Then we'll have to fight our way back up the peninsula to rid Luzon of the Japs.

"I figure once we get today's load to the railhead at San Fernando, there's another ten miles of track heading down toward the peninsula, see. We take us a boxcar load and have Johnny and Manuelito waiting with the half-track and a truck.

"We locate some places along the way to our assignment down in Mariveles at the tip. Bury some cases of canned goods and rations from one of them boxcars. Spot our location real careful and each carry a map. That way if we need to escape from the Japs, hide out or whatever, we'll have some food. This man's army has already proven they don't care diddly whether we starve or not."

"The officers seem to be always fed. You notice that?"

"You're talking to one, remember?"

"Yes, sir, Norman, sir," Lucian howled. "Forgive me if I don't salute. My hands are busy," he laughed, as he tossed a load of coal into the fire. "How'd you come up with this harebrained idea of burying food?"

"Harry. Remember how Mary Jane and Harry always seemed to have some of the best meals in town?"

"Yeah. Go on," Lucian drawled contemplatively as Manuelito took his turn shoveling coal into the fire.

"Harry showed me on my first visit to the house there on Main Street how he stored food. He had dug these root cellars about ten feet down or more and kept produce, canned goods and dried meats real fresh for months. Other people went without, but not old pioneer Harry Harrison."

"We could throw some stuff out of the train and mark the spot. Maybe even stop, but bury it? Come on, Norm."

"Hey, we could find some hillsides. There are plenty. Cover our little caves with palm fronds and rocks. It's canned goods. They'll do better than a warehouse with some dope that has to have paperwork filled out before he lets a starving soldier at it."

"Good point."

"We leave half a boxcar off the tracks into our lines enough that the Japs won't get there for a month, but not so far down that we give it away to the army. They'll bungle this load of supplies like they always do, Lucian."

"You're a sorry excuse for a loyal officer, Lieutenant, sir."

"Family and friends first. So we leave it off, see, with Manuelito here and cousin Johnny and his weapons to guard it. Men and supplies are all strung out to hell and gone. When we get to the end of the line, we each grab a truck and head on back to help Johnny dig and bury it.

"We are still officially on MacArthur's staff. I guess we wouldn't be missed. We can turn the platoon over to one of the other guys. Say Palinsky. They're just diggin' in anyway.

"Besides, we got these." He pulled out his special orders signed by MacArthur's staff officer in charge of quartermaster personnel. "We are legal. We are supposed to handle supplies."

"How far does this rail line go?" Lucian drawled, tired and hot, leaning on the coal shovel.

"We're nearing the end of the main line. I figure a shortline down the peninsula ought to take us another ten miles at least, maybe more," Norman replied from his seat at the engineer's control panel.

"I'm goin' back to talk to Johnny about this. We got the half-track on the flat car. I'll have him ready for action at the first stop you figure we can unload some of this stuff. Get Manuelito ready." Lucian hopped onto the remaining coal pile in the tender car and did the circus balancing act he had performed so many times before in Oklahoma.

He crawled atop the cars and worked his way back to his cousin.

"You hear what we were talking about, Manuelito?" Norman called.

"Sí. I hear. I agree. We are going to need this stuff. I hang out with Johnny. Besides, it be a whole lot better for me to disappear for a few days. Maybe my friends in Capas complain to the army and figure me out."

"Well, I wouldn't worry. What's the worst they can do? Send us to the Philippines to fight Japs?"

The shorter Filipino roared at the American humor. "I like you, Lieutenant Parker. You a good Joe. Maybe I stay and fight with you. I hate the damn Japs."

"I think we make a good team," he replied.

"Sí. A good team."

"Say, Manuelito. I've been meaning to ask. How come you use Spanish words so much and not Tagalog?"

"I speak Tagalog, Spanish, and English. Me a real smarty pants, no?"

Norman let out an uncontrolled roar of approval. "Sí, you are real *smarty pants*. Go on." He smiled, chuckling at the offhand remark.

"My mother, a mestizo, she insisted. Only

maybe ten percent still speak Spanish but she was from a noble family and my father, his family spoke it at home. Tradition from the colonial years. Landowners, the mestizos, did not want to change. So I speak Spanish; English I learn at school as a boy; and Tagalog I know. Maybe I learn Jap?" He smiled.

"You definitely are a valuable member of my little army. I say you have just been drafted into the New Mexico National Guard. What do you say?"

"Yes, sir!" He saluted with a broad grin.

"Okay. Here's where we stop," he said, pulling on the brakes. "You take this map. You and Johnny get busy and unload all you can with Lucian. Just as fast as you can. Just toss the stuff off. Then Lucian and I will hightail on out of here and be back in a few days."

"Yes, sir, Lieutenant," he called as he prepared to jump from the slowing train.

"Norm! We're ready to go!" Lucian called above the screech of brakes as the ancient steam locomotive ground to a halt.

Norman acknowledged with a thumbs-up.

They hurriedly tossed as many crates as a thirty-minute stop would allow then took off with a wave to Johnny who was tossing as much into the half-track as he could and making for the bushes off the tracks.

"Great machines them half-tracks. I suppose once this fun is all over we'll be back to our infantry platoon. Wait for the Japs to attack. Be regular fighting troops," Lucian called across the cab as they picked up steam.

"Suppose so."

"Next big holiday is Easter Sunday. Holidays don't seem like much here do they?" Lucian returned as they reversed the train to go back to the original destination, San Fernando main line station.

"Nope."

"So what did the Easter Bunny say to make the hen so mad?" Lucian called back.

" 'I ordered these months ago and you promised orange eggs with speckles. What happened? You were supposed to be a special hen.' And the hen said, 'If you think I'm not so special why don't you stand in line and take a number along with all them other roosters.' "

"Did Pa really make that stupid line up?"

"Repeated it every year like it was the funniest line in the world. I used to laugh just because he'd get such a kick out of his own homemade jokes. The more I'd laugh, the more dumb one-liners he'd do. Sometimes he'd go on for a whole hour repeating one-liners he'd heard at the loadin' docks some-wheres on the Santa Fe line."

"Mama sure didn't care for that Easter line much. Remember how she'd swing at him?" Lucian laughed. "But Pa was simply trying to make her feel like a special hen, I sup-pose. He always said he felt like he had to stand in line to get her hand. He surely did love her."

"He surely did," Norman agreed somberly at the thought of his beloved mother and her care for them as boys. "He was a funny old rooster." Norman brightened quickly with the kind of smile only memories of home bring to a soldier's face. "Wonder what he's doin' right now?"

"Eatin' Sunday supper I suppose. I'll bet Mary Jane fixed up something real special."

"A mighty fine woman. You're lucky, Lu-cian."

"You got over that? I figured you were just hidin' your feelings. Being the good boy you are and all."

"I don't have much time to think, being an

officer and all," he laughed, wanting to avoid the issue. He had transformed his anger over losing Mary Jane to gunfire against the Japanese. Every time he killed he did it for all the right reasons, he supposed.

"You've changed, Norm. I'm proud of you."

"Yeah. Me too. Pull that whistle real loud, Lucian. I want to hear some noise. They say that sound travels until it is absorbed somehow. Let's give this a whistle for Pa. Let him know we're comin' home."

"You figure he'll hear it all them miles to Oklahoma?" Lucian laughed, remembering how they had always blown the whistle just short of the depot. "We always tried to see how far out we could blow it and still get Pa to hear it. Remember?"

Norman nodded with a smile a grown man's memory keeps in supply for moments like these. "*God willing, he'll hear it,*" Norman voiced solemnly.

"Say what?" Lucian replied above the noise.

"I say pull for Pa!" Norman hollered back.

Lucian grinned and pulled. *Three whistles. Two whistles. Three whistles*—Lucian's code. "Just like bein' a kid again." He grinned.

CHAPTER 47

Two Months Later, March 12, 1942,
the Philippines

"MacArthur left Corregidor," Johnny reported to the platoon.

"Says who?" Corporal Jimmy Palinsky called back from his foxhole above the distant thunder of artillery explosions.

"I just overheard it at company HQ. Norm and Lucian are there now," he answered.

"How would he leave? Those guys over on Corregidor are getting plastered just like us. They got no planes. A seaplane maybe?" Palinsky responded.

"Nope. Submarine."

"So *dug-out Doug* is hightailing now that the Japs have us cut off and surrounded?" Thatcher interjected sarcastically.

"The president ordered him to Australia. And he didn't want to go," Johnny Mead loyally countered.

"As if the president cares about the rest of us. We're 'expendable.' Heard that on the radio broadcast some guys in supply are getting from San Francisco," another soldier threw in.

"They could still get reinforcements and supplies to us. You just gotta have faith," Mead proposed earnestly.

"Look at you, Mead. You are skin and bones. When you don't have the runs you got malaria. I got to hand it to you, you are a dreamer. We haven't had meat for five weeks. We got cut to half rations two months ago, cut twice since that. We are down to survival rations! Maybe a thousand calories. No protein. Not fightin' rations! Guys are eating bamboo, elephant grass! So when they gonna 'reinforce' us? When we're dead from dysentery? Starvation?" Thatcher shot back, unbelieving. "Hey Palinsky! Pull out that harmonica of yours. You know 'Yankee Doodle'?" Private Thatcher called out above the backdrop of thundering guns on the battlefield surrounding them.

"What? That's kid's stuff. Of course," he answered.

"Play it for me," he asked. Palinsky began.

"No, not 'Yankee Doodle.' I meant the other one. What's the name of the hymn of the republic?"

" 'The Battle Hymn of the Republic,' you pea-brain," Palinsky replied and began to play. Thatcher began to sing the poem that had spread across Bataan like a bad virus. Soon the entire platoon chimed in.

We're the battling bastards of Bataan;
No mama, no papa, no Uncle Sam;
No aunts, no uncles, no nephews, no nieces;
No pills, no planes, no artillery pieces;
And nobody gives a damn!

"Hey, who wrote that?" Palinsky laughed.

"Some war correspondent. This piece of paper says Hewlett is the name," Thatcher replied.

"Well you guys make fun. But MacArthur said, '*I shall return*'," Johnny Mead protested patriotically.

"Well if he don't bring some food, bullets, and fresh troops it won't matter much if he does return," Thatcher countered.

"Ah, you guys just remember Valley Forge. They were starving and they won," said the young optimist Mead as he walked away.

Bataan Peninsula was a deathtrap. With the sea surrounding them on all sides, the Japanese advancing from the north and having landed on the east coast, the hundreds of thousands of military and civilians had already eaten anything that moved.

There wasn't a carabao, the big common water buffalo, to be had. Men had resorted to eating the few horses the cavalry had brought, dogs too. Military brass had left and destroyed tons of rice, rations, and canned food in warehouses from Manila to Clark Airfield. The men were down to fighting with poor food, poor ammo, and raw nerve.

"Norman, it's HQ," Lucian said, handing the walkie-talkie over to his platoon leader twin brother.

"Yeah, this is Parker, go ahead," Norman called back. "We're down half strength, sir," he replied. "We're beat up pretty badly, sir," he answered again after a pause. "Roger that, sir," he said clicking the conversation off.

"Looks like we're the one's going in to do the dirty work again," he whispered to his staff sergeant brother.

"What is it this time?" Lucian asked above the din of distant artillery, rain now pelting them in sheets.

"We've got Jap spotters out there on the hill marking their artillery. Battalion HQ figures we are the closest ones to them. We have to send a man or two out, load him up with grenades and take them out." He paused, looking at the sorry sight of skeletal eighteen, nineteen, and twenty-year-old men huddled in foxholes half filled with muddy water.

"Damn, I hate sending these boys to die. Who's it going to be, Norman?" Lucian asked, turning to his twin who had already grabbed the walkie-talkie from him and was talking to one other man—Thatcher. Lucian grabbed his rifle and began to load grenades into his trouser pockets.

"Lucian, we need you. You can't go," Norman said, yanking at his brother's sleeve. "We've made it this far, and—"

"We can't let these kids go out there, Norman," he spit back, cutting him off.

"You're married and I'm not," Norman replied, grabbing the grenades the Thatcher kid had brought up. "I'm going alone. I'll make it."

"No, dammit! This is my mission! Get out of my way," Lucian demanded, pushing his brother aside, grabbing the handset walkie-talkie. "Take over for me. Help Norm out," Lucian called to Johnny Mead who now appeared as he charged over the top of their protective makeshift bunker.

Just then an explosion behind him from incoming enemy fire threw Norman, Thatcher, and Johnny Mead to the muddy ground.

He checked himself out and then got up tentatively, looking around him to the men scattered over a fifty-square-yard area.

"Dammit, Lucian." He scowled, looking around himself for his Thompson submachine gun. "Palinsky!" he yelled. "Get over here," he screamed above the noise of the monsoon wetness and artillery fire toying with the battlefield like the tympan section of the orchestra—off and on again, never sure what to expect next.

"Yeah, Lieutenant," answered the lithe but sturdy Corporal Jimmy Palinsky from Las Cruces, scrambling low over the muddy encampment.

"Take this handset and see if you can raise Sergeant Parker. I'm going out there to relieve him. Johnny, you're in charge now."

"Norm, I don't think . . ." Johnny stammered but understood and cut his statement off.

"What's he doing outside the perimeter?" the young corporal with the radio handset queried.

"We got some Japs out ahead, maybe one hundred meters on that rise just above us. We got to take them out if we want to survive this 105-mm barrage."

"Norm—I mean, Lieutenant," Palinsky countered. "I don't think it's such a good idea. I mean the two of you, brothers and all. I mean what if . . . you both . . . you know . . ." He didn't finish his question as the rain suddenly ceased.

Like a malignant growth, spreading, doubling, and choking out life as it did, an oppressive eeriness crept over the suddenly silent field they were assigned to defend. They talked in whispers now.

"Listen. Do as I say. I promised my pa." He winked and slapped the young soldier on the back. He gave a thumbs up signal to Johnny Mead, now in charge of the platoon.

Just then a burst of automatic gunfire exposed the brief muzzle of silence that had bridled the battlefield. The rules of war wouldn't allow silence. A grenade, screams, and more gunfire came from the hill ahead of them.

Norman, just about ready to crawl out into the blackness, rolled back down the incline that offered cover and took the handset.

"Lucian! Come in! Lucian! This is Norman. Lucian, come in!" he breathed urgently. "Lucian! Damn you, Lucian, say something!" he ordered into the handset.

"Lucian . . . Over . . ." the strained reply came back.

"What's your situation?" Norman whispered back.

"One hundred meters east. The rise. Rocky area before forest. Yeah, I got two of them. But I caught some in the shoulder from a grenade." He ended with a sudden

and unexpected scream mixed with the unmistakable sound of a Japanese voice.

"Lucian! Lucian! Dammit, Lucian, come
in!" Norman demanded in a panicked voice.

"American die. All American die!"
screamed the broken English voice with a
heavy Japanese accent over the handset.

"Bastards!" Norman yelled as he dropped
the walkie-talkie to Palinsky and threw himself over the ridge.

He rolled into one water-filled crater after
another under a steady stream of artillery
and mortar fire which now probed both sides
of the line. The incoming and outgoing
noises of death were so much screams of
hot metal piercing the night sky—screams
even before they mutilated the bodies of the
young soldiers—as they soared high
enough for him to run, hit the ground, and
roll into another muddy crater in desperate
search for his brother.

The darkness became filled with every
kind and size of artillery. Now illuminating
the field with every fifth round were the tracers arching overhead. Added to that were
flares bringing a pulsating strobe-light movement to even the dead—whether men,
trees, or the rocky stillness of boulders.

Everything seemed to move and only God knew if Lucian was alive in the midst of it.

Machine-gun fire followed Norman, kicking at his heels as he dove into a muddy ditch. He spotted the flashes and pulled the pin from a grenade, his breath heaving as he offered every ounce of strength he could muster. He waited. The next flash of muzzle fire found him lobbing the grenade from a prone position with deadly accuracy. Two Jap soldiers blew apart twenty meters away.

He crawled, whispering as he went, "Lucian? Lucian? You hear me, Lucian?"

A moan straight ahead alerted him. Then another one. Norman bellied his way to the groaning sound knowing it could be a Jap trick, submachine gun ready in his right hand, bayonet unsheathed in his left.

He rolled into a water-filled crater on top of two bodies. "Norm," he heard one gasp as he pulled the dead body of a Japanese soldier with a bayonet protruding from the man's rib cage.

"I don't think it's too bad. Help me up," Lucian moaned. "You should've stayed put, Norm," he whispered.

"Shut up, Lucian. Just shut up." He put

him over his slender shoulders and rolled out of the hole.

"I can run. It's my shoulders and not my legs. I was just so spent. I didn't have an ounce of energy left after fighting that crazy Jap."

"Okay. On three we get up and hightail it together."

"I love you, Norm," Lucian responded weakly, innocently.

"Yeah," he answered as he huffed from the exertion he'd used to get here. "One, two, three . . . go!"

They both ran through the mud and mire back toward their lines. Enemy gunners spotted them through the silhouettes their bodies created against the flashing of artillery close by.

"Ahh!" Norman grunted from the impact of a single bullet to his skeletal upper body throwing him forward.

"Norm!" Lucian called, crawling over to him just under the hail of fire skirting the air a foot above them. "Norm, you okay?"

Norman looked himself over and felt the hot burning sensation filling his upper arm and shoulder. "Hit right shoulder. I'm beat, Lucian. I don't know," he added, confused.

"My turn," his brother replied. "I only got a few pieces of metal pokin' me. Here, you hop on," he ordered his brother. Norman climbed onto his prostrate twin's back. Lucian inched forward on his belly under the steady stream of fire that was trying to discover where the two Americans had fallen, making sure they had been killed.

"Just a bit more, Norm," he whispered. "You still with me?" Lucian asked, out of breath.

"Yeah. I think we lost those Japs."

"Hang in there. We'll get you taken care of," Lucian whispered.

"You act like you just got scratched," Norman muttered in reply.

"You caught a big slug, Norman. A man can bleed to death from a slug like that. I did just get scratched. Almost there now."

He slid over the embankment as they both rolled down the muddiness to the waiting hands of Johnny Mead and the others below them.

"Oh Norm! Lucian! They got you both? Oh! We got to get you boys to the rear," Johnny Mead urged, looking helpless.

"Well, that can't be too far since the

ocean's just a piece down the hill," Lucian offered sarcastically, out of breath.

Norman moaned. "Johnny, you stay. Take over. Palinsky and Thatcher. Get a couple of others to carry us to the medics. We got those spotters. The artillery should ease up a bit."

"Hey, Norm?"

"Yeah, Lucian?"

"Thanks."

"That's what a brother's for."

CHAPTER 48

April 9, 1942, Bataan Peninsula

"Over ten thousand of us are supposed to just up and quit? Just give up? Never in the history of the U.S. Army have ten thousand men surrendered at once!" Lucian growled, pacing back and forth in agitation at feeling trapped. His wounds had healed surprisingly fast while Norman, who rescued him that night a month ago, was wounded in the shoulder and instead of getting better was deteriorating.

"We must have ten times that many Filipinos here in Bataan with us. If MacArthur could just get us some food, more guns, and ammunition. I'm not givin' up, no sir," Lucian grumbled as he continued to stomp up and down the aisle in front of his brother's hospital cot.

"We need food. We can't hold out. We've just eaten every carabao on Bataan. Horses have disappeared, cats, dogs. Men are killing monkeys, eating rats, lizards, bugs to stay alive. Maybe they'll treat us good like their leaflets say," Norman offered sickly, hopefully.

"Those damn leaflets! You don't believe they would, do you? And look at you! You still recovering from the gunshot wound to your shoulder a month back. Malaria crazed out of your head last night. We're out of quinine. I'd be surprised if we had a bottle of it on all the peninsula. I had to steal what little we got between us. It'll be gone in a couple days. Guys are dropping all over the place. We just need supplies that's all. And need to kill more of them sons-a—"

"Lucian," Norman interjected, pointing across the tent to the sickbed of their cousin. "Johnny," he said. "He needs help. Maybe they'll give us some medicine. He's going to die without it. Dysentery just about has him."

Lucian paced back and forth looking somewhere for an answer. He knew Norman was right. Norman was always right. Rechecking his watch every couple of minutes he realized that if they were going to make a break, the three of them, and hide out in the mountains with the guerillas they had but a couple of hours left.

At twelve hundred hours all hostilities were to cease and weapons stacked in piles. Then the men were to wait for the Japanese to arrive and take them prisoner. Outfits were all broken up now. Men looking out for themselves and their close buddies. Too many were sick and wounded.

"The Japs are brutal demons, Norman. I've seen 'em up close. In Lacay they took this young Filipino, not a hundred yards from where we were holdin' that bridge and shot him. Cold-blooded murder in the head.

"Then they took his little wife and daughter, bayoneted them, and while they were still screaming tossed them over the bridge. Screamin' and all I tell ya! That was women and children! We swung that .50-caliber mounted on the half-track and mowed those mothers down on the spot."

"Where was I?" Norman groaned.

"That was right after the night we had to get them Jap spotters. You were kinda sore from that bullet to the shoulder. I was dazed by the shrapnel but it turned out a few pieces were taken out and I figured you needed the rest more than me. So Captain Miller, seein' my predicament, let Palinsky handle what was left of the platoon and sent me and Johnny on a special bridge guarding assignment. Lost the half-track that day." He shook his head.

He paced some more, searching for a way out. "Only reason we held back on them Japs on the bridge at first was because of those Filipinos in the way of our line of fire. No, Norm, they won't treat us good. They're mean-spirited little morons."

Norman rolled upright from his cot, coughing. "Come on, help me with these boots," he wheezed. "Let's make our way out of here. Get our canteens, some rations. Grab that litter over there and put Johnny on it. Time to go dig up some buried supplies. Where's Manuelito?"

"Off with some Filipino guerilla unit I suppose. I hate this, Norm. I surely do hate this," he complained.

Norman knew something about hate. He

had transferred all his pent-up emotions and anger he'd stored at losing Mary Jane to these merciless legions from the Empire of the Rising Sun.

He was hungry, sick, and tired as most of the ragged American forces were, but he wanted to keep fighting, killing, and lose himself in the anger. He felt justified, it was legal to be angry, mad as hell, and kill these murdering Asian bullies.

Norman motioned tiredly to his brother. They both gingerly lay their emaciated first cousin on the stretcher. Hospital medics and surgeons where too busy caring for the seriously wounded and others who had signs of surviving. Private Mead was given less than 10 percent chance of making it through the week.

"We're gonna act real calm, Lucian. Like nothin's wrong when those Japs come bustin' down this road. We're gonna take Johnny, one on each end so they won't separate us. By the way, you look like hell," Norman offered with a dark laugh—a coughing, malarial, plaintive laugh reserved for those soldiers who could stare at death with cold indifference.

"At least I still got some meat on me.

Guess you haven't seen a mirror in awhile," Lucian replied. "Come on. One, two, three," he said as they lifted the light cargo. Johnny Mead was a mere one hundred pounds.

"Thanks, boys," the wasted cousin weakly offered. "But I can't go on. You fellas just leave me be," he groaned.

Norman laid his end down, followed by Lucian. "As long as you are breathing you're going with us, Johnny. What's our promise, the Mead and Parker family motto?"

"Keep . . . the . . . faith," he replied, struggling with each word.

"What's that mean, cousin?" Norm asked tenderly as he squeezed water on Johnny's forehead to cool him off then placed the wet rag over his temples.

" *'Fight the good fight'* like the good book says. We don't let down the other . . . Ohhh, I can't . . . ," he gasped, holding his stomach. His bed, trousers were soiled from constant diarrhea. "I'm a dead man, Norm. Leave me be. Please?" he cried weakly.

Norman motioned to Lucian to pick his end up and they started out the tent door. "Johnny, the other patients are complaining. You stink too much. They told us we had to get you out of here or else."

"Thanks, Norm." The dying soldier laughed sardonically in spite of it all. "I know what you're tryin' to do," he groaned.

"Yeah," Norman answered. Lucian didn't answer a word. His eyes were too wet with rage and his throat too dry to say what he was thinking.

CHAPTER 49

April 1942, Warm Springs

Jason had taken a train run to Amarillo and had not been able to get back to Warm Springs on Easter the week before. Mary Jane had promised they would celebrate Easter when he returned. It had meant a lot to him, that she would help him celebrate a day so filled with significance. He needed refreshing and encouragement and at least the thoughts of Easter and what it had always meant to the Parker family offered that.

Mary Jane struggled to smile, speak, become animated in any way about this day they were celebrating as a rebirth. She placed the ham on the small dining table and sat quietly in her chair.

Jason Parker had never felt more alone, more abandoned, and less able to say a prayer, even grace for this meal. But he had to. He was alone more than Mary Jane could understand, but he had to be strong for her and his boys. He began:

"Dear God, our Father in Heaven: It is with . . . a grateful heart . . . ," he stuttered, trying to bring himself to feel what he was saying, *". . . that we bow our heads to offer thanks for this Easter feast."*

"Thank You. Thank You for all Your loving kindness. We ask You to bless this meal before us . . . ," he said, not knowing if he should conclude or go on. After a long silence he cleared his throat.

"We are mindful of the first Easter day when Jesus came out of the tomb and became the first fruits of the resurrection for all mankind. We are comforted to believe we will see our dearly departed loved ones again because of this miracle," he said with a sigh of genuine longing to be heard.

"God my Father, I've never prayed a

prayer like this one," he voiced sincerely. *"We request a sign, a knowledge, a feeling, anything, that will help us know our boys are alive and alright amidst the terrors and brutalities of war. That's all we can ask for now. We commend our lives to You and trying to remember Your goodness and patience with our human weaknesses. In Jesus' holy name. Amen."*

"Thank you," Mary Jane offered in a low whisper.

"I lost my Maria Linda. I can't lose my boys too," he replied almost inaudibly. They ate in quiet reverie of meals that had been, when there was laughter and every seat at the table had been occupied by a loved one. At length Mary Jane brought in a warm vanilla pudding. "Grandpa's favorite," she observed.

She mechanically tuned the radio dial and turned up the volume as the evening's CBS radio broadcast opened. The deep throated voice of the announcer began:

We are just getting confirmations of reports that on April ninth at approximately twelve P.M. *Manila time the combined forces under the command of General Douglas MacArthur with headquarters in Australia surrendered unconditionally all allied forces on the peninsula of Bataan in the Philippines to the Japanese Fourteenth Army. The surrender was effected by General Edward King, Army AirCorp, the acting commander of U.S. and Filipino forces on Bataan.*

The last American holdouts, some thirteen thousand, remain grasping to a final hope of defense in the Philippines two and one half miles off the tip of the Bataan Peninsula under the Command of General Jonathan Wainwright on the island of Corregidor also known as 'the Rock' for its fortresslike tunnels and fortifications.

The Japanese herded the starving, sick, and besieged Americans and Filipinos alongside the coast road, starting in Mariveles on the southern tip of Bataan.

It is estimated that approximately ten thousand American soldiers have surrendered along with seventy thousand Filipino allies. This sets a historic precedent as the largest surrender of Americans in any war during its proud history. Those last rescued by submarine were nurses who confided to reporters that the conditions were dreadful, lacking in medicine, sanitation, and food. Neverthe-

less the men's fighting spirit held to the end and only then did they reluctantly lay down arms under direct command of their superiors.

This station asks all Americans listening to offer a prayer to God for the safety and well-being of these brave Americans. Never has such a calamity befallen our military in this magnitude before. May God rescue them and go with them.

Jason Parker sighed heavily, then broke down like a child as he moved to the table radio and slowly turned the dial off. He needed to compose himself for Mary Jane's sake, for his own. His eyes bled moisture like a tap needing repair, but no repair could fix what he had. All his loves; his wife, his sons, his dreams for them were being systematically destroyed by a cruel and unforgiving world.

He didn't blame God but he didn't know how to pray to someone so far away who looked down upon the affairs of men and allowed some to live, others to be taken before their time. But he had no one else to turn to.

He posed the new question of his faith to

himself as he stood, back to Mary Jane, face to the wall, peering deeply in the patterned wallpaper as if the answer lay hidden in the design somewhere. He was deaf, dumb, and blind, to how he could help his boys, and mitigate the awful tearing sorrow that had engulfed him and the sweet lady of his boys' life, Mary Jane.

Maybe this was how it was when God sent angels. Where would he be now? All alone at the depot. At least one soul, this young woman, gave him someone to talk to, someone to share his grief.

He took in a deep breath and then slowly released it as if to exhale his emotions so colored by the events that had torn his loved ones from his bosom. His only solace was found in that he had loved a woman who gave him these boys and she had loved him in return. *At least I have known joy. At least*, he sighed.

His innermost mourning became a supplication from deep within the soul, from his heart in words not capable of being formed. It was a father's prayer for his sons. Did God understand what he felt?

He felt ashamed of the thought, for the day this Sunday represented, even though he celebrated it late, was all about a for-saken son. But that was then . . . He wanted to feel that God understood his tender concern and abject feelings of abandonment, hopelessness.

"Am I hearing things?" he turned suddenly to Mary Jane. "Did you hear that?"

"What? I didn't hear anything," she responded.

"The whistle," he beamed. "The boys always blew it when they were coming home from a trip somewheres. When I couldn't go, when my sick wife needed me, they'd blow the whistle to let me know they were almost home." He beamed. "They're safe!" he rejoiced, running to the window filled with the rays of early morning light. "They're okay!" he excitedly exclaimed as he looked out to the tracks. "I can hear the whistle! It's Lucian's call. I can hear them! They're coming home Mary Jane! Dear God in heaven, my boys are coming home!"

CHAPTER 50

"Johnny, we're setting you down. Just for a minute," Norman exhaled, heavily sweating from every pore what little moisture was in him from the effort. Pale and dizzy with heat exhaustion, weak from dehydration, face blistered from the scorching sun, Norman needed a breather.

He was down from his normal one hundred and sixty pounds to one hundred and ten. All together he was aware that a few weeks difference were all that separated him from the condition Johnny Mead was in.

"Thanks," Johnny groaned weakly. His pallor suggested that the stench of death filling the air around them would soon include their tender-aged cousin.

Lucian shook his head bitterly. He still had fight in him. He didn't know where he was getting it from but he didn't want to, wouldn't have surrendered, if it were not for his brother and dying cousin. He was mad at the whole mess, not to mention the fact that a lot of military decisions at the highest level led to this.

When Lucian and Norman Parker were sent on a trip north two months earlier, just ahead of the Japanese advance, to reconnoiter and find existing stores of food supplies that hadn't yet been recovered from camps and bases along the route, they were turned back my military authorities who had told them they didn't have the proper authority, the right forms, paperwork.

The idiots who brilliantly turned away their own American men from rescuing foodstuffs were forced to abandon them days later to the advancing enemy. Americans and Filipinos were starving to death by the hundreds every day now.

Now it was survival of the fittest and everyone for himself. Most of the old 200th and 515th were spread out all over the Bataan Peninsula, over on Corregidor, fighting wherever they had been needed. They all served as infantry in the end along with everyone else. But as a cohesive unit they were dead.

Lucian picked up one of the leaflets that were dropped by the Japanese on a bombing raid days before and that were now generously littering the fields and roads. It offered extravagant terms of surrender to any American who turned himself in.

"To all American and Filipino troops," it read. *"It is not a dishonor to surrender. Surrender and you will be treated humanely! Enjoy the comforts of women, good food, the hospitality of the Japanese soldier who understands your courage. Why die for a cause that is lost? Bring this leaflet with you and surrender to the first Japanese soldier you see and live with dignity."*

He spat on the leaflet. "Good for toilet paper and nothing more, Norm," he said angrily, tossing it away. "They laughingly and indiscriminately kill, torture, rape, and pillage the Filipinos," he muttered. "We sure as hell are walking into a deathtrap as sure as staying here is one," he complained.

Norman couldn't respond. He was

drained. He just nodded and panted, trying to gain breath and strength to move ahead with his cousin on the stretcher.

The word was passed along to the thousands of men gathering near the highways, off the roads and in the fields.

"Cease-fire will commence officially at noon. You are to wait for the Japanese to accept the surrender. Pile your weapons in one location. It is advisable to follow whatever they ask of us. We are to be considered prisoners of war under the Geneva Convention," one officer stopped and read from a jeep with a bull-horn every hundred yards or so.

"To hell with you and the Japs!" Lucian obstinately shouted for anyone to hear.

"Johnny! Stay with us Johnny. We're gonna go for that food! Listen, Johnny," Lucian whispered as the Japanese soldiers surrounded the several hundred men in the area they had camped in. "These illegitimate yellow scums are gonna make us march north right past where you, me, and Manuelito buried the food. All you got to do is hold on. We're gonna get some food somehow and hide out in the jungle. Make you better."

"Ohh, Lucian. I can't," he sighed, barely audible as he strained at the mild effort to respond.

"You got to! That's an order!" Norman countered, weak and dizzy himself from the exercise of carrying the litter with dysentery, constant diarrhea, dehydration.

Malaria attacks would get him soon if he didn't get some more quinine. Quinine was worth a month's pay now and hard to find. He slumped under the blazing sun at the screams of the power-hungry Jap guards eager to show their captives what a victorious soldier could do on a whim. Lucian swatted at the flies impatient to eat the deathly ill Johnny Mead alive.

A Japanese soldier with a fixed bayonet attached to a rifle larger than himself, prodded them to their feet and yelled something, pointing his rifle to the stricken cousin.

"We carry," Lucian said, gesturing as he did.

The smaller Japanese guard reared his rifle butt to Lucian's jaw, knocking him to the ground and lunged at him with bayonet barely missing his legs.

Norman quickly rolled over to his brother and shielded him from the next thrust. Expecting it to enter his back and end his misery he was stunned to hear the scream coming from Johnny.

The enemy guard forced another bayonet thrust through the chest of the screaming young man, quieting him. He laughed as he removed it, wiping the blood on the trousers of the dead boy.

"I'm gonna kill that son-of-a-bitch," Norman spit out with considerable struggle as he helped Lucian to his feet.

"How?" Lucian bitterly asked. "You can hardly stand. I'll kill him. I swear, I'll kill him. Don't you worry," he huffed as they both moved to the boy who was lying peacefully for the first time in weeks.

The guard had lost interest in them and had moved on to his next victim, a sick sailor who screamed at the first thrust of the bayonet and was quieted, as was Johnny, on the second.

"They're murdering scum just like I told ya, Norm," Lucian grunted angrily. "That Jap is a dead man!" He nodded as the gleeful enemy guard wiped blood from yet another bayonet thrust into a helpless sick American.

"Animals," Norman groaned, still suffering from dysentery, weakness, malaria. "They aren't gonna get us, Lucian. We gotta make it out of here. Look at little Johnny," he cried in a broken voice of a child whose entire world has just been devastated.

The boy from Albuquerque lay still, eyes skyward, mouth agape with an expression that seemed to ask, "Why?"

"I'll kill him, Lucian. I'll get better and I'll find that no good bastard and I'll kill him," Norman muttered, mopping at his eyes.

Lucian couldn't pay attention for the moment. He suffered to regain his wits. He felt his jaw which had received the butt end of the Jap rifle just moments before. He felt inside his bloody mouth and pulled out two teeth. "So much for dental care," he said sarcastically, bravely. The jolt had about rendered him senseless.

"Lucian, we got to hang onto each other until we figure out how to get to the food. Johnny was a gonner. I'm still gonna kill that lousy Jap for Johnny, but now I need your help," Norman moaned. "I can't walk without your help."

Shots rang out as a group of men started to run into the thickets surrounding the sun-scorched clearing where the hundred men had gathered. Bodies fell. Japanese guards didn't waste additional bullets. They showed a propensity for the bayonet by using it on each of the half dozen fallen men.

"They're trying to show who's boss. Get our attention. I think it's gonna work," Lucian finally responded to his weaker brother wiping at the blood oozing from the split lip, broken teeth given him moments earlier. "Come on. Let's just fall in line. Here, take one of these. We got to conserve water but you'll need this more than me," he said, putting the last two salt tablets he had hidden into Norman's hand. "Drink 'em down fast," he added, taking the canteen on his web belt and bringing it to his brother's lips.

"Grab those dead fellas' canteens, Lucian," Norman pointed. "We got to have water."

Lucian followed his brother's advice and brought the partially-filled canteens to their spot. "Two apiece," he said, as he hooked them to each others' belts.

"We got to bury Johnny," Norman groaned under the stress of his own sickness.

"We pray for him, brother. That's all we can do." They both closed their eyes as Norman prayed first, followed by Lucian.

"I haven't prayed since I was a boy, Norm." Lucian wiped at the saltiness stinging his eyes. "I loved that boy," he offered, still gurgling blood in his throat from the sudden loss of teeth.

Norman raised his canteen with great effort to his trembling brother's lips. "Take," he said weakly. "Drink," he ordered. Lucian obeyed like a small boy, helpless, emotionally wrung out at the loss of control, Johnny, the lives of friends around him.

"Where do you think they'll be taking us?" Norman groaned, seeking to bring Lucian back into composure.

Lucian picked up a tin helmet someone had discarded and placed it on his sickly brother's head to shield him from the sun. "The Rock hasn't surrendered," he said wiping away tears, washing the grime from his soiled face. "The Japs still have to attack Corregidor across that two miles of Manila Bay from the shore here," he said, still wiping at his running eyes and nose, drying the blood oozing from his lip with a soiled handkerchief. "They'll stage it from here for sure.

So I figure they'll move us up to one of the abandoned bases. Probably near a rail-head. Clark Airfield maybe. Maybe Camp O'Donnell. That's what I'd do in their shoes. If they don't just decide to kill us on the spot instead."

"You think they'll bring trucks? I can't walk far," Norman responded dizzily. "I need to ride."

"I don't know, Norm," Lucian reponded under more control. "These guys are swarming in here now that we gave up. Looks like the caravans are all headed in this direction south, not north. I sure hope so." Lucian picked up a discarded poncho and draped it over the dead body of his cousin. "So long, Johnny," he said, then standing looked down the dusty road to the growling Jap soldiers coming their way again.

"What do we do with Johnny? Just leave him?" Norman asked again, incredulous that their lives had come to this.

"He's dead, Norm. I'll take his dog tags. We can't do a thing about it unless we stay put for the night. Come night, if we're still here, maybe we can sneak him off the road to them bushes and bury him with some loose dirt or something. I can't think what else we can do. I'll tell ya what, Norm. I'm watching that Jap guard. If he's even fifty feet alone from another guard tonight, he's a dead man."

"Good. I'd kill him, but I . . ."

"I know. I'll do it. Don't worry," Lucian replied coldly. "They even look like they're gonna touch you and I swear I kill until I haven't got an ounce of life in me. I swear."

The Japanese guard stood proudly before them, intimidating them. His broad grin belied missing front teeth, his cheek a long scar from a battle wound.

"I'll get this guy. No matter how long it takes. I'll remember him," Lucian whispered to Norman as the guard walked on looking for another victim. "He's a dead man!"

CHAPTER 51

Third Day, Bataan Death March

"God in Heaven," Norman groaned as they lay in an open field under the blazing sun the third day into their march. "Any water left?" he asked.

Lucian didn't answer. They were seated next to an artesian spring. "Water spigot and all," Lucian whispered to himself.

He had just watched a Japanese officer draw his sword from his sheath and behead a young man, delirious for water, who had rushed out of line to the spigot. Now the

Japs forbid any of them from filling their canteens.

"You must all obey!" the Japanese officer yelled angrily. "You live because the emperor is gracious to spare you! Any man who does not follow orders exactly will be shot. To surrender is to be worse than a dog. You are cowards. Cowards deserve to die! No more water today!" he screamed and stepped back into his captured American jeep.

The Japanese guards, all uneducated privates, gleefully used the man's decapitated body for bayonet practice, laughing fiendishly at each thrust.

The scene of wanton murder was hourly. Hundreds who had fallen out of the march were summarily shot or run through.

"Officers, enlisted men, the Jap guards show no stinking defference to anyone, Norm. They killed three officers yesterday for having Jap money. Remember?"

"I heard shots. I can't remember nothin' anymore. I can't make it, Lucian. Just let me die," Norm moaned.

"One step at a time. They won't do anything unless we fall out of the march. Just keep hangin' onto me. I'll get us some water somehow."

"Food? We got to have food. We haven't had anything since we left Mariveles."

"We are about two kilometers from the last place we buried those canned goods. Two or three cases of fruit and some rations. I'm gonna make a break for it tonight, Norm. We just quietly roll into the underbrush and let them be on their way in the morning. They won't even miss us."

"We'll just get recaptured."

"Maybe. But we'll have some food in us by then."

"How much did you guys bury up ahead?"

"A few cases. Covered it with palms and elephant grass. I remember this spot because of the water spigot. We used it to fill our canteens, and the radiator. That nipa hut over there?" He pointed. "I recall making a mental note. We are close, Norm. Just one step at a time."

"Okay. One step at a time."

They continued, dragging one foot ahead of the other. Lucian's head was aching from the rifle butt he'd received when the Jap soldier killed Johnny. His throat parched, he tried not to think any further than one more step. One, the next, the next, the next . . .

Norman was delirious, being dragged slowly forward by the sheer determination of his twin. After hours of walking in the merciless hundred-and-ten-degree tropical sun, breathing the dust of the road as parched and dry as their own throats, Lucian stumbled. A hand reached for him then for Norman. From both sides the brothers were helped to their feet.

"Bogan, is that you? I thought you was dead?" Lucian mumbled through swollen lips, his eyes darkened and swollen almost shut by a blow to the face, as he tried to distinguish the man who picked him up. "Who's this?" he asked pointing to the man holding Norman up on his other side.

"That's Pedro Villalobos, E Battery. We been together since San Fernando in January."

"Thank you, Pedro," he allowed with a dry throaty sound.

"This is where being an Indian from the Southwest comes in handy. Look!" They watched in horror as a young private ran for the filthy ditch water to the side of the dusty road. Full of bloating bodies, animals and men, brown with fecal matter and disease, the young man drank. Another broke ranks until a half dozen found themselves splashing the filthy liquid over them for relief from the sweltering rays of the sun. It was the second day without water and delirium was epidemic among the dying bedraggled prisoners.

"You can't get like that, Parker. You got to be like an Indian. Take a drink next time we fill up the canteen, swish it around in your mouth and hold it. Let it slowly drain down your throat. No gulps."

"Here," Pedro offered, giving each brother one sip from his canteen.

"They're stopping us. They're letting men fill the canteens!" Lucian turned his swollen face to Norman. "Thank God in Heaven! We're gonna make it now, Norm."

"Thank God," Norman weakly offered. "And you," he whispered through cracked dry lips. "Thank God for you," he said collasping into Lucian's arms.

CHAPTER 52

Present Day, American Military Cemetery, Manila

Aged Lucian Parker from Warm Springs sighed and relaxed his voice for several minutes as Vincente waited. The cemetery didn't seem so ghostly now, to Vincente. These crosses with names were suddenly taking the form of faces and personalities. The names had strengths, human weakness, hopes, and dreams.

Mead, Bogan, Martinez, Stiles, Parker. All names until now. The Filipino had sat at the feet of the American in rapt attention as a schoolboy does upon hearing a tale weaved by a master storyteller.

"It was there I was reunited with your father, Manuelito," the aged Parker brother said. "San Fernando. The march lasted six more days from the time Bogan and Villalobos picked us up, rescued us from certain bayoneting, until we reached the rail-head town of San Fernando. The one we had retreated from with the train loads of supplies four months earlier. It was there the Japs were registering the POW's names and then herding us into oven-like metal boxcars so tight men had to stand. Many died that day."

"How did you survive the next six days? I hear thousands died. Maybe ten thousand Filipinos, many thousand Americanos. No?"

"The prayers of loved ones and the grace of God I suppose. The unwillingness of my brother, Bogan, and Villalobos to let me fall to the ground. I love those men more than I can say. More than I can find words to describe.

"The Japs were butchers, you know. But our minds were numb, our bodies sore, heads blistered, lips swollen, minds gone. It was a nightmare we couldn't wake from. The Japs even killed each other.

"One time, I don't recall which day, one Jap soldier dropped out from heat exhaustion. A Jap sergeant makes some grunt to two of his men and they drag this sick Jap soldier into the bushes. We hear a shot. Then we knew for sure life meant nothing to them."

Lengthy silence followed as the gazing eyes of the old veteran were suddenly transported to the land of dreams, where nothing makes sense but everything seems real.

"Most died because they gave up," he abruptly started again.

"They either fell down and were bayoneted, left for dead, or shot. There was zero tolerance or mercy given us. Prisoners, men who surrendered, were considered worse than dogs by the Japs.

"A lot of Filipinos marching with us died drinking the ditch scum, the diseased filth in the water found in puddles created by feces-filled carabao tracks. It was awful. Awful," he said quietly, almost reverently, as he hung his head in reverie. "Just more terrible than I can describe. They would fall over in fits of pain and agony and die along the roads soon after drinking it. Hundreds of them every mile," he said, eyes moistening. "Probably ten Filipinos for every American."

Silence reigned again.

"The clouds are coming but I don't think they bring monsoon." Vincente pointed to the moonlit sky momentarily bringing the old man Parker back to the present.

"A little rain then would have saved us. The dust along the road choked us, as if the sun didn't almost bake us. We were walking zombies covered in our own filth, excrement, needing desperately to lay down, find some water, food. Most men hadn't eaten for nine days. It was a miracle anyone was alive," he continued, oblivious to the younger man's comment.

"We found ourselves standing near the edge of the clearing we had been herded into at San Fernando. There was jungle, shade, trees. A few men ventured to sit under the shade. The guards apparently were as beat as we were. There Manuelito, your father, appeared. Our salvation!"

CHAPTER 53

Ninth Day, Bataan Death March

The Parkers, Bogan, and Villalobos waited for a chance to make a break into the jungle. The Japanese guards had not yet herded their group of resting men into the boxcars.

"Psst. Señores Parker," Manuelito whispered from the jungle underbrush. "I got food. Remember, we buried food," he rolled several cans their way. "Peaches. Beans." He threw a knife.

Bogan scrambled on hands and knees for it and scooped up the cans under him. He gathered the men in a tight little group.

"We got to look out for ourselves. We got four cans here. We got no choice," he said. "I'm gonna open them and then you guys eat it as fast as you can. We share each can, then the next, and so on. We won't get another chance. No one is payin' attention. Norman you first, then Lucian, then Pedro, then me."

Manuelito remained hidden with two other Filipinos in a ravine, a small dip in the landscape in the trees just feet beyond the prisoners. Bogan popped the lids off the cans quickly with the small pocket knife then sliced a flap into the side of one of his boots and slid the knife in to hide it. The men gorged themselves and tossed the cans into the bushes before anyone paid attention.

A table was set up in the clearing and soon a Japanese officer appeared shouting instructions.

"We got to sign our names in some book," Bogan ascertained for the group now laying prostrate in the shade. "Once they got our names there is no turning back. They'll count us. If we turn up missing they may shoot some of the others just to teach a lesson. It's now or never," he said and as he did he and Pedro rolled off into the bushes for their escape.

A Jap guard seeing the commotion in the bushes yelled and soon the two were being pursued. Shots rang out and the excitement had the guards distracted by the jungle chase of the two escapees, away from the brothers.

"Norman. This is where you get off," Lucian said, revived from the fruit and protein, and pushed his brother as hard as he could down the small incline into the ravine where Manuelito waited. "Go with Manuelito. *Keep the faith.*"

The men gathered themselves with the guards and were herded like cattle to the metal boxcars. Lucian looked toward the jungle one last time before stepping up into the train where more death followed the band of prisoners. Norman weakly gazed at the scene, too tired to move, waiting for dark to make his move with Manuelito.

He followed his Filipino rescuers into the bushes and crawled to a stream and small carved out cavern barely large enough for the four men. But it was heaven. He fed upon the canned goods, drank the water and then found himself carried, exhausted beyond anything he understood a living man could know, into the mountains and the camps of American and Filipino guerillas.

Manuelito had escaped a Japanese attack on a patrol he was on with a Filipino scout platoon one month before the surrender of Bataan. All ten of the other men had been killed.

"I thought you were dead, Manuelito," an exhausted Norman Parker finally said after having slept for two days straight.

"Here. Take. Eat." He smiled, handing Norman a piece of wild boar meat and a bowl of rice. "Sorry, no forks." He grinned.

Norman Parker ate with abandon. He downed the mild tea Manuelito had prepared and lay back on the rugged grass mat that had served as his bed.

"You smell pretty bad, lieutenant," Manuelito said, nodding to his clothes stacked in the corner. "We cleaned those in the stream two days ago. You ready for a bath? I take you there."

"Yeah, I stink. I need a bath, a shave. Any razors around here?"

"Sure thing, Lieutenant Parker. We buried all kinds of goodies that day. Remember?"

Norman let out a hearty laugh. "Any Wrigleys chewing gum? Some Colgate toothpaste? A toothbrush maybe?"

"I see what I can do." He smiled. "Come. Let's go. I show you around."

He soothed his aching, bruised body under a trickling clear stream of water falling over rocks from above him and showered with a bar of Lux soap for hours. Simple, clear, plain, everyday jungle stream water. Something he had never considered a luxury. *A pure and simple gift from the Almighty*, he thought to himself.

The Filipinos enjoyed watching him revel in it. Allowing his mouth to be filled, his body soothed, the soap to slowly take its time as he carefully scrubbed every inch of crusted filth from himself.

Cleaned, smiling, he dressed and went back to camp. A roasted chicken, some rice, comotes—sweet potatoes—he felt new strength surge through him.

"Manuelito. Do you know where they took Lucian?" Norman asked, as he gorged on a drumstick.

"Yes. Old army camp named O'Donnell. It is not good. Hundreds of men dying every day. No food, little water. Sickness. Executions. I very sorry for you Joes. But the Filipinos dropping like flies too. A real crime. Now we organize. Tomorrow we fight."

Lucian had survived the first year. Surviving the daily sickness, lack of food, beatings, and arbitrary executions was a miracle in itself. Now the men survived by their wits and learned the art of bartering, trading, stealing, and bribing guards for survival.

He had hidden his final valuable, the one thing that really mattered, the family heirloom. When being stripped of all personal items during the Death March, he at first had hid the gold ring in his mouth, determined to swallow it and look for it later during a latrine stop. He was fortunate to scrounge some thread and sewed the ring into his shorts. He was sure the Jap guards wouldn't check there.

He had tried to give it to Norman but Norman was so far gone, delirious. Norman couldn't entertain any thought except telling one foot to move, then the next.

On the fourth day of the Death March he mustered up all the energy he had to string enough words together under the torture of the broiling and brutal sun, waterless and foodless days, telling his brother as they limped along: "Norm, if something happens to me, toss my body off the side of the road but keep my underwear. I'll explain later."

He smiled now recalling how Norman almost died from the convulsions the unintended humor had created. Norman, his mouth dry, his throat parched, laughed uncontrollably with a high-pitched squeak that caused them to hug each other to keep from falling to the ground. They both cried that day, tears of hysteria.

The superstitious Jap guards left them alone, sure they were crazy for laughing under the conditions. It was one solitary bright spot of the ordeal.

The ring meant he was alive. Making sure Norm got it if something happened to him meant the vow to *keep the faith* of the Parker clan would live.

He had wormed his way onto a work crew shortly after being sent from O'Donnell to Cabanatuan. Getting out of the camp meant possibilities. Smuggling a banana or a sweet potato could mean the difference between life and death. Now at the Cabanatuan POW camp he was a few hours train ride from Manila.

"Hey! American stop now!" a Jap guard had yelled. He had walked toward a stalled train at a crossing during a road trip to work on a bridge repair outside the camp with fellow prisoners.

"Fix train. I fix train." He motioned with his hands to the guards. After some time trying to communicate driving and fixing the train, the guards relented. In thirty minutes he had it going and was from then on an engineer. Well fed, but working sixteen hour days, he still was half the man of his former self.

Now he wrangled ways to get supplies into Cabanatuan. Two Jap guards, intent on getting rich off their jobs, worked well with him. He looked out for them, and they looked out for him by turning their backs. They got hard currency supplied by the underground in Manila. He got the supplies siphoned off from each load the Japs shipped north to Cabanatuan, a junction for enemy troops stationed throughout northeast Luzon.

It worked well until the two cooperative Jap guards were transferred. Now he had to use skills of subterfuge. If he was ever caught he'd be a dead man. He couldn't find a friendly Jap in the whole company that guarded the train and camp now. Maybe in time, but not a greedy enemy soldier had surfaced yet.

Escape wasn't an option. He would love to join Norman. He had opportunities since being on the train. But the Japs had proved they were serious when they threatened they would kill ten Americans for every one who escaped.

They did. More than once. He had been in a group that five men were picked out of for execution in the first days of internment. The experience had cured any idea of escape from then on.

Today he was being permanently transferred to a prison at Fort Santiago. A three-hundred-year-old dungeon—everyone knew someone who had gone there. No one knew of any who had come out.

He was still a train man though. Valuable. He had to survive long enough for MacArthur to keep his promise, to return to the Philippines. He'd seen American planes recently. Had heard bombings. It couldn't be long before Norman made a move and liberated him, before American troops actually stormed ashore to their rescue.

He knew of one thing he wanted above all

others. To get the ring to Norman. To see his face once more. To tell him he loved him. To make sure Mary Jane understood he had done his best. The ring would assure that.

"American. Get up. Go now!" he was urged at the point of bayonet. He was aboard the train for Manila but for the first time since the Death March ride from San Fernando to the old U.S. Army Camp O'Donnell two years ago he was in a boxcar filled with other men, not in the cab as engineer.

CHAPTER 54

February 1945, Raid on Cabanatuan

Norman had waited two and one half years for this moment. The last news from Manuelito was that Lucian had gotten back to the camp after a week of work detail under Jap guard on the north/south rail-run from the POW camp at Cabanatuan to Manila.

Rumor was spreading like wildfire throughout the Philippines. "The Japs are killing their prisoners before the Americans get here."

It had happened so often, the wanton killing, the senseless spur of the moment murder of POWs by guards. He knew it could easily be true. He had to find Lucian and get him out.

The Americans had landed in Leyte Gulf far to the south of Luzon and MacArthur, his old boss, had returned as promised. Surviving with guerillas in the hills, following Lucian from Camp O'Donnell to this camp, then making forays with guerilla protection as far as the outskirts of Manila, Norman had kept an eye on his brother as best he could. Through Manuelito he had gotten messages to Lucian and much-needed quinine for malaria, money to buy food on the black market, and sulfa for wounded Americans.

Norman knew Lucian had developed a rapport with two greedy Jap guards, one at the camp, and one who rode the train with him. He'd pay them off. They eagerly accepted and secretly were friendly to prisoners. But two guards out of two hundred couldn't assure that Lucian wouldn't be hurt or murdered on the spot for the smallest infraction. Especially if he was found smuggling food and medicine in to the Cabanatuan hellhole.

Only five hundred POW's remained now

at the camp. The thousands formerly living here, survivors of the Bataan Death March and the disease-ridden Camp O'Donnell had been shipped to other work camps in the Philippines, Japan, and Manchuria. Thousands had died since those days on Bataan and they continued dying daily en route to other camps, or they were executed, or disease finally caught up with them, or they were drowned at sea during transfers in Japanese "hell ships" unwittingly torpedoed by American submarines.

These few living prisoners represented the embodiment of a promise MacArthur had made. "I shall return" meant he wouldn't abandon them. The American army was now determined to get the five hundred or so American men remaining at Cabanatuan home safely before the Japanese carried out their plans for massacres.

Norman checked his watch. He was in the company of the 6th Rangers, a special army battalion assigned the task of rescuing these prisoners of war before the Japanese slaughter commenced. And although it was not unusual for Norman to be behind enemy lines after thirty months of it, there had never been this many Americans sneaking through the jungle on a forced march sixty-five kilometers behind the lines.

Their job was simple. Kill all two hundred or so Japanese camped at Cabanatuan and bring the prisoners out on their backs if necessary. Leave no one behind.

Norman's job was simpler. Find Lucian and bring him home. If he could find his brother the war would be over for them. Maybe as early as tomorrow.

This rescue was being effected by roughly one hundred and twenty men of the 6th Rangers. They were highly trained and motivated jungle fighters who were eager and ready for action. All of them knew the odds. No one would be able to come to their aid if detected. They would have to fight their way out or be killed.

There had never before been a rescue attempt of this magnitude in the history of American combat. This was one of historic proportions which, if successful, would go down in the books as the greatest mass POW escape of all time.

"Lieutenant Parker!" the ranger captain whispered in an urgent tone. He motioned with his hand for the veteran guerilla fighter to aid him in his study of the map.

"Approximately five kilometers past this point on the river. The river is only feet deep now. But if a monsoon hits suddenly, the water level could be up to our necks in no time. We can't delay," Norman told him.

"Delay isn't part of the ranger motto. Look, Lieutenant. There is going to be a lot of gunfire. A lot of killing. You have been through hell. You've done more than your part in this war. There is no need for you to risk yourself in the raid. We'll be able to get your brother. I'm sure of it."

"Well, I appreciate that, sir, but those men are in hell still. I got to go for my brother. He'd do the same."

"Well I can't order you to stay now can I?" He grinned.

"No, sir. No one can order any of us Bastards of Bataan to do anything we don't want to do."

"Bastards of Bataan? I've never heard it put that way before. Why do you say that?"

"It was a song we sang. '*We're the battling bastards of Bataan. No mama, no papa, no Uncle Sam,*' was one of the lines. '*And nobody gives a damn,*' it ended. See, we felt we were abandoned by our country; expendable. We fought, those men in there fought, without food, ammo. We'd have thrown sticks and stones before surrendering but were too weak by then. We felt like motherless illegitimates, sir, and I'm not going to abandon my brother to fate. If he dies, I die. That's all there is to it."

"Very well. The men rested?" whispered the ranger leading the raiding party to his master sergeant.

"Ready when you are, sir."

"Stick close to this man here, Sergeant. I want to see him and his brother alive when this is over. Move out," he commanded in low voice. The word was passed carefully along to the entire company of men with hand signals.

They crawled through waist-high cogan grass for the final one kilometer, avoiding detection by enemy guards in the towers surrounding the enclosure. The rangers were deployed. Each with his assignment.

Kill the guards in the towers.

Shoot the lock off the front gate.

Take the encampment of Japanese out while they slept.

Kill all who awaken with overwhelming fire power and the element of surprise.

Other teams would shout, "American soldiers! Get to the front gate now!" clearing each hut and building as they went, killing anyone who opposed them, lifting the sick and weak upon their own shoulders if required.

The whole operation couldn't last more than twenty minutes without alerting the thousands of Japanese troops quartered within the five kilometers of the camp.

"I'm going in those buildings, Sergeant. Here on this map," he pointed to a piece of crumpled paper containing the layout of the camp, "is the last hut my brother was reported to be kept in. I'm headed straight for it. You can come with me if you like."

"Don't see as I have a choice, do I?"

"Nope," Norman replied, emotionless, folding the paper up and stuffing it in his trouser pocket.

The sound of a sniper rifle taking the guards out at the towers was followed by the staccato burst from a submachinegun shooting the locks off the gates. Explosions and automatic gunfire now added to the general confusion as more than one hundred Rangers fired, followed the designed plan of action, screamed out to the prisoners that they were free, and killed every waking and sleeping enemy soldier in sight. Grenade blasts followed by screams of terrified and confused Japanese soldiers being mowed down filled the night air.

Dazed, deathly slender Americans peered out from their bamboo prison barracks sure that the massacre they had anticipated at the hands of the Jap guards had begun.

"Lucian! Lucian Parker!" Norman yelled as he entered the first, second, and third barracks building. "You seen Lucian Parker?" he asked, grabbing a skeletal bearded man in loin cloths. Teeth missing, hair askew, he was the personification of bewilderment.

"Who? What are you doing here?" the dazed prisoner asked, boggled by the men in olive green uniforms, strange guns, hat styles, and helmets he had never seen before.

"We're Americans!" Norman sped past him as the sergeant behind him issued orders to him and each prisoner they encountered to get to the front gate.

The gunfire, screams, and pandemonium of the moment mounted even though no more than five minutes had elapsed. "Lucian Parker! Lucian!" Norman, full of adrenalin, screamed.

"Get out! Out now!" the sergeant yelled to each new American as they came out of hiding. "You're being freed. We're American Rangers! Get to the front gates now!" the sergeant called above the noise of mayhem as the dazed and sickly POWs struggled to comprehend what was happening.

Norman ran into the courtyard in the direction of the hospital. He knew from the map where it was.

Pop, pop, pop, and then *zing,* he felt the spin of bullets pass his ear coming from the direction of the barracks off to his left.

He leveled his new M1 Garand at the enemy soldier charging him with a drawn sword and angrily unloaded the entire clip into the man's chest, dropping him within ten feet from when he started his screaming charge. Another Jap charged at him with fixed bayonet. He dove for the dead Jap's samurai sword and side-stepping the new menace swung for the head of the smaller attacking enemy soldier.

Whoosh! the blade sliced the air, smacking squarely against the throat of the enemy soldier. An expression of amazement turned to blood squirting in all directions from the enemy soldier's severed head. Norman felt nothing. Heart pumping, he threw the saber down and picked up his rifle, loaded a new clip, and resumed his hunt.

"Lucian Parker!" he yelled as the last of the sick prisoners were being carried and hustled out by the strong and sturdy Rangers. He followed them out to the front gates in a dead-run as bullets whistled through the air.

Enemy mortars had now zeroed in on the gate and three Rangers fell from a barrage of explosions. He dove to the ground and kept his eyes searching each man that hobbled by, sure one of them had to be his brother. Blood oozed from his left shoulder caused by the mortar explosion but there was no time for attending to that now.

"Come on, Lieutenant! There's no one left in there. Just a few angry Japs our teams are flushing out and killing. You can't stay here," the sergeant urged as Norman stood up, confused, wounded, trying to decide where to look next for Lucian.

"Come on, Lieutenant. Maybe he's out in the group that's made it outside. We got to go." The sergeant tugged at Norman and then pushed as he reluctantly left the camp through the gates and fled north, back toward friendly lines sixty-five kilometers away.

CHAPTER 55

Present Day, Manila

"I want to tell you now, Vincente, what it meant to me to have for a friend a valiant man, your father," Lucian Parker pointedly said. "This is important to me. You see I couldn't thank him directly for what he did for me and my brother. But you, his son, I can thank," he concluded.

He sighed a weary breath for having been so sleepless with the scenes of war revisiting his mind here where it all took place. Having at least this man to recount it to, share it with, was as if God had heard his silent plea for redeeming grace.

To know that Manuelito, somewhere in the realm beyond, knew he was grateful seemed certain to him now. And to believe that God understood his deepest thoughts and cares, was reassuring to him in the very strange but real chance meeting of the two men this very night of sleepless nights.

"I always had your father to count on for the entire time I was behind enemy lines while my brother played the part of prisoner to the Japanese."

"But you say Norman was with my father. Lucian was prisoner, No?"

Vincente asked. "You are Lucian. How could you be in POW camp and behind the lines too?"

The man from Warm Springs sighed. "I am going to clear that part up shortly. Very soon. What is important for you to know is what heros your people are to me. Right here," he replied patting the center of his chest with his right hand.

"They put their lives on the line, sí?"

"Very much so. All of them would have been shot. Your mother and older sister too," he answered matter-of-factly.

"Why you stay away so long? My mother talked of you Parkers much. My father was never there for me when I grew up. You have so much information for me. Things I always wondered. I guess you had reasons for not coming back to the Philippines?"

The old Oklahoman groaned inwardly as he studied the confused look on the face of his new Filipino friend. It was his private war that kept him away but he couldn't expect this young man to understand that. No one could understand why he needed to bury the past. It was too hard on him to recall the terrible memories and too hard to forget them. Then of course there was a secret shame. He hadn't been ready to clear that until now.

"So many reasons. Yes, so very many," he began. "I have been ashamed of some things I did during the war. The hardest part has been to think I let my brother and your father down. Coming back wouldn't have changed things. And I never wanted to think of the death and killing again.

"But it was no use. The nightmares have never ended. Ghosts have haunted my days and nights. I have never even told my wife the story I've shared with you this night. She only knows my brother and I left from Warm Springs, I endured a war, and came home without him."

"I want to know how he died. Was my father courageous? Did he think of us? What was the final thing he did? Said?" Vincente probed.

"I understand," he replied. "Courageous? Manuelito Salazar was the most courageous man I ever knew." Lucian nodded as he looked to the cross with a name inscribed on it that shouldn't be there. He would finish the story for the young man. He owed Manuelito that. And it brought all the fears he had in telling this story to their proper resting place. Here, in the cemetery.

The elderly railroader had thought that he couldn't possibly go on this night. The thoughts had weighed on him for so long they were like a well-worn book, a mentally worn-out book with page after page handled, frayed, spent in going over the same story again and again and never seeming satisfied with the ending.

Over five decades had passed and Vincente Salazar was the first to hear it all. It surprised Lucian how therapeutic it seemed now.

He softened to the young man almost thirty years his junior and began recounting the final pages of a personal history, his story, to which he had not yet added the words *"The End."*

CHAPTER 56

1945—Final days of war, Outside Manila

Lieutenant Norman Parker was on a private mission and he did not return the sixty-five kilometers to safety with the Rangers. They had boldly accomplished their mission with just three of their number killed and two hundred and fifty enemy soldiers killed in the battle for Camp Cabanatuan.

All the American POWs were brought out alive. The Rangers, especially the three dead, were heroes deserving the greatest of honors, but Norman didn't have time to share in the triumph or accolades.

Norman, with the aid of Manuelito Salazar had finally located Lucian. He had been kept prisoner in the dungeons at Fort Santiago just outside the Inturmuros. He was being used for train maintenance. Once the Japs were done with him, once it appeared that the Americans would be entering Manila, and especially the old fortress city of the Inturmuros, Lucian would be executed. There was no question of that.

Norman had used his extensive underground Filipino contacts to smuggle him to a hamlet just outside of Manila. Now with the Americans on the island of Luzon, the Filipinos took new courage and aided the Americans in every way possible against their common enemy.

Manuelito had not accompanied Norman on the raid but had left word with his wife in Santa Rosa a few kilometers down the rail tracks from Cabanatuan how to get in touch with him. Norman hid in the Salazar home until Manuelito and six other loyal Filipino guerrillas had arrived.

All were motivated by anger at the tortures and executions of family and friends and without exception were eager to exact revenge. The Japanese had learned there was no more dangerous enemy than a vengeful Filipino. Hundreds of thousands of their countrymen had been slaughtered during the three year reign of terror by the Japanese. The Japanese had promised freedom from the imperialist American rule and had graciously granted the Philippines inclusion in their "Greater Asia Co-Prosperity Sphere" as they called it.

"Prosperity with a gun to my head," Manuelito said. "It is time to kill every Jap on Luzon. Then in the rest of the Philippines."

"First we rescue Lucian and the people with him. Then when the American army reaches Manila we go in and take no prisoners," Norman agreed.

"Okay. Here is what I know. My contacts in Manila say that Lucian is running the daily train to San Fernando. Taking supplies to the Japs and bringing wounded Japs back. It is on the return trip I think we strike. Hundreds of Japs on the train die.

We get message through my contacts at the Manila station and then near here, Santa Rosa, we blow the train up."

"I don't want Lucian hurt. Nor any Filipinos riding the train," Norman demanded.

"Of course. But we can never be certain in war. You know that, Lieutenant Parker."

"I know. But if I can get Lucian to blow the train then maybe we can spare lives. Blow the engine. Sabotage it. There are ways both he and I know to blow up a steam engine. Real quick. When it goes the Jap soldiers can be killed by your guerillas."

Manuelito agreed. They set out for the ambush the next day.

"You come now!" a Japanese guard yelled at Lucian as he fought the malarial attack that had caused spasms of uncontrolled shivering, sweats, and delirium.

He struggled to his feet and tugged at the diminutive Filipino who was his fireman. They stood clinging to each other for support at the door of the dark and damp six-by-six-foot dungeon cell. The Filipino fainted helpless at Lucian's feet.

"No! Only American! No Filipino!" the Jap guard protested as Lucian lifted the struggling man to his feet. "You go now," he ordered, waving a rifle in the direction he expected the emaciated American to head. The Jap guard offered a toothless, evil grin. A scar ran the length of his right eye to his chin—Lucian had seen this Jap somewhere before. Utterly worn out, he couldn't recall, his mind fogged from sickness and lack of sleep, he could only concentrate on this moment. But he knew this guard.

Lucian slowly took each step up the concrete stairs with great effort. *One at a time. Just one at a time*, he commanded himself.

Pop! Pop! Pop! He stumbled at the echoing sound of gunshots from behind him. "Go now!" the Japanese guard ordered to Lucian as he stood over the lifeless body of the Filipino.

"*I'll kill him. I'll kill that dirty yellow bastard! I swear it if it is my final act in life*, he vowed silently as he got back to his feet and made his way into the blinding sunlight of the old Spanish courtyard.

His malaria attack subsided with the penetrating rays of the sun upon his shivering wet body. He stood swaying, putting complete effort into remaining on his feet as he waited for the guard. Feeling the poke of a bayonet in the small of his back he dutifully moved forward and onto a waiting truck. Minutes later he was at the train depot that three years before he, Norman, and Johnny Mead had been assigned to guard.

"You get water." The Jap guard pointed.

A Filipino came to Lucian, purposefully bumping into him and spilling a cup of water on him. He slid a piece of paper into his hand with the empty cup and guided him to the faucet in the waiting room for it to be refilled.

"This note. Read quickly and destroy," he said, filling the cup and handing two quinine pills to the sickly American. "Take these quickly. The Jap not looking."

Lucian eagerly swallowed and focused on the note held close to him.

"To L P. I am at SR. Look for MS. Blow boiler at highway xing return trip. I will be there to get you. N P."

"Norm is at Santa Rosa. It's over," he sighed quietly.

"You drink water," the guard yelled.

Lucian put the small crumpled paper in his mouth, chewed, and swallowed with another cup of water. He decided to continue drinking until the guard ordered him back.

"Tell my brother I got the message and understand," Lucian whispered to the Filipino messenger. The man nodded and quickly departed. "Thanks," he offered tiredly. The Filipino nodded without expression.

The quinine must have been sent by Norman, he thought. *Thank you God! Thank you!* He struggled back to the rails, waiting for the engine to come up the tracks to where he stood with the guard. A Filipino would be engineer with him. He guessed the Japs didn't totally trust the Filipinos and wanted an experienced American.

The antiquated steam engine, identical with a few exceptions to the one owned by his pa in Warm Springs, made its way to the loading platform where he waited. He thought he knew the man at the controls and at gunpoint found his way into the cab with the Filipino almost half his height.

"Say nothing, Lucian," Manuelito urged. "You don't know me."

"But how?"

"Papers. I showed my Filipino Certificate of Operations and asked for work. I told them I want to help Japs. They agreed to give me the train today. I almost didn't get it. Good luck I guess. Shhh," he whispered. "Guards coming aboard now. I load fuel. Be fireman. You sit and drive."

Lucian was grateful to the faithful friend who had been a benefactor so often. Through Manuelito and his contacts Lucian had been able to smuggle food, medicine, and hard currency to the prisoners at Cabanatuan for over a year. Manuelito had risked his life. And although he had never seen Norman since the Death March he knew he had been behind the smuggling. He had received notes, quinine, sulfa, and other items that had made it possible to survive the tortures of prison life.

The familiar-looking Jap angrily approached Lucian. Lucian studied the face carefully for any hint of where he had seen it before.

"Go now!" the Jap guard ordered him. He raised his rifle menacingly then mocked him with a sinister grin.

"Johnny," Lucian muttered under his breath as he recognized the man's face, the missing teeth, the scar. "*I told Norm I'd kill him.*" He nodded silently with satisfaction.

The ill-tempered killer of Lucian and Norman's cousin stood guard with rifle at the ready on Lucian's side of the engine compartment. Another guard stood facing out on Manuelito's side. Their backs to the fireman and engineer so they could look out of either side during the ride to San Fernando, Lucian and Manuelito talked by sign language, whispers, and hatched the escape plan and destruction of the train.

It was simple, really. All Lucian had to do was run the boiler tanks low of water, release a valve, and then allow the heat to build pressure in the tank. Then it would blow up.

"The coal box water level has to be above the crown sheet," he explained in whispers to Manuelito. "If the water level falls below a certain level the crown sheet ruptures and we have a catastrophic explosion. We have seconds to get off before it blows."

"Your brother said you would know how to do it. Critical we do it at the Santa Rosa highway crossing. There we can jump and my boys have machine guns, mortars. They will kill all Japs and get us out safe."

"I understand." Lucian nodded in whispers. "What about these guys?"

"I push one and you push the other. Look at them. So sure of themselves. One hit with the shovel, one push with the hand and they go flying off the train." Manuelito Salazar smiled as he loaded coal from the tender into the burning coal box.

Lucian smiled confidently at the small man's plan. He held a pipe wrench up. Left inside the cab carelessly by the engineer's seat, Manuelito knew Lucian's intention, how he planned to use it, and nodded.

"What's keeping them?" Norman grumbled, hunched over in the underbrush closest to the tracks.

"Maybe Americans hit train from air," replied the Filipino who Norman called Geronimo for his features and savage ways of getting revenge.

"Let's hope not. Good thing it's getting dark. It will help." Norman looked down at his watch. Nineteen hundred hours—the sun was setting.

Norman picked up on it first. The slight perception all train men pick up on. A vibration on the rails, a rumble of the tracks, followed by the thunder of a locomotive. Even miles away a real train man knows when the track is filled with thousands of pounds of a steam engine headed his way.

The whistle blew faintly but distinctly in the distance. Geronimo gave his men hand signals. Once Lucian and Manuelito were clear of the train and it blew they would open fire.

A full moon was all that would offer enough illumination to tell who was who when the actual escape took place. But Norman was certain Lucian would be at the controls if Manuelito had made it aboard. They would have heard from Manuelito by now if he had failed in his plan.

The whistle was clear now. Two, maybe three kilometers, down the line. *Three blows . . . followed by two blows of the horn . . .* pause . . . *three blows* . . . "It's him!" Norman grinned excitedly.

Norman was impatient. His hands wrung with perspiration. Two and a half years since they had held onto each other in the Death March. Lucian saved his life then. He waited anxiously to do the same for his brother now.

"Come on, Lucian. Lower that water pressure. Blow that baby!" Norman instructed inaudibly. "Make those rivets pop! You can do it!"

Norman could smell the familiar but pungent odor wafting his way from the smokestack. One minute later the locomotive's headlamp was clearly visible, appearing from a bend in the tracks. The guerillas looked at their watches. They had ten minutes to pull this off and then escape into the forest before local Japanese army units were alerted by the sounds of gunfire and explosions.

Manuelito trustingly looked over at Lucian working on the gauges. He watched Lucian's eyes as he monitored the sight-glass and pressure guage.

Lucian had told him the water pressure must drop rapidly under two hundred pounds per square inch. Now he was sweating profusely from the heat in the cab and the pressure of needing to do this right. It was their escape and the final payment to Japs who had imprisoned and killed so many of them. Especially this Jap guard who deserved to die. Promised revenge, the payment for Johnny Mead's death, was coming due.

Lucian nodded and grinned to Manuelito as the gauges told their story to him. Manuelito pretended to load coal into the fire.

Lucian moved his lips and worded his message to Manuelito who paid close attention. It was all timing. Important and crucial timing.

"When I count to ten with my fingers we push the guards out the door and follow. This thing should blow within a hundred yards either side of the crossing. You have to move as fast as you can. When it blows it's gonna send pieces of this train in all directions. It's one big bomb under immense pressure. You understand?" he whispered.

Manuelito nodded and readied himself to give the Jap guarding his door of the cab a wack with the handle of his coal shovel. He looked forward to the moment. Lucian handled the large pipe wrench kept at the engineer's control panel. He would help this lousy murdering scum Jap into the next world with pleasure for what he had done to his cousin more than two years ago. With a crack to the back of the skull or square in the face, it didn't matter to him.

He'd enjoy this payback as he buried the wrench in his head, shoved him out, then followed with a jump. Then he would clear the tracks before any of the Japanese riding in the box and flat cars knew what was happening. He'd let the train head on down the tracks and explode. Then he'd look for his brother and together they would find their way north to the American lines.

His heart beat now with anticipation for the escape and the reunion. They had made it! Over half of all men captured were dead now and they were both alive! It felt like every child's Christmas gift rolled into one.

He blew the whistle long and loud now that the crossing was in sight. He was sure Norman would recognize his game. Three yanks on the whistle followed by two followed by three. An old code they had used back in Oklahoma. Norman would know it was him.

Lucian reached for the heavy pipe wrench, looked at Manuelito who nodded, then tugged at the trousers of the Jap who had killed his cousin.

"This is for Johnny!" he smiled coldly as the startled guard turned to face him. Lucian swung hard with both hands grasping the hammer like tool. The stunned guard staggered and began to crumble from the solid blow to his mouth and nose. Blood spurted from the place where teeth and nose had been. "Time for you to go," Lucian announced with satisfaction, giving the crumpled body a kick with his feet and then watching as it rolled like a broken doll into stagnant pools of water off the track. He turned to see how his companion was faring.

"Manuelito! Look out!"

Norman smiled and looked over to Geronimo. "It's him. His signal. Let the men know. Nobody fires until I get him off the tracks and safely under cover. Understood?"

"Sure thing, Joe. You hurry. We gonna kill lots of damn Japs tonight."

"When the boiler blows on that train it's gonna kill a lot of Japs too. You just finish the job. My brother and me will take off to the agreed rendevous north of Santa Rosa."

"No sweat, Joe," Geronimo nodded and passed his signal along. "Nobody fires guns until I fire."

"Good. Okay. Here we go," Norman replied. "I'm goin' for my brother," he said and darted from cover along the tracks in the direction of the oncoming train.

He huffed heavily with anticipation of seeing Lucian fly out of the cab and roll off into the tall grass along the tracks. The elephant grass he was running through offered excellent camouflage for both of them once he pulled his brother under his arms.

He was carrying a Thompson submachine gun on this trip. The army had air dropped the guerillas a new cache of weapons just days before. He was angry and ready to kill but Lucian was his top priority.

He was almost to the point where he expected Lucian to knock the guard out and follow him. The last time they were together Lucian had supported him from collapsing during the Death March. He had held him up. Lucian had been the strong one. Now the roles had changed. Norman, wounded at Cabanatuan, had treated his own injuries, removed with Filipino help the shrapnel from his shoulder. This time, this reunion of the brothers, was Norman's turn to carry the load.

Hunched down in the grass now he stopped short one hundred yards away as the train approached. Fifty yards. One guard out and down on the tracks! "Good job Lucian!" he said happily against the oncoming noise.

Manuelito struggled with the Jap guard who had turned suddenly at the commotion in the cab caused by Lucian's quick dispatching of his guard. Manuelito pulled a knife from his boot and jabbed deeply into the enemy soldier's chest, a surprised look of shock registering on the enemy as he looked down to see the Filipino plunge the knife repeatedly into his body. The Jap guard finally crumbled and fell out the door as the train kept moving down the tracks.

"Lucian! You go! Go now! Jump!"

"The boiler! Something's wrong. The pressure is all wrong. The gauge shouldn't be reading this. It should be down fifty more pounds! The sight-glass shows the water is escaping. This thing is gonna blow but I . . ."

"Lucian you go now!" the loyal Filipino repeated and pushed him to the the opening. Lucian hesitated.

"Sorry, Joe. But you going now," Manuelito said, shoving him off the slowing train. He turned and put the brakes on and then readied himself to jump.

"Lucian! Lucian! Over here!" Norman stood tall in the grass and waved as he began running toward his limping skeletal-looking brother.

"Norm? Thank God. Norm!" He strained

as he limped off the tracks, headed in the direction of his sprinting brother. Even the night couldn't disguise the form of his twin image.

Lucian stopped to see the train go by wondering why it hadn't blown and realized Manuelito was still in the cab working the release gauge.

"Manuelito, get off! Jump! Let it go! Get off!" Lucian stood and yelled as the engine passed. The little man saw him, nodded, and then headed for the door opening.

"Lucian, get down!" Norman yelled as he dove for his brother. Covering him, he raised his head to see the image of Manuelito in the door. Then the fiery yellow explosion ripping the engine to shreds caused the loyal Filipino to completely disappear in a fireball engulfing the engine.

"We got to help Manuelito!" Lucian struggled, trying to raise himself and run to the wreckage.

"Lucian, dammit! He's gone. It's gone! The train ain't no more. If he made it he'll meet us. Come on!"

"Okay. Okay. Norm. Is it really you?" he asked, breathing heavily, stumbling to his knees and then up again to make the run.

Tears, confusion, joy, all mixed freely as they held each other tightly.

"It's me. Come on." Sounds of rage and weapons filled the air as the Filipino troops fired on the Japanese soldiers trying to escape from the boxcars. They were cut down, each as he moved to the door. The massacre had begun and this time the good guys were doing the job of slaughter. An explosion from a dynamite charge sent a flat car loaded with soldiers hurtling into the air. As quickly as the cacophony of violence filled the countryside air it ceased.

Norman hustled his brother off the tracks and into the bushes. They stumbled for several yards before the unexpected took place. Standing in a line of wonderment at the sudden explosive commotion so close to them, a patrol of Japanese soldiers began to move into their path heading for the tracks.

"Hit the ground!" Norm commanded Lucian, letting him fall from the support of one shoulder. Taking his Thompson off his other shoulder he lowered it at the stunned Japanese soldiers and began firing staccato bursts, dropping them quickly.

"The SOB's didn't stand a chance against the Parker brothers," he offered mockingly, coldly, as he helped the shaken and nervous Lucian to his feet. "Come on. Let's head off in another direction."

"I'm proud of you, Norm," Lucian strained to say as he nervously, flimsily, got to his feet and grabbed hold of Norman for support. He turned his head to look back at Norman's handiwork just paces from the dead Japanese soldiers.

"Norman!" he screamed, putting himself in front of his brother.

Pop! The clanking of a bolt action sounded from behind as Lucian lurched forward, taking the shot meant for his brother.

Pop! Blasting again from the movement of the enemy rifle's bolt action. Norman was down now.

Norman rolled away from his brother to draw the fire to him. He dropped the sling from his shouldered Thompson submachine gun, turned, and aimed into the darkness. A wounded but determined shadow, a Japanese soldier, headed for them. Norman let go a burst of rapid fire upon the shadow, crumbling the enemy soldier in a heap to the ground.

Lucian groaned. "Oh dammit, Norm. They

got me good this time. They up and got me good!"

Norman felt at his own head. He'd been grazed and was bleeding. The single bullet created a neat and bloody crease cutting along his temple above the right eye and into his scalp. A fraction of an inch more and he'd have been dead. His left hand stung and bled. He grabbed a well-worn handkerchief from his trousers and instructed Lucian to hold it to his wounded upper body.

"Okay, Lucian. My turn. We gotta run for it. I'll go a few hundred yards and put you down to dress the wound. It's gonna be a long night. We got to get away and we got to move fast," he said, scooping his brother into his arms. "Doggone it Lucian. You hang in there. It's almost over."

"You get the ring?"

"Huh?" Norman huffed as he brought his slender and frail brother up to his chest from off the ground.

"I gave Manuelito the ring. He was supposed to get it to you."

"Hush. I got ya now. Forget the ring. It's over now. It's all over with," he grunted and began running with his wounded twin through the jungle brush for the appointed rendevous.

CHAPTER 57

February 1945, Army Field Hospital
Outside Manila

"Lucian?" Norman whispered. "Lucian," he struggled again with all the energy left in his war-worn body.

"Yeah," his twin brother exhaled heavily.

"I want to go home," he said.

"Me, too," Lucian struggled to say.

"We can do this—we can make it. I want you to make it—not give up. I'm not leaving without you," he said.

"I'm tryin', Norm. It hurts. The Japs got me good this time. I'm so tired. So very tired."

"It's almost over. You can do it. Remember what Mama always said? When we'd leave for a trip on the rails with Pa?"

Lucian's trembling hand reached out and held on to his brother's across the narrow aisle separating the two cots in the field hospital outside Manila where the fighting still raged.

"Keep the faith," he responded, repeating it over and over. "Keep the faith . . . keep the . . . Ohh, it hurts." He winced, struggling for breath like a sprinter catching his air after running the fastest mile of his career. "Did Manuelito get you my letter and the ring?" he finally forced from his lungs.

"Manuelito didn't make it," Norman strained in a throaty effort to encourage his twin. "Hold on, Lucian. Just a little longer. We got Pa waitin', expectin' us. Pa needs us for the shortline—the steel beast—it's paid for. The land, it's gotta be all paid up by now. We gotta go home," he squeezed out, gritting his teeth against his own fatigue and pain. "Mary Jane's waiting," he encouraged.

"Norm?" Lucian's malarial voice begged. "Norman?" the gravelly throat stumbled again. "We sure showed 'em didn't we? I killed the Jap who killed Johnny. Did I tell you?" he struggled to say.

"Nope. That's good, Lucian. Real good."

"Yep. Kept my promise, didn't I," he coughed, trying to smile. "We didn't give up, did we Norm?"

"Sure enough didn't, brother. You hold on," Norman replied softly but with great effort.

"Mary Jane . . . if I don't . . . you tell her, give her . . ." Lucian sighed shakily before falling into well-deserved unconscious slumber—the chills, shakes, fevered perspiration, fleeing from him as suddenly as they had come on.

Norman gazed over at his twin through moist battle-weary eyes. Wounded days before while leading American Rangers to the jungle prison that had held his brother for almost three years, he was relieved to see the end of their nightmare. He groaned in pain from the shrapnel wounds he had ignored to save his brother, wounds now ravaging his already skeletal upper body. And then there was the bullet creasing his skull—offering the mother of all headaches and mental confusion.

Every contagion under the Philippine sky

had rained on him, his brother, and other army survivors of the death camps. He still suffered from dysentery. Both he and Lucian dealt with malaria as best they could now.

"Nurse. Nurse," Norman called. "Morphine? More morphine for my brother and me? Please?" he begged as the slender woman passed their cots, clipboard in hand.

She stopped and bent over, checking his head. Her hand was the touch of angel to him now. "Mary Jane," he whispered. The nurse smiled and promised to return shortly.

"Norm?" Lucian roused, breathing almost inaudibly now. "Norm—I love you like life. We showed 'em. We never gave up, did we?" His lips were dry as he struggled to wet them to form the next words. "Mary Jane . . . you won't forget?" he groaned.

"When I forget how to think, breathe, smell the air of home," Norman answered, wearily taking the limp right hand of his brother in his left. He whispered the promise again like a sacred vow, "I won't forget."

"Norm?" Lucian roused, suddenly turning a weak head toward his wounded brother. "You got the ring? Manuelito?" he asked with a groan.

"I . . ." Norman was suffering as much delirium, fever, and fighting for life as was Lucian. He understood what the ring had meant to his brother. It was the family keepsake, their symbol of trying to make things work out between them with Mary Jane.

"Never forget," Lucian broke in, his muttering more subdued now.

"What?" Norman groaned in reply.

"Why . . . the   ring . . . How   much   I loved . . ." he sighed as expression from his face released, air deflating from his lungs.

"I love you, too. God knows I do," the tired dysentery-riddled Norman offered to his sleeping twin. "Don't worry about Mary Jane or the ring," he replied tearily. "This is our ticket home. That's all. Just our ticket home."

CHAPTER 58

"The survivor of three family members from the New Mexico National Guard is that one over there," a nurse pointed out to the chaplain and lieutenant colonel.

"Lieutenant Parker?" the colonel inquired to the recovering young man who looked ten years older than his real age.

"Yes? Oh, yes, sir." He stood and turned solemnly toward the man, offering a tired salute. "I was just thinking. Didn't see you come in."

"No salute. It is I who must salute you!" The colonel snapped to attention and offered a sharp salute followed by the army chaplain.

"I am Lieutenant Colonel Oliver Forrest. And this is Chaplain Curtis. We have some information from the War Department that we believe you should have before you return to the States."

The chaplain spoke first. "I want to tell you, Lieutenant Parker, that it is a great honor that I meet with you knowing the courage you have displayed and the fact that your cousin Corporal Johnny Mead and your brother Sergeant Parker both died in your arms."

"Padre, I respect that feeling. But I just did what anyone would do for their brother and cousin. Anything else I did during the war was to survive and out of duty. A lot of men did the same."

"Lieutenant Parker, I understand your feelings. Perhaps I should allow Colonel Forrest here to offer his items of business and then, should you require them, I have come to offer my support and prayers at this time."

"Thank you, Padre," the Parker brother offered without emotion, still confused as how to play out the secret he had adopted earlier that day.

"Lieutenant, this is overdue, but this small case here contains your captain bars," Colonel Forrest said, extending a small cardboard box that fit in his hand. "Not only that but your rank has been adjusted to reflect the years you spent behind the lines. You will be receiving back pay for that time at the new rank of captain."

"Thank you," he replied reluctantly, nervously. These men were causing him more confusion about the decision he had made earlier. Now he didn't know what to think or do.

"What about my brother and his promotions?"

"Sergeant Parker has been promoted posthumously to the rank of lieutenant along with his military citations. They have already been processed and sent ahead to his home in Oklahoma.

"Not only that but this paperwork indicates that General MacArthur himself will present you and other survivors with the gratitude of our nation before you leave for the States at a special ceremony to honor the men from Bataan this week on Friday at his field headquarters. These are very high honors, Captain Parker, as the paperwork indicates." He smiled as he pointed to the awards.

"So Sergeant Lucian Parker's papers have been sent on ahead, and he, my brother, is being made a lieutenant?"

"That is correct." The colonel smiled.

"Then I'd better return these," he said, handing the gold captain's bars back to the colonel.

"I don't understand," he responded, confused.

"See, we are twins. Something must have happened to the paperwork," he said, as he made up his story on the go. "I am Lucian Parker. So I guess I'll just wear this bar here." He pulled out his silver bars. "My brother Norman's, sir. I kept all his personal effects. I would appreciate it very much if I could just go home, skip the ceremonies and all.

"You know, an army foul-up in paperwork can cause a lot of delays, confusion, and I got a family—wife and pa—waiting. Sir, you do understand? Besides, if that paperwork gets to my pa or wife before I do, you could give them a lot of confusion and hurt that, well sir, just isn't necessary."

"Lieutenant Parker, my apologies for this mess up. I'll see to the changes immediately and I'll offer my explanation to the general's staff in charge of this citation ceremony. You go to Division Processing immediately with this." He scribbled a note on the back of his card. "If they have any questions tell them to call me. And this will authorize a cablegram home so that any confusion caused by the army may be corrected immediately."

"Thank you, sir," he replied with a salute. "Padre, thanks for the offer, but I guess with all this confusion I'd rather just thank God on my own and be on my way."

"I understand, son. God bless you."

"Thank you, Padre. I need that."

He sat on the bunk in the processing barracks and contemplated this new twist. It had played nicely into his already made plans. The switch was a sign from God. He was sure of it.

He had no desire to relive this war with his pa, Mary Jane, talk about his brother's death, his cousin's. He wanted to bury the terror of it all. Just go home and start over.

"If it is God's will, then . . . ," he whispered without finishing the sentence. He took his own dog tags off and searched through his brother's personal effects, putting his brother's on. He waited. No change. No bolt of lightning. Felt just the same.

He was muttering to himself now as he sat in the barracks alone, trying to sort out in his tired mind his present course of action.

"One more thing to do after processing the paperwork. Then I'm goin' home. Thank you God," he voiced aloud but low as he took a long look at the photo of Mary Jane standing on the steps of the small chapel in Redemption the day of her marriage.

"I am Lucian," he vowed. "I am," he said, tucking the photo into his shirt pocket.

CHAPTER 59

He watched, emotionless, as the last shovelful of earth filled the spot where his brother's emaciated and weakened body had been laid to rest. It didn't feel right. It didn't feel like his brother was really in there.

It wasn't even the Jap bullet that had killed him. His body just couldn't deal with the injury and sickness—heal—it wouldn't come back from the brink of death. Many of his friends were already dead from the same thing—Johnny Mead was dying that way until the Jap bayoneted him.

In the case of the prisoners of war who had endured the two and a half years of brutality, there was all too often nothing left for the heart to pump blood to. Starvation, beri-beri, chronic dysentery, rickets, and malaria all weakened a man's internal organs so much that a good steady breeze could knock him over and the result would kill him.

But Lucian had always made a comeback, he thought, stunned that the box contained his brother. This death didn't seem at all real. Not this one.

A twenty-one gun salute followed the final shovelful of Filippino soil upon his brother's metal casket. He shook with each *pop* from the M-1 rifles the soldiers were carrying.

Taps. The bugler on burial detail had a full-time job playing taps these days.

A captain came to him with a folded flag and saluted him smartly. "On behalf of a grateful nation . . ." he had said. They were doing everything they could to make the Bataan Death March survivors know they hadn't forgotten what they went through.

He stood there pondering what he was about to do. He had answered, "Yes ma'am, that's right," when the army nurse had his release papers drawn up from the hospital. He carried both brothers' dog tags with him. He just didn't want to lose his brother, his identity, the thing that made him such a hero.

And then there was Mary Jane. The anger over that died so long ago it seemed like a lifetime now. He'd killed enough of the enemy to assure that every ounce of anger had been satisfied. *She was his in the first place, wasn't she?* Lucian and Mary Jane Parker were married as long as Lucian returned.

And going home there would be Pa and the shortline to run. The Dearborn place was all paid for. A fine spread of over one hundred acres to run. It was all he had ever dreamed of.

Mary Jane. *Would she recognize him?* He was skin and bones. Sure the army was stuffing him with anything he asked for. Steaks, hamburgers, ice cream, mashed potatoes; he'd already gained ten pounds over the last couple weeks.

So all he needed to do was another physical checkup in San Francisco, process out of the army, and go live "happily ever after" in Warm Springs with the girl he loved.

Easy. Nothing to it. "I love you, brother," he said. Then, saluting, he walked away promising to not look back, to not shed a tear. There were no more tears left. If he ever cried again it would have to be for shame and he felt none now. As a matter of fact, he felt nothing at all.

CHAPTER 60

March 1945, Warm Springs, Oklahoma

Mary Jane read the note with trembling hands. She hadn't heard from her husband for almost three years. Whether he was alive, dead, or a prisoner had never been assured. The letter had been preceded by a Western Union telegram letting her know he was safe, but the letter itself had just arrived, and at that it was more than one month from the date inscribed.

Though wounded and sick, Lucian Parker had been rescued! His brother, Norman, was wounded but alive as well according to the letter. Perhaps that was why this letter was addressed, "Field Hospital, outside Manila."

She read each brief line over and over again to assure herself she had not dreamt this:

Darling,

A kind nurse is writing down my words for me. I have no way of knowing if you have received any of my other letters since I was taken prisoner by the Japs in April 1942. Norman had escaped at the beginning and we are finally back together again. The fighting is still raging, darling, and I am awfully sick. Over half the boys who came over here with us died. Malaria, dysentery, starvation, murder by the Japs—it is too horrible to recount to you now.

I am slightly wounded. Norman too. Norman came to rescue me with the help of Filipino guerillas at a train crossing. I can't say in words the love I feel for him now. We would die for each other and almost did.

How's Pa? Is he well? Are the Kelly boys still helping our pa run the shortline? Hope so.

I guess the army will try to fatten us up

before shipping us home. I'm afraid we aren't a very pretty sight. No real food for three years. Freedom is hard to describe. I'll never complain again as long as I live, I can promise that.

Norman is in a lot of pain right now. I have to go. Time is precious. My love for you is eternal. This war has changed me. Hope you can recognize me when I get back.

Your loving husband,
Lucian

Mary Jane held the thin onion-skin envelope to her breast. She could barely recall which of the two brothers it was that she had married, her emotions had been so entwined with both. Lucian had held her in his arms for but two days of marriage. It all seemed so long ago now.

It was hard to tell the two apart. They were twins of course, but they were different. In manners Lucian more playful, Norman more serious. Lucian chewed tobacco and hated coffee. Norman loved coffee and hated tobacco. But both could grin, and unless one knew the sly teasing grin from the other, they could play "who's who" against a person all day long.

She had loved Norman at first. Funny how it goes, she sighed leaning back into the soft cushion of the small sofa situated in the cottage near Main Street.

How would she tell Lucian about his pa, the train man, Jason Parker. How would she see them both here at the train depot, without his strong frame, loving arms welcoming them in his embrace? She wondered if they knew. Wondered if the army had delivered all the mail she had faithfully sent each week.

The train was repossessed now by the Santa Fe. The depot was in disrepair. Norman, no doubt would take care of that and live out his dream, if he returned well enough. Lucian on the other hand . . . probably still dreaming of California, as she did too.

Who could that be? she mumbled to herself at the unexpected knock at the door.

"Hello, Missy. Got a call from someone on the West Coast, says he knows you. Says he'll be in Redemption in three days. To meet him there," the drug store owner, Mr. Kelly, smiled, handing her the scribbled note.

"Oh!" she squealed. "You think?" she ventured a wordless question.

"Sure 'nuff sounded like him, Missy. I sure am happy for ya, Missy. This war mess has been too much for too long."

"What about Norman?" she asked nervously.

"Didn't say here nor there, Missy. Well, best be gettin' back to the store. Sure was good to hear one of them Parker boy's voices again. Like a ghost from the past . . . I mean . . ." he stumbled to say.

"I understand. You go along. And thank you, Mr. Kelly." She smiled, shutting the door slowly behind her. She held the letter close to her bosom, sure of her husband's safety, sure she would hold him again. Sure all was going to be right . . . with Norman too.

CHAPTER 61

April 1945, Near Redemption, Oklahoma

He gazed out the window of the passenger train as the Texas prairie rolled by. How many trips had he taken through this dry country with his brother? With his pa en route to Albuquerque?

It was four years ago now. The last trip was in summer 1941 just after the two of them had gotten into it over the marriage to Mary Jane. That was all dead, ancient history. He had no such feelings now, just a numbness, a persisting and penetrating sorrow for what the war had done to him and his brother.

He had avoided all the hoopla about returning from the war. The bands, well-wishers, banquets. New Mexico had turned out for their returning sons at every stop. He did check in at Frankie's Grill to have a bite and tell Luisa the bad news about his brother not coming home. She seemed stunned, searched his eyes, but he wouldn't look back at her, not squarely into her eyes anyway.

Now he just wanted to get home and forget about the years he had been gone. Rebuild the depot business with his pa. Live the dream that so long ago had eluded him.

He was different. He wasn't the same boy who left Oklahoma and New Mexico four years before. He had grown up. He was old in his mid-twenties. Tired, weak, he had nearly died, been wounded more than once; he had aged fifty years since then. He couldn't smile anymore. He didn't know how.

Even though his heart still skipped a beat at the thought of her, would he be able to smile when they locked eyes? He didn't think so. Not without his brother coming home. Not with so many men he cared about dead. Not now having become a cold and angry man-killer. And the truth was, killing didn't bother him.

It just wasn't going to be the same.

He guessed the rail bum Skully was right. His remedy for anger had worked. He felt anger no more. None. He'd used the anger up in the bloodbaths of the Philippines. He had washed his hands in it.

What did he feel? Dull. Sobered. Grown up.

Innocent? No, but not guilty either. He'd lost his innocence for sure. But was he the cause of all the killing? The pettiness that had been? The former angers that had consumed so much time? He mused and pondered it over and over again until his head ached from so much thought.

It was the army that had given him his present identity. A piece of paper said so. A colonel and a chaplain said so. A cemetery marker in the Philippines bearing the name of Captain Norman Parker said so. Rank, name, and serial number. He wasn't lying to call himself Lieutenant Lucian Parker. Norman had died. He died in the killing fields of

Luzon. He died when he lost his heart, when it turned into a stone cold killer. He was dead. Lucian was alive. The man who belonged to Mary Jane was alive.

CHAPTER 62

April 1945 Easter, Warm Springs

"Hello, Mary Jane," he smiled, setting his duffel bag down beside him on the front porch of the tiny white bungalow on Main Street.

"Oh! Oh my! Lucian? Lucian darling? You were supposed to be . . . I was supposed to meet you . . . Ohh!" she cried, throwing herself into his arms sobbing, curlers in her hair, half-dressed.

He hadn't felt the touch of love for so long. "I . . . I'm sorry. The train arrived early. I couldn't wait in Redemption. I hitched a ride," he said apologetically, awkward as they held each other.

She stood back, embarrassed, putting her hands over her curlers, apologizing for how she looked.

"You are the most beautiful thing I have seen in four years," he assured her in a solid stare of admiration.

"Don't just stand there. Come in. Come in darling. Sit. Let me fix myself up. I'll be right back," she promised, blowing him an excited kiss and retreating to her mirror and bedroom.

He walked in and took a deep breath. The smell was the essence of home, like her. Some things were missing, but this fragrance brought all the feelings from that first day back. The first time he saw her at the springs, when he and his brother disagreed on how to handle the sight of the bathing beauty.

He walked over to the nightstand at the end of the sofa. His eyes had caught sight of a photograph she must have kept there for all these years. There was one of the three of them, Mary Jane, Lucian, and Norman, laughing at the depot. Some silliness his pa had caught on the box camera before they had sent Mary Jane on her way to California in the fall of 1939. He looked at Lucian in the photo long and hard. He wished he had never known anger now.

Then there was the wedding photo. Summer 1941 and the steps of the small chapel in Redemption. He studied it. He'd forgotten how he had felt that day. It had been buried in his memory during the years of war.

He wondered about Harry. About his pa. Harry was dead he knew, but how had Mary Jane handled the loneliness here without him? He sensed the old man's presence as if a lingering scent of pipe smoke still greeted a visitor to this house.

He had come straight here. Right past the quiet and still depot. So unlike his pa to not be here if Mary Jane had passed the word along. Maybe he should go home to the depot, surprise the old man, his father. Maybe he was busy on a ride somewheres and on his way back to Warm Springs this very minute.

Maybe he'd be gone. It wasn't like him though. Times were tough without him and his brother to help out. He hadn't seen the old Baldwin steamer in the yard as he drove past. Maybe . . .

"Well!" she said, releasing a long and

happy sigh. "How do I look?" she asked, spinning herself in the brightly patterned Easter gown.

"Like a dream," he whispered admiringly. "Just like an angel," he said softly, setting the photo down and coming to her.

"Mary Jane, I . . ."

"Shhh," she whispered as she brought her lips to his. "We've got a lot to talk about but right now I need you to hold me."

"Me too," he assured her as he held her head, the fullness of blond strands against his own. He wanted to feel love again. Something driven from him so many years ago. "I need you, Mary Jane," he whispered into her ear as his tears descended to mingle with those already streaming down her tender cheeks. "I need you like water, air . . . I can't go on anymore like I have been. I've been so lost. I've lived in hell," he stuttered, seeking composure. "I . . ."

"Come with me," she offered, wiping moisture from her own eyes and taking his hand and leading him to her room.

"I'm not sure I am too good at this. I just need you in my arms. Will you understand if . . ."

She nodded to interrupt his questioning. "Let me be with you now. Quietly."

CHAPTER 63

"I had no way of knowing if you got my letters," she remarked quietly as Lucian finished his supper. She raised her eyes and watched him poking at the food, slowly, stirring it around, mentally far away from the kitchen table where the two sat for their first meal together in almost four years.

"I thought you knew about your pa," she offered again. "He was real proud of you, and Norman too," she spoke up. She hoped he would raise his eyes to her and find a way to unburden his feelings.

"I'm sorry. I don't feel much like talking now. I'll come to terms. Did he suffer?" he asked, finally breaking the influence of the silent spell he had been under.

"The Kelly boys found him slumped over. The engine was going. They were going to ride with him into Redemption and then on over to Albuquerque. He was real excited after hearing the army had landed in the Philippines. He died there aboard the train. He's buried next to your mother. Maybe we should go there. Go for a walk. The weather is fine for a Sunday walk."

"Did he talk about us much?"

"All the time. It's all he talked about. I remember . . ." She stopped and smiled with a glint of tears in her eyes. "I remember it was the week after Easter Sunday, 1942. We had just heard of your surrender on the radio and he asked for a sign. He was pretty broken up. And he prayed asking God to offer something that showed you and Norman were alive and coming home."

She paused, emotionally overcome at the thought of the dear sweet father of her two twin loves. How Jason Parker had sorrowed so very much to feel there was a reason for all the suffering and tragedy going on.

Lucian looked up at her and reached

across the table for her hand. "Go on, Mary Jane. Finish, please."

"He said he heard a train whistle. He got all excited and ran to the window like a little boy would at the coming of an unexpected visitor. He said, 'They're comin' home. My boys are comin' home.' "

"He heard a whistle?" Lucian asked with a childlike perplexity. "We blew a whistle real loud once, right before the siege in Bataan by the Japs. So loud we joked Pa would probably hear it." He smiled at the thought of the two of them recounting the Easter joke their pa would always tell about the bunny and the hen. "I guess he heard it then." He smiled.

It was his first smile since showing up on the doorstep earlier that day and the first he could recall having for years.

They had cleared the dishes from the table, and hand in hand walked the country road to the cemetery where her Grandpa Harry and Lucian's parents were buried. No talking transpired as Mary Jane allowed her husband to take in the newness of all that was after nearly four years of separation from Warm Springs.

"Where's the train?" he finally asked.

"The man from Santa Fe was apologetic but said he had no other option but to take it back for lack of final payment. He had it shipped up to Oklahoma City."

"It's comin' back. That is, if you don't mind. I'd like to go pay it off and bring it back. It was the last thing we all—my brother and pa—had together. I got enough pay and more to clear it off, this land too, if needed." He nodded over at the old spread where Mary Jane had grown up. "Three years of back pay at officer rates is a pretty good chunk."

"I think that would be wonderful. Maybe we could build that house you and I talked about. Right near the springs with a big front room to gaze out upon the place. A large yard for the children where we could watch them easily as we sit there on the covered porch. Remember the night we got married? Remember how we talked about it right after . . . well you know." She giggled.

His face flushed red as he turned away from her. "Yeah," he said, simply unable to cope with any memories of that day.

They came to the white picket fence which surrounded the small well-cared-for town cemetery on the bluff overlooking Main

Street. His feet froze in place. He was all alone. He was the last Parker alive. It was up to him to carry the legacy. This made it all real.

"Come," Mary Jane urged, pulling him forward to the headstones. He read them carefully, still seeking comprehension of how his world had changed so very much in the space of four years.

He knelt down at the grave of his father, reading his name carefully as if to be sure this could be true. "I'm sorry, Pa," he whispered. "I tried to bring him home with me. We almost made it. I love you. I . . ." He stumbled with a sudden rush of emotions that swept through him and unlocked the dam holding back any hint of the sorrows that had built inside him. He hadn't allowed emotion during the war. Just anger. Just the anger necessary for killing. Now he wept like a boy not understanding how everyone could leave him like this.

Mary Jane knelt next to him and held his head against her breasts, gently caressing his short crop of hair. She allowed him all the time he needed.

"Lucian?" she asked quietly after some time. He was frozen in a distant far off gaze she was totally unprepared for. "Lucian?" she prompted again.

"Huh?" he finally allowed, awakening as if he had been in a trance.

"We should go now. It is getting late. You should rest."

"Can I come back tomorrow?" he queried like a boy would to a parent seeking permission.

"Yes, darling. But it's hot and you should get some rest."

He followed her out the gate and took one look back. "Tomorrow," he assured and then walked hand in hand back to the small cottage on Main Street.

He lay asleep on the sofa as if he hadn't slept in weeks but with an unfamiliar inquietude. He couldn't seem to just lie and sleep deeply. He talked now and then calling out "Lucian, Johnny, Manuelito." But strangely he didn't call his brother's name. She hadn't heard "Norman."

There was no doubt he had seen horror too abundant to describe. He had asked her just before falling asleep to never ask him about the war. That he wanted to forget it. That it was a nightmare. She thought she could understand, but also knew unless he described what hell he had gone through she really never would be able to comprehend.

And she wondered about the secret love she had for Norman. Did he suffer? Did he think of her?

She looked at him and didn't see the man she married. This man was the flesh and blood resemblance but the war had so scarred him, so marked him that she wondered if Lucian would ever really return home. She really needed to know, to have some answers.

At length she got up and went to her nightstand where she kept the stationery and began to write a letter to him. She had a sudden awareness that crept into her heart that this was perhaps not Lucian at all. She observed him in his fitful sleep and dismissed the thought.

"No. It's Lucian," she mumbled to herself as she began to write a letter to him. She stopped and looked at him carefully, praying in her heart to know who he was now, and how to be the wife she should be. The nagging realization of the former thought from minutes before suddenly surged through her like a jolt of electricity.

"It's you! Isn't it?"

CHAPTER 64

Present day, American Military Cemetery, Manila

"Lucian?" she called gently. "Lucian, it's me, Mary Jane," she tenderly announced. "Lucian? Do you hear me? Can you hear me?" she softly voiced with a throaty plea.

"He's been like that for an hour or so Mrs. Parker," the Filipino interjected. "He ended telling his story to me. About my father Manuelito and . . ."

"I've heard that name before!" she interrupted, surprised at the sudden thought shooting back in time.

"I need your help. You brought my husband here in the night?"

"Yes," Vincente answered.

"And you are a son of someone my husband knew from the war?"

"Yes, Mrs. Parker. Amazing as it may be to hear it. I was a simple taxi driver stopping at the Manila Hotel last night on my final round. Today, this morning, I am a different man. I know things because of Señor Parker I never knew. He told me who I am. It is as if God has answered my prayers of a lifetime."

"Perhaps his, too," she mumbled under her breath, touched by the scene. She was confused, surprised at this man's story, but knew she could query him more and get the complete picture of all that had transpired last night with patience, some more questioning later. Now she needed to help Lucian and help herself resolve the issue that had silently grown like a cancer for fifty-five years.

She pushed a dozen small objects aside in her carrying bag looking for the time-yellowed envelope. She thought a thousand times she would show it to him.

Smudged now with the one hundred fingerprints from touches seeking courage to hand it over to her beloved, she retrieved it from the bag and held it outstretched with trembling hand as Vincente looked on.

"Lucian," Mary Jane tried again. The sun was now evaporating any moisture left from the gentle rain of the previous evening. She watched with concern as her husband gazed transfixed at the stone object before him.

"I'm so, so sorry," he finally voiced, inaudible above the squawking of the song birds, sounds of life, and morning traffic passing outside the gates of the hallowed ground. "I couldn't have lied except for love," he pleaded as if the white stone cross over the grave would say something to ease his pain.

"Lucian."

"Don't call me that," he answered.

"Darling?" she mouthed with a gentle hand upon his shoulder. He was bent over, kneeling. Eyes closed, fist clenched, head bowed, he epitomized every painting ever brought to life on canvas of a man in mighty petition to his maker.

"Oh God, hear me . . ." he moaned softly, clutching at his abdomen as if suddenly struck by some horrible blow.

"Lucian!" she gasped, frantic to comfort him. She came to him, lowered herself to the moist ground with him and held out her arms, still clutching the time-aged envelope in one hand.

He didn't look up but responded with heaving chest and the stuttering sobs of a little child unable to break the cycle of terror, fear, and remorse that filled him.

He sought her, placing his head and frustrations in the softness of her waiting arms and breasts. She responded with motherly affection for a boy desperate to tell his secret but not knowing how needed. This was a very different kind of love only a deeply caring woman can ever understand.

He was traumatized beyond anything she had witnessed and knew she had to just hold him, reassure her aged husband who had slipped from his seventy-nine-year-old present to his youthful, terrorized past. She held him, stroking his soft gray hair, waiting for him to ask for the help he truly needed.

She kissed his forehead unashamedly, ready to confess her guilt, waiting for him to reveal to her his long-buried troubles.

She repeated her deep awareness of his emotions with trembling words as he lost himself to the past that he had carried with him like some sort of ball and chain; tied to this place, to his brother, to her, for fifty-five years.

"I understand. I know darling. I am so sorry. I understand darling," she said softly, her tears mingling with his.

"No, Missy. You don't understand. How could you?" he finally responded between the sobbings that had seized him. His weary swollen eyes looked up at her from where he lay his head, upon her breasts, eyes now peering deeply into hers.

"I lied," he mouthed meekly, searching her for forgiveness.

She hung her head and a slight moan escaped from deep within her. "I lied too," his wife offered quietly.

"What?" he answered searchingly. "No sweetheart. I forsook my brother, my loyalty, my honor. I took something that wasn't mine. I . . ."

"So did I," she interrupted.

He wiped at the moisture that had so thoroughly cleansed his bloodshot and weary eyes with the work-worn hands of a small-town train engineer. Hands that had for so many years tried to prove his loyalty and love, hands that had held his brother's in the last tired moment of his life. "You know?"

"Oh Lucian . . . I mean . . ." she said, sadly shaking her head. "I have something for you. You read this," she said, handing the envelope over to him.

He looked at the envelope as if it were sacred holy writing. "Norman" was scribbled in the unmistakable handwriting of his younger wife.

"What is this?" he questioned humbly, lips trembling.

"A letter. A letter from a woman to her husband's brother returning from war. A letter I should have given you the first month you came home from the war but I was vulnerable, weak-willed. A letter about someone we both loved very, very much," she said simply, arising to her feet and taking the arm of the diminutive Filipino taxi driver who had been the companion to her man for the entire long night. "Come with me. He needs a moment alone."

Vincente Salazar understood. He had learned something this night he could not have in any other way. His history, what happened to cause his father's death, and about the mysterious ring. He took her arm in his and escorted her away toward the waiting cab.

"Mrs. Parker. I beg of you something. I have something that is yours, your husband's, I mean. I must go to my mother's home in Santa Rosa, north of Manila. There I will get for you something I think is very important to this man," he pointed, "and to you."

"We will be fine. We can call for a cab from the caretaker's office." They both turned suddenly at the throaty moan coming from the grave site.

"Oh dear God! Lucian!" the twin cried to himself as he shakily struggled through the words of the letter.

"Come," she tearily but mildly adjured the taxi driver. "He'll need me, but first he needs his brother."

He read the words meant for his eyes fifty-five years ago. If he had read these words then, before making the decision to continue to hide the facts from Mary Jane, the townsfolk of Warm Springs, all of this wouldn't be necessary.

He had tried to comfort himself in the belief that God's hand had made things right, the way they should have been in the first place with Mary Jane, but he couldn't. God deals through faith, not lies, and he had not *kept the faith.*

Dearest Norman,

You are asleep. I am watching you as you stir every so often and cry out from nightmares you brought home from the war. Warm Springs isn't the same as when you left. You are not the same. We have both lost something. Not only have you lost your father and brother but an innocence. It is hard for me to describe to you what I am feeling, what I am seeing.

It is you, Norman, isn't it? When I kissed you to welcome you home I felt the same way as I did that night in Los Angeles. Remember? Thinking you were Lucian, I kissed your lips to realize a difference. What it was I can't explain, except it had happened once before, long ago outside a diner on Santa Monica Boulevard before the war.

Only now I want what you want. I have had both of you to love. But I am a widow, am I not? We should not fool ourselves, but I watch your terrible struggle and think, "If this will make him happy, make him feel closer to his brother, then all right. Let it be."

Then I think, "No, it's not right."

I weigh out the meaning of this lie of ours and wonder if it is worth it. You are Norman and not Lucian. I can tell not by looks but by feeling. But I really don't care. At least I have one of you back and I loved you both so dearly.

Upon reading this I expect you to take me to Redemption for a church service that we both deserve. I expect the people who have welcomed us home to know the truth.

I love you darling. I always have. How could a woman be so lucky to have had the two best men in the world to love?

—Mary Jane

He bowed his head, tightly clutching the fifty-five-year-old letter to his chest. He began to wipe at the name upon the grave marker. Darkened by humidity and time he wiped furiously as if he could rub the name, CAPTAIN NORMAN B. PARKER, out somehow, right the wrong, make it correct.

"I love you, Lucian," he cried in a child's tone, asking for understanding. "God in heaven knows do! I didn't mean to betray you! I . . . I wanted what you had so bad! Did I cause you to die?" he sobbed. "You didn't give up because of me, did you?"

"I mean that day when Manuelito and you—the train escape at Santa Rosa. Could I have changed it? Did I try hard enough to keep you from getting shot? Or did I want Missy so bad that . . . Oh no!" he wept, burying his head in his gnarled and worn trainman hands, ashamed, embarrassed at his thoughts of lies and betrayal. "Too much—this is too much," he weepingly lamented. "No, Lucian. I would have given my life for yours. You know that, don't you?"

"I tried to make up for it, Lucian. See?" he started again like a defendant at trial seeking to explain some actions he had taken. "I took some shrapnel coming to get you out of there, looking for you at Cabanatuan," the seventy-nine-year-old offered, pleading for understanding.

"I looked everywhere for you. I was ready to die for you!" he mourned in an attempt at forgiveness.

He continued to tearfully explain, rubbing at the stinging eyes, at the cloudiness of hot salty moisture that veiled them and kept his mind from seeing clearly. Mumbling words of regret, sorrow, wishes that he had tried harder, done differently, not lied—he begged, feeling he still had not found the words that would make it right.

"I tried to make up for it. All these years. I thought, see, if I was you then I couldn't hurt you anymore. I thought if I was you all my anger, all my memories would go away. I thought you wouldn't mind. But I lived your name well, brother. I never hurt your name.

"I . . ." His words melted to sobs as a lifetime of anguish spilled out of him in an instant. "I lost so much in the war. I grew so damned cold. You understand? See, the old Norman died there somewheres. See? You understand why I took your name?"

In grief he bowed himself to the earth to supplicate the God of goodness for redemption, for forgiveness. He had said it all, had spilled it all out except for one solicitude to someone he quit talking to privately five decades earlier:

"I am Norman, *Lord*! I have always been Norman Parker! I have lived a lie! Oh *God* in heaven, hear me! *Please!* I need you!"

CHAPTER 65

Vincente Salazar raced through the streets of Manila as if he were a man on a rescue mission. He hoped to secure the object that he was certain his aged mother had hidden safely away at the end of the war. She had told him of his father's final instructions before he died.

But only once, when he was a very small boy, and then had passed on. He had forgotten until now. The old Americano, the "trainman" as his mother had referred to him, had revealed something this night of great importance.

There was an object of great meaning to

the Parker twins when they were young. An object of such value that the dying words of one to the other included, "Did Manuelito get you the ring?"

All these years the honored painting of Christ had hung on the wall in the family home and he had forgotten that anything lay behind it. He couldn't be sure now if it was a vivid memory or his imagination. But if there was something there, if it was not just an overactive imagination, then what he would find belonged to Lucian Parker. And the old Americano fighter, his broken-hearted brother, needed it now.

"This package is for the twin brother to the trainman, Señor Parker. His name is Norman Parker," Miranda Salazar pointed to the name on the enveloped letter with a bulge in it. "I want to show you where it is, Vincente, if he should return to the Philippines for it."

He thought he could see himself, no more than five or six, not very interested, but when his mother had said the "trainman" something had clicked.

There was also a photo of the brother named Norman with Vincente's older sister during the war and one of his father and both Parker brothers taken just before the fall of Luzon to the Japanese. He had always wondered what these men had meant to his father. These photos were almost sacred to his mother for she kept candles lit every holiday near them.

His mother had taken him to the wall in the *sala*, and above the statuette of the Blessed Virgin she removed the portrait of Christ holding heart in hand. To have such a painting was not unusual. Every Catholic home kept a similar portrait prominently posted in the main *sala*.

She had pulled at the cardboard backing to reveal a thin envelope with a slight bulge. He had been more interested in playing with his friends. *But if it were true! If something was really there!*

He wondered if he could make the more than two-hundred kilometer round-trip, find the object, and return by nightfall to Manila. He didn't care at all about Mr. Parker's money, his cab fares for spending the night. Vincente Salazar now possessed a portion of life and love he never could have imagined. He possessed the firsthand account of his hero father, his determination to see a job through, *to keep the faith* as the old Americano kept saying.

Norman Parker felt like he had been reborn. Just the admission, the plea to God and his brother seemed to wash him clean. All the scrubbing in the world couldn't do that before. Now he knew. Plain and simple. He didn't need any outward sign from God to know that his offering, his confession, had been accepted. He had something burned into him at Lucian's grave.

An undeniable wave of peace, tingling from his head as if entering at the crown and traveling through him to his feet and up again burned as hot as any fire he'd known. And he'd known fires, lots of them. But a warm, comfortable, pleasing, happy fire it was. He was redeemed immediately from any torment and he knew that he was being loved from someone beyond the seeing world.

Now, when he smiled at his beloved Mary Jane, it was the eighteen-year-old that did it. That same boy that still resided within the worn-out flesh and bone. That very same boy who first saw her at the springs and fell completely and instantly in love that hot summer day in 1939.

It took some explaining as he and Mary Jane gathered their children around, but he was able to do it, relive the war at long last without shame, without the nagging terror that had shadowed him for fifty-five years.

Seeming bewildered, amused, and befuddled by it all, his grown children simply smiled, hugged him and told him they loved him. Lucian or Norman Parker, he was still just "Dad" and that love never had any conditions attached.

The family agreed they would bill the marriage ceremony in Redemption as "recommitting to a love affair of five decades." Now that day for the ceremony had arrived. Mary Jane met her man at the altar while Pastor Briggs invited all in attendance to be seated.

Pastor Briggs began:

"Dearly beloved, we are gathered here on this sacred occasion to witness Norman B. Parker, also known by the name of Lucian, and Mary Jane Harrison Parker take each other by the hand and affirm to the world that they are forever one, united as man and wife.

"By taking these vows they testify that

they have loved each other with all their hearts and promise to do so until the end of their mortal lives. And if love is divine then by this sacrament of marriage they will keep a promise to love eternally.

"Norman B. Parker do you take Mary Jane . . ."

Vincente Salazar was perplexed. Why had his sister, Rosita, offered a stranger the small envelope from behind the portrait? And how did she know it was even there? He waited anxiously for her to return from shopping.

His nephew had explained to him about the young-looking Americano who so pleasantly and politely had just hours before visited the home inquiring for the tiny package.

He knew the connection with this object had greater significance than ever now and the fact that his father had given his life for these two brothers meant that he too had a duty, a responsibility to take care of the item, with his life if necessary.

"Rosita!" he called as she entered the door carrying a bag of fresh produce from the market. "Rosita, I came from Manila tonight for something special. My nephew Julio tells me . . ."

She cut him off. "It can't be the small envelope?"

"You didn't give it away to a stranger, did you? I can't understand this. What did he look like? How did he know about it? What did he say? And by the way, how did you know about it?"

"You don't think you were the only one Mamá told, do you?" the graying and dignified Filipina asked him.

"No, but Rosita. I have just had a special occasion to know the owner and . . ."

"What do you mean, owner? This man said he was the owner."

"Rosita, a young Americano comes to the door and knows about this secret hidden behind the portrait of Christ for fifty-five years? And you believe him? Ah!" he announced with frustration. "Hey! Maybe the old man . . . yes, maybe he sent him!"

"I don't know who sent him or what this is really all about but he said he was a friend of Papá's and I had the strangest feeling. Everything he said felt so good. He was so kind. So pleasant. I couldn't resist such a man with so much knowledge."

"What do you mean?"

"He sat with me almost the entire evening. I haven't slept. He told me all I ever wondered about Papa and the war, what he did, how he died for the trainmen and about the two brothers who made an agreement."

A chill swept through Vincente as an unanticipated pleasant cool breeze brings on; suddenly, without warning. He wondered at his sister's story and fell back into the sofa to listen as she continued and recounted detail for detail the story he had heard from the lips of the old veteran from Oklahoma.

An hour, two, three, then four went by. They shared the common experience with childlike excitement in a wonderment reserved for the spiritual awakening that happens perhaps once in a lifetime.

Vincente fixed his gaze upon the glass-covered portrait of Christ with a new appreciation. He had taken this token of family heritage and belief for granted. The painting of Christ holding his heart suddenly had meaning, a refreshing new meaning.

He understood and yet could not quite comprehend how the magical event that had happened to him and his sister could be possible.

"What did this man look like?" he finally asked. "I mean specifically. Can you describe him?"

Rosita sat there, teary-eyed and drained from all that had transpired. Yes, she could describe him.

"Vincente, I think you should see this," she said softly as she pulled from her wallet a photo she had kept safely encased in plastic. "After he left, I thought he looked so familiar. Then I remembered this. I think you should see it and tell me if I am imagining this," she said almost reverently.

"You mean this man? The one in the photo taken with you behind the *casa*? And this one with Papá taken during the war? But Rosita that could only mean . . ."

The wedding vows were as joyful to the aged couple as to newlyweds just starting life. Though the ceremony lasted only minutes, to Mary Jane and Norman Parker it was the dream of a lifetime. A beautiful culminating moment that crowned them as a reward for a rich life so well lived and deserved.

The children and grandchildren threw rice and handed Norman the tickets for the train from Redemption to Dallas/Ft. Worth International Airport and then on to an undisclosed and secret rendevous with romance, a honeymoon never known by his true identity until now.

Using the MasterCard with *Norman B. Parker* was like using a toy that gave a child great pleasure every time he plunked it on the counter to purchase something, pay for the hotels. Spend he did. Like a man out of his mind he used that name, *Norman B. Parker.*

The Parker children had gone their separate ways. Now home from their romantic weeks together, Norman and Mary Jane found themselves standing on the railroad passenger platform in Redemption enjoying a soothing breeze, a pleasant Oklahoma sunset.

Time had vanished and Norman rested his gaze upon the most perfect picture of peace and beauty he could have ever imagined. They held hands tightly only as two young lovers do.

"I feel eighteen," he softly voiced. "I feel as though I could walk on air. Oh, Missy!"

he whispered. "I feel free and full of love like I have never felt before!"

"I understand darling. I truly do." She smiled with eyes that danced happily as they locked with his. "You are the most handsome man on earth, Norman!" she said in a gleeful girlish tone. "It feels so wonderful to say your name . . . *Norman.*"

They brought to each other a fire reserved for youth and in that instant as lips met they knew they would forever be as young as they desired.

"Love does that," Norman assured her.

"Does what?" She smiled as if she were admiring a man she had just fallen in love with.

"Keeps you young," he replied with a nibble to her ear.

"Uh, humm . . . Mr. Parker?" a man standing off to one side cleared his throat. "I apologize for the interruption," the cheerful middle-aged train-station manager announced.

"Oh hello, Steve. How's the train business today?" Norman replied happily.

"Just dandy as usual. People love these old steel beasts. Howdy do, Mrs. Parker?

What's got Mr. Parker so cheery?" he laughed.

"Why he's always been that way. And I am feeling wonderful as well. Simply marvelous," she replied radiantly.

"May I just say that in all the years I have known the two of you I do not believe I have ever seen you a happier couple." He smiled. "They say love just gets better." He smiled again.

"Thank you, Steven." Mary Jane blushed. "He is a handsome man!" she offered, pulling close to Norman as she did.

"Again I do apologize for interrupting two little love birds in action. You know displays of affection are so highly regarded here in Redemption that we have laws forbidding getting carried away in public. Don't make me call the sheriff," he chuckled as they held each other joyfully around the waist.

"Is that what you came out here from your office to tell us?" Norman laughed like a man without a care in the world. "Steve, what do you have there?" He pointed to the curious small envelope, painted a rusty lemon color by time. A tiny bulge accented its age.

"Oh. Why, I almost forgot the reason I came to greet you. I have something for you.

A young man said you would know what it
was." He paused thoughtfully as he questioned something about Norman's countenance. "Well, I'll be," he said, looking intently
into the face of the smiling old train man. He
stood back and just shook his head.

"What? Steve, what are looking at?"

"Very curious. Your smile," he pointed out.
"If you were fifty years younger I'd swear . . .
Remarkable!" he said, scratching his head.
"Well, just a coincidence I'm sure. I hope
you have a superb trip," the friendly depot
manager from Redemption offered, handing
the envelope over to the suddenly serious
and sober man.

"Good day, Steve," Norman said courte-
ously as the man cheerily whistled and
walked away with a wave of the hand.

"What could this be?" Mary Jane posed in
a tone mixed with concern and bewilderment.

Norman shrugged and began to shakily
open the tired and thin looking envelope. It
had a distinctive appearance, even a smell
that easily drew his mind to the battlefields
of the Philippines; a place he had so completely forgotten, disengaged his thoughts
from for many days now.

"Careful," Mary Jane urged as he gently tore at the envelope.

A shiny circular metallic object rolled easily from it and into his hand. His gaze welled with moisture as if a heaven sent flood had flashed across the plains and caught him wide eyed in it. He held it up, examining it. A cruel hoax?

The sun shimmered off the ring held between his thumb and index finger causing a spectacular gold sparkle to radiate from it in every direction.

Mary Jane gasped, hand to her mouth. Trembling they both moved to the nearby bench to support the emotions and questions now overwhelming and coursing through them.

Unsteadily Norman reached into his coat pocket and placed his reading glasses on. He pulled a single soiled sheet of onionskin writing paper with aged and smeared ink blotches from the envelope, and read:

Dear Norman,

I think this belongs to you now. If you see this note it is because you made it home and I did not. You kept the family motto and it was you who rightly deserve to have it. You kept the faith! I was kind of selfish growing up, always looking out for myself, you know. You never were. You deserve this.

Keep it safe and if I don't make it back, make Mary Jane put it on your hand. In this way part of me will return home. Wear it with honor and pass it on. Keep the family faith alive.

I love you like life, Norman. There isn't anything I wouldn't do for you.

Your brother,

Sergeant Lucian Parker

P.S. We sure showed 'em didn't we, brother?

"We sure did, brother. We surely did," he whispered in a gravelly voice, wiping at the tears that had become so common these past weeks.

Mary Jane reached for the ring and made him give his left hand to her. It slid on easily, as if no time had transpired from the last time he had tried it on, 1941. The etched letters "KTF" glistened from the light of the afternoon sun.

"Keep the faith," he whispered. "I did, didn't I?" he asked Mary Jane with an innocent boyishness.

"Yes, darling. You did. You really did!" she answered tearily. The stately silver-haired woman he had adored with all his heart was really his now.

With a sweet kiss to his lips and firm arms placed around his neck she gave a silent witness to her belief that Norman Parker really had kept the family trust and faith, and would keep passing it down forever.

EPILOGUE

Easter Sunday—One Month Later at Home in Warm Springs

Norman struggled to lift his head from his bed situated in the center of the living room where he could gaze out to view the panoramic vista of the land he had loved so well.

"Here darling, let me help you," Mary Jane said, reaching for his head and fluffing the pillows up so her fragile husband could ponder all that his eyes beheld.

"I'm thirsty," he whispered in a voice hoarse with dryness.

"Here you are, sweetheart," she offered,

struggling with the emotions of letting go of her beloved who each hour seemed to be drifting further away from life and from her. She held the tumbler and the straw to his lips and allowed the cool iced water to soothe his parched throat.

"Reminds me of the Bataan Death March." He pointed weakly to his throat. "Dry. Very dry," he gurgled as he strained to sip from the straw.

"Oh, Norman," Mary Jane voiced softly as she stroked his head, kissed his moist cheeks, wet from eyes tenderly offering what words his lips couldn't form. "Why, Norman? Why do you have to leave me?" she asked in the innocent voice of a child seeking guidance, understanding from a wiser, older one. "Why now? We finally . . ." She couldn't finish as she looked into the eyes of the man intently gazing past her, beyond her, through her to the distant rails bordering their property, and the lonely depot he had first known with his pa, Jason, mother, Maria Linda, and beloved twin, Lucian.

She tried to alert him to her presence to no avail. He was lost in one of his moments of reverie that he lapsed in and out of so often in the past few days. But he was weaker now. His breathing shallow, his heartbeat faint. It was no use lying to herself. Not anymore. The doctor told her it would be days at best. To make him as comfortable as she could.

"Norman?" she breathed shakily. "Norman!" she cried as she stroked his head and sought for someone to give her solace. Her children were on the way. Yet she was alone waiting to be comforted, waiting for companionship in this final hour of marriage.

She picked her head up from off his chest where it lay seeking one final embrace from him. "Are you going to leave me again, darling?" she whispered.

He smiled and yet looked through her gazing eyes as if she wasn't there. "Norman? Can you hear me?" she begged placing her face directly in front of his.

"I'm seeing things." He smiled with shallow breaths. His gaze fixed into and through the ample picture window.

"What's that?" he asked, a quizzical expression written on his sunken, tired face.

"For me?" He grinned through a pain-conquered grimace he had worn for so many hours now.

"Why?" he asked like a child would to an adult standing over him. "To make me feel comfortable? If you are here I am comfortable." He smiled softly, breathing eased, countenance radiating a confidence Mary Jane hadn't seen since he and Lucian were young and alive.

"Norman? Dear? Can you talk to me?" she gently probed. She wondered if he was hallucinating about his parents, going back to his childhood. Or was he thinking the children had arrived?

He had wanted and was anticipating the children who were on their way to spend the final moments with their father. She had promised him the day before and he was eager to see them. Now he wasn't making sense. Mary Jane turned to look out the window expecting and hoping to see the children coming up the long driveway from the road bordering the rails. No one.

"Who, darling? I don't see them. Who are you seeing? Talking to?" she asked, turning to him again, fearful of this moment.

His pupils dilated as if beams of light had been directly placed upon them, then removed. "Sure! I can hear you. Clear as a bell," he whispered back, to someone unseen by Mary Jane.

"Whistles. You mean when I hear them?" He smiled, eyes sparkling from the light shining brightly from outside the large picture window.

A sudden childish grin energized him. "It's true! It's really true!" he laughed as excitedly as his worn and frail shell could muster.

"It's beautiful!"

"Really? I didn't think they made those steamers—not like that! How?" He conversed in self-talk as a child to an imaginary visitor.

"Just for me? Oh my!" he responded to what only his ears seemed to hear.

"Well yes, I can go. When do I get to see you?" he whispered throatily but contented, voice falling off.

"Norman? Darling? Are you leaving me?" Mary Jane complained weakly. She really didn't expect an answer. She had never seen anyone die. Was this death?

"Fine. Surely am ready. Surely am," he sighed, eyes closing. "Missy? Oh fine, she's real fine," he answered to the unseen questionare so low Mary Jane strained to make out his words.

She was shaken, unsure of herself. Her life had been filled for so many thousands of days with Parker men she could barely remember being anyone else before those days.

She couldn't hold the dam restraining the deep moisture building behind the walls of her eyes. As it burst, her trembling lips sought to form words.

Trembling, her aging hands reached for his thin but still very distinguished graying head, to stroke his temples, offer him a soothing touch of love as she had thousands of times during countless sleepless episodes of war memories, recurrences of malaria, tormenting nightmares.

Nightmares no more. Her man was acting as if he were headed home. As if other arms were there to greet him, to take him away from her.

"Mary Jane." He suddenly spoke lucidly as he directed his failing gaze upon her.

"Mary Jane Parker. I love you!" he offered with urgency. "Can you hear it? Listen," he implored with what strength was left in him. "Can you hear it?"

"Hear what darling? I don't heat anything."

"Listen." His eyes urged and then closed.

He smiled and sighed, contented with the approaching sounds.

"I knew he would come for me," he whispered, relaxing the tenseness that had occupied his sickly body.

"We always—kept the faith for each other. Hear that?" He opened his eyes tiredly once more to the window, pupils dilating again to the dazzling light penetrating them.

"Ticket?" He smiled to an image growing larger in his view. "Here," he offered in weakened gasp as he allowed the bright metallic wedding band to slide from his skeletal finger and into the palm of his outstretched hand.

She gazed out toward the depot but saw nothing. "Oh, Norman!" she cried, looking desperately for what he was seeing, hoping, wanting to believe.

"Lucian!" he sighed as the breath released from his lungs. "Lucian . . . Lu . . ." His right hand, extended to the light in the picture window, fell limp to the side of the bed and a bright gold ring rolled out from it easily, onto the floor, and toward the same picture window he had gazed through moments before.

"Oh darling, Norman," she cried. "You can

go now. You can go, darling," she offered, kissing his cheeks, mingling her tears with the moist drops draining from his still and closed eyes.

"What!" Mary Jane swung around to the familiar noise coming from the tracks. She gazed intently, calmly, suddenly serene as an indescribable peace bathed her, swept over her, with sounds from the rails. It had always been Lucian's call. He always let his family know when he was almost home.

Three whistles . . . two whistles . . . three!

She smiled, looked back to Norman's still and now empty frame. Tears freely mingled with creases from unexpected an smile trapping the lips which she had used to kiss the two men of her life.

Gasps of loss from her lungs mingled with an incredible and intense bliss. She turned back toward the sounds of blasts from the locomotive that didn't, couldn't really, exist.

She blew them a kiss and spoke her heart and mind aloud for anyone to hear. "Farewell, my darlings," her halting voice offered to the invisible reaches beyond Warm Springs.

She bent to the floor and recovered the

ring they had both worn in display of their love for her.

She held it to her breast and gazed miles beyond this place. The fleeting rays of day broke through clouds as if to encourage her, give her comfort.

"Please come, take me home soon. I loved you, Lucian Parker, and oh, *how I have loved you, Norman!* With all my heart and soul . . . *I have loved you so very much!*"

AUTHOR'S AFTERWORD

Why I write on the theme of
love and war

I am often asked how I come upon my stories and why I particularly choose the generation of my parents to honor. My stories are based first on strong personal beliefs and second on the fact that the years the World War II generation lived were pivotal and transitional to creating the world we now enjoy. As such they offer an unparalleled backdrop for drama, romance, and tragedy—all elements which combined make for interesting, believable, and engaging characters who can offer us insights no other living generation can.

I believe, for example, that love alone will save this world from a destruction to be caused ultimately by lack of it. I confess to being an incurable romantic.

I believe in romance in all of its dignity—most cherished of all the soul's dreams are to truly love and be loved. My view of personal dignity in romance, the gentleman's code of honor which includes how he looks at and treats a woman, may seem quixotic to some. They would not be very far from the mark. What women would not want to feel valued, prized, and worthy of true love—safe—a Dulcinea?

I believe in virtues taught to me by my parents and so many others of their generation. They are timeless in their power to build healthy relationships and heal the challenges which confront us. Naive? If so, I'm perfectly happy to skip through life believing wrongs can be righted with integrity and honor.

My stories are of *love* from the perspectives of a generation who has lived long enough to be authoritative about it, not from the scholar or therapist, but from those who said "I do" and did.

With this novel completed I have penned a trio of love stories. Starting with *The Last Valentine*, about timeless love and determination to keep promises, I chose to again take a step back in time with *The Lighthouse Keeper*, a tale of deep devotion showing how the flame of love gives us the brightest hope to deal with tragedy, loss, and come to terms with what matters most.

Finally this story, *Ticket Home*, takes us on a journey back to youthful days of innocence, loss of innocence through war, and the power of love to salvage dreams. Different in focus from the previous two, our heroes discover love's immense power to cure sickness of the mind and heart. It is a tale of healing and redemptive powers.

All three novels in the series honor the triumph, tragedies, and loves of a generation which news anchor Tom Brokow has coined and introduced to us as, *The Greatest Generation*, the title for his national bestseller. I personally feel driven to show them my respect and gratitude in fiction as he has in nonfiction.

With *Ticket Home* I hope to entertain, inspire, and inform, using the backdrop from this generation's days, months, and years which most closely mirror the complete history of our twentieth century than any other generation. In some measure, and with profound respect, I hope to keep this "greatest generation" alive in our memories through my writing.

They are looking back now, often wondering what happened to time. They entertain grandchildren who have no concept of a devastating universal economic Depression, a world at war, making do or doing without. We still have much to learn from them.

They lived both in a violent time and a gentler slower-paced world. They saved a world engulfed in wars created by madmen in the center of a century, and united they reshaped forever the map of the world and destinies of nations.

There are many in their generation whose stories of life never fully blossomed. They were cut short by the most destructive war ever to have occurred in the history of mankind. These brave souls cut short in their youth were neither given a lifetime to fill with love nor were they given years to train the next generation.

A few readers have complained that the stories include so much war. One reader recently wrote: "You lost me when you started into the war stories," to which I wrote back, "Sorry."

It is intentional that I include the war years and I do feel sorry for any reader who wishes to remain uninformed about those dead and living to whom she or he owes the right to choose what they will do each day with their freedom. It is a shame that some will choose to skip over character-cultivating history. The main characters and protagonists are from that generation for all the reasons previously ascribed. So I do feel "sorry" if a reader loses interest.

To understand how the character representing our parents and grandparents develops, becomes, changes, one must view his or her life from that character's point of view, dilemmas, historical perspectives, and so on. Find anyone of the "greatest generation" who has not been significantly affected emotionally, spiritually, or physically by the war years and you find someone who lived in a shell or on another planet.

There were more than sixteen million American men and women in uniform during World War II and over one half million dead and missing. There were more than one million wounded, some so severely their lives were altered forever. We talk about Vietnam's MIAs still in the realm of two thousand, and the Korean War with some eight thousand MIAs and what a tragedy that is. It is a tragedy for one to be missing in war. In World War II there are still over seventy-three thousand MIAs! Each missing man's life has a story behind it!

All three of my novels to date honor and remember those courageous men and women who faced the steel of two brutal militaristic empires so that we may enjoy the freedoms we all too often fail to recognize, including what to read, think, do with our lives, and enjoy. These freedoms cost someone his or her blood.

More particularly, I have placed this story's heroes among the more than eighty thousand Americans and Filipinos taken prisoner in the fall of the Philippines in April and May 1942.

In particular I have chosen to honor the New Mexico National Guard units, the 200th

Coastal Artillery, and the first new regiment formed during combat in World War II—the 515th Coastal Artillery. Also the 6th Rangers and Alamo Scouts, who so gallantly risked their lives to free some 500 Americans at Cabanatuan POW camp, were mentioned and our hero Norman Parker placed among them. They were the first to fight against the sea, air, and land forces of the Japanese empire in World War II. Why did I choose these groups of fighting men and other Philippine war veterans to honor?

As a young boy I was both fascinated and filled with terror reading about the tens of thousand who would not return from the battle for Bataan, the Bataan Death March, then Corregidor, the prison camps O'Donnell, Cabanatuan, Bilibid, the forced labor for coal and copper in the mines of Japan, China, and Manchuria.

Thousands died at sea in cramped, stifling, miserable, unventilated holds of "hell ships" without food or water in transport from the Philippines to Japan and other labor destinations as prisoners of war. Each had a love, a life, a personal story to tell.

What happened to these men represented among the worst deprivations, most heinous acts of brutality and barbarisms suffered by men at war. I do not recount in detail the trials of these captive Americans of World War II but the heroes of the story necessarily are placed in the brutal circumstances and their lives and loves are forever changed.

By even briefly exploring their descent into what you or I would consider the very depth of hell they represent what that great generation endured, and thus we may explore even love, in a way we might not have ever appreciated it otherwise.

While *Ticket Home* is a work of fiction, many of the places described, times of battles, units who fought there, are real. Some are fictionalized to represent a mosaic of experiences endured by our fighting men and those who waited for them.

To these survivors, living and dead, we owe a heartfelt debt of thanks and love for surrendering their youthful lives to brutality and a loss of innocence so others might live. They suffered and died in the belief that democracy, honor, and duty were values as real as the hearth-taught values of home, family, freedom, and God.

This is not a story about war, nor has it

treated the battles and history of those times in an exhaustive manner. But it is a story illustrating the effects war may have on personal history, the lives of the characters, and creating in them the crisis and resolution, offering a window into their decisions that forged men and women of heart and steel.

In the end all of us who face crisis in life in one way or another will come to resolutions which change us forever. Perhaps in examining these characters and what they faced we may find meaningful answers to some of life's most challenging questions for ourselves.

No attempt has been made to connect true names of combatants with the fictional characters or the places they fought; rather, the composite experience of all the combatants and prisoners of war studied in preparation for the war scenes can be summarized in the lives of the heroes of this story. Also, although Don Bell *was* an announcer at KMZH and he reported the attack on Pearl Harbor, his actual words are not represented in this book, rather they are a dramatization from reports of what it was thought he said.

While only those who lived it can truly comprehend the bravery, courage, and unyielding honor it took to survive days, months, years of war as combatants and prisoners, we may be able to imagine it in some way and by so doing honor them.

The costs are finally memorialized in thousands of homes, at cemeteries, in the hearts of millions, as they realize their beloved brothers, husbands, and fathers, while dying nobly, still died and are not coming home.

To benefit from this and all stories with elements of war, (including love stories which my trio of books claim to be) we look into the abyss of hell, the darkness of man's meanest spirit. We must not glorify it, but we must render it awful, in all its brutality, so that we may abhor it, then eliminate it, and never act the part of aggressors in it.

Peace and love are the antithesis to war and hate. Dramatizing the contrasts of love and hate, war and peace, through storytelling, allows the reader an extraordinary journey of the mind, an opportunity to vicariously live through the characters and thus grow and draw conclusions from the actions portrayed.

Finally, we must be true to the details of war and its terrible consequences as they are so briefly treated in this and my other novels. This is so that we may remember it required the ultimate of those who only wanted to be in their loved ones' arms again and find their *Ticket Home*.

AUTHOR'S STATEMENT

I have read nearly one dozen different accounts of World War II fighting as it occurred in the Philippines by authors of nonfiction historical books and editors of personal war journals.

I have tried to maintain a sense of accuracy without any characterizations which might lead one to think this story has been based upon any individual or set of soldiers. *Ticket Home* is a fictional story and the most important elements within its pages are the feelings portrayed by its characters and not specific facts, details, or related war events.

If any similarity exists between the characters of *Ticket Home* and any personal accounts from the war known by readers it is purely coincidental.

I have written this story which focuses on the times of World War II and considers the jargon of the times in referring to the American enemy, imperial Japan. The news, the soldiers, and the American public all referred to the enemy soldier from Japan as "Japs, Nips, and Tojos."

By referring to the World War II enemy of the United States in terms natural to the people of the times I only depict it as it was. I do not wish to be demeaning to anyone of Japanese ancestry or descent.

I also apologize to any reader feeling that any expletive used was unnecessary. I never look for ways to include an expletive, pejorative, or profanity in any way. Rather, I look for every possible way to exclude them and still allow the characters to come through with the emotion, personality, and individual qualities which make them human and move the story forward.

Accurate character portrayal and realism demands a dose of words from time to time that the best dictionaries don't have definitions for. They convey urgency, stress, anger, even bad manners, and do a much better job to conduct the feeling the character has at the moment than a string of words might otherwise.

Thank you for your understanding.

To learn more about World War II history in the Philippines and other battlegrounds you may wish to visit the author's Web site and look under "Recommended Reading" at www.jmpratt.com and www.thebestsellers.com or write to him at: PO Box 970189 Orem, Utah, 84097